GW00382108

IVOR'S GHOSTS

A Novel

ANTHONY MCDONALD

Anchor Mill Publishing

Anthony McDonald

All rights reserved. Copyright © Anthony McDonald
2014
www.anthonymcdonald.co.uk

Anchor Mill Publishing
4/04 Anchor Mill
Paisley PA1 1JR
SCOTLAND
anchormillpublishing@gmail.com

Cover photograph © Stephen Gee

Cover design © Charles Coussens

For Tony Linford, *in memoriam*

And for Nigel Fothergill

Acknowledgements

The author would like to thank Jane Mowl, Sarah Parnaby and Joachim Vieritz

ONE

Ivor had no memory of it. He'd only been four. He knew only his mother's and grandmother's accounts of what happened. Though in time he came to know the story very well indeed: they repeated it endlessly to him throughout his childhood – until his grandmother died, and a few years later his mother moved up north.

It was a big, tall house, they told him. It stood high on a bank beside the London road, among fields, but partly hidden by wild hedgerows from which sprang full-grown trees. Violet had taken Norma and Ivor on nearly all of her house-hunting trips, although it was not intended that they should share her new home with her. Twenty-year-old Norma had her own small flat above the antique shop where she worked, and she lived with Ivor there. But it was as a party of three that they arrived at Welstead House, left the car in the driveway and climbed the last few uphill yards to the front door to which the estate agent had happily given Violet, his respectably white-haired customer, the key.

The house had stood empty for six months, they'd been told. Yet coming into the lofty hallway in the chill of a November afternoon they had the feeling – at least the two adults had – that they were entering a place that had been unoccupied for much longer than that. 'Victorian with Elizabethan pretensions, I'd call it.' That was Violet's swift verdict. They'd seen from the outside its Dutch gables and dormers with their ogee-curved copings, all pricked up with spiked finials on their peaks.

All in silver-grey stone ... or stone cladding, Violet thought. All windows diamond-paned.

Norma opened the nearest door. It led into an echoing front room, roughly square, with two bay windows facing south. At the windows' edges diamond panes gave way to a surround of small square amber ones which transformed the sunlight slanting towards the floor into curtains of gold air where dust motes gleamed like worn threads. 'Oh, Mum, look at this,' Norma said. She had crossed the bare elm floor and was standing by the room's other exit, running her finger down the crack between door and jamb. 'Look. Masking tape. Parcel tape. Whatever it's called.'

Violet came over and looked, and Ivor came and looked too, though it was never discovered afterwards whether he knew what he was looking at. 'The doors have been sealed. Well, this one has.'

'Draughts, I expect,' said Violet, unable for the moment to see other possible implications. 'Place like this.'

'They wouldn't seal a connecting door with tape, surely? This must lead to the kitchen or somewhere. They'd use draught excluder. The only people who seal doors with tape...' Norma glanced at her son before selecting the words. Then she half spoke, half mouthed them. 'The what d'you call them. Psychic research people.'

'Nonsense,' Violet said. But they didn't try to break the seal, and returned the way they'd come to visit the rear of the house. Quarry-tiled kitchen, pre-war bathroom and scullery inspected, the women began to climb a narrow set of stairs that led up from the hall at the back. But Ivor, a hollow-eyed child, thin and thoughtful, who would have been well cast as one of Dickens's waifs or strays, shook his head and stayed put. 'All right, then,' his mother told him. 'Just stay downstairs. We'll only be a minute. Look all you want to, but don't touch things. Don't get dirty.' They left him, standing still and unprotesting, looking up at them with solemn eyes as they made their way upstairs.

They peered into bedrooms that were chill and empty, though Violet did remark enviously on the deep fitted cupboards in the recesses next to the chimneys in three of them. Then in the last room they came to they found an old spinning-wheel standing on the floor, as well as an antique cradle, like a tiny oak coffin on transverse rockers. 'They must be worth a bit,' Norma said. She'd known nothing about antiques four years ago when Violet had persuaded the Spraggens to take her on as a shop minder, but by now she knew a little. Even a bit more than that. 'Why would those get left behind when everything else has gone?'

'I can't imagine,' Violet said.

'And here's another door sealed with tape,' Norma announced. Though this door's seal, unlike the one downstairs, had been broken. But they were conscious of having left Ivor for a good two minutes and of having heard no sound from him in that time, so they didn't linger but headed back down the stairs. Ivor had moved a few steps from where they'd left him: back through the open door into the kitchen. He was looking away from them, he seemed to be staring hard at something, but he turned to face them, hearing their approach. 'I want to go,' he said.

'We're going in a minute,' his mother told him. 'We'll just have a look into the dining-room on the way out.'

'I want to go now,' the child said, all of a sudden fierce. 'Don't want to see dining-room.'

Norma looked at Violet. 'It's no fun for him. I'll take him back to the car. You join us in a minute.'

Once they were outside Ivor's spirits revived and he wanted to see the big gardens which ran all around the house. They were full of hide-and-seek corners created by crowding trees and shrubs, and by the long deep shadows that the sinking sun was causing to tilt and lance across the damp unmown grass. By the time Violet came out to join them Ivor was happily running off in all directions, disappearing behind hedges or into caverns of shade and then emerging with explosive whoops from a different quarter in order to give the grown-ups little surprises and frights.

Back in the car Ivor quietened down again, becoming the silent introspective boy he more often was. They'd gone a mile or more, Violet driving, Norma in the passenger seat and Ivor in the back, before he spoke again. 'I didn't like that house.'

'Neither did we, sweetheart,' his mother said, turning round. 'Don't worry. Nan's not going to buy it. We only went to look at it for fun.'

That was true. It wasn't a house that Violet would remotely have considered buying, even if she'd been left better off. Recently widowed, her thoughts ran more to a small easily-maintained bungalow with a Kleenex-sized garden, at Cooden Beach or Bexhill, and that was what she bought in the end – although a little further east, and nearer to her daughter – at Winchelsea Beach. But she had caught the house-hunting bug, and her modest intentions had not stopped her, these last few weeks, from viewing properties of every kind along the whole coast, and some distance inland too, all the way from Eastbourne to Deal. She'd already inspected an oast-house conversion, then deep in chestnut woods a time-locked Tudor farmhouse, whose single lavatory boasted a mahogany double-seat, and a house near the South Foreland, almost on the beach, that had once belonged to Ian Fleming and would have cost three times her entire estate.

'I didn't like the people,' Ivor said.

'What people, lovey?'

'When you upstairs they come into the kitchen.'

Norma and Violet exchanged a glance over the gear lever. 'Who did?' Norma asked. 'How many people?'

'Lady and a boy. They was laughing together. They walked into the skull.'

'Scullery.'

'Then they gone.'

'Did they speak to you?' Violet felt it was her turn to ask a question. 'Did they ask who you were?'

'Don't think they saw me.'

'Can you stop a mo?' Norma asked her adoptive mother. Violet pulled up beside a field gate. 'Now tell us everything you saw.'

Ivor went through it. Dutifully, dully, in the same stony dead way in which he would be responding, in a year's time, to questions about what he had done that day at school. He'd been in the kitchen. The woman and boy had come in behind him from the back hall, laughing and talking together. They'd walked right past him, ignored him completely – no, he hadn't tried to speak to them either – and then gone through the open door into the scullery. Then he didn't see or hear them any more. Perhaps they'd gone out through the back door into the garden? Ivor didn't think so. He hadn't heard the outside door open. The laughter simply stopped and they weren't there.

'What did they look like?' Norma wanted to know. 'What did they wear?'

'Lady had a coat over her head. Couldn't see face. Put her arms round boy.'

'And the boy? How old was he?'

'Bigger'n me. Like Danny and George.' These were a neighbour's children, aged eleven and nine. 'He long short trousers, and under – like mum wears.'

'You mean, like tights? How odd. What about shoes?'

'Lace shoes.'

'Lace-ups.'

'But funny.' Ivor demonstrated, touching places on his own short legs, that the shoes were ankle-boots, and that the shorts came down to just below the knee: not a fashion seen in the streets of Rye at that time, which was the late seventies.

'He's describing Edwardian costume,' Violet said. 'A woman in a riding cape and a boy in knickerbockers. Have you been reading him E. Nesbitt?'

'No,' said Norma, who rarely read him anything. She asked him, 'Have you seen people dressed that way in pictures? On the telly?'

'Nope.'

Norma thought for a moment. The Railway Children hadn't been on TV recently, as far as she remembered. By then the conversation had come to an end. Ivor said nothing further about the strange house and its stranger inhabitants, and his mother and Violet agreed that if he didn't want to talk about it, it was best not to open the subject up. That went not only for the rest of the car journey home but for the time that followed. Norma and Violet talked about it between themselves, asking each other what if anything Ivor had actually seen and what it meant, and told their friends, out of earshot of Ivor and always with the warning that the subject wasn't to be broached with the boy in case it disturbed him. Even when they drove past the house, high on its bank, as from time to time they did, they never pointed it out.

That changed a few years later, when Norma and Violet judged that Ivor was old enough to deal with such things, and then the story was told to him again and again. But by now Ivor had no memory of the incident at all.

TWO

Rye was a picture, everyone said. But what appealed especially to Gemma was that it was a picture you could get into and then, peering out of it, make more pictures still as the crooked streets of the town became viewfinders and frames for the landscapes beyond. In this it had more in common with the hill towns of Italy – even if it was a molehill in comparison with those – than with most other market towns in England's south east.

Making pictures was what Gemma did. She had just graduated from art school in London, and had come here, tagging along with her sister Sarah and Sarah's boyfriend Jeremy, on their camping, cycling holiday on the Kent-Sussex border. Gemma enjoyed the cycling – the camping less so – but the main object of her visit was to draw, paint, scribble – whatever best described the medium in which she worked. That fitted in fine with the more energetic cycling plans of Sarah and Jeremy: Gemma knew what the word gooseberry meant.

It was Gemma's first time in Rye. Summer 1982: a time when Britain briefly felt good about itself in the afterglow of the Falklands War. The winding little streets were full of painters with their easels, which they had difficulty in making stand upright among the round flint cobbles and on the steep camber of the bumpy ways. The pavements on either side were mere inches wide, so that every time Gemma passed another person one of them had to step off into the uneven road, and the other say sorry or excuse me, and both would smile. It created a sociable atmosphere that was almost party-like.

Favourite of views, to judge from the number of easels set up there, was the one from the top of Mermaid Street looking down. One of those streets in which the rooftops and chimneys at the bottom of its very steep slope lie below the eye-line of someone standing at the top, its appeal to Gemma was obvious and immediate. Eccentric half-timbered cottages and houses lined it on both sides. There was the world-famous Mermaid Inn – rebuilt in 1420, according to a sign at the front – which stood halfway down; then at the bottom the street's abrupt end framed a view of old tarred warehouses on the river quay and a wooded cliff rising behind, which led the eye upward till it rested on the open sky above. But there was no room for Gemma's easel this morning. Too many others had got here first. She told herself to get up earlier another day.

She walked on round the corner, noticed she was passing a sturdy brick-fronted Georgian house. A blue plaque on it read: Henry James, Author, Lived Here 1898 – 1916. She approved. Writers and painters alike had colonised the town over the years, and Henry James, by being American and English at the same time, was a suitable role model for herself – she with her English mum and American dad. Not that she was a writer like Henry James, or even a writer at all, but she knew what she meant.

Suddenly she was in Church Square. The narrow lane had opened into a wide space, a grassy sunlit churchyard with a yew tree in it and other trees besides, and lichen-covered tombstones that might have been older than the yew itself. Round three sides of the square were the same type of black and white cottages that put the quaint into Mermaid Street, and on the fourth side stood a huge and handsome medieval church. With the sun at her left shoulder she set up her easel and at once began to work.

She used a medium that would have invited snorts of derision had she been anything less than a superb draughtswoman: coloured Biros. She would use them to give intermittent outline to the shapes she wanted and then give them mass by filling the spaces with rapidly executed loops and figures of eight – rather like a French-polisher – in whatever combination of colours she chose. Anyone watching her doing this would have been reminded of the sight of a child scribbling, but somehow it worked.

She made rapid progress with the stonework of St Mary's church and the tombstones in front, and she planned to use the top of the low flint wall that separated the churchyard from the cobbled street for the bottom horizontal of her view. She had no thought for anything these days but the making of pictures: it was the way to stave off panic. She had left art college with no other plans for making a living, but had had no work offers, nor had she made much of an effort to seek them out. Her life had hardly been hers for the past three years: she'd shared it, plus a rather nice flat, with a fellow student called Michael, whom she'd believed she loved. But the end of student days culled relationships ruthlessly: only a few survived transplanting into the colder world beyond. Her one with Michael had not been one of those. The flat had gone. She was living at her parents' house, *sans* job, *sans* prospects, *sans* Michael, *sans* everything.

A cat came walking along the wall towards her, then sat down on it, turning to face her, a little to the left of the centre of her view. Afterwards Gemma liked to imagine that the cat knew this area of her paper was still blank. She decided to include the creature in her composition.

There had always been cats at her parents' home. The current one was called Nicholas II. A silver-grey animal, he was the successor to Old Nick, a sooty black, who had died at the impressive age of sixteen and a half. In her teens Gemma had once had a dream about Old Nick in which the cat had jumped onto her lap and spoken a few words in English.

'Oh Nick,' she'd answered him, 'I've known you all these years and you've never spoken to me before.'

'Oh, but I have,' replied the cat. 'But not out loud, of course.'

It was probably Gemma's memory of that dream, more than this day's invasion of her picture by the impertinent feline, that caused her to dream again that night about a talking cat. It was a less clear scenario this time, the details garbled, images muddled. Somehow potatoes were involved.

Gemma woke up, sat up even, in her rucked-up sleeping-bag to hear herself saying, 'Give the cat potatoes and it'll talk.' Fortunately there was no-one to hear her. She had a single tent; Sarah and Jeremy shared a larger one alongside. Only a groundsheet lay between her sleeping-bag and the lumpy turf beneath. Perhaps that very lumpiness had sown the potatoes in her dream.

The town was full of low-ceilinged pubs hundreds of years old; Jeremy had to duck between the black, ex-ship-timber beams. Each ancient inn was decorated with old ships' lamps and all boasted shaggy green hop bines from the last year's harvest, strung among the beams for luck. The Standard, The Union, and others besides provided snug sitting-rooms for their evenings. But they weren't open for breakfast. For that they would cycle up from the camp-site outside the walls to one of the tea and coffee shops in the town centre: tea-shops that like the pubs were fashioned out of ancient black-beamed houses but minus the hop bines and the beer. They had two favourites, next-door to each other, crowding against the church's north door: Simon the Pieman's, and Fletcher's House – the latter the birthplace of that dramatist in 1579 – and they frequented them on alternate days so as not to give offence to either. The smallest drop in temperature was an excuse for blazing log fires in the inglenooks of the two establishments, and both provided high quality home-made cakes that were served in massive slices. The look of them was enough to make the mouth water. The price did the same for the eyes.

'I thought I might do a series of pictures of the Rye streets, each one featuring a cat or two,' Gemma announced to the others this after-dream morning between mouthfuls of a chocolate cake almost as rich and sticky as a French mousse.

'A bit twee, don't you think?' Sarah said. 'And look at the shops in the town. They're already choc-a-bloc with sketches of Mermaid Street, the church and everywhere else. Water colours, oils, the lot.'

'Not with cats in them, there aren't,' said Jeremy quietly. Gemma gave him a mental gold star for that. 'But you'd be up against massive competition – in terms of quantity at least.' The gold star award stood. Just.

'Nothing ventured,' said Gemma brightly.

'In your dreams,' said Sarah.

Outside a small crowd was gathering in the street, its eyes raised to the clock on the side of the church tower. The crowd gathered at fifteen minutes past, and again at fifteen minutes to, each hour in order to witness the Quarter Boys, a pair of naked gilded cherubs about six feet tall, who stood either side of the clock-face, striking two bells with small gold hammers, producing a dull metallic clang. Crowds who gathered expectantly at the approach of the hour or the half went away disappointed: the Quarter Boys worked strictly to the dictates of their title. 'Oh, look at that,' Gemma said. She didn't need to point to the member of the crowd who'd attracted her attention: a stout woman in middle age and a bright floral dress, with a truly enormous broad-brimmed sun hat.

Jeremy said, in that drawl of his that hinted at the public-school upbringing he might have wished for but hadn't actually had, 'How is it that towns like Rye always end up producing these eccentric spinsters – or matrons, whichever she is? And *who* is she?'

'She's someone's aunt,' said Sarah. 'Isn't she wonderful? That hat!'

'Aunt Hattie,' said Gemma, laughing. 'She someone's Aunt Hattie.' They watched her, hat bobbing and ducking among the little knot of tourists, until that knot came undone and fell apart and the hat went with it, flopping and bouncing down the street.

Gemma had no intention of telling either Sarah or Jeremy about her absurd dream but she thought about it after they'd parted for the middle part of the day, the couple to cycle the undemanding flat lanes of the Romney Marsh, Gemma to continue scribbling her pictures in the town. She bought postcards to help her remember scenes she wouldn't have time to finish during her stay at Rye. She also climbed the tightly wound staircase inside the church tower until she stood behind battlements at the top and looked out over the close-knit orange roofs below, at the wide expanse of the Romney Marsh on the seaward side, and then up the river valleys that reached into the hilly countryside like outstretched fingers of the Marsh's dead-flat hand.

She also found herself looking down into a big and well-tended walled garden, which must have been hidden from the street, in which tourists (she presumed) were walking to and fro. She was able to work out that the garden belonged to the house she'd noticed the day before: the one that had been owned by Henry James. Lamb House was its name. She descended from the church tower and crossed the square, paid her fee to the National Trust at the door, and went in.

Typical, she thought. You could never see the most interesting parts of these properties. The bedroom where George I had spent the night after being rescued from shipwreck on Camber Sands was not open to the public. Nor were the kitchens. The panelled dining-room, though, she liked, as well as the humour of the telephone room, a panelled sanctuary that was exactly that – a tiny room with a wall-mounted phone in it – and had been kept for posterity in a state that James would have known. The gardens were lovely, even if James's beloved garden-room was no longer there: it had been demolished by a bomb in the Second World War.

It was a place you'd like to live in, Gemma thought. You couldn't buy it now, though. The writers who had inhabited it more recently, even Rumer Godden after her farmhouse was destroyed by fire, had been tenants of the National Trust. Still, you could always dream.

Rumer Godden had seen a ghost in that house, so had Henry James, and others had seen the ghost of Henry James, all of which had a satisfying kind of symmetry. Gemma left the house with a feeling, she couldn't have explained it, that everything was about to happen, that things were on some kind of brink.

She returned to her pictures, composing feverishly all afternoon. At one point she saw a small boy climbing the street towards her, aged perhaps eight. He was a striking-looking little fellow, with very large blue eyes framed in starbursts of black lashes and with a shock of black curls that had got rather over-long but which – Gemma imagined sympathetically – his mother probably hated to see cut. She was just wondering whether she should incorporate him in one of her sketches when he disappeared through the doorway of a shop. Gemma remembered, with a feeling of surprise, that it was an antique shop, its window, which she'd glanced through several times in the past few days, full of Jacobean and Georgian furniture and glowing Afghan rugs. The boy did not come out. Perhaps his parents owned the shop. He ought to have a bicycle, Gemma decided. Probably did have one, come to think of it. Parents who owned an antique shop would have made sure of that. They'd have given him a smart name too. Something like Vincent, which his friends would shorten to Vince.

An idea was coming to her, an idea that had never crossed her mind before today, even today hadn't crossed it until after her visit to Henry James's house. The boy would be in her pictures. So would Aunt Hattie. She'd be his aunt. She'd have a different – but always extreme – hat in every picture. The cat would be her cat – or his. He'd have that bicycle. The bicycle would take him places. And her project would not be just a matter of pictures. She went down to the High Street where there was a big stationer's shop and bought three A4 notepads, spiral-bound. Later that day she began to write.

The antique shop was Ivor's playroom when he was very small. That might have been a worry for Norma, or the shop's owners, the Spraggens, but it wasn't. Ivor was very respectful towards the shop's contents. He might trace the outlines of carved rosettes on an Elizabethan chest with a finger-tip or stroke a Persian rug as other children fondled pets, but he would never have allowed himself to break or even scratch any of the precious objects that furnished the shop above which he lived. Because he was a careful and quiet child – so different from what Norma remembered of herself at the same age – she began to think of him as precociously wise and thoughtful, a nice child, an easy child, an all-round good boy.

That changed when he went off to school and the complaints started coming in. Ivor stamped hard on the other boys' feet and twisted their arms, even if they were a size or two bigger than he was. He did those things to the girls too, and pulled their long hair till it came out by the roots. Took hold of his classmates' exercise books and tore them to shreds. But he started school in an age when teachers could still impose their authority and will by force. Although not without difficulty, and a few stern warnings to his young mother, they did eventually manage to clamp a lid on his antisocial behaviour – inside the classroom at least.

Although bright, he didn't do well at school. He was one of those children whom teachers classify as lazy when the reality is that they can not see the point of the tasks they are set and regard most of their school work as a waste of time. There were two exceptions: art and woodwork, both of which he took to with a fierce aptitude, almost impatiently, as if he were angry at not having been shown these things before. His teachers were impressed, if not startled, by what he could do, almost untaught, while his mother was more than delighted by the creations he brought home.

It was very important to Norma that she should show these things off to Violet. Ivor's early drawings and daubs, his balsa-wood models and later his delicate fretwork constructions: cranes, drawbridges, fairground roundabouts that worked. 'You must admit that's amazing,' she'd say, 'for a boy of six.' Then seven, then eight. Violet did agree that his achievements were better than the average for his age but was not prepared to offer fulsome praise. 'It's all very well, dear,' she said more than once. 'But it's the three Rs he ought to be making progress with, and you know as well as I do that he's not.'

Norma's insistence on the positive stemmed from a fear that Violet was growing to dislike the child. She was aware of the weakness of her own position: no ties of blood linked her to Violet. Ivor on the other hand was irrevocably hers, yet she was afraid that she too was not managing to like the boy enough. He was more than usually cute for a small boy, and seldom did anything actively to antagonise her, yet she felt the presence of something in him, something beyond her power to define, that she would not be able to trust.

In the earliest years of Ivor's existence the three of them had been very much a family unit, three generations together, going places, doing things as a team. In and out of each other's homes: the flat above the shop, Violet's neat and tidy bungalow four miles away at Winchelsea Beach. But with time this changed; visits between them grew more sporadic, more formally arranged: Sunday lunch at grandma's, or Saturday tea. Looked forward to with mixed feelings on both sides.

If Ivor was aware of Violet's growing distaste for him he never showed it. Not that he showed much in the way of affection towards her either, or to his mother, come to that. He would submit dutifully to an embrace or cuddle, but never instigated or asked for one himself. The words *I love you, Mum*, or *I love you, Nan*, did not come readily to his lips. Yet there were a number of things about Violet that he appreciated very much: they were to be found in her garden shed.

When Violet's builder husband Peter had died his business died with him. As he worked mostly alone there were no partners or permanent staff to take it onward and upward. Violet had handled the paperwork for years but could hardly take over the physical labour of an actual builder, and the same went for her adopted daughter. Peter Wingate's workshop didn't really amount to a going concern that could be sold on, even if you took into account the goodwill of his customers: people's ties to their local builders tend to be personal and not easily transferred. So the heavy equipment and stocks of timber, cement and such were sold, but the hand-tools, mainly for sentimental reasons, Violet kept.

She had them carefully transported when she moved to Winchelsea Beach, and they were now stored in her shed. There was a workbench with a vice attached to it. There were G-clamps and try-squares, chisels and saws, mitre-boxes and other devices for helping you saw at precise angles. There was an oil-stone in a mahogany case, and spoke-shaves and planes, and other mysterious things whose names Violet was unable to pass on to Ivor when he began to show an interest in the collection, because she didn't know them herself.

Ivor wasn't allowed to play with the chisels and saws unsupervised, but he did anyway when the adults' attention was elsewhere. Once Violet caught him in the act of tightening the vice slowly on his thumb. 'I want to know how much pain I can stand,' he said sullenly. He was seven.

Violet was both frightened and shocked. 'You mustn't inflict pain on yourself,' she told him. 'If it comes your way that's different. Then you can offer it up to Jesus.' Every so often Violet did speak to him in this puzzling way about Jesus, but only when Norma wasn't in earshot. Norma did not approve of his being 'indoctrinated'. 'It's all right him being told about Jesus at school,' she told Violet. 'There he can take it or leave it. But I don't want it forced on him at home the way you did with me when I was little.'

Violet was a regular attender at the Catholic church in Watchbell Street. Norma had stopped accompanying her in her mid-teens and had never taken Ivor there or had him baptised. It was a matter of sadness to Violet. She wondered whether, had he been brought up to have a bit of religion about him, he might have been less inclined to displays of shocking behaviour such as testing his pain threshold in a vice. She wondered whether, if she'd insisted on Norma's coming to church with her she might not have got pregnant with him at fifteen to begin with.

The carpentry tools had pride of place in Ivor's thoughts, but they were not the only things in the shed to claim his attention. On a stack of shelves sat dusty jars and tins and packets that contained every kind of product for use in the garden and Ivor, though not given to the reading of books or anything much else, was well able by the age of seven or so to discover what those packets and tins contained. It seemed to him that they fell into two distinct categories: one lot was for making plants grow bigger, the other for killing things. They seldom moved from their allotted places on the shelves. If there had been a bottle of Miracle-Gro in the third place from the left on the lowest shelf when Ivor was five, there it or its replacement still was when he was eight, and if he picked it up to look at it he would see revealed in the place where it had been a perfect circle of dust-free wood.

Ivor was particularly interested in a packet of something called Weed and Feed. Ivor was conscious of its singularity. It was the only one among all those packets and jars that didn't fall into either of the two categories he'd already identified: the nurturers and the killers. This one was both. It was intended for application to lawns. Ivor wondered whether it would also work on the fish.

Violet's garden contained a small brick-surrounded pool which was home to a collection of goldfish. When he was younger and just learning his numbers Ivor had made a game out of trying to count those fish but after a few weeks of never reaching the same total twice he had given up. They hid themselves so in the weed. Violet often used to say, especially in the height of summer, that there was too much weed. There were also too many herons. Violet's bungalow at Winchelsea Beach – not just a beach but a full-sized modern village complete with pub, church and shop – was halfway between two nature reserves, both containing several lakes and other bodies of water which were fished by numbers of herons. Their flight path between the Pett Level lakes and those of the Rye Harbour reserve provided a conveniently fish-stocked way-point in the form of Violet's garden pond.

Violet placed a net over the pond from time to time, but thought it unsightly and would remove it when visitors came, then she would forget to replace it after they left and a heron would fly down and make off with one of the fish.

Ivor, unconcerned by the fate of the goldfish, rather enjoyed the visits of the herons. They gave him a chance to study their angle-poise outlines and bold markings, which he would reproduce with confidence in his drawings later. As their colour scheme was almost entirely grey, white and black they lent themselves well to the medium of the pencil sketch. But he had in his mind now a sketch of something more dramatic. He didn't know exactly what the drama might consist of, but experienced a new thrill at the thought that he had it in his power to set it in motion himself.

All poisons and even mildly dangerous substances carry the warning: Keep out of reach of children. But no parent can be a vigilante twenty-four hours a day, and Ivor was now nine – no longer of an age to be swallowing garden fertiliser from the packet. Kill the weeds and feed the fish, he told himself. His motives were entirely honourable, he told himself. But deep down he knew that these were simply the explanations he would offer to people when asked for them. They could believe him or not, as they chose. It didn't worry him that they probably would not. Even so he did make sure that Violet and Norma were not in the garden but busy in the kitchen when he went to the shed and took the packet from the shelf. And he made sure they hadn't re-emerged when he came out of the shed, packet in one hand, sketch-pad and pencils in the other, and made his way to the goldfish pool.

He began by dropping a few pellets into the water. They were large, and sank, and the fish darted around a bit, keener to avoid the hail of missiles than to find out what the pellets actually were. So he crumbled a few more of them in his fingers and dropped them gently onto the surface as he had seen Violet do with ants' eggs. It worked. One by one the fish came, their round mouths gibbering silently, tasting the new treat. It didn't taste good, evidently, as one mouthful was all that any of them took before shimmying away. Ivor noticed that the whole pellets he had thrown to the bottom just a minute earlier were breaking up and dissolving in the water. Encouraged by this he tipped in the entire contents of the packet.

Violet and Norma, coming out of the house a few minutes later, were pleased to come upon Ivor sitting beside the pool, sketching on his cartridge-paper pad. Peering over his shoulder they were impressed by what they saw. Ivor had skilfully captured the look of the water-lily pads, like pie-charts that show ninety-five percent of something, yet with a little uplift to the last couple of percent that stopped the surface of the pond from being entirely flat. Then there were the fish, some peering curiously up at the world above the water's surface, others open-mouthed in wonder at it. Yet others lay on their sides as though ready to expire. One or two, fins akimbo, already floated upside-down.

Norma was the first to look at the actual pool. The carnage there was now more advanced than in Ivor's sketch. 'Oh blimey,' she said.

Violet looked and saw. She saw the empty packet of Weed and Feed. She yanked Ivor to his feet with such force and suddenness that he wet himself, though he didn't cry. But it was to Norma that she spoke. Shouted through rising sobs. 'Take him home. Take your bastard child away from me. Go now. Never bring him here again.'

THREE

The success of The Cat Who Loved Potatoes by Gemma Palmer was not of the overnight variety. It was better than that. It built over the months, and then over the years. It was more than she could have dreamed of when she began to draw that fortuitous cat in Rye, and saw the boy who became Vince. Vince Harris.

Gemma had taken pains to find the right surname for him. Harris hadn't popped into her head like his first name. She had read somewhere that Beatrix Potter found inspiration for her characters' names in tombstone inscriptions in the churchyard at Hawkshead. Nutkin had been one serendipitous find – though presumably without the given name of Squirrel. Dickens had done the same thing. With this in mind Gemma had explored the churchyard in Rye during that first visit, in search of the unusual. She found the name Twort on the war memorial, but something told her it would be in questionable taste to use a name from that source for what would essentially be comic effect. The name of Ethelbert Mittel on a nineteenth-century tomb had possibilities, but she thought it would do better for Dickens's purposes or in a Monty Python sketch than for the story she had in mind. But then another stone happily offered her the beautifully ordinary name of Harris, and so that was who Vince became.

The book was turned down by the first three publishers she sent it to. They took the view that children's books about talking cats had had their day and that she should try to be more original. But the fourth editor to look at it saw potential – which the others had possibly missed – in the wit and energy of Gemma's illustrations.

A month after its publication Gemma moved out of her parent's house near Tunbridge Wells and into her own flat in London. It was not just the book which sold. The Cat Who Loved Potatoes began to feature on tea-towels, kids' pyjamas, coffee mugs, cereal bowls, cats' feeding dishes and bedroom curtains. Nowhere more than in the town of Rye itself: its landmark buildings were the background to all the pictures after all.

The town was in the process of exchanging its High Street of butchers and bakers and gentlemen's tailors, which had supplied its inhabitants' wants without fuss for generations, for shops that offered trinkets, teddy-bears and bric-a-brac to growing tourist hordes. Gemma had mixed feelings about this: all her romantic and artistic instincts deplored the change, but it coincided most happily with the arrival on the scene of her Cat merchandise to fill those very trinket shops and provide her with a gratifyingly good income.

Gemma visited Rye often. She got to know the owners of the shops and book stores that sold the things she'd created. She was called on to give talks, read from the book in the children's library, sign copies of it in the shops. She began to make friends in the town. She loved Rye, not for mercenary reasons but because its streets had provided her inspiration in the first place: picturesque scenery, a grey cat, a woman in an outrageous hat and a boy in a doorway. Also because, for all the changes that time was bringing to the place, she still found it charming. She began to think about living there. Buying a house in the town. Or maybe in the countryside beyond its walls.

Her plans might have been rendered obsolete by the arrival in her life of a man called Dieter. He was German, a painter ten years older than herself, with twinkly blue eyes and sporting a neat goatee of blond beard a few years before everyone else decided that such a growth was fashionable – though from another angle, of course, he was wearing the thing some decades after it had gone out of favour the last time around. He was introduced to her by ex-art-school friends in London. He was very taken with her intelligent grey eyes, her neat nose and sensitive mouth, the grace of her movements and the overall slim trimness of her. When she spoke she made people smile. Not every woman he'd met could do that

For her part Gemma was equally attracted. Dieter had perfect manners, nearly perfect English, was handsome and sexy and had paid her the compliment of falling in love with her work, despite the fact that it had been written for children, before he'd even met her. She had always been impetuous where men were concerned. Only a few weeks of dating and discovering each other further in the bedroom passed between their first meeting and Gemma's moving, with most of her belongings, into the house and attached studio he owned near Koblenz.

But Dieter on his home turf proved a less emollient, easy-going fellow than he'd been in England. He wanted meals cooked for him when *he* wanted them, he decided what time they had to get up or go to bed, who used the studio when and for how long, how often they went out and with whom they socialised. When Gemma resisted, he involved his mother who came all the way from Frankfurt to lecture her daughter-in-common-law on the way that German men needed to be kept happy. On top of all this, Gemma failed to return the compliment Dieter had paid her of admiring her work. He had a very high opinion of his merit as a painter, Gemma did not. She was back in England before two years had passed.

But her time in Germany had not been wasted. The Rhineland landscapes around Koblenz, where vineyards grew up mountain slopes as steep as leaning walls, where turreted castles danced with the shadows of the clouds on the crests of the hills, had provided a haunting setting for her second illustrated book for children, Nicholas II and the Castle of Rats. By the time she returned to Rye, this time to look seriously for a house to live in, copies of the hardback edition were already in the shops.

Arriving back in England homeless, except for her parents' house and her sister's, Gemma made neither address her first refuge. Instead she hired a car at the airport, drove straight to Rye and booked in at The George. The following morning she went after breakfast to an estate agent's in Cinque Ports Street, where she asked the staff to find a small flat for her to rent for a few weeks while she looked for something more permanent.

As she left the estate agent's office she saw walking towards her one of her old Rye acquaintances from two years before. This was Jane, ten years older than Gemma, a potter and sculptress whose work was exhibited nationally and who, like Gemma, had occasionally appeared on TV. They might not have had much in common as individuals: the bond between them was a shared consciousness of belonging on the same plane of artistic achievement – even if in Jane's case it was the financial support of the Guy's Hospital surgeon she was married to that enabled her to stay there.

Despite exchanging nothing more than Christmas cards for two years, within minutes of meeting they were sharing news over hot coffee in Fletcher's House. It struck Gemma as a very Rye thing, this easy sociability, one of the things that had propelled her straight back here to lick her wounds, even if she hadn't been conscious of that till now.

'You missed Rye's latest moment of fame,' Jane told her, once Gemma had got the whole Dieter debacle off her chest, and laid before Jane her reason for being here. By this time they'd moved on from coffee at Fletcher's to lunch at The Mermaid. 'They did Mapp and Lucia for TV while you were away. Two series. We had Prunella Scales and Geraldine McEwen practically living here and they were wonderful fun.' Jane didn't go on to say that she had met them personally so Gemma presumed she hadn't. 'Then when the series were shown the tourists simply flocked. Lamb House didn't know what had hit it. He called it Mallards in the books of course.'

For a moment Gemma thought Jane meant Henry James. Then she remembered that E.F.Benson, the original creator of Mapp and Lucia, had also occupied Lamb House. She hadn't read his books. 'Oh yes, Lamb House,' she said, and remembered how years ago she'd imagined herself living there. 'I don't imagine the National Trust have decided to part with it, hmm?'

'Sounds as though you're house-hunting in a pretty big way,' said Jane, with a little flicker of mascara-ed eyelashes, more interested in Gemma's plans now that she thought she'd got a glimpse of the scale of them. Two days later, and for many days after that, they were setting off in Jane's car because, as Jane said, you couldn't just leave it all to the estate agent, to scour the countryside for a suitable property.

Gemma was in a state of readiness to fall in love with every attractive house they drove past, whether it was for sale or not. During their first drives around the area Gemma was saying ooh and aah to everything and, *If only that was for sale*, or *What about that?* After a few days of this Jane, slowing the car to a crawl in order to peer sideways at her, her mouth turned slightly down at the corners as it always did when she had something particularly serious to say, told her, 'I know you've just come home and everything looks wonderfully rose-tinted, but if you don't mind my saying so, you do seem a bit unfocused.'

Gemma took this on the chin, partly because Jane was ten years her senior but mainly because it was true. They were driving through the lanes that threaded the high ground above the Tillingham valley, and at that moment were slowly passing the gateway to a farm whose buildings, which included a pretty white-painted house, could be seen a hundred yards up a track. Its name was on the gate: Birdskitchen. Gemma turned to Jane and said very seriously, 'Stop a second. You're right. I must get my idea straight.' Jane stepped daintily on the brake pedal and they halted in the middle of the lane. 'All right then.' Gemma pointed along the farm track. 'What I would like to live in would be an old farmhouse. One like that.'

Jane looked at the house and then back at her. 'A farm? Isn't that going a bit far?'

'I meant one without land attached.'

'Even so,' said Jane. 'It'd still be far too big – and isolating. Since you're not currently attached either.'

The farms that dotted this landscape were mostly of a type. Their common features were a huge timber barn, clad in tarred weatherboard, an oast house with one or two white-cowled roundels apiece for the drying of hops, and a farmhouse, usually weather-boarded, white-painted, of indeterminate age and in shape much longer than it was high or deep, with the comforting appearance of a rustic loaf. Some were still the headquarters of working farms but others had parted company with their land and other buildings in the course of the twentieth century and were simply picturesque private dwellings. Most, of course, were not for sale.

But the very day after Gemma had her previously unknown wish revealed to her by Jane's question and the sight of Birdskitchen Farm the estate agent telephoned her. He was calling to say that a farmhouse called Gatcombe, three miles from Rye, had come onto the market. Gemma drove out to it with Jane the next day.

The morning air was crisp and jewel-like, its warmth poignant with the end of summer. Hops were being picked in the river valleys below, where a little mist still lingered, clothing the snail-paced tractors and the men working alongside them in a light veil. Gatcombe stood on a shallow hillside, a little way up from the floor of the Brede valley. A short lane connected it with the main road that ran west along the ridge from Rye, and if you pursued the lane downhill it would take you back to Rye, or Winchelsea, by a more devious route. The valley bottoms of the Tillingham and Brede had a landlocked, inland feel to them, yet climb just a few feet up any hill and the sea rushed headlong into view, and the rooftops of Rye, clustering up their molehill-mountain site, would appear unexpectedly, sometimes above and sometimes below you as you rounded a bend.

Gatcombe also came into sight unexpectedly, and round a bend. Its white paintwork and rust-red roof appeared almost shocking in the sunshine against the green. Its pair of oast kilns, a farmyard's breadth away, stood watch over the house's roof – like two sentries with pointing guns, Gemma thought. Or did they remind her more of giant champagne bottles? Soda water siphons? There would be sketches of them in her next book.

The house was slightly but pleasingly asymmetric, the front door not central: there was one window to the left of it, two on the right. The main chimney punched its way out of the roof top from a couple of strides behind the front door. Gemma wondered how the rooms were laid out inside. She knew already that she wanted this house.

They parked the car and got out. 'It's picturesque in the extreme, I grant you,' said Jane at once. 'A truly lovely spot. The house looks almost exactly like that other one you liked – Birdskitchen. And the name – Gatcombe. You could turn it into Catcombe with one stroke of a brush. But you can't be serious about living here. On your own. The size of it! It's a farmhouse for a family of eight.'

'I'll fill it with children,' Gemma said at once, though she hadn't entertained that thought before this moment.

'Your own or other people's?' Jane enquired.

'Either or,' said Gemma with a laugh. 'Both if necessary.' She had the money: she could do with the place as she liked.

'But the oast,' Jane went on. 'What would you do with that, for heaven's sake?'

'It wouldn't be mine,' Gemma said, slightly impatiently because the question betrayed a lack of attention on Jane's part. 'We've already talked about this. I'm not so crazy as to go buying a whole farm. The house was sold off separately, apparently, a generation or more ago. Farmers don't want their old houses these days, the agent told me. Especially if they've been expanding over the years and would now have three or four of the things. Why hold on to three high-maintenance seventeenth-century pads when you can have a big bungalow built for a song on land you already own? The family who own this place,' she gestured to the farmyard, the oast, other buildings and the land around them, 'are called Jameson. They have a modern house at the top of the lane.'

'Well, I hope they've got a tractor that can dig you out of the snow when there's a winter,' said Jane.

They entered the front garden through a wicket gate in the waist-high wall that divided the garden from the lane. The white-painted door ahead of them was open.

That evening Gemma telephoned her sister for the first time since her return to England. Sarah, forever two steps behind where Gemma's life was concerned, kept asking what was happening to Dieter. 'You can forget him,' Gemma said. 'I'm buying a farmhouse. How soon can you get down to see it?'

Ivor moved up from primary school to the local comprehensive, the Thomas Peacocke. His contemporaries, some of whom had come from his old school with him, found him aloof and unsociable. He talked little and seemed not to care much whether people liked him or not. He was seldom bullied by older pupils. Though not very big he was strong for his size and immensely tough, and as the years passed and provided a supply of smaller, weaker boys than himself to pick on he did so without hesitation. On the sports field he was respected, in the same way and for the same reason that, walking a country footpath, you'd respect a bull.

He had long grown out of pulling girls' hair. What he now tried to do when the opportunity arose was to undress them. At least, to begin to. He seldom got very far. Squeals of protest would bring other people – teachers or contemporaries – running, but curiously his attentions were seldom resented in the longer term. The twelve-year-old girls in his class might not want him to strip them naked just yet, and certainly not inside the school, but they agreed, talking among themselves, that he had some weird kind of appeal. Perhaps they sensed a danger about him that was not limited to the football pitch. It helped, of course, that among all his peers he had the most striking looks. While from his point of view his precocious interest in the complex business of removing female clothing would stand him in good stead in times to come.

Violet died when Ivor had just turned fourteen. It happened very suddenly. She was buying hand-cream in Boot's. She had reached the till and was fishing in her purse when an almighty headache ignited like a tank of petrol beneath her skull. The pharmacist called to his assistant to phone for an ambulance at once. To Violet he said, 'Don't worry. You'll be fine.' But she wouldn't be. She gave a little gasp as if she was starting to laugh, but it was the last wraith of a breath that would ever leave her body. Before the ambulance arrived they had closed the shop.

They told Norma that it had been a type of brain haemorrhage called a sub-arachnoid, which was one hyphenated word more than Norma had really wanted to know. On the other hand there soon came the more pleasing discovery that she was the owner of a bungalow at Winchelsea Beach and a balance of savings and investments that, while not amounting to riches, left her with more money to her name than she had ever had to do with before. For his part Ivor was pleased that he would have access once again to Violet's garden shed and his grandfather's woodworking tools.

Among Violet's small collection of jewellery Norma discovered a little silver chain with an adjustable clasp and a tiny cross attached. She asked the jeweller to whom she sold those items that she didn't want for herself if it was some kind of rosary without any beads.

'I take it your mother was a Catholic,' the jeweller said, frowning through spectacles. 'I think she may also have been a member of Opus Dei. This is, I think, a *cilice*. It would be worn around the upper thigh, quite invisible to anyone else, but intended to mortify the flesh.' When Norma looked at him in open-mouthed incomprehension he added, 'I suppose, to remind people of the suffering of their Saviour.' He gave a shrug. 'Not my cup of tea, but there you are. I'm not sure if there's much of a market. But I'll take it off your hands along with the other stuff if you don't want it around the house.'

'I never had any idea she was a member of anything like that,' Norma told Ivor afterwards, with a mixture of squeamish disgust and grudging admiration.

'What a turn-up,' said Ivor. 'Who'd have thought the old cow had any feelings to mortify in that bit of her body?'

'Don't talk like that about your grandmother,' Norma flared at him. 'That's worse than horrible. You should wash your mouth out.'

'What she said to me last time I saw her was just as horrible,' Ivor countered coolly. 'That time of the accident with the fish. She called me a bastard.' Ivor had hardly mentioned his grandmother since that day. He had seldom referred to the event either. On the rare occasions that it did come up he would insist on the word accident.

'Well,' said Norma more thoughtfully, 'if we can't forgive people after they're dead I don't see there's much hope for any of us.' For the first time in her life she heard herself sounding like Violet as she spoke.

Gemma heard about the woman who had dropped dead in Boots. It happened a few months after she moved into Gatcombe Farm. Angela told her. Angela was one of her new friends from the chamber choir.

When Gemma first saw Gatcombe it had been at the centre of great activity. Hop picking was still going on and the tractors were driving past the side of the house and into the yard every half hour with their trailer-loads of bines. After hops came the apple harvest. But after that the action stopped. The lovely Brede valley went abruptly to sleep for the winter. Occasionally a flock of black-headed gulls would draw Gemma's eye to a solitary man on a tractor, ploughing a distant hillside. But that was that. Which explained the chamber choir.

She also picked up the viola she hadn't touched since school orchestra days and joined an amateur string quartet in which Jane the sculptress played the cello. She drew and painted in the part of Gatcombe that had become her studio. And met her friends for coffee or lunch, as she was meeting Angela now, when she went into Rye. Rye was well-stocked with people like herself, poets, painters and potters, women of all ages who were intelligent, creative, and exhibited a strong vein of independence.

'Did you know the woman?' Gemma asked Angela.

Angela delicately chewed, then swallowed, her mouthful of early asparagus. They were lunching at The George. 'Which woman?'

'The one who died in Boot's.' Gemma took a sip of wine.

'Not really. I know people who knew her. She was the widow of a builder in Northiam. She had a daughter, I believe, who works in one of the antique shops.'

'Which one?'

'One of the ones in Lion Street. Why?'

Gemma ignored the why. 'Does she have a son?'

'The daughter, you mean? I've no idea.'

Gemma hadn't seen any child in Rye, either before her time in Germany or since, who might have been the little boy who'd disappeared into that antique shop and then turned in her imagination into Vince. But then she had never again seen the woman in the flamboyant hat who had been the inspiration for Aunt Hattie. Come to that, she hadn't seen the grey cat either.

Six years had passed. Cats died. Buxom lady tourists went home and didn't return. Children changed out of all recognition. They grew up.

*

Norma gave up the little flat above the shop and moved out with Ivor to Winchelsea Beach. She took driving lessons – she had inherited Violet's car, after all. – and in a few months was freed from having to use the bus to travel to work or anywhere else. She bought Ivor a bicycle. And Ivor was secretly relieved, though he never said so, not to have to pile up his bedroom with a shed-load of woodworking tools.

The bicycle might have been a mistake, Norma began to think before very long. It gave Ivor the freedom to truant from school whenever he wanted without being easily caught. He cycled off by himself with his sketchpads on the Marsh roads, along the miles of sea-wall between Winchelsea Beach and Pett, and up the narrow lanes around Icklesham and Brede. Patiently he watched the birds, the marsh birds, the coast birds, the field and hedgerow ones. A pair of binoculars had turned up among Violet's things and was anexed by Ivor without discussion. He sketched whatever he saw at lightning speed and later would make paintings at leisure, using the notes about colour that he'd made.

That was during daylight hours. Evenings he spent with a group of youngsters who theoretically went to his school, though he didn't think he ever saw them there. They hung around the station yard and the kebab shop till all hours, and as their conversational resources were not large, fell back when they'd exhausted those on daring each other to break the windows in the bus shelters or the phone-box, and outdoing each other in the obscenities they hurled at the police when they came to move them on.

The first time Ivor stayed out all night – sleeping on the living-room floor of an older member of the gang – Norma was beside herself with worry. Then she was angry with him when he turned up at the shop next day. But getting angry never worked with Ivor. He just shrugged his shoulders and carried on, seldom bothering even to argue back. He stayed away again, and then it became routine, and eventually Norma just shrugged her own shoulders and carried on.

One morning in May of that year, when Ivor had turned sixteen without maturing into a loving son or a lovable one, a man walked into the antique shop, where Norma was on her own. He was dressed in a smart suit, had a seventies-looking mane of dark hair, and looked about fifteen years older than Norma's thirty-one. He asked if Norma was the shop's owner, which always went down well with her. She was less fond of customers who asked at once for her to fetch the manager on the assumption that that person could not possibly be she. Neither Mr nor Mrs Spraggen would be back until the afternoon, she told him. He said he'd come back then, but in the meantime he didn't seem in much of a hurry to go. He stayed and talked antiques. He was furnishing a chain of country house hotels in the north, he told Norma, and was in Rye on the lookout for good things. Norma showed him what was in the shop and then, since it was one o'clock and the shop was about to close for an hour, he invited her to lunch at the Union Inn.

FOUR

Every summer the fifth form at Ivor's school was given a 'map-day'. Modelled on the orienteering hikes that scouts, guides and cadets practised, it involved pairs of boys or girls setting out in different directions armed with Ordnance Survey maps, and instructions to make their way between a series of grid reference points, reporting back on what they found at each one. The mystery destinations were carefully selected by the teachers and allocated to the youngsters so as not to send them in the direction of their homes. This year it was the turn of Ivor's class.

Ivor was paired off with a boy called Mark: he'd known him for years, though not particularly well. Ivor didn't think they'd ever shared a private conversation. Now they were to have a whole day of them as they set off on a ten-mile bus ride to New Romney, an ancient town like Rye and a fellow member of the Cinque Ports.

Normally Ivor was disinclined to carry out tasks that other people assigned to him but the idea of today's activity touched something in him, and he found himself – rather to his surprise – as meekly ready as Mark was to follow the instructions they'd been given. They got off the bus in New Romney's broad main street and, after a bit of head-scratching and turning the map this way and that, made for their first grid reference point. It turned out to be the church. Mark read out their instructions. 'Here are tall pillars. Dark stains mark them. How high (estimate) do the stains reach? What caused them, and when?'

The pillars were inside the church. 'Norman,' said Ivor, who knew next to nothing about churches, but he did know this. They were darkly stained to an even height of about four feet above the ground.

'But why, and when?' said Mark. 'Hang on.' He pulled a notepad and a Biro from his backpack. 'They put notices at the back somewhere, giving the place's history.' Ivor looked at him blankly. 'Well, they do in most churches.'

Mark was right. A plastic-covered card on a table at the rear of the building informed them that the stains marked the depth of the water that flooded the town during a great storm in 1287 and left the church choked with mud for years afterwards. They were awed enough to delay the lighting of their first cigarette of freedom until they were back in the sunshine and ambling southward on the High Street.

'You ain't got a girlfriend yet, then,' said Mark. It wasn't a question.

'I don't do the girlfriend bit,' Ivor answered. 'I screw around.'

'Yeah, really?' Mark wasn't sure if he believed this. He had a girlfriend called Becky but she hadn't let him go the whole way with her yet. 'Who've you screwed?'

Ivor wanted to say 'Becky' out of sheer devilment but, conscious that Mark was an inch taller than him and slightly more advanced in muscular development, resisted the urge. 'Why would I tell you?' he said instead, with a bit of a grin to show he was being jocular rather than rude.

'There's a fuck of a lot of pubs in this town. You notice?' Mark said next as they walked along. He didn't normally pepper his speech with the f-word but was feeling that in the company of a boy five months younger than himself who 'screwed around' he probably should. Ivor agreed there were a lot of pubs for so small a place; they were of an age to start being interested in pubs, though still both a bit too small to risk going into one and suffering the ignominy of being immediately thrown out.

They agreed New Romney's High Street was a handsome one, its houses – pubs included – a mix of Georgian brick and Tudor black and white. Almost unknown to himself Ivor was developing a taste for architectural style and harmony. He wished for a moment that he'd brought pencils and sketchpad. But if you were on a hike with someone like Mark, who was five months older than you and already had a girlfriend, you couldn't bring the whole thing to a halt – and risk your cred – by sitting down and drawing the streetscape like the elderly women you saw in Rye. Perhaps he'd bunk off school another day and come here with his sketchpad on his own.

Abruptly the street disgorged them into open countryside: the un-hedged, sheep-flecked fields and flat horizons of the Romney Marsh, through which poked up at intervals a church tower or a clump of trees. They stopped briefly to eat the sandwich each had brought with him and to smoke another cigarette. Then they followed a footpath, which was not all that easy, to their next target: a small airfield where a few light aircraft sat on the tarmac.

'What if we nicked one of them and just took off in it?' Mark suggested. 'They couldn't stop us.' The idea appealed enough to Ivor to make him snigger but both knew they wouldn't attempt it. How did you fly a plane? Even start the engine?

They had questions to ask at the information desk. What had the airport been called in its hey-day? What airline had used it? Back in the 50s and 60s, they learned, the place had been called Ferryfield, the airline Silver City. There had been flights to France, in car-transporting Bristol Super-freighters, every fifteen minutes during the summer months. Mark wrote this down. Ivor watched him then, with a shrug, got out his Biro and did the same.

Another footpath brought them to the town of Lydd. And here the odd thing happened. Perhaps the oddest in Ivor's life so far. Or at least the second oddest. As they came along the footpath Lydd could be seen ahead of them, its tall church tower, New Romney's twin, rising above a line of trees that hid most other buildings from their sight. The trees were brilliant with the freshness of May, the poplars and aspens among them flashing silver as the wind pawed at their walls of leaves. Behind them they heard the buzz of one of the light planes they hadn't stolen, accelerating down the runway and lifting into the air.

They reached the end of the last field. There was a stile and the path continued through the ring of trees that surrounded the town. As they moved among the trees the noise of the plane abruptly ceased. 'Reckon it's crashed,' said Mark deadpan.

Ivor though he was serious. 'We'd a heard the bang.' Just for a moment they couldn't see through the trees to the buildings beyond, though they'd had glimpses of them a minute before. But then their path widened to a track, they came out of the trees and saw, where their path met the street beyond, a cluster of small buildings less like houses than shacks. And then they were in the High Street. They stopped in puzzlement.

'I've been through Lydd before,' said Mark. 'In the car. I thought it had a street like New Romney.'

The street was like New Romney's in being straight and long and broad. But not otherwise. There were short rows of huddled cottages, with gaps between the rows. Some were half-timbered, others fronted with bare board. Whether they had been painted at some long-past date was not easy to see. They looked up the street and down it. Nobody was there that they could see. 'Spooky,' Mark said.

'It's like Watchbell Street,' Ivor said. 'Church Square and that. But like no-one's fixed anything or repainted in a hundred years.' Both boys felt their spirits sagging, though for no obvious reason, and lit a cigarette each to counter the sensation. They walked up to one house and peered through a front window, cupping hands and leaning on the sill. It was hard to see in, even though the room they looked into was lit by another small window at the back. The window panes were very small and thick, and tinged with a sea-water green like in some of the tea-shops in Rye. They could see an open staircase rising from just behind the shut front door. The room looked as if no-one had been in it for years. There was no colour anywhere: no carpet that they could see, no paint on walls. No stick of furniture except a chair. A bare, heavy, solid wooden chair. Ivor remembered the simple chairs they'd seen in New Romney church, but this was more crudely made. That sagging of the spirits he was experiencing began to intensify: he felt the kind of depression that takes hold of you when you're going to be sick, though he didn't actually feel nauseous; he wasn't in danger of throwing up.

Walking on they passed a vacant lot where brambles had mostly taken over but in the middle of which was a weedy pool. A heron stood there, motionless, peering into the shadowy water. 'Well, at least there's one thing alive here,' Mark said.

'Even if it doesn't seem to want to move,' said Ivor, also trying be flippant.

'No pubs here,' said Mark. 'No shops.' He looked around again. 'No dogs or cats. Shit, this is weird.'

'No, there's a shop.' Ivor pointed. 'Over there.' He was almost desperately pleased there was a shop. They crossed towards it.

It was very hot for May. The sky was so deep a blue they could hardly bear to look up. Right overhead it would be bronze. Ivor thought the word furnace: a word he knew, a thing he'd never seen. The trees looked strange. It was as if they had suddenly acquired the heavy deep foliage of late summer; the aspens no longer quivered but were still; they seemed flat against the sky like in a painting.

'Funny old shop,' said Mark. But Ivor thought again of those places where, years before, his mother and Violet had used to take him for tea. Small window-panes again and difficult to see through. But here, decrepit and un-repaired.

Mark was the first to cup his hands against the glass and peer in. He sprang back at once. 'Fucking shit, man,' he said. Ivor was unnerved – a rare occurrence – by the look he saw in Mark's eyes. He saw Mark's hands shake. It was his turn to look in.

It was a butcher's, though empty of customers and staff, and very closed. No trays of meat were in the window, there was no counter, no butcher's block. It was only the row of hooks hanging near the back wall that told them what it was. That and what hung from two of them, the headless carcases of two steers or cows. But there was something wrong. 'Oh Jesus,' Ivor said. 'They're rotten. Stinking, putrid. Look at the colour.' The carcases were dark, like polished leather shoes, except where streaked and blotched with phosphorescent green.

'I think I'm going to be sick,' said Mark quietly.

'Get out,' Ivor said. He wouldn't be able to trust his voice if he said more.

'Which way?'

'Same one we come.' They turned and walked with deliberate strides along the street, trying to behave like people in TV westerns. But in no time they were at a quick march and a moment later running, racing each other to the corner where they'd come into the street. Then they ran up the track through the trees, and didn't stop till they'd crossed the stile and were out again in the open field.

A feeling of horror and dread still had hold of Ivor. He knew without asking that it gripped Mark too. They walked halfway across that first field in silence but then the feeling slipped away from them. They heard larks singing. You could tell it was May again. The drone of a light plane sounded overhead.

They began to talk, excitedly. About what they'd seen. And, more significantly, about what they hadn't. It seemed important now to remember all the details. 'There were no cars.' 'No noise.' 'Did you see lines in the road? Was it tarmac-ed?'

The road had been like compact earth, they thought. They remembered lots of dust. Thatch or tiles on the roofs? Neither could be sure. They remembered holes in some roofs, and weeds growing on them. At last they dared to turn round and stare back at the place they'd come from, a quarter of a mile away. 'Look.' Mark pointed to the church tower, tall and proud above the trees and golden in the sun. 'Where the fuck was that? In the street we didn't see the tower.'

'Hidden by trees, maybe,' said Ivor, though there was uncertainty in his voice. By what trick of perspective could the smaller trees they'd seen inside the village conceal something the size of that?

Mark said, 'When I was here before – OK, it was just driving down the street once, and it takes about a minute – but there were brick houses in among the really old ones. The brick ones were old too, but like in Romney. What are they called?'

'Georgian,' Ivor said authoritatively.

Mark looked at him. A hint of surprise, a hint of respect. 'Well, where were they today?' he asked. 'Lydd's the spit of Romney, or was when I saw it before. What's happened to the place? Even from here you can see more buildings than we saw when we were inside. Bigger ones. Barns, garages...'

I saw ghosts when I was little, Ivor thought. Or I was told I did. Have I just seen the ghost of a village today and Mark's seen it too? He didn't want to voice this. He murmured, 'It's hard to remember what we saw and what we didn't.'

'Well, I'll never forget the sight of those green dead things on hooks,' Mark said. 'That's sure.'

They crossed the approach road to the airport. Looking along it they could see the terminal buildings just as they'd seen them earlier, could see planes on the tarmac and a few ant-sized people walking about. They didn't turn in that direction a second time. Ahead of them the church tower of New Romney rose above its ring of trees, while its almost mirror image at Lydd receded behind them. 'Reckon the same thing'll happen at Romney when we get there?' Mark said. 'It'll all be falling down and empty?'

'Like in a kid's story?'

'It happened at Lydd,' Mark answered a bit sharply. 'That wasn't a kid's story. I don't know what we saw but we didn't not see it.' Ivor agreed with just a nod and a grunt and they both fell silent. When they arrived at New Romney everything looked as it had when they left it that morning: it was reassuringly busy with people and cars, its High Street lined with handsome old houses of various dates and still full of pubs.

Ivor noticed something else. 'The houses have flowers in the windows. Window-boxes and stuff. Curtains. Lydd didn't.'

Mark's certainty about what he'd seen began to waver. 'Maybe it wasn't Lydd we went to. We read the map wrong, went somewhere else. Saw the wrong town.'

Ivor made him turn round. 'Look back where we've come. Lydd church a couple of miles away. Nowhere else like it in sight. Where could another village be hiding, down here on the flat? Even without a church.'

'So what happened then? We walked into the past? Or the future? Piss off!'

'Maybe,' said Ivor slowly, trying to think, trying to make sense of things, trying to keep hold of reality, 'maybe they'd rigged it for a film or TV. Like when they did Mapp and Lucia in Rye.'

'So where were the cameras?' Mark asked. 'We saw them in Rye. Actors in costume, the lot. Where was everybody today?'

'Dunno. Lunch break?'

'In Rye they covered up a few street signs. They didn't rebuild the whole town.'

Ivor had run out of suggestions. 'They didn't evacuate it either,' he conceded.

Their bus came and they climbed on board, waving their return tickets in the general direction of the driver. 'It'll be something to tell old Phipps anyway,' Mark said as they took their seats. Then they looked at each other as the same realisation came to them both.

'He'd think we're mental,' Ivor said, and Mark nodded slowly.

They sat in silence for a few minutes as their bus wound its way back to Rye, which became visible almost at once across the flat distance, perched on its hill. Then Mark said, 'Nah, we imagined the whole thing, both of us.'

'What, both of us? Two people imagine the same thing?'

'Crowds of people have mass hallucinations sometimes. I read about it.'

'Yeah, but...' Ivor wasn't sure what he wanted to think about what had happened. He didn't believe in ghosts, though he believed that people saw ghosts – which was not the same thing – because he'd seen two himself. Or his mother and Violet said he had. But now there was this. Could you really walk into another piece of time? The idea was absurd. So was he simply delusional? He thought he'd heard that word somewhere: it meant crazy, loony, mad. Imagination was another thing, though. Artists had imagination. He was an artist. So he was a man of imagination. But were imagining and hallucinating the same thing? He had never heard anyone say they were, or that they were not. He mulled these things over as the bus bounced him nearer to Rye. None of the possible explanations that he could think of gave him any comfort at all. The only thing that did, or might do in time, was the fact that whatever had happened to him had happened to Mark also, to someone he hardly knew. He supposed that was better than nothing.

'Best try and convince ourselves it never happened. Yeah?' said Mark, who had presumably been thinking along similar lines.

'Yeah, you're right,' Ivor said, and they didn't talk again till they got to Rye.

Back at school Mark spoke to Mr Phipps first. He talked about Romney and the flood marks in the church. Ivor then spoke up, unusually for him, and surprised Phipps – who was geography – by being articulate and interesting on the subject of Ferryfield airport. Then it came to what they'd seen in Lydd. The two boys looked at each other, then Mark took a great gulp of air and said, 'Lydd was a limb of Romney during the later years of the Cinque Ports. Before that the estuary of the River

Rother ran between the two towns – across where the airport is now – and their harbours faced each other across the water. That was before the great storms of 1287 shifted the Rother's course over to Rye and eventually, as the centuries passed, left both Lydd and Romney high and dry.'

Ivor looked at him in astonishment. He felt oddly betrayed, although they hadn't had any sort of conversation about what they would say to Mr Phipps, only what they wouldn't. 'Where the f...? Sorry. Where did you get that story from?'

Mark said evenly, 'On that info thing in the church. We both read it.' It must have been in the history they'd looked at in the church at New Romney. Ivor had skipped parts of it.

'Actually, what we saw in Lydd was the way it looked in the medieval ages,' Ivor said in a rather truculent tone. 'All hovels and mud and stuff. And a butcher's shop with rotting animals.'

Now Mark looked at him as if he'd been betrayed. But Mr Phipps laughed. 'Well, well, well. You've got a bit of imagination after all, Wingate. Never thought you had that in you. Hope you'll find a use for it in the big wide world. But if you have anything to do with history or geography you have to stick to facts, I'm afraid.' He turned to Mark. 'Right?'

'Right, sir,' Mark said.

The teacher looked at his watch. 'Anyway, a day well spent. Well done, both of you. Now get along home.'

Arriving at the bungalow Ivor found himself for the first time in years – maybe for the first time ever – wanting to confide in his mother, to share with her the strange experience he'd had. It had been Norma more than Violet who'd so enthusiastically bought the idea that he'd seen ghosts when he was small and who had kept the memory alive when his own mental processes had buried it. He actually began to feel a kind of tenderness towards her, something else he hadn't felt in years, as he got off the bus at Winchelsea Beach and made his way to the front door.

When he got inside he was taken aback to find his mother sprawled in the arms of an unknown man who was himself sprawling on the sofa. Two glasses of gin and tonic or something similar sat on the coffee table. His mother leapt to her feet at the sight of Ivor entering the room, while the stranger, a man with more hair than was decent for one of his age, and the sharpest knife-edge creases to his trousers Ivor had ever seen, sat up on the sofa as rapidly and straight-backed as if he'd just been yelled at for slouching.

'Ivor,' his mother said, 'I didn't expect you back for ages, if at all. This is Michael. Michael Harding. He's buying antique furniture for up north.'

The man got to his feet. 'York,' he said, and then held out his hand. 'Ivor, it's nice to meet you.' His accent was also from York.

'Get yourself a juice or a coke and come and join us,' Norma said, but Ivor stayed where he was, with no particular expression on his face and not moving his hand towards the outstretched fingers of the visitor.

'Nah,' he said. 'I'm off out.' He turned and left the room. They heard him run upstairs and dump his school bag, then run down again and leave noisily by the front door on his way to get the next bus back into Rye.

Ivor decided to turn the lie he'd told that day to Mark into a piece of truth. He took the preliminary step of buying a packet of condoms from the machine in the gents' on Strand Quay, then located his old gang playing at throwing lighted matches onto the boats moored in the Rock Channel. With a jerk of the head he invited one of the female members of the group to step apart. He told her gruffly, 'I want you tonight. Where can we go?' He didn't think she'd make any difficulty about this or shout out to any of the other boys in the gang and she didn't. People said that she'd go with anybody and all the slightly older boys claimed that she'd gone with them. That was why he chose her. She was called Meryl.

'This way,' she said simply, and led him up the steps of The Needles, a narrow short cut between Cinque Ports Street and the Mint. At one point the alley narrowed to a tunnel beneath the upper floors of neighbouring houses and here Meryl stopped. Ivor hadn't needed to buy the condoms. She fished one from her bag and said, 'Put it on. Make sure you do. I'm watching you.'

Dealing with Meryl's clothes presented no major problem: she'd been one of the girls he'd practised on years earlier. He wedged her into the corner of a doorway, the way some sharp-billed birds wedge a nut into a fork in a tree in order to attack it more efficiently, and then just got on with it, to the accompaniment of laughter and noise from a pub that was just a wall away. Nobody came walking past and when the job was done it was done.

'You done all right,' Meryl said as she returned herself to the condition of the fully dressed. 'That your first time then?'

Ivor snorted. 'No way. Don't be daft.'

FIVE

During the three years that followed her purchase of Gatcombe, Gemma extended her social life a little way beyond the chamber choir and the string quartet. Though only in certain directions: she had not had the luck to find a suitable new man. She had said to Jane all that time ago that she would fill the house with children, but that didn't happen straight away. Cats were a different matter. She began with four.

Since she couldn't emulate Henry James or E.F. Benson by living in Lamb House she did the next best thing and joined the band of volunteers who manned the door and did guide duty when the building was open to the public. One day a week. One other day every week she did a job for money. She travelled up to London and gave advanced drawing and painting classes at the American School in St John's Wood. She had been a pupil there herself and later had given some classes while she worked on her first book. Back then she'd had to beg for the work. Now she was an established author and illustrator of children's books and it was they who had come courting her.

It was from the American School that children eventually came. A retired teacher had for some years offered holidays to some pupils in her home in the New Forest. There were always a few teenagers who, for whatever reason, could not join their parents for the school holidays, or whose parents thought it would be good for them to have an experience of British life outside London. Now, pleading age, this former teacher was bowing out. And, although she'd had no thought of doing so until the moment came, Gemma found herself offering to take her place. Gatcombe would be just as good as the New Forest, she informed the principal of the school. The Jamesons at the top of the lane gave riding lessons, one of her friends from the string quartet offered music coaching, she herself would give guidance with painting. And if the kids wanted to make holiday money, she explained, there would be temporary jobs, in the summer at least, on neighbouring farms. After some discussion, and a flying visit to Gatcombe by the school's welfare officer, her offer was taken up.

The first group of more or less bewildered American teenagers had arrived at the end of the summer term. Most bewildered – if that word may be used as a polite synonym for recalcitrant – had been fifteen-year-old Feri. She was American in the wider sense of the word: she came from Colombia, or rather her parents did. Although her mother had been sent to an English convent school, she had then settled in New York, where she'd met her businessman husband. Now Feri in her turn had been transplanted, at least in term-time, to England while her parents got on with the task of getting divorced.

London, where she had lodged with an aunt since her arrival at Easter, suited Feri not too badly: she saw it as a pallid imitation of New York, recognizable enough for her to handle with competence. But the countryside appalled her. Gemma met her off the train with the others. She was conscious of Feri's silence in the car on the way to Gatcombe, a silence that seemed more ominous with the passing minutes and in its contrast to the eager chatter of the other youngsters. On being shown her room in the farmhouse she went into it, barricaded the door with bedroom furniture and, except for trips to the bathroom, stayed there for thirty-six hours. This would have been a long enough self-incarceration to test the mettle of almost any hostess, but Gemma proved a match for her: she simply ignored her and got on with settling the others in. Two had riding lessons booked and one of the boys set off at once in search of work picking soft fruit at a neighbouring farm called Tibbs.

Feri eventually did emerge: hunger could not be ignored for ever. She joined the others for lunch on her second day. She ate in a silent fury; the others, taking their cue from Gemma, spoke among themselves but not to her. Feri found her situation intolerable; it was beyond anything she'd ever imagined happening to her, and beyond her powers to deal with. Nobody would speak to her, there was no-one to phone, nowhere to go and nothing to do. After lunch she stamped out of the house and off down the lane. Neither Gemma nor any of the others called her back, remonstrated with her, or asked if she was all right. Which made it all worse.

She strode along the lane, a small walking fortress of solid rage. She meant to stop at the first phone-box she came to, phone her father and demand he cross the Atlantic right now and come to take her home. Had she climbed the lane towards the main road she would have reached a call-box after half a mile, but she didn't. She turned right, down the hill into the valley where no phone-box would come in sight until she reached Winchelsea station a good two miles away. But by the time she got there she no longer wanted to phone her father, no longer wanted to fly to New York. And by the time she got back to Gatcombe, just in time for supper, she was a different person: one who was, among other changes, oblivious to the blisters on her feet.

She had walked the lane in baking sun at first, then was conscious of the friendly enveloping shade beneath tall hedgerows and under trees. In the middle of the afternoon stillness – to begin with it registered as a silence so intense and threatening that it hurt the ears – she began to notice the orchestration of small sounds around her, like a symphony playing at the dynamic of a child's whisper. She heard the free-wheeling bicycle noise of the grasshoppers in the just-cut hay, the rattle of a corn bunting on a wire, the call of a little yellow bird that popped its head out of the top of a low hedge: the one that goes, *A little bit of bread and no cheese*. Smells came to her too, as if half-remembered from some vanished past: the smell of greenery in sunshine, the smell of drying brown, of lying hay that was the colour of lemon juice and scented warmly like the clean but pungent fur of a domestic pet.

Then Rye appeared. It simply slid out from behind the line of low hills, almost cliffs, that formed the valley's side. One minute it wasn't there, and then it was. Toy-town size at two miles' distance: a mole-hill mound on the dead-flat pasture. Red rooftops crowded together, an upheaval of irregular tile; the houses seemed to be trying to make their way up the gentle slopes of the mound until they'd got wedged together as in a traffic jam, or like a herd of bison, and were forced to stop. Sticking up above the topmost ... (houses? cottages? What did you call dwellings that looked like that?) ... was the squat tower, capped with a mini-pyramid of slate, of the church. All Feri had taken in on arriving at Rye was a station that was disconcertingly small and a supermarket nearby that made the same poor impression.

Then a tiny bird, brown and grey but with a crimson cap and a crimson patch on its pale chest that was shaped like a heart, appeared on a fence post a couple of feet away. 'Then it sang like it was doing it for me,' she said later. It had been: it had been trying to warn her away from its family or nest, but Gemma didn't have the heart to tell her so. At supper Feri managed to weary her contemporaries, though not Gemma, by repeating and repeating that she had never in her life felt more alive. She ate enough for three.

A week later Feri was working as a strawberry picker at Tibbs Farm just the other side of the hill. As the summer passed her skin tone changed from New York milky to South American almond, while her face had shed the look of acid disdain it had worn on her arrival and carried more often a pearl-toothed smile. Gemma hadn't noticed at first that Feri was beautiful, but now she did. She had the high-cheekboned, fine-chinned face that is sometimes called catlike, while her eyes were so dark a brown that they were often mistaken for blue – a dark blue that no human eye has ever been, but is seen on grapes and plums and sloes. At the end of her stay at Gatcombe Feri announced, 'Know what? I'm going to live down here one day.'

'Really?' Gemma answered, smiling. 'Living on what?'

'I shall marry an English farmer.' Like many people whose first language is not English she was more pernickety about her shalls and wills than most natives. 'And I shall do what you do. Paint and draw to make a living.'

'Hmm,' said Gemma. 'I've been one of the lucky ones. Not many of us do that. So don't give up on the farmer idea. You may need him to be a rich one.' Though it crossed her mind that for someone with parents as well-off as Feri's were that might not be a concern.

In the autumn Feri joined Gemma's art classes at school. She did have talent, Gemma saw. In the New Year she came down to stay at Gatcombe again and after that she came for a part of each school holiday. As she got older she helped Gemma organise activities for the younger kids. By the time she left school and started at Gemma's old art college, St Martin's, the two young women were firm friends. Gemma would have said Feri had become more like a sister to her than her real one. They exchanged man stories and commiserated with each other when appropriate – though Gemma became painfully aware of the difference: Feri's tales of rapture or woe, or rapture that turned to woe, were very current; Gemma's were receding into the past.

'I looked in the mirror today,' Gemma said as she turned out of the station car park one May evening in 1989, 'and didn't like what I saw.'

'You look kind of fine to me,' said Feri, turning to look at her profile from the passenger seat.

'Side view doesn't count. I'm only twenty-nine and I'm turning into Aunt Hattie.'

'Don't be silly, Gee. Aunt Hattie looks fifty or more in your pictures.'

'That's what I mean. It's only by the absence of outsize headgear that you could tell us apart.' Feri laughed. Gemma told her, 'It's all very well for you, just eighteen and no need to worry about losing your looks for ages.'

'I hope I won't be worrying about that when I'm your age either. And you've no need to be. It's not your looks that are the problem. It's how you feel about yourself.' Despite the gap in age between them only Feri could talk to her like this. 'Down here with only your elderly friends.'

Gemma protested. 'Elderly! None of them's more than forty: that's no older than me than I'm older than you.' But she was secretly pleased. Feri called those friends of Gemma's, the Janes and Angelas of Rye, the Fogresses – a coinage that Gemma, although ashamed of the disloyalty to those older friends it implied, couldn't help wishing she'd thought of herself.

'Oh, look at those kids,' Gemma said. They were driving across the Tillingham river bridge. In the dusk a group of youngsters were flicking lit matches onto the moored boats. The silhouette of one youth was pursuing the silhouette of a skinny girl into an alley. 'Don't you despair sometimes?'

But Feri was too young to despair of teenagers only a little younger than herself and let the question go unanswered. 'You should write something,' she suggested. 'Too many pictures of cats. It's doing your head in. Write something grown-up. That'll keep you feeling young.'

'Interesting you should say that,' Gemma said. 'I'd been thinking on those lines. I don't want to end up like Louis Wain.'

'Who's Louis Wain?'

'He drew sentimental pictures of cats at the beginning of the century. Ended up in an asylum, creating crazy kaleidoscopic canvasses with huge fierce cat eyes staring out of them.'

'I see,' said Feri. 'Looks like we'd better spend the weekend finding you a subject to write about. And maybe a man to pay the bills while you're doing it.'

'A murder might do,' Feri came back to the subject while they finished their pasta supper at Gemma's oak dining-table. 'A country-house murder. Since you live in a country house.'

'My agent told me a few months ago I ought to have a go at something else. She said romance or murder. I'm not in a romantic frame of mind right now, so I did toy with the murder idea. Not a country house, though. That's been done to death, by abler souls than me. And don't suggest vicarages either.'

'I'm not sure that country house was what I meant,' Feri clarified. 'I should have said a house in the country. With a farm attached. Plenty of scope. Lots of weird characters...'

'Have you read Cold Comfort Farm?' Gemma asked, her eyebrows slightly raised. It was not only Feri who was allowed by the terms of their friendship to indulge in a little gentle mockery. But she took Feri's point. Farms were natural death-traps. Powerful machinery was often used by very inexperienced people with little or no supervision. There were rickety buildings. And unpredictable terrain, with hidden ponds, steeply sloping banks, half-buried objects lying waiting for the unsuspecting to stumble over them. A farm could be a very unforgiving place. 'Tell you what,' Gemma said. 'Tomorrow we'll take a tour of the barns and the oast house. See if anything inspires us.'

'I already know the barns and the oast house,' Feri said. 'In case you've forgotten, I've picked hops here for the last three summers.'

'I know,' Gemma said. 'But you haven't examined them with the eyes of a murderer.'

The days were gone when women and girls sat in the open among the growing hops, stripping the papery hop cones off the twelve-foot bines. These days the bines were loaded onto a trailer and carted back to the farmyard, where a barn full of machinery awaited. The bines were hung ignominiously upside down – Gemma could never help thinking of Mussolini – on a moving chain of hooks, then dipped to dangle between revolving flails which stripped them of their opal flower cones, and unceremoniously dumped outside the barn on the other side. Meanwhile a small number of women – who had included Feri for the past three summers, as she had just pointed out – picked over the hop flowers as they bobbed along the belt, removing stray leaves and bits of stalk.

Gemma and Feri stood in the un-peopled barn, gazing at the silent machinery that ran the whole length of one wall, and which had been gathering dust since the harvest of the previous year. 'You could drop a man into that,' said Feri, pointing to the funnel-like structure that housed the flails, 'and there wouldn't be much left of him.'

'True,' said Gemma, 'but even if someone got hooked onto the chain by some freak accident, they'd be seen and heard and the motor would be stopped before they could fall in.'

'Not if it was the middle of the night,' Feri argued.

'Someone would have to start it up specially. If anyone lived near – like me – they'd wake up.'

'By then it would be over except for the screaming.' Feri looked at Gemma very earnestly, and Gemma looked back at her equally seriously for a second. Then they both dissolved in laughter.

It was fun to be with Feri, planning a fictional murder together. Gemma no longer felt remotely like Aunt Hattie when she was with her youngest friend, but like a teenager again herself. It was as though some of Feri's youth and her desirability in men's eyes rubbed off like the coloured dust on a butterfly's wing to bedeck and rejuvenate her older friend. 'Let's go and look in the oast,' Gemma said. 'It won't be locked.'

The oast house was a two-centuries-old brick and timber structure about the size of Gemma's house and with a matching red-tiled roof. At one end stood the two conical towers or roundels that formed the drying kilns. Till twenty years before they had been powered by massive coal fires and fed by a stoker as on a ship; now they ran on oil. They worked like upward pointing hair-driers, only two thousand times as big.

Gemma pushed open the door into the building. The lofty ground floor was nearly empty out of season; just a few carts and attachments for tractors sat about on the ground. A set of wooden steps, not much more than a ladder with a handrail, led to the upper floor. A few yards further on was a circular hole cut in the dirt-grey boards of the ceiling. At harvest time the ten-foot-long hop pocket – an elongated jute sack with the farmer's name printed on it – would hang in that hole to be filled with the dried hops when they were shovelled out from the drying floor above. 'You could do something with that,' Feri suggested.

'I'm not sure,' Gemma said. 'Isn't there a press up there that would get in the way?'

'That might stop your victim falling down the hole,' said Feri. 'But he could still be pressed through it into the hop pocket, couldn't he?' She laughed again. 'I don't know why I'm assuming it's a he.'

They climbed the rickety stairs to inspect the press more closely. 'Oh,' said Gemma, giving a start as her head arrived above the level of the upper floor and she discovered that they were not alone. Bob Jameson, owner of the farm that surrounded her house, was kneeling by the tall press, doing something with a screwdriver. He turned at her arrival. 'Sorry to make you jump,' he said, grinning through a greying ginger beard. 'I'd have jumped too, only I heard you talking as you came up. About victims falling down a hole. You planning to do somebody in, then?'

'Only in fiction.' Gemma laughed and finished climbing the stairs, allowing Feri to follow her onto the hop floor. Feri greeted Bob, her sometime and occasional employer, with a wave. Gemma said, 'Feri thinks I should be writing murder stories. I'm not sure I agree with her, but we came up to look at the possibilities for a setting. I hope you don't mind.'

'You were thinking of the hop press and the hole under it, were you?' Bob got to his feet and stepped aside to let them inspect it. 'Just a little repair I've got round to after six months,' he said, explaining his presence and the screwdriver in his hand. The press, these days an electrically powered ram, straddled the hole in the floorboards, its piston nearly blocking it. There was space to shovel hops into the hole, but it would be difficult to push anyone down through it unless they were already dead or at least beyond struggling. 'You could drop a corpse into a hop pocket, I suppose,' Bob said helpfully, 'and sort of smuggle it out. But you'd have to get the corpse up here in the first place. Come and look at the kiln, though.'

He walked to the far end of the hop floor, Gemma and Feri following. Bob slid back the massive door that opened into the conical top half of one of the roundels. Inside was a living-room-sized space whose floor was a grid, covered with a net, on which the hops would be spread to dry, knee-deep, for ten hours or so while the oil-burners below got to work. The space still smelt of last year's hops, perhaps of generation on generation of hops: clean, peppery, pungent. Daylight came from above: a tall isosceles triangle of sky, framed in the white wooden cowl, the 'witch's hat' that characterised the countryside of Kent and this Kent-hugging strip of Sussex. 'Shut someone in here and they'd be well kippered,' Bob said. He added quickly, ''Course, these days there's an emergency handle inside just in case somebody did accidentally get shut in, but if you were setting your story a century back there wouldn't have been.'

Gemma thanked Bob for the information. Bob asked Feri if she'd be back for the current year's hop picking, and she smiled an options-open maybe. Then they went back down the stairs, leaving the farmer to his task.

They'd missed a phone-call, they discovered when they got back inside the house. Gemma's mother's voice was on the answering machine, sounding stressed and strange and asking her to call back at once. Gemma's heart started to beat very fast as she dialled the number.

And when she got through it was to be told that her father had died suddenly, of a massive stroke.

'I'll have to go,' Gemma told Feri. 'There's times when you...'

'I know that,' Feri said. She had the same kind of cold-war relationship with her own mother as Gemma had with hers. But she too would have rushed to her mother's side, halfway across the world, if anything bad had happened to her. 'Would you like me to come with you?' It was not the sort of thing that non-family members were expected to say in this particular situation, but Feri was refreshingly unaware of some aspects of bourgeois conventionality. Gemma liked that. She accepted Feri's offer and phoned her mother again at once to tell her – not ask her – to expect Feri, whom she'd never met, to arrive in the car with her within an hour.

Feri managed to win over her friend's mother's heart. While Gemma and her sister tussled with death certificates, lawyers and the bank, Feri quietly rolled up her sleeves in the most natural way and kept the household going by cooking and shopping, washing and ironing – all those tasks to which even death can't put a stop. But Feri was wise enough not to stay on till the funeral. After two days she returned to London, and her boyfriend Carlos. There was no more talk of murders in oasts.

SIX

Ivor and Mark began to be friends in the days that followed their visit to Romney and Lydd. Friends was perhaps an exaggeration, at least in Ivor's case. He didn't really have friends, just as he didn't really have girlfriends. The opening of the heart to another person whom you'd learned to trust a little, and the discovery in the process of the treasure of another's heart laid open to you was outside his experience, and he was unaware that that sublime exchange of self defined for many people what it meant to be human. Perhaps it was surprising that Mark and Ivor didn't become enemies: after all, they had each tried to torpedo the other's story when they accounted for their day to Mr Phipps. Or perhaps it was the knowledge of that mutual betrayal, confronted unblinkingly by them both, that cemented them together.

That and the secret they shared. For they didn't speak of their experience at Lydd in the short weeks that remained of that summer term. Not even between themselves, let alone to others. Yet something extraordinary had occurred, whether it was indeed a visit to a distant point in time or simply a trick played by the brain: it was extraordinary not least because it had happened to the two of them together, and to no-one else.

During breaks they gravitated together, which they hadn't done before, to smoke a cigarette companionably behind the kitchen block and to talk about ... well, not much. Last night's TV perhaps. Mark's new air-gun. But Mark did ask a big question, one of those morning break times, puffing grey smoke over Ivor's shoulder. 'What are you going to do with your life? Leaving school at sixteen, and then what?' Mark would be staying on to do A levels and then go to agricultural college at Wye, as most local farmers' sons did. Not Ivor. His school-days were almost at an end.

'Make something of myself,' he answered promptly. Defiantly. 'Set up in business. Make money.'

Mark's big grey-blue eyes tended to bulge when he heard something interesting or surprising. They did now. With his round ruddy cheeks and rather thick lips he had the appearance, which was far from unpleasant, of a slightly debauched cherub. 'What, make money drawing pictures of birds?' That was the only skill of Ivor's that Mark was aware of.

'Nah, woodwork. Remember I do that too?'

'I know you do. Even so...'

'I'll be a carpenter. Build houses. Restore old ones.' He hadn't known he wanted to do those things before Lydd. Seeing those old houses in such a tumbledown state had had a curious effect on him: he wanted to find them again and make them nice. There had been a rustic chair in the room they'd peered into... 'And make classy furniture.'

Classy was a new word on Ivor's lips. And it was probably there because of Mark. Mark had middle class written ... perhaps not all over him, because he was born on the land and already worked it in his spare time, so that his surface was overlaid with the scent of silage and a Kent-Sussex burr of an accent ... but right through the centre as in a stick of Hastings rock. Not for him were evenings spent hanging around the bottom end of town by the station and kebab shop. Losing his virginity would not be accomplished in a shop doorway in a cold street but in a bed perhaps, when parents weren't around, or at least in a haystack's relative comfort and warmth.

As for Ivor, he couldn't say to what class he belonged. He didn't know who his father was: he'd never bothered asking Norma, nor had she volunteered the information; she'd even withheld it from Violet. His mother, for all that she worked in a 'classy' shop, had been adopted as a baby and so had no idea as to the social plane she'd come from originally. All Ivor knew for certain was that his adoptive grandmother had been the wife of a local builder. If he thought about this occasionally he would round off the discussion with himself with a phrase he was growing fond of: *Work that one out.*

Getting to know Mark, even a little bit, had a sudden and unexpected effect on Ivor: it gave him a startling adrenalin rush of aspiration. His GCSE results would be rubbish, he knew that. Staying on at school to do A levels had never been an option. What a fool he'd been, he suddenly thought, not to profit from those years, now ending, of forced incarceration in classrooms. What a bloody waste!

'How does the public library work?' he asked Mark.

'What do you mean, how does it work?' His eyes performed their bulging trick again.

'I mean, you get to borrow books. I know that. But how?'

'You go in and get a form to fill in. Name, address and so on. You get it signed by a magistrate...' Ivor's jaw dropped. The movement was almost imperceptible but Mark was looking carefully. 'Only kidding. Get any teacher to sign it. Then you borrow any books you want. For three weeks. Up to a certain number.'

'Have to pay?'

'Only if you return the books late. Not otherwise.'

'Hmm,' said Ivor. Many people's education finished on the day they left school. Not his. On that day his would start. He wasn't sure, looking at Mark's grinning cherub's face through the cigarette smoke, whether this resolution was entirely due to the new company he was keeping, or if it was another thing that had been triggered by that out-of-time experience at Lydd.

He began to tell Mark about the new man in his mother's life. 'Michael his name is. Michael Harding. He was only spending a few days down here. Went back up north after that. But mum's head-over-heels. She don't talk about him much but she is.'

'How do you know?'

'Just do. There been no man in her life since before I was born. Not really, I mean. But now she's all, you know, completely different. It's like she remembered she got a vagina all sudden.'

Mark winced. His relationship with his own mother was chivalrous and close. He didn't know anyone who'd talk about theirs in this way. 'And what is he?' he asked, to get away from that aspect of the matter. 'Single, divorced, married?'

'Divorced. You see the danger.'

'Don't sound that dangerous,' Mark said. 'Looks like she might be falling on her feet.'

'I meant dangerous for me,' Ivor said sharply. 'What if she dies and leaves him all she's got?'

Frown lines appeared on Mark's forehead; there was no indication that they'd ever been there before. 'How old's your mum?'

'Thirty-one.'

Frown lines gave way to startled eyebrows. Even to Mark that seemed indecorously young. 'She's not going to die,' he told Ivor firmly. 'How old's he?'

'Fifty-odd.'

'Hell, man, you've nothing to worry about. He'll go long before she does. Blokes always do. Anyway, you shouldn't be worrying about what folks are going to leave you. Not yet.'

'All very well for you, mate,' Ivor said, sounding offended. 'Everything on a plate. A farm and ninety acres coming to you...'

'Don't make me laugh, Ivor. Anyway, you know the saying: a farmer's only rich when he's dead.'

'Well, there you are, then,' Ivor said, managing to invest so much conviction in his non-sequitur that they both ended up feeling he'd somehow scored a point.

It was easier for both of them not to go over the Lydd experience in their conversations. It would have been unsettling, posing a Pandora's Box of questions that neither of them wanted to ask, let alone have answered. Easier to follow the strategy Mark had eventually employed when dealing with Mr Phipps. Lie point-blank. Then will themselves into believing it hadn't happened, or that they'd simply imagined the whole thing, or remembered wrongly. Nevertheless there remained something in Ivor's otherwise pragmatic mind that couldn't entirely accept this. It was this that compelled him, a few days after the event, to make a series of sketches from memory of what he and Mark had seen. He showed the sketches to no-one, not even Mark. Nor did he tell him about them. But he was careful to keep them safe.

It was thanks to Mark that Ivor got his first job. Mark told him that a farm across the river from his father's would be looking for workers in July, right after the end of the school term.

Reedbed Farm lay on the southern side of the Rother Valley, near Iden. It looked across to the steep-sided Isle of Oxney, whose slopes between Stone and Wittersham had been farmed by Mark's family for generations. But Reedbed was not what town-dwellers would have considered a typical farm. Though it grew a certain amount of soft fruit, and there were mushroom sheds, dark and pungent, its principal activity was buying in fresh produce from neighbouring farms, processing it through a high-tech freezer plant, and then shipping the store-ready product by freezer truck to a distribution centre near Sevenoaks, forty miles away.

Ivor began with broad beans. He stood on the back of a parked trailer which had arrived loaded with full sacks, and emptied those sacks one by one, hour after hour, into the funnel of a machine that stood beside him. The bottom end of the machine spat out the chewed-up pods on one side, and their precious cargoes of pearly beans on the other. The beans mounted up inside massive plywood crates which, once full, were whisked away on pallets to a blast freezer.

The bean pods were dark green on the outside and lined with soft white fur within. The beans themselves were a delicate pastel green. The Hessian sacks were orange-brown. So Ivor never understood how, in the course of a day engaged in his particular task, he managed to get so black. His hands and face were black. His arms and shorts-clad legs were black. Even the bits of him that he didn't see till he got into the shower were black. And the water he washed his hair in ran black too. Ivor learned, a little to his surprise, that he was unafraid of hard, physical work. It was the dirt he hated. He wondered how the full-time farmers put up with it.

Ivor dealt with beans for three solid weeks. It was a seven-mile cycle-ride morning and evening from Winchelsea Beach, though he didn't do it very often, preferring to crash with those old acquaintances – he never thought of them as friends – who still hung out evenings in the station yard in Rye. On one of the few occasions when his mother did see him she broached the subject of an August holiday, paid for by Michael Harding, on which Ivor had been invited too. 'A holiday with that arsehole?' he said. 'No way. You go, though. He seems to suit you all right.'

Norma bit her lip before replying in a measured tone, 'You can't stay here, all on your own.'

'Why not?' Ivor said. 'I'm sixteen. Old enough to marry, or get killed in a war.' He chuckled without warmth. 'Much the same thing really.' So Norma went – in spite of forebodings that Ivor would invite his gang round in her absence and she'd find the place trashed on her return – while Ivor stayed: the master, for a short time, of Winchelsea Beach.

Luckily for his mother Ivor had no interest in inviting people to his home. True, he did entertain the thought once or twice of getting Meryl back to the bungalow. He still had sex with her occasionally in the alleyways of Rye and wondered at times what it might be like to do that in a bed. But instinct told him it would need to be the right person when that eventually happened, and that person would not be Meryl. The peculiar dynamic of their connection was better served by dark doorways, so that was how things stayed.

At Reedbed broad beans gave way to raspberries and blackcurrants. Now Ivor was no longer black all over but crimson-handed all day then, when he washed, the crimson turned to indigo, as indelible as print. Meanwhile, at weekends, Ivor had another job. For several years he'd helped out occasionally in the antique shop over which he used to live and where his mother still worked. At first he'd simply cleaned and tidied, but as he moved up through his teen years he'd gone on to polishing the furniture. Even, under supervision at first, French polishing. Then, as his skill in woodwork developed he was given the odd repair to do: nothing too sensitive at first; he wasn't let loose on damaged Second Empire inlay but, where a cross-brace beneath a gate-legged table had become detached, or the bottom panel of a drawer showed signs of cracking, Ivor could be trusted to set those things right.

It was because of this experience, in part anyway, that he'd developed an awareness of style and period in architecture as well as furniture. That was how he had managed confidently to pronounce the buildings of New Romney Georgian when he'd gone there with Mark. The visit to Lydd and the sight of the weird old houses there had sharpened his eyes further and increased his interest. Antiques made money for the Spraggens. Old buildings could probably do the same if you found a way to exploit them. But he needed to know more. How did you recognise early Georgian from late? And how was it different from Queen Anne? Ivor joined the library and began his education again from scratch.

He had no intention of relearning all they'd tried to teach him at school. Literature and maths, foreign languages and history would play no part in his new, self-imposed curriculum. His disciplines were furniture making (history of, and skills in) the construction of old buildings, and the world of antiques.

From the library he borrowed A Pictorial Encyclopaedia of Antiques. He read Sir Banister Fletcher's History of Architecture on the Comparative Method, and although he didn't notice it at first, the ghosts of maths and history and the English language haunted their pages, and visited him too. He read Nathaniel Lloyd's History of the English House, and was jubilant at the discovery that nearly half of the buildings photographed as examples could be found within cycling distance of Rye. Not only that but Lloyd had restored and then lived in a medieval hall house – Ivor hadn't known what that was, but it was now very clear to him from the text and pictures – called Great Dixter. It was just seven miles away.

He cycled to Dixter one Saturday afternoon. To his surprise it was open to the public and fluttering with tourists. The house was surrounded by enormous and, he now discovered, world-famous gardens which were tended by Lloyd's son Christopher. The things that everybody around Rye seemed to know, but that he didn't.

There was an entrance fee, which struck Ivor as exorbitant, even though he knew it didn't apply to him. He crawled in through a badger-sized hole in a hedge. He gave the brilliant, scented gardens a few minutes of his time but then slipped into the house itself when the beady-eyed lady checking tickets inside the back door had her attention distracted by someone else.

He had never seen a house like it. Without ceiling or first floor, the central hall rose the full height of the house to the ridge pole. Windows that filled one wall from knee-height to the eaves let in a heart-warming quantity of summer sunshine. The whole frame was of timber, massive beams of old oak, in-filled with white-painted plaster, wattle and daub. Where the tree-trunk rafters met overheard they were black with the smoke of the Middle Ages, accumulated through the generations before anyone thought of installing a chimney. In two of the curved central beams that held up the king-post could be seen the bored-out nest chambers of medieval woodpeckers. Only at the extremities of the hall had a first floor been inserted. The narrow windows of those upper rooms peered down upon the hall below like ancient eyes. The whole experience gave Ivor a curious feeling – a potent mixture of excitement and dismay – that brought back to him, if only in pale imitation, the emotions he'd experienced in the street of Lydd. He walked round the hall again and again, noting the devilishly clever construction, and the carved details, of the hammer-beam roof. He climbed the stairs to the solar and peered down through the little window he'd earlier looked up at. Even this upper chamber was not that small. It was full of handsome furniture and glowing rugs like the antique shop in Rye. 'I could live here,' he heard himself say out loud.

Another illustration in Lloyd's book was of a house even nearer home. A Georgian one this time, and less than a hundred yards from the antique shop where he'd lived. He'd never given it more than an approving glance before, but in the light of his growing knowledge he decided he would favour it with a full visit.

When she was on duty at the door Gemma could see from the window everyone who passed in front of Lamb House. She enjoyed trying to guess which of them were simply walking by, which were arriving purposefully with a visit in mind, and which ones, the more casual tourists these, were on the brink of passing by but at the last moment would change their minds, decide to stump up the entrance fee and approach the door. She also tried to distinguish between those visitors who turned up because of their interest in Henry James and those who came on account of the E. F. Benson connection – or perhaps more precisely, the Mapp and Lucia TV series of a few years before. This was more difficult to guess correctly, not least because many of those who'd been led here by the charming TV pictures were loth to admit this, and made a show instead of their devotion to James. Yet other visitors were interested in neither writer, but had simply had their eyes caught by a handsome double-fronted Georgian town house, in a quiet angle between two prettily cobbled streets and were running out of things to do before dinner was served in their hotels.

The teenage boy who came through the door that August Saturday – Gemma's first day back at Lamb House after her father died – seemed to belong to none of those categories. She'd seen him stride almost urgently up the steep cobbles of West Street, and when he came in through the door she was struck at once by his looks: finely chiselled facial features, thick curly hair that was coal black like his eyebrows and lashes, which framed scarily bright blue eyes. 'Student,' the boy was saying to her, rather aggressively she thought.

'Have you a student card?' Gemma asked him sweetly.

'No,' the youth snapped. 'I'm a student of architecture.'

'Where?' Gemma asked. She was genuinely interested, even if he did look a bit young to be embarked on any kind of degree course.

'Self-study. University of life.'

Gemma laughed, quite loudly, warming to him. 'That applies to us all, you know. We can't all get in everywhere we want to go without paying the entrance fee. Look,' she went on without pausing, 'what interests you about Lamb House?'

'It's in Nathaniel Lloyd's book.' Ivor had stopped sounding impatient. He didn't object to the way Gemma was talking to him. 'I've seen Dixter and it's brilliant. Now I wanted to see this too. Early Georgian.'

'Yes,' said Gemma slowly. 'You're right. It is.' The boy had impressed her. There was something more about him than mere good looks. 'All right, I'll do a deal with you. I'll let you have the tour of the house for nothing, but you have to come back and tell me what you've learnt. Deal?'

'Blimey,' said the boy. 'You sound like a teacher.'

'I am a teacher,' Gemma said. 'I teach art at a school in London.' It was refreshing to be saying this for once, rather than coyly admitting to people who'd seen her on the television that, yes, she was indeed the author of the books about the cat. This boy had probably never come across those books, nor noticed her designs in print on half the tea-towels for sale in Rye. 'Deal or no deal?'

'Deal,' said the boy, as if reluctantly accepting a low offer for a car he was trying to sell.

'Tell me,' Gemma said to him as he tensed his muscles ready to move away from her, 'How did you blag your way into Dixter?'

Ivor turned back to her. 'I didn't.' He smiled for the first time. 'I crawled in through a hole in the hedge. I did some sketches.' Then he turned away and followed a little covey of other visitors into the panelled dining-room. It was only then that, with a sudden rush of blood to her head and neck, Gemma realised who he was.

'I can tell you one thing,' he said when he returned thirty minutes later. He made his shoulders swagger as he said it. 'Some water's got in behind the sash window in the dining-room and rotted part of the sill. I can do a splice repair, make good and repaint, for two thirds the lowest quote you can get from anybody else.'

Gemma was almost too astonished to answer. She had sometimes indulged her imagination in wondering what might have become of her creation Vince by the time he was sixteen, but it had never come up with this. She found an amused but also collusive tone in which to answer, after a moment, 'I'm not the person who makes these decisions. I'm just a volunteer here. You'd have to see Mr or Mrs Goderich if you're seriously touting for trade.' She appraised him quickly. Did he really know what he was talking about? At his – mid-teen – age was he capable of doing a professional carpentry job? Or was he simply a blagger, or indulging in a bit of childish fantasy? 'You need to know,' she went on, though still smiling at him, 'this is a listed building. It's owned by the National Trust and can't be repaired by just anyone without their approval. Or,' she thought back to her own battle three years ago to have a northern light cut into the roof above her studio, 'I imagine, without the approval of Rother Council.'

'Replacement of like for like, running repair, don't need approval from anyone.' Ivor's face had gone surly again, though his voice was smooth.

Hearing the 'don't need', Gemma's ears had expected 'from nobody' also and she was almost as startled by the 'anybody' as she was by the answer as a whole. 'Have you done work like this before?' she asked him. None of this was remotely her business but after the astonishing fact of his walking into the middle of her afternoon she was loth to let him out of it, probably never to be seen again.

He didn't spot this. Why would he? 'I've made a chair. From scratch. You can see that.'

'I'm due for my tea break now,' said Gemma, continuing the conversation seamlessly while thinking that the whole situation had become surreal. 'Why don't you come and join me in Mr James's kitchen and you can speak to Mr or Mrs Goderich, whichever of them happens to be there.' She paused only a split second before adding, 'There's always brilliant chocolate cake from Fletcher's on Saturday.' She was quite sure that the prospect of tea with a handful of mainly elderly voluntary ladies would have been enough to frighten him out of the front door. But she also had a shrewd suspicion that he was not yet too old to be blackmailed by a hefty wodge of chocolate cake. She was right.

SEVEN

Ivor had been stretching the truth when he said he'd made a chair. The reality was that he was in the middle of making one. He promised to bring it along to Lamb House to show it to Mr and Mrs Goderich in a week's time, when the potato harvest was finished.

At Reedbed Farm summer work was drying up. The beans, raspberries and blackcurrants were all over; there remained only a couple of fields of potatoes to be dug. So Ivor spent his last fortnight at Reedbed grubbing on hands and knees along the furrows, like someone doing a medieval penance, for the tubers flung up by the spinner as the tractor inched its way up and down the rows, and throwing his harvest into a sack which he dragged behind him. The mud, the dirt, the rain turning the clay to sludge... This was not how he intended to spend the rest of his life.

At the antique shop those repairs and restorations too complex and sophisticated to be entrusted to Ivor were dealt with by a professional joiner and cabinet maker named Albert Gutsell. He was sixtyish, with wispy grey hair and a long, ascetic face, like one of the more curmudgeonly saints painted by Zurbaran. He had a workshop in Udimore, a few miles outside Rye on the Battle road and not all that far, by the back road, from Winchelsea Beach. Ivor went to call on him.

Mr Gutsell had known Ivor by sight since he was a child, but neither as child nor teenager had Ivor given Gutsell any reason to like him. So he was surprised when Ivor turned up at his workshop one hot afternoon in August and said, without even the preamble of a good morning, 'Will you take me on as an apprentice?'

Mr Gutsell had a very accomplished old assistant who was due to retire at the end of September, and he was wondering whether to take on someone new to replace him or not. For that reason he did not immediately tell Ivor to get lost, as he would have done otherwise. But he didn't give him the Prodigal Son's welcome either. He pursed up his thin lips in an extraordinary way, which Ivor had never seen anybody do before, and said, 'Can't say I'm looking for one right now, son. Tell you what, though. Go away and make me a chair. When you've done that bring it here and I'll have a look at it. Maybe I'll have something for you then. Maybe not. Good afternoon now.' He didn't let Ivor say yes or no to this rather one-sided arrangement, let alone protest. He moved to the door of the workshop, held it open just enough for Ivor to pass through it, then, when he had done so and in spite of the August heat, bolted it shut behind him.

Gutsell had noticed that Ivor arrived on a bicycle. He knew that few people in the world could, without instruction, make a chair that wouldn't come apart when sat on. And of those that could, not many would be prepared to transport one up the three-mile incline that was the Rye to Udimore road on the back of a bike.

Ivor got the timber he needed from Alsford's, down on the Undercliff where Rye's wharves ran. He chose a sturdy gauge of hardwood: some serviceable kiln-dried stuff that was unlikely to shrink or split. Mr Gutsell had said, make me a chair, not, make me an elegant chair, or a beautiful chair, or something carved out of ebony and rosewood. Ivor knew what he was being tested on and he wasn't taking more chances than he had to.

'You got a rubber stamp with the company's name on?' he asked the assistant who helped him select the timber. The assistant gawped at him. 'You know,' Ivor prompted, 'like for stamping documents?' The assistant gave a reined-back, doubtful nod. 'Can you stamp each length in three or four places? And then can you sign and date them?'

'You want me to sign your timber?' the young man said, wondering if this was a wind-up.

'Yeah,' said Ivor. 'I gotta make a chair for a test. Don't want to give the bloke any chance to say I faked it. You with me?' The assistant went off to look for the rubber stamp.

Fortunately Ivor's route from the Undercliff to Winchelsea Beach was totally flat; there was no need to wind laboriously up into the streets of Rye and back down again. Ivor rode steadily round the bottom of the town, crossed the Tillingham bridge onto the Hastings road and wobbled slowly home, his two-metre lengths of hardwood balanced across his handlebars, veering in and out of the path of every driver coming from the opposite direction for the entire three-mile journey, and terrifying the life out of each.

The old shed in the garden, still full of the equipment once owned by Violet's husband might have been waiting all Ivor's life for this moment, this day. He already knew what the chair would look like in overall shape and structure. It would be an approximate copy of the chair he'd seen through the window in that spooky house in Lydd. But now, laying paper on the workbench, he made detailed drawings that showed the workings of the mortices and tenons that would hold it together. Then he set to work. Choosing his dimensions carefully, and remembering the carpenter's mantra of *measure twice, cut once*, he sawed his timber to length with all the care and reverence of someone carrying out a religious rite.

Later he sawed away at the ends of the horizontal members until the tenons materialised – or *were revealed*, he thought: the way a sculptor reveals the human or other figure that lies dormant and imprisoned in a slab of stone. Then painstakingly he drilled and chiselled out the mortices into which those tenons must snugly fit. The task took up all his evenings for two weeks. He knew he had only one chance to get each joint right. Coated with glue and banged in with a mallet, the joints would either fit perfectly, lock tight as a boilermaker's rivets, or there'd be no chair.

They all fitted. Perfect, every one. Ivor hardly dared to believe it. But now he had to be patient overnight, giving the glue time to set before he could test the chair's strength and toughness. He hardly knew how to wait. But morning came eventually. And there the chair was. He sat on it. He wriggled gently. The chair did not. As the seconds passed the reality of his achievement seemed to flow gradually through his being, like a rising tide. He'd done it. He'd made a chair. The feeling was better – far better – than sex. This was the best moment of his life.

Ivor thought carefully about which of its two appraisals his chair should go to first. He decided to take it initially to Lamb House. Mr and Mrs Goderich – and that younger woman on the door who seemed to have taken a shine to him – might examine the chair carefully, might even pull it and poke at it a bit, but they would be unlikely to try testing it to destruction. They wouldn't attempt to pull it limb from limb, whereas Albert Gutsell, Ivor strongly suspected, might. And if he did succeed in wrenching Ivor's creation apart there would be no point in taking the resulting bundle of firewood to show off at Lamb House. Going there first would at least leave the piece ready to face its second and more important trial intact.

It looked like something you might find in a church, Gemma thought, when Ivor plonked it down in front of her in the big hallway of Lamb House. Like something that might have inspired Pugin to copy its naïve purity of form before going on to artily-craftily decorate it. This boy had done nothing to decorate his work, which rather pleased Gemma, though she didn't know quite why. On the other hand, it was covered with ink-marks from a rubber stamp, and someone's signature, as if it had been travelling and had its passport validated everywhere it went. 'What's with the signatures and stamps, then?' Gemma asked.

'Proof of when and where I bought the timber to make it. Otherwise people might think I bought it ready-made.'

Nobody would imagine that, Gemma thought. Nobody supplied chairs that looked like this, hewn out of untreated wood, like something from the Middle Ages. She said, 'Are you used to people not trusting you? Is that it? I think Mr and Mrs Goderich will take your word it's your own work.'

'Yeah, but I got to show it to someone I'm trying to get steady work from. Mean bastard. Any chance to say he don't believe I done the work myself, he'd take it.'

'I see,' said Gemma, eyebrows slightly raised.

Mr Goderich arrived. 'Well,' he said, looking at the chair carefully. 'It looks pretty well put together to me.' He sniffed importantly. 'You said you'd done some repairs for Eric Spraggen at the antique shop. Well, I saw him the other day and asked him.' He saw Ivor's expression darken. 'Come on. You'd hardly expect me not to. It's called taking up references. Anyway, he says you're good. He also told me the going rate for the particular job you're touting for.' He named the figure. 'You make as good a job of it as you've done with this chair and I'll give you the full whack. Not just the two-thirds you asked for. The full whack. Do you follow me? But it's got to be a damn fine job. Not two tins-full of plastic wood.'

'I'll do it,' Ivor said, in what struck the others as an unnecessarily surly tone. 'I'll do it tomorrow.'

'That's Sunday,' said Gemma.

'No extra charge,' Ivor said.

Ivor's hunch had been right. Albert Gutsell did try to pull his chair apart with his bare hands, using all his might. He turned very red in the face in the process. (Which made two of them. In Ivor's case this was the result of pedalling three miles uphill on an August morning, with his chair tied on behind him.) But the chair refused to be torn in pieces and Mr Gutsell, who needed an assistant anyway, could find no other good reason not to make that assistant Ivor.

'When can you start?' Mr Gutsell asked him.

'Tomorrow,' Ivor answered. The next day would be Tuesday. This afternoon he had to go back to Lamb House and give his splice repair on the window-sill its second coat of paint.

'I can start you end of September. Not before. I got old Alec to keep on salary till he retires at the end of the month.' A rather spindly, grey-looking man was busy doing something in the gloom at the other end of the workshop. He hadn't come over to introduce himself, and neither had Gutsell thought this a good use of anybody's time.

'What am I going to do till then?' Ivor asked.

'Not my problem, that one,' said Gutsell without smiling.

To Ivor's surprise old Alec joined the conversation. 'I reckon Jack Eason over Birdskitchen might have a use for you, hopping. Heard him say in the pub he were short of pickers, and they'll all be starting next week.'

Ivor turned up at Birdskitchen half an hour later, chair and all. Between them Gutsell and his assistant had managed to give him directions there, down a steep lane and up another one, and once there the lanes would lead him back to Rye by another winding route. The farm was easy to find. The short track that led to it passed by the front of the handsome farmhouse before opening out at the business end, the farmyard itself. Ivor liked the look of the house. It was of a type he was very familiar with: asymmetric, with two windows to one side of the front door and one to the other. From the outside these houses all looked attractive in a similar way: their tin-loaf shapes were softened by old roofs of red or orange tile that were never exactly straight but undulated faintly where the timbers beneath had moved over the centuries. The roofs cascaded right down to first-floor level over the kitchen at the back: you could reach up and touch the lowest line of tiles when you walked out of the back door, and look up to see an uninterrupted ski-slope of roof climbing to the ridge. Some of these farmhouses had dormer windows let into the roof at the rear, or at attic height at the front, some had had their front walls rebuilt with glowing eighteenth-century brick. Most had wood-framed casement windows, a few retained their original leaded lights. This one had the bottom half of its front wall made of, or cased in, old pink brick, the upper half faced with white-painted weather-board. Ivor went up to the blue front door and knocked.

A sallow-faced and very thin woman came to the door. 'Are you looking for hop pickers?' Ivor asked.

'You'll need to see Robbie about that,' the woman said. 'He's the hop man here. Hop man and drier. He employs the pickers. You'll find him in the yard.' She pointed out of the door and to her left, then rubbed her hands down the front of her skirt as if that might make Ivor disappear more quickly. He did remember to say thank you, while she closed the front door firmly in his face.

There was only one person to be seen in the yard, a big man in his thirties with very shiny straight black hair and eyes to match – like pieces of coal. He had on a string vest, dark corduroys and boots. In answer to Ivor's, 'I'm looking for someone called Robbie,' he said, 'You've found him.'

'Heard you might be wanting pickers for next week,' Ivor said. 'And I'm looking for a few weeks' work myself.'

'Are you, now?' Robbie said, peering through narrowed eyes at the chair on Ivor's bike as if it might be some kind of trap, like the Wooden Horse of Troy. 'Who said we was looking for hoppers?'

'Albert Gutsell the cabinet maker. I'm starting work for him next month. I need something till then.'

'And where did Gutsell hear that, I wonder?'

'Well, his assistant heard. In the pub, he said. He mentioned Jack Eason.'

Robbie lifted up his chin and snorted like a pony. 'Yep. Figures.' He looked again at the burden on Ivor's bike. 'And you've brought a chair to sit on while you work, have you?'

'It's a test piece. That got me my job with Gutsell.'

'Hmm.' Robbie tried not to look impressed, but he was. 'Well, if you can make a chair I reckon you can pick hops, and Gutsell told you right, we could use an extra kid. Start Monday, seven a.m. You up for that?'

Ivor said he was, and then they were joined by another, older man, who had come to see who Robbie was talking to: some kid with a chair strapped to his push-bike.

'Who are you?' the new arrival said to Ivor.

'Fine and dandy,' Ivor answered.

'I said who are you, not how,' the older man shot back fiercely.

'He's coming hopping with us next week,' Robbie explained. 'He hasn't told us his name yet.' He turned to

Ivor. 'This is Mr Eason, sonny. Owner of everything you can see, except the sky and the sun in it. And your name is...?'

'Ivor Wingate. Monday at seven. I'll be here. But no chair next time.' Ivor, who was still standing astride the cross-bar of his bicycle, now slid up and back into the saddle, turned the handlebars towards the exit and pedalled away.

When he got back home he was surprised to find his mother there. 'I did phone you, Ivor,' she told him. 'Again and again, but you've never been in.' Only businesses had answering machines back then, while mobile telephones were an expensive rarity that weighed a kilogramme.

'Been busy,' Ivor said. 'I got two new jobs today.' He told his mother about them, the temporary and the long-term. Her relief showed in her face. She had not been looking forward to having an unemployed son knocking about the house, once apple-picking was finished, for the foreseeable future. Though her son was not her most important preoccupation these days. Her affair with Michael Harding had not petered out. The just-ended holiday with him in the Algarve had felt more like the start of something big than anything before in her life. Now she'd come home to tell Ivor that she was very shortly setting out with him again, this time on a Mediterranean cruise. She told him she'd arranged for someone else to fill in for her at the antique shop, and that Ivor would again have the run of the house. All this, which she had rather dreaded having to explain to him, became much easier now that the boy had work lined up. There was nothing like having a job, Norma believed, for keeping young men out of trouble.

Gemma had been able to find no reasonable-sounding excuse for calling at Lamb House on the Sunday Ivor fixed the window-sill there, though during the week she did pass by in the street outside. From there she noticed with relief not only that the repair had been carried out but also that it looked perfect, the joins invisible under the new paint. When she went there again on Saturday to do her voluntary duty on the door it was not she but Mrs Goderich who brought the subject up.

'Your little find did a splendid job last weekend. Ralph made a point of inspecting the work before the first coat of paint went on and could find no fault with it. He said a carpenter with twenty years' experience couldn't have done a better job, and paid him the full amount he'd promised. Not the most personable of young people, I couldn't help feeling, though that may simply be the age he's at, but what a craftsman!'

'Well, I'm not sure I can claim to have found him,' Gemma said demurely. 'It was more like he found us. And actually I could do with someone like that for a couple of little repairs at home.'

Mrs Goderich tilted her head a little and assumed an oh-dear, what-a-pity expression. 'I fear he may be a bit busy for that. He told us he's off hop picking next week, and in a month's time he's starting work as an apprentice cabinet maker. That chair he brought us was his entrance exam, apparently. Pity. We might have wanted to use him again too.'

'You didn't get any sort of address for him, I don't suppose?' Gemma tried.

'We didn't think to, which was a bit silly, perhaps. Ralph paid him cash and got him to sign a voucher. But, wait a minute.' Mrs Goderich's expression brightened. 'There's always ways to track people down if they're local. He and his mother used to live over the Spraggens' antique shop in Lion Street, though they don't any more.' Gemma wanted to shout, I knew it, I knew it, but contented herself with an interested nod.

'His mother still works there – though he told us she's away. He told us the name of the farm he's going to work at, though I can't bring it to mind – and that the cabinet maker he's going to work for lives at Udimore – just near you. Now what was his name? Goodsell?'

'Gutsell. Albert Gutsell,' said Gemma. 'I know his workshop – and his name's up outside.'

'There you are then. If you want to find him in a month's time then you'll know where to look.'

EIGHT

Once he'd been handed his oilskin coat and hat for protection against the drenching September dew – whose early morning gallons doubled the weight of every hop bine – Ivor saw little of Robbie the hop drier or Jack Eason, his boss. They were both busy in the oast and the machine shed, where the women picked over the hops on the conveyor-belts with rubber-gloved hands. Ivor was one of a team of eight men who would be spending the days out in the fields, the hop gardens, cutting the bines, piling them on trailers, and seeing them driven off to feed the gobbling machine.

Two tractors worked in relay, four men with each. When Ivor's tractor was delivering its load to the farm, the group he worked with walked the next avenue of hops, slashing with bill-hooks to free the bottom ends of the bines at waist height. When the tractor returned it nosed its way between what had now become two dangling curtains of hops; Ivor and the other pickers rode in the empty trailer behind. One member of the team clung to the top of a girder tower – the crow's nest – which was mounted on the trailer, and cut the top of each bine, sixteen feet up, as he brushed past. The other men below caught each falling bine and stowed it on the trailer. There was a special way of doing this so they didn't all tangle up.

In the crew of strangers to which he now belonged it took Ivor a while to discover who was a farm employee and who was hired for the duration like himself. The latter group were mostly college students, the former numbered just three. There was young Andy, who drove one of the tractors: he worked freelance for Jack Eason as a 'man with tractor', on hire to any local farmer who needed heavy work doing. Second was Frank, Eason's ageing pig man, and third – though first in the hierarchy – was the foreman Heinz. Heinz had lived in England for years but had never been taught the language properly. This resulted, the very first morning, in an incident which amused Ivor very much.

The driver of the second tractor was a university student on vacation. He had never met Heinz before. Navigating the hop gardens, thick and deep as forests, needed expert knowledge – or a command from Heinz. 'Don't turn left,' from Heinz, delivered in a sergeant-major's bark, caused the novice driver to abandon the turn he was just beginning with his full trailer-load, down a promising-looking avenue with a full view of the farmyard at the end of it, and to continue ahead down the edge of the field, despite this route's disappearing down a narrowing track which a guy-wire cut down across diagonally just a few yards ahead. To save himself from decapitation the driver threw himself face-down across the steering-wheel, which was smart of him, but that didn't save the exhaust pipe – one of the kind that pokes upwards – from being neatly folded in half by the guy-wire as it crossed its path. This completely closed its vent and stopped the engine. Struggle as they might, no-one could bend the funnel back by hand, and eventually someone had to be despatched back to the farm to get a hack-saw with which to chop it off. During the resulting stoppage everyone sat on the ground, relaxing and watching the other team and tractor go about their business, while Heinz kept up a murmur of German invective under his breath.

'It's his English,' Frank the pig man confided to Ivor. 'He gets his yes-things and his no-things mixed. Don't mean no harm by it.'

Ivor remained fascinated by the Easons' farmhouse. He'd been to its front door once, only to have that fauxpas pointed out to him by the gesticulating, apron-smoothing behaviour of Mrs Eason. Now, doing the lowly job he did, he was unlikely to be asked in. Nevertheless, riding back from the hop garden on the piled-high trailer, last load of the day, he managed to get a few glimpses in through the front windows. He saw big rooms, three along the front, with shabby furniture within. He imagined how they'd look if cleaned and painted, and filled with the rich furnishings of Great Dixter. The place would look superb.

He did get inside the back door once or twice, when a message or something else had to be taken indoors. From here he glimpsed a warm old-fashioned kitchen with a smooth-worn red-brick floor, immensely long, running almost the full length of the back of the house. There was an Aga... But the door would always shut before he had time to focus on anything else.

It was a mystery to Ivor why these houses – for he knew of many in the district – lacked symmetry at the front. Those two rooms on one side, but only one on the other, of the big chimney and front door. The Georgians would have deplored the layout; they only relinquished symmetry reluctantly – on a cramped town-centre plot, for instance, or to avoid matchbox-sized rooms. But here, in open country, those seventeenth-century builders – for Ivor presumed that was when these farmhouses had been built – had no such excuse. He thought again of medieval Dixter ... and then it hit him.

Birdskitchen Farm and all those others were not seventeenth-century in origin at all. They were conversions. In the heart, or rather in the skeleton, of each, could be found a medieval hall house, like Dixter, though in humbler, miniature form. That central room had been the open-hearthed hall, open to the roof above, the front door placed to the side of it so that on entering you wouldn't walk into the fire in the centre. Buried in the plaster of the bedrooms and lofts above there would be a king-post roof... Ivor saw himself laying the past bare, as had happened at Lydd. His imagination placed him suddenly in the great hall of such a house, king-post above, himself a little king within. He looked with newly understanding eyes at the familiar frontage of the farmhouse. Locked up inside it, beneath the wallpaper and the plaster, were the ghostly timbers of the Middle Ages, which had blindly witnessed the history of seven hundred years.

There were two standard ways for Ivor to get from Rye to Birdskitchen. But now he had the bungalow to himself again he realised there was a shorter cut that didn't involve a detour through Rye at all. So he took the crooked little lane that went past Winchelsea station and then ran gently along the floor of the Brede valley before punishing him with the whole climb to Udimore in its final half mile.

The first time he did this he found he had to dismount and push his bike – it was no mountain bike but just a hand-me-down from one of the Spraggen's now grown-up children – up the steepest part of the hill. From the point of view of any cyclist that steep edge of the Brede valley had something of the character of a cliff. But as he climbed he found himself passing, just a little way from the road, a house and farm complex that was almost identical to Birdskitchen. And hop picking was clearly in progress there too. The house itself was the spit and image of the Easons'. Another hall house, Ivor thought, and the idea pleased him: here was another house that had had an earlier incarnation in a vanished past. The name on the gates, of both house and farm, was Gatcombe.

Ivor passed this house twice a day now on his way to work, and turned his head to look at it approvingly each time. It wasn't till the Friday morning of his first week's hopping, though, that he encountered Gemma, who had driven her car out into the lane but then stopped there, realising that she couldn't go any further without wiping the heavy dew off the side windows. She was busy attacking the wet with the remnant of an old skirt which she kept in the glove compartment for the purpose, when she saw Ivor stomping and bumping up the hill.

Ivor recognised her at once, though he was surprised to see her in this new context. He registered her proximity to the farmhouse that he so admired, so that once he got level with her his first words were, 'This your house, then?'

'Yes, it is,' said Gemma, taken a little by surprise, but not to the point of losing her sang-froid. 'And a very good morning to you too,' she said pointedly.

'Good morning, miss,' he replied huffily, as though to a teacher who had mildly rebuked him for something.

'On your way to work, I see,' Gemma went on smoothly. 'Hop picking now, isn't it? You did a good job at Lamb House last weekend.'

'Suppose I should say thank you for putting that bit of work my way.' It sounded quite a major effort.

'Your thanks accepted,' Gemma said, pleased to receive them, wondering how such a small thing as a thank you could apparently cost him so dear. She smiled faintly. 'I won't delay you now, but there might be a job, something similar, that you could do for me here some time. That is, if your other work doesn't keep you too busy.'

'What sort of job?' Ivor hoped it would be indoors. He wanted to see inside that house.

'Call in when you're passing on your way back from work one day. If the car's here, then so am I. I'll show you what it is then and you can decide whether you want the job or not.'

There was something oddly persistent about Gemma, Ivor thought, which he couldn't account for. Something intense about her. But other people had worse qualities than that. Somehow he couldn't make himself dislike her.

Her car wasn't there when Ivor returned from work that day. 'She might have said, don't come this evening,' he grumbled half aloud. But he got off his bike all the same. It was a good opportunity to have a look round. The hop pickers here had left for home now, just as he had, and there didn't seem to be anyone else about. If someone caught him he would simply say Gemma had invited him to call and he'd been looking for her.

He walked slowly up the brick path that cut the front lawn into two sail-shaped pieces and cupped his hands against the window to the left of the front door. He saw a room sparsely yet imaginatively furnished to a modern, careful taste. On a carved bare-wood table that looked delicately Egyptian was a ceramic vase, blue, purple and white, that looked expensive as well as exotic. A polished walnut desk was occupied by a home computer – a rarity back then – while the floor was covered with a patterned carpet that glowed so warmly that its reflected light seemed to come from within; Ivor thought it was from Morocco, perhaps, or Afghanistan, like the ones he'd seen at Dixter. The right-hand wall was largely occupied by an inglenook fireplace.

Ivor walked back, past the front door. He could guess, thanks to his encounter with Mrs Eason at the front door of Birdskitchen, that behind this door too lay a small lobby, with hooks for coats, whose back wall was the side of the massive chimney – a structure that had been implanted when the medieval hall house was modernised in Tudor times. Looking through the window to the right of the front door he saw the even bigger inglenook – the other side of the great chimney stack – that he'd expected would be there. It was the same at Birdskitchen. Here though, the walls still showed their oak-beamed frames; either this room had never been papered or, in an act of painstaking restoration, the wallpaper had been stripped off. The room was furnished with satisfyingly solid Jacobean oak, including a massive dining-table with chairs – plus a few modern easy chairs and sofa to give comfort at the sitting end.

Expecting the third and final window along the front of the house to light a third reception room as it did at Birdskitchen, Ivor was surprised to find that here instead was now the kitchen: it looked quite newly equipped. He wondered what the long back of the farmhouse was used for – it was the kitchen at Birdskitchen and most other houses of this type.

As he walked round the side of the house he spotted a cat which, after observing him disapprovingly for a second, darted through a flap in the kitchen door. By now he was out in the farmyard and had to get back onto Gemma's land by means of a tall gate in a hedge. The single-storey rear wall was pierced by two doors and a number of windows. Except for one frosted one that presumably lit a toilet, all looked into an enormous artist's studio, one that was clearly much in use. On an easel he could just make out the detail of a partly completed picture in an idiom he seemed to recognise. But he'd been here long enough, he thought. If you had to make the excuse that you were looking for someone you could justify one quick walk round their house, but not a studious prowl.

He slipped out through the back gate, found his bicycle where he'd left it half hidden under the opposite hedge and pedalled down the hill. It wasn't until he was passing the junction with Dumb Woman's Lane that he realised why the picture on the easel looked familiar. There were pictures, and prints of pictures, in the same style in every arty shop and on every tea-towel and every calendar in Rye. There had been since he was very young. Whoever this mysterious young woman was she must be worth a mint.

As the hop harvest progressed at Birdskitchen, so the aspect of the hop gardens began to change. At the beginning the gardens were dense forests, sixteen feet high. You worked along viewless tunnels of green, where the hanging leafy tendrils drenched you with dew in the early morning, and scratched you to pieces in the afternoon, leaving angry red weals round neck and wrists. But as the gardens were denuded of their clambering hop bines the landscape around began to reveal itself, like a jigsaw puzzle taking shape, piece by piece. One day the tower of Wittersham church surprisingly appeared, five miles away, springing from the hillside of Oxney out of fields and woods. Another day, while working in the highest hop garden of all, Ivor was startled to see the sea. It too must have been five miles distant but in the clear bright midday it was as if you could stretch out and touch the sparkling substance of it, framed in a U-shaped valley between hills, contained there like champagne in its saucer-glass.

The crop was getting heavier now. They'd moved on from the plantations of Golding hops to the higher-yielding Fuggle variety, and the trailers were now struggling back to the yard with two men on board, lying on the high loads to stop the topmost bines bouncing off. Ivor liked the name Fuggle and thought it comic in an Archers-ish sort of way. He was told it was a traditional Kentish name – Kent began only two miles away after all – and that there was a Mrs Fuggle who worked among the local women in the machine shed, scrabbling among the hops on the conveyor belt. She was a grey-haired hedgehog-like lady of politely indefinite age.

Robbie collared him one lunchtime as he ate his sandwiches with the others outside the oast. Robbie virtually lived in the oast during these days, drying the morning hops in the afternoon, and the afternoon load overnight, cat-napping through the morning, only spending time with his wife and children at weekends. Now he stood before him, yawning and scratching, his abundant chest hair bushing out through his string vest in diamond-shaped thickets, like vigorous plant growth through a trellis. 'Heinz says you don't mind hard work, kid. What d'you say to a couple extra hours after the others have gone these next few days? Heavy loads this week, and we need a bit more manpower in the oast, early evenings.'

'I'm up for that,' Ivor said. 'Same rate?'

'Bit more as it happens,' said Robbie, and walked away.

So Ivor found himself working alongside the regular staff: Robbie, Heinz and Andy the freelance tractor man, and of course Jack Eason himself. Old Frank the pig man wasn't there: he had his pigs. This little crew now tossed the bagged fresh hops onto a grain-elevator, then followed them up to the storage floor of the oast, emptied the pokes out and shovelled the contents through the hatch onto the circular drying floors of the kilns. At the end of his first evening of this extra work, Andy asked Ivor if he'd come to the pub with him. Ivor, knowing that Andy drove home by tractor, frowned and said, 'There's my bike.'

'No problem, mate,' said Andy, who was a wild-blond, red-faced giant of a young man. 'We'll stick it on the back.' And so they entered the car-park of the Cock Inn at Peasmarsh on Andy's tractor, with Ivor riding high on the rear mudguard and his bike impaled on the raised lift-arms behind.

They hadn't been in the pub very long before Heinz wandered in, looking as if he'd meant to go somewhere else but had found himself here through some momentary lapse of concentration. A little later came Frank the pig man, and finally Mr Eason himself, who had the look, Ivor thought, of a man who'd already been drinking elsewhere. When his pint was drawn, Eason pulled it across the counter and, before putting it to his lips, dipped a finger into the foam and tasted it thoughtfully, as if checking for poison. Ivor had only been inside pubs a couple of times, but he'd never before seen anyone do that.

Ivor was conscious of his youth, compared to the others, and was careful not to draw attention to it by drinking an imprudent amount. Afterwards he was delighted to find that Andy lived halfway back towards Rye, that he was happy to take Ivor plus bicycle that far on the tractor with him in the oncoming dusk, and that he would then have only a short way to cycle home.

That was the routine of the next few days, and nothing happened to disturb it. In the pub on those evenings there were no alcohol-fuelled conversations that Ivor would remember all his life. At least, not until Friday... It was then that Frank the pig man, his hand wrapped as tightly round his pint glass as if it had been a diplomatic bag, said out of the blue, 'They've had people over that house again. Crawling over.'

Heinz said, good-naturedly, 'What people? What aren't you talking about?' (Ivor no longer had consciously to reverse the meaning of Heinz's utterances: it happened now automatically in his head, the way the brain reversed the images on his retina.)

'House on the Rye road. Welstead House.' That made Ivor prick up his ears. 'One with the ghosts an' all. They've had the psychiatric research folk back again. All over it again, I heard.'

'Nobody don't find nothing when they don't go looking,' said Heinz – and despite his experience Ivor did need a second or two to work that one out.

'Nothing but a load of old hooey,' said Jack Eason slowly, before putting his lips back to his pint mug.

'No, no, no,' said his pig man, almost combatively. 'Folks did see things. Only never when they was looking to see what they saw. Folks don't see what they want when they go looking. Only folk see what they don't want when they don't go looking.' This was almost worthy of Heinz, and Ivor found himself doing mental backflips as he tried to tease out the meaning.

'I know someone who saw something there,' said Andy. He spoke quietly and very deliberately, as though he wanted what he was going to say to be free from any ambiguity whatever. Ivor felt the frisson that comes when you realise that someone else is about to reveal something that you'd thought was known only to you. 'Son of the family who've the farm next my dad's. Harris at Stone in Oxney.' Ivor was listening intently, remaining very quiet indeed and trying not to look as if he had more than a casual interest in whatever story was about to be told. But he couldn't stop showing his surprise in the tiniest twitch of the mouth at the mention of the Harris family: they only had one son and that was Mark. Andy saw this and said, 'Know them, do you?'

'I was at school with Mark. That's all.'

'Then maybe you know this story already.' Andy looked slightly disappointed, as everyone does when they're robbed of the opportunity to tell a tale.

'No,' said Ivor firmly. 'We never talked about things like that.'

Andy cheered up visibly. 'Well,' he began, settling happily into storyteller mode. 'This was when young Mark was a kid. I mean a real kid. He went to a party there. You know, a kid's birthday party or something.

Someone he was at first school with. They moved on years ago. Anyway, at some point he wanders off from the rest of the party, maybe going to look for the toilet or what not, and he finds himself in the scullery.' The scullery, thought Ivor and then, absurdly, the skull, the place of the skull. He made himself attend. 'And there's no-one there,' Andy was saying, 'and then suddenly there is. A woman and a boy have come in behind him. And they're like, wearing funny old-fashioned clothes. She, the woman, puts an arm round the boy's shoulder, like she's his mother, and then they walk off together, laughing and saying something Mark didn't catch. And they – this is the bit...'

'Aw, come on Andy,' said Jack. 'Kid's party. Mothers and their kids. Fancy dress...'

'No, but listen,' Andy pressed on. 'This is the bit. They disappear.' Even to his own ears that didn't sound much of a climax. He repeated it. 'They disappear. They just fucking...'

'Yes, OK,' said Jack, grinning. 'We got the point.'

'Yep, yep,' seconded Heinz. 'Everybody didn' get the point.'

Andy turned to Ivor. 'Mark never told you that?'

'No,' said Ivor crisply. 'Did he tell you?'

'No,' said Andy. 'I mean why would he? Kid half my age... Oops, sorry, didn't mean...'

'It's OK,' Ivor said.

'No, he never wanted to talk about it, his mum said. He told her but then nobody else. I got the story from her.' Andy looked at the circle of faces around him, which were studies in different degrees of scepticism, belief and half-belief. 'Well, there must be something in it, don't you reckon? If they had the psychiat ... psychic research people there that first time and, according to Frank, again now... Don't you think?' His face fell into a frown as he willed his audience to believe.

'I believe you,' Ivor said. 'I mean, I believe Mark's mum told you, and I believe Mark told his mum. But what he saw...' He didn't finish the sentence. He'd said enough. He'd pleased Andy by saying he believed him. He didn't need to tell him why.

NINE

It was because Ivor was working those extra hours at Birdskitchen that Gemma received no visit from him in the week that followed their chance encounter in the lane. She resigned herself to the idea that he wasn't going to come. He'd got a full-time job, after all, and probably didn't need, let alone want, to spend his spare time doing trifling repair jobs in other people's homes. She asked herself, did she mind? She oughtn't to mind, certainly. A repair man was just a repair man and plenty existed. And yet... She couldn't rid herself of the idea that she had somehow conjured this boy into existence by the fact of turning him into Vince and putting him in her books. In a sense he had two existences: as the slightly idealised child in her fiction, who had an aunt, a cat and a bicycle; and as the surly yet somehow appealing youth of the real world who did carpentry, picked hops – and had a bicycle. Perhaps it was enough just to know that.

Then, late on Sunday afternoon, he knocked at her door – the kitchen door, following the custom of old-fashioned tradesmen. Gemma found that unexpectedly touching. He carried something in his right hand. Gemma might have expected it to be a box or bag of tools, but it looked more like an old music case – the kind that appears to be fastened with a knitting needle. She glanced down at it only briefly. Either she would learn in due course what it was or she wouldn't. 'Thank you for calling by,' she said and gave him a cheerful smile. 'Come in.'

He took up the invitation but, as he crossed the threshold, gestured back over his shoulder at the farm buildings across the yard. 'Them oast and barns belong to you?'

'No,' said Gemma. 'I just have the house.'

'Who farms, then?'

'Bob Jameson. He lives a bit further up the hill. He has three farms, strung out along the valley.'

'Reckon his kids went to my school. Guess Jack Eason'd know him.'

'Who's Jack Eason?' Gemma asked.

'Bloke I'm hopping for. Other side of Udimore. Birdskitchen.'

'Birdskitchen.' The name brought back the memory. Seeing the house at Birdskitchen while house hunting with Jane all that time ago had made her want to buy a house like it. Had led her to buy Gatcombe.

'House looks just like this one,' Ivor said, as if prompting her from a script.

'I know it does,' Gemma said. 'I saw it years ago, before I bought this. Anyway.' She looked around the kitchen. 'I'm afraid there's no chocolate cake, but let me put the kettle on before I show you this job that wants doing.'

'Tea'd be nice,' Ivor said, then, 'Nice kitchen you got.' He was clutching his music case tightly, Gemma noticed, as though it contained something he particularly cared about.

'It's a nice house,' she said, 'though I had to do a lot to it.' Then she remembered that he'd originally introduced himself, pre-emptively, as a student of architecture, so she said, 'Would you like to see round it?'

'Be nice.'

'I'll show you the work that wants doing while the kettle boils. You can say no to it if you want. You'll still get the tea and the house tour.' Surprising her, but pleasingly so, he actually laughed – a friendly, unguarded, youthful laugh that was at odds with the rest of his behaviour, or what she'd seen of it up to now.

Gemma crossed the kitchen and opened one of two doors in the far wall. It opened into an enclosed stairway, the main access to the first floor. She walked up the two lowest steps and put a foot on the third tread. It groaned in protest. 'It's loose,' she said, 'and so's the riser. Think you could do something with it?'

'Should be able,' Ivor said. Allowing her to come down out of the way, he knelt down and felt about under the stair carpet. 'Need to get the carpet off to see properly. See if we need new timber or can just tighten up what's there.'

'No time like the present, I suppose,' said Gemma. She glanced again at the case he was carrying. As a source of carpenter's tools it looked unpromising.

'Didn't bring tools with me,' Ivor said. 'Should a thought. No screwdriver. Do you...?'

'Under the kitchen sink are a few elementary things.' Together they went to fetch them, then, very carefully, Ivor began to remove the carpet from the stairs.

'Needs a little fillet,' Ivor said, after a brief feel and inspection. 'See? Just there. Nothing difficult, but I'll want to come back with wood and tools another time. Won't cost you much, though.'

Five minutes later, with the stair carpet tacked back in position, Gemma and Ivor were sitting in two of the easy chairs in the big living-room with biscuits and tea. Ivor was looking enquiringly into the back of the inglenook. There was no fire this warm afternoon, but the room smelt enticingly of wood smoke. 'It's a Charles II fire-back,' Gemma explained, guessing the object of his interest. Ivor looked almost too impressed so she added, 'Of course you and I know it's not really a Restoration piece. They were mass-produced in Victorian times, weren't they, but it's still nice to have.'

Ivor hastily exchanged the awed expression on his face for something more suitable and agreed with a nod. 'You're an artist, right?' he said.

'A bit of one,' Gemma answered. 'How did you know that?'

Because he'd gone peering through her back windows a week earlier, but he could hardly say so. 'Mrs Goderich told me,' he invented seamlessly. 'At Lamb House. She said you done all them pictures of Rye with cats in you see everywhere.'

Ivor didn't understand why Gemma laughed at that. She said, 'It began with books. Two books for children about a cat called Nicholas II and a boy called Vince. I began to draw cats in Rye as illustrations for the first one. Then it all sort of took off.' She paused for a moment, watching him keenly. If he had read or even seen those books this was the moment he would say so. He did not. She smiled at him again. 'The books would be rather young for you, to say the least, though you might still think the pictures quite fun.' She had gone as far as she could without saying, *the pictures of Vince were based on you*. 'Perhaps when you have children of your own.' She stood up. 'Come on, let's have this tour of the house.'

As Ivor got up he pointed to one of Gemma's cats, which had been asleep on another armchair all the time they'd been drinking their tea. A second cat had walked in from the kitchen during that time and then gone out again but Ivor had taken no notice of either of them. Now he said, 'What are your cats called?'

'That one's Debussy,' Gemma told him. 'Just now you might have seen Tiramisu. There are two more: No Knickers and M'pusscat.'

Ivor spluttered a laugh of surprise. 'No Knickers? Funny name for a cat.'

'There were two,' Gemma explained. 'Twins. Fur Coat and No Knickers. Sadly Fur Coat met with an accident, which just left the one, so it does sound a bit odd.'

Ivor didn't follow, having never heard the expression before, but he let it go. 'It's a hall house, your house,' he said next.

For a second Gemma thought he had said something totally different and dreadfully offensive, and felt her cheeks flush, but realised just in time to save them both embarrassment what the actual word had been. Back on track now she was able to say, 'Really? I didn't think it was so old. I was told, seventeenth century.'

'Yeah, but the basic structure is probably miles older. Like Birdskitchen.' Since the day he'd made his major discovery – or guess – about the ancient origins of the local farmhouses he had found his idea supported by a book he'd got out of the library, and was now fully confident of his theory and with the vocabulary that expressed it. 'They're Wealden Halls, also called Yeomen's Houses. Date back centuries. You tell by looking in the roof. If there's a king-post up there, what some books call a crown-post, you got a medieval building.' The excitement in his voice was exchanged for regret. 'I couldn't check this out at Birdskitchen.'

Gemma was interested in what he'd said, but much more so in the fact that he'd come out with it at all. She hadn't heard him sound this enthusiastic about anything before. She said, 'Well, we can go up there in a minute and look. Meanwhile, here you've seen the living-room. When I bought Gatcombe it was, as the ad put it, "ripe for renovation". I bought it from a couple in their seventies who needed something smaller. They'd made no alterations to the place in thirty years, but this room at least was more or less as I wanted it, silvered oak beams in white plaster walls.' She tapped on the oak dining-table and indicated the Jacobean sideboard and chairs.

'Happily they sold me these.' She led the way through the lobby between front door and chimney stack into the third front room. 'They still called this the parlour: it was wall-papered – a dreadful pattern in different shades of brown, and full of glass-fronted cabinets and yellowing photographs in frames. The room was obviously never used. I had the walls emulsioned white before I moved in. It's my writing room now, as you can see.'

Ivor had to remember that Gemma thought he was seeing the ground-floor rooms for the first time. 'I like this room. And your kitchen,' he said, 'but what's round the back, where the kitchen usually is?'

'Come and I'll show you. I'm glad you like the kitchen. There was an old flat stone sink there when I moved in, and an ancient black range. I felt a bit guilty about getting rid of the sink, but putting in the Aga... No hesitation.' She took him into the enormous studio behind. As Gemma walked in front of him Ivor noticed that, though she talked like someone older than her – what, thirty years? – her slim figure, and the graceful way she moved seemed to belong to someone younger, someone little older than himself, for instance. For all her seniority she was a real looker, he thought. Compared to someone like Meryl, anyway.

'When I arrived, this was a disused dairy and there,' she pointed through a doorway, 'a bread oven, which the previous owners hadn't gone near for years. This lovely brick floor was sprouting ribbon fern in little tufts like plumes. I haven't done anything with the old bake-house, except to show it to interested visitors, but the dairy's become my studio, you see. And the council let me put in an unobtrusive skylight.'

Ivor couldn't get enough of this house. Furnished as it was, it was Birdskitchen as he wanted Birdskitchen to be. But this was Gatcombe. He found he wanted Gatcombe now, just as it was.

Upstairs were four bedrooms with two more in the attic above, these rewarding you for the climb, on a fine afternoon like this one, with the distant sight of the sea. And there, embedded in the wall between the two rooms Ivor found the king-post of his dreams. The short braces radiating from the top of it, then disappearing through the ceiling on their way to support the nearest rafters, did indeed look a little like a wooden crown. Again Ivor saw himself living in a house like this in splendid state. Lord of the manor in his hall. Or yeoman at least. Whatever a yeoman was. 'There it is,' he said. 'King-post. Crown-post. Whatever. It's like having the past coming to life in the middle of your house. Like a ghost.' He turned to Gemma with another boyish chuckle of a laugh. 'Fun, yeah?'

'Wow,' said Gemma. 'You've shown me something I didn't know.' Then, suddenly aware that she was alone with him in a bedroom at the top of the otherwise empty house, she said, 'Better go back down now.' She let him precede her through the door and down the two flights of boxed-in stairs.

When they were standing on the floor of the living-room again, and it was the moment for Ivor to say that he was going, and to name the day of his return to fix the stair, he instead threw himself down in an armchair and said, 'I've got some pictures, miss. I want you to see them.'

That explained the music case, which he now had on his lap and was tapping nervously with the flats of the fingers of his left hand. 'Show me them,' Gemma said, sitting down herself, opposite him. She didn't know what to expect, but half-guessed he might have a case-full of architectural drawings, or sketches of historic furniture, those being the only interests of his that she knew of. She was more than surprised when he pulled out of the case some dozen watercolour studies of wild birds on A4 cartridge paper. 'Good heavens,' she said.

'Why good heavens?' he asked, back to his sulky voice.

'Because they're extraordinarily good and they took me by surprise. Are they really your own work?' She regretted the words as soon as she heard them, though it was already too late. She remembered the timber merchant's stamp and signature plastered comically all over the chair he'd brought to Lamb House. She added at once, 'No, no, that was rude of me. Forget I said that.'

Ivor had flushed slightly. He looked displeased. 'I can prove it to you. I'll sketch one of your cats.' He pulled from the case a blank sheet of cartridge paper and a pencil, and did a rough, quick sketch of Debussy, who was still lying, curled and asleep, in a spare armchair. It took him just two minutes. Then he got up and presented it to Gemma who, having made a point of not coming round to peer over his shoulder, was continuing minutely to study his paintings of the birds.

'Well,' she said, examining the new sketch approvingly, 'you've certainly cracked that. Tabbies are notoriously difficult to do – the stripes go one way and the fur lies the other. But you understand that, of course. I think I told you I teach art at a school in London. If you were one of my students it might not be easy to find too many things to teach you. Did you have a good art teacher at your school, or did you get to this standard all by yourself?'

'Bit of both, miss,' said Ivor, trying not to show how fiercely pleased he was to hear all these compliments.

Gemma tapped one of the bird paintings she was still holding in her hand. 'This duck, though. What kind is it?' It was mottled grey for the most part, with a chestnut shoulder patch.

'Don't know, miss.'

The implication of this astonished Gemma. 'You mean you don't have a bird book? You've never looked at a picture to check the detail?'

'No,' said Ivor. 'You meant to?'

Gemma thought for a second. 'Most of us would need to. Perhaps you're one of the rare souls who don't. I've got a bird book. We can look it up in a minute and see. And by the way, I don't think you need to go on calling me miss. I have a name, which is Gemma. My friends call me Gee.'

During his final week of hop picking Ivor was still putting in the extra hours at the end of the afternoon. Andy continued to drive him and his bicycle halfway home after the early evening pint in the pub – and what an easy habit that one was to get into, Ivor thought. Not only that but Andy insisted on buying him his drink as well. Ivor knew exactly why this was: it was because he'd told Andy he believed his account of Mark's seeing ghosts at the big house on the London road. He took a big lesson from that. If you presented a face to people that corresponded to what they wanted you to be, or thought you ought to be, they would be so pleased with themselves that you could wrap them round your finger. He wondered why he'd never thought of this before.

He went back to Gatcombe the day after hop picking at Birdskitchen had finished, on the Saturday afternoon, with a proper bag of tools and a few off-cuts of timber, to repair the wobbly stair. This time there was chocolate cake, from Simon the Pieman's, along with the tea. 'I've never asked you where you live,' Gemma said to him. 'But in case I need your services again...' She had examined his completed repair very carefully; he had done an excellent job.

'I got a bungalow at Winchelsea Beach,' he told her.

'What, all on your own?' Gemma said teasingly.

'Pretty much,' Ivor said. 'No brothers or nothin'. My mum's on a cruise with this bloke from the north she's picked up.'

'And your dad?' she asked, more gently.

'Don't have one. Never did have.'

Well, of course he'd had a dad at some point, but Gemma understood what he meant. She was taken aback to discover that he was fending for himself, alone in his mother's house, at the age of sixteen. That wasn't at all her world. 'Well, I hope she comes back after her cruise,' was all she could think to say. Then, 'Of course I live mostly on my own too, but not all the time.' She told him about the teenagers she took in during the school holidays.

Ivor was a bit disconcerted by this. He hadn't imagined those lovely old bedrooms haunted by rowdy young Americans. 'When are the next ones?' he asked.

Gemma laughed. 'Christmas holidays. A long way off.' She had seen that look of concern cross his face and wondered what it meant. But he seemed satisfied by her answer.

To Ivor also Christmas seemed a long way off. It wasn't a bridge that needed to be crossed yet. He was thinking, as he ate his cake, about Gemma's wonderful studio. He'd been more than impressed by its possibilities. It was quite big enough for two. At a pinch his woodworking tools and workbench would go in there – should anything happen to the bungalow at Winchelsea Beach. By this he meant, if his mother decided to up sticks and run off to Michael Harding in York. But all of this was running ahead.

They talked about hop picking. 'I got promoted in my last week,' Ivor told Gemma proudly. 'I got to be crow's-nester, if you know what that is.'

Gemma did. 'The chap up on the tall tower thing at the back of the hop trailer, who gets to cut the bine tops.'

'Sorry. Of course you'd know. Hop picking going on right under your nose out there.' Ivor gestured through the wall in the direction of Gatcombe's oast. 'Are your lot finished, then?'

'They finished when yours did, I think. Yesterday midday. They had a bit of a party. Drinks and sandwiches.'

'Us the same. Tom, the hooker-on, chain-smokes even when he's eating. It was a right laugh seeing him gobble peanuts from the palm of his hand, still keeping a lit ciggie between his two fingers.' Ivor did a mime to show what this had looked like. 'We had a load of crazy people, really. Dead funny foreman. He was quite old and he was German. Well, he'd been German once. Had trouble with the English.'

'English people, you mean?'

'English language. If he meant "you must" he said "you mustn't" and if he meant "you should" he said "you shouldn't". If he told people to do something he'd say "don't do it". Caused tons of trouble with people that didn't know him.' He told Gemma the story of the tractor driver who'd believed he'd been told to drive under a wire, which bent the exhaust pipe over and made the engine stop. Gemma was amused. She liked seeing Ivor animated like this, as he had been when he discovered the king-post in the bedroom, and when he'd shown her his paintings of birds. 'Once he said to someone, "What didn't you do with those wellingtons I didn't give you yesterday?" God knows why.'

Gemma thought she knew. 'Perhaps he taught himself English,' she said, 'and got one big thing wrong. In German, when you say "you must" to people you know very well, you say "du must", which sounds quite like "you must" in English. But if you're talking to people you don't know so well, like at work, you have to say "Sie müssen". It's considered polite. But it does sound a bit like "you mustn't". So he must have mistaken the negative for the polite form and applied it across the board. It does seem rather funny, as well as a bit sad. All those years and no-one ever corrected him.'

Ivor screwed up his face. 'He wasn't the sort of bloke anyone corrected.' Then, 'Hey, you speak German, then?'

'Up to a point, yes. I actually lived in Germany for nearly two years. Last time there was a man in my life. He was German.'

'What happened to him?'

'I'd like to say that after we split up his life fell apart, he did drugs and took to drink and ruined his talent... Only joking. Actually, he's got a nice German girlfriend, settled down, and his paintings – boring as I personally think they are – sell rather well over there.'

'Why'd you split up?' Ivor asked. He took an interest in things that went wrong for people.

'Oh, lots of reasons, as there always are. I think that when I told him he must have learnt to paint in the army that probably sealed it.'

Ivor laughed, as he was meant to. He thought it was funny, but wasn't quite sure why.

'On the subject of painting,' Gemma went on, 'I've been doing some thinking. I think I'd like to show your bird pictures to my agent. That is, if you had no objection.' She looked quite intently into his eyes, looking for his reaction. It came in the form of an infinitesimal nod. 'I might be doing myself out of a job, of course, even though our styles could hardly be more different, but there it is.' She looked at him carefully, to see if he'd notice she was joking.

He didn't. 'I wouldn't want that to happen,' he said, looking at the carpet.

'I was only half serious,' Gemma said. 'But I do think your work could make you a bit of money. Though I'm afraid I'm not thinking of the Royal Academy. At least, not just yet. I'm not thinking of that for my work either, by the way.'

'I'd like it if my work was seen by your agent,' said Ivor.

'How do we get it to her? That's the question. She's up in London and I don't imagine you'd want to let your portfolio out of your hands for very long.' Gemma was being perfectly serious about this.

'Perhaps your agent could come down,' Ivor suggested. 'Look at them here.'

Gemma smiled. 'I'm afraid that's not very likely. It's not the sort of thing that agents do, unless you're David Hockney or Damien Hirst, and even then not at the beginning.'

'Reckon I could trust you to take them to London yourself,' Ivor said slowly. 'I don't think you'd get them lost or stolen.' He was a bit reluctant, but didn't think there remained any other choice.

'When does your apprenticeship with Mr Gutsell start, Ivor?' Something that hadn't seemed obvious a moment before now seemed so. 'Monday, or Monday week?'

'Monday week.'

'Then maybe we could go up together, if I can get an appointment for us one day next week. I'd pay your fare and you'd only have to pay me back if we sell your paintings. What do you think?'

They met at Rye station and took the train up. For Ivor the day passed like a dream. He'd been taken to London twice as a child: once to the zoo and once to see the Crown Jewels, and it had rained both times. This time things couldn't have been more different. The sun turned London's grey buildings yellow and pink with light.

They went to a big office block and were treated like important people by the receptionist. Gemma's agent, Marianne, a businesslike woman with businesslike grey hair which was cut very short, examined Ivor's paintings minutely and for some time. 'What's this one?' she wanted to know, indicating the mystery duck. 'A gadwall drake,' Ivor was able to elucidate. They had found a picture of it in Gemma's bird book, between the mallard and the scaup. 'I'd like to keep these for a while,' Marianne said and, seeing him stiffen, added, 'I promise they'll be in very safe hands. I'll get the right people to see them and we'll see what happens next.' She stood up and smiled and Ivor, who didn't think he was very good at this sort of thing, realised the interview was over and that he had to get to his feet too.

Gemma bought him a celebratory meal in an Italian restaurant near Notting Hill Gate. With a little guidance from her he had chosen the half-bottle of wine they shared with their steak. Then at last the day was over and they caught the train home from Charing Cross. Arriving at Rye station, Gemma asked her protégé, a bit carefully, since she knew he still spent some of his nights crashing with friends in Rye, and didn't always go home to Winchelsea Beach, 'Can I drive you home?'

This was the moment, and Ivor knew it. People spoke of a 'tipping point'. This was the tipping point, after which everything would either come right or go horribly wrong. Ivor seized the tail end of this so-far lucky day. 'I'd like to come home with you, Gee,' he said.

TEN

'What do the Fogresses think?' Feri asked.

'I haven't told them yet,' said Gemma. They were walking through Russell Square, in hazy autumn sunshine on the way to lunch at Pizza Express. It was their first meeting, their first face-to-face conversation in nearly a month.

'But they'll find out. People in small towns always do. Even in London...'

'Oh, you can be sure I'll tell them. It's just that finding the right approach isn't that easy. You're actually the first person of all who I've told.' That sounded clumsy, Gemma thought. Still, she wasn't writing a book. And she should have protested about that Fogress word that Feri still used when referring to Gemma's slightly older friends in Rye. But she hadn't done; she'd gone along with Feri by using that complicit 'them' in her responses, relishing at that moment the conspiracy of youth that she still enjoyed with her. And now, of course, that she also shared with someone else.

Feri hadn't come hop picking this year. Her relationship with Carlos was becoming all-consuming. Feri wouldn't have wanted to leave him behind even had she gone for a short weekend at Gatcombe, and as for travelling down with Carlos in tow, she wouldn't have been prepared to share her beautiful man even in that very limited way. She also had the nous to realise that taking your very-much-in-love-with-you boyfriend, your can't-take-his-hands-off-you boyfriend, down to the house of a best friend who at that time didn't have a boyfriend at all would have been a cruelly insensitive thing to do. Instead, she and Gemma had met a few times in London since Gemma's father had died. They'd met, as they were meeting today, when Gemma had come up on some business or other, for a simple lunch and a walk. But this was the first time that Gemma had arrived with such momentous news.

'Darling, a toy-boy! And living in! How very up to the minute!' had been Feri's uproarious first reaction to hearing the news. The t-b-word was one that Gemma had refused to use herself, even in her own mind, but she couldn't stop Feri using it, and couldn't deny the tiny thrill it gave her when Feri did. But she'd replied to Feri that toy-boys were what older women had. What she had found in Ivor was a boyfriend, plain and simple. Though plain and simple were hardly the right words for Ivor who, she explained emphatically to Feri, was both a highly complex character and an absolute dish. By the time of this pizza-lunch meeting the affair was five days old.

Once you had told one person, Gemma found, telling the others became slightly easier. Angela spotted Gemma and Ivor getting out of the car together in Rye one day and asked Gemma, when they next had lunch at The Mermaid, who he was. Which gave Gemma an opportunity to smile a Mona-Lisa-like smile and say, 'I was just about to tell you. He's Ivor, my new boyfriend.'

Angela's face delivered all by itself the Good Lord, or Heavens above, that she only just managed to stop herself voicing. She said, 'How very wonderful for you. And for him. He looks splendidly youthful.'

Gemma enjoyed delivering her answer. 'Oh, he is. He's not quite seventeen.'

As for Jane, she had heard the news from Angela by the time Gemma next ran into her. Did Gemma have time for a coffee and a catch-up at Fletcher's – or Simon the Pieman's? Jane had had time to digest the new tit-bit, and was more prepared than Angela had been to voice an opinion on the matter. 'I agree that it's all wonderful and unexpected. Like something in a classical myth. But the beauty of it all is going to count for nothing once you start getting hurt by him, as I'm terribly afraid you will be.'

'I do realise that,' Gemma said. 'I may be an unwise, foolish non-virgin, but I'm not a stupid one. But sometimes a moment presents itself in life that you have to seize with both hands. You know, the kind of thing that will happen to some people only once, and to many not at all. And when it runs its course, as I'm perfectly well aware it will, I shall take a leaf out of the Marschallin's book, in Der Rosenkavalier, and let him go with dignity and grace.'

Jane pursed her lips as though doubting this. 'Well, only you can know what's best for you. But you're not just looking at a rather bleak future (though I suppose it's good you realise that), you're turning your back on something *now*. The chance to meet a good man your own age, to settle down with...'

'In Rye?' Gemma interrupted, mock-incredulity in her voice. Or perhaps the incredulity was real. 'Where's he been hiding all these years?' She gave a little laugh. 'You tell me!'

A fortnight passed before Gemma got round to telling her sister about the new situation. She did this on the phone.

'You must be out of your mind!' Sarah said. 'Mother will have a fit!'

'I've absolutely no intention of telling Mother, and I'd be glad if you didn't either. I haven't forgotten what she was like about Dieter all that time ago, and I'm sure you haven't.'

'All right,' Sarah said. 'I won't pass the news on. But that's in the cause of protecting her feelings, not yours. And it's still a very big thing to ask, you know. Since she'll find out one day anyway, and then want to know how long I've known. I do think you're being more than usually selfish.'

'And how is our mother going to find out, if neither of us tells her?' Gemma challenged.

'Don't be naïve. Your neighbours will know by now. Your friends in Rye.'

'Because I've already told them,' Gemma said calmly.

'Before you told me. Thank you! But I'll let that pass. You won't have told everybody, though. Not the lady in the dry-cleaner's. Not the postman, or the man who comes with the milk. Not the tellers in the bank. But they'll all know now. They won't tell you they know, but they'll tell each other. And because you have a public face – OK, you're not that famous, but you're the author of children's books that everyone's heard of – one of them at some point is going to report you to the News of the World. Cradle-snatching children's author.'

'I don't think report is the right verb,' said Gemma stonily.

Sarah ignored this. 'And even though Mummy doesn't read the News of the World, other people around Tunbridge Wells do, and it will come to her ears from somebody. And your publisher and your agent will get to know from somebody. And the American School... What about the kids that stay with you in the holidays? It'll be Christmas in a couple of months What's to happen then?'

'It won't be in the News of the World,' Gemma argued back. 'It's true that some people round here will be shocked; even some of my friends are shocked, though they pretend not to be; it's a very respectable neighbourhood. But in the best as well as the worst way.

That very respectability means that none of them would dream of going to the papers.'

'Don't you believe it,' said Sarah. Gemma thought her sister would have run at her down the phone line if she could.

'As for Christmas, Ivor knows about Christmas. He's going to go back to his mother's while the kids are here. We've discussed it like the adults we are.'

'Adults! How can you? You're behaving like... I won't say a child, but like someone who's lost their reason. As for the boy...'

'At sixteen he's entitled to get married or die for his country.'

'Boys of sixteen don't marry women old enough to be their mothers. But if you're so damn sure of him, why don't you discuss that too? What on earth does his real mother think?'

'I really don't think she gives a fig what happens to him. She's on an extended cruise in the Med with some businessman from the north. She wrote to Ivor, telling him they were getting engaged.'

There was no answer to that that Sarah could think of. Gemma heard the phone at the other end being put down.

Gemma would never have considered seducing a sixteen-year-old boy. She was not naturally sympathetic towards Mrs Robinson in The Graduate, and despite her liberal attitude to other people's sexual conduct, not to mention her own, she couldn't help tut-tutting inwardly when she read of cases where mature people – often teachers – ended up between the sheets with someone else's teenage son.

She regarded her own case, hers and Ivor's, as utterly different from those. She had not seduced him, nor had she even considered the possibility. Any fantasies she had entertained concerning him were centred on the idea of Ivor Wingate's being the grown-older Vince Harris of her stories: the idea of sex between herself and him had played no part in them.

But then had come that day of the trip to London, when everything changed. It had been a wonderful day from the beginning. She had enjoyed watching Ivor's childlike pleasure in everything that had happened to him, beginning with seeing London in the sunshine for the first time. Then in the tempting possibility, not actually voiced by Gemma's agent, but nonetheless allowed to hover in the atmosphere of the friendly interview between them, that he might enjoy a career as an illustrator that was as lucrative and successful as Gemma's own. The celebration meal in the restaurant afterwards where, as Gemma's escort, Ivor was treated by the waiters as well as by herself as a young grown-up and given the ritual task of tasting the wine before the glasses were filled. And the day had ended so extraordinarily, first with his request to come back home with her – she willed herself, as they drove back from the station, not to think about where this might be leading – then with his kissing her boyishly when bedtime came, but the very next moment, with his thumb and forefinger alighting, then pausing, on the top button of her blouse, asking, 'Can I sleep with you tonight?'

Ivor was her creature in a way that he could not possibly imagine. She had taken him years ago and moulded him into Vince. Without him there would have been no Cat Who Loved Potatoes, no Nicholas and the Castle of Rats, no Gatcombe Farm, no London agents and TV appearances, no lifestyle that was anything like the one she now enjoyed. But Vince, or more truthfully Ivor, had breathtakingly returned the compliment by wanting to be her lover. She could hardly deny him that. If she had the power also to shape his career, to nudge forward his development as a commercial artist, or as an artist or craftsman of any kind, then that was yet one more good thing. It gave the whole unlooked-for, incredible narrative a wonderful symmetry that was awe-inspiring, heart-stopping.

Gemma did not fool herself into imagining that Ivor had fallen in love with her. She knew that he never would. But she knew he liked her well enough – the passing weeks held plenty of evidence of that – and with that she could be content. She was fond of him, would happily nurture him and share her bed with him for the short time that he would continue to want it (she had no illusions about that either) but she would take the greatest care not actually to fall in love. The warning stories were engraved on her heart: not just Der Rosenkavalier; there were Isis and Galatea, Pygmalion, Coppelia, and more. She knew that what had started so beautifully would one day painfully end. She would deal with that when the moment arrived. For now she was more than happy simply to enjoy an episode of beauty in her life.

'Where did you get your education?' Ivor asked her out of the blue.

When she was surprised by something, or particularly amused, she had a special small laugh that was like toy sleigh-bells, or the tinkling call of linnets or goldfinches in flight. Ivor liked it. She did it now, then said, 'At school. Same as you.'

'Except I didn't listen,' Ivor said gruffly.

'I wasn't that good a student either,' said Gemma. 'But even when I didn't listen some of it got through. I can still tell you the chemical symbol for tin. Big S, small N. Information I've never had any need of but there you go.'

'Yeah, but when I didn't listen, I didn't listen – big time.' He took a gulp of beer. They went to pubs together sometimes. To the King's Head at Udimore, or the Red Lion at Brede. Although Ivor was exceptionally good-looking, and not particularly tall for his age, his face didn't automatically shout under-age at every moderately attentive barman, and no-one had made any difficulties to date. Today they had walked through the fields, crossed the footbridge over the Brede, stopped, looked and listened before crossing the railway line, and climbed the hill to Icklesham, to the Queen's Head.

'There aren't all that many things you really need to learn,' Gemma said, more to herself than to him. Then, 'Shakespeare?'

'Don't think we did that.'

'Oh, for heaven's sake!' This time she laughed in a heartier way. 'We must go up to London some time. I'll drag you there. You need to see Hamlet at the very least. Macbeth first, perhaps, to get you used to the idea.'

Ivor felt that he'd done well for himself. If he had to be the toy-boy of a woman nearly twice his age – because he'd become obsessed with the house she lived in – he could have done a lot worse than Gemma. She cooked better than his mother did, and she knew how to satisfy him in bed. Bed. That in itself was a new pleasure. Ivor had plenty of sexual experience, but only in doorways and against the walls of alleys. He'd never known this degree of comfort. And if his new life was all a bit domestic, so be it. What had his social life consisted of previously, after all? Evenings of hanging around outside the kebab shop in the station yard, smoking dope, inventing sexual exploits to brag about to the other boys – who weren't people he cared for anyway – and smashing the glass in the bus shelters when the wellsprings of conversation ran dry.

When he ran into those people in Rye these days they would ask him what he was doing with himself and he'd answer that he was shacked up with a rich bird in a big house in the country. He saw the same sceptical smirks appear on all their faces. So what? He was wiser than to add too much detail in an effort to make them believe. He never told them his partner's name or occupation, or that she was well-known in her field and in Rye, that her designs were all over their parents' tea-towels. He never told them the name of Gatcombe Farm, or said in which direction it lay. And by unspoken agreement, he and Gemma never went together into any of the pubs in the centre of town.

'What about books?' Gemma was asking now.

'I read about houses,' Ivor said. 'Architecture and stuff. And paintings. Painters.'

'Yes, I know,' Gemma said. 'But I meant, well, for want of a better word, literature. Novels and so on. Good ones.'

'Nah,' said Ivor. Then a thought struck him. 'Is that part of your education too? Is that what makes you sound so clever when you talk?'

'Thank you, darling, and, no, I don't know. Books don't suit everyone. You can be very well educated indeed, I should imagine, and never have opened a novel. But if you were to read just one – one in all your life – you should make it Crime and Punishment. Written over a hundred years ago by Dostoyevsky.' Ivor pulled a face at the name. 'He was Russian,' Gemma pleaded in his defence.

The Queen's Head was not unusual among the local inns in being hundreds of years old. But unlike most it had a hilltop garden with a view that extended for miles. Across the valley the white frontage of Gatcombe could be seen, its two bonneted oast-kilns peering over its roof. The wind had caught the protruding vane of one of the cowls and turned it round, but not the other, so that the two white bonnets appeared to be having a conversation. Further off lay Winchelsea and Rye, on their mole-hill mounds above the Marsh with, far beyond them, the shingle spit of Dungeness, a tongue that poked the sea, and distant Dover's cliffs. Even this October Sunday lunchtime the garden was a sun-trap, to which Gemma and Ivor were just two of many locals to have made their way. Now, coming in through the garden gate and giving them a searching look before walking in through the front door of the pub, was Albert Gutsell, Ivor's new boss. Which gave them both a jolt.

'What the... What's he bloody doing here?' said Ivor. 'He doesn't drink.' Gutsell and his wife were Methodists, they both knew. Their Sunday mornings were spent at the Chapel in Brede rather than in local pubs.

'Does it matter?' Gemma said. 'He has his Sunday, we have ours.'

'Yeah, but all the same.'

Gemma knew that Ivor disliked his new boss. Gutsell had made Ivor spend his first few days doing nothing beyond sharpening an endless store of chisels, gouges and planes on an oil-stone. Still, Ivor was determined to learn everything he could from him. He'd stuck at his job a whole month now, and seemed in no mood to quit. Gemma admired him for that. A few minutes later Albert Gutsell emerged from the pub, carrying an old oak table with the help of one of the staff. Despite the awkward load they were carrying Gutsell remembered to turn towards Ivor and give him another glare. Outside the gate they manoeuvred the table into Gutsell's van, and Gutsell drove off. 'Mystery explained,' said Gemma. 'And now you know what awaits you in the morning.'

'Too right,' said Ivor. He felt an unfamiliar rush of affection for Gemma just then. She was good company, and indulged him. She made him laugh. She was always making silly little jokes about everyday things that tickled his imagination. Nobody in his life had done this for him before. She'd say that the fridge contained "a mouseful of cheese", or there was nothing for lunch but "a tin of puma chunks". A certain kind of angel-hair pasta was "tangliolini". Those jokes might already be written down in those famous books of hers, but he'd never opened a copy to look inside. 'This Russian bloke,' he said suddenly. 'Are his books anything like yours?'

'Dostoyevsky? Not in the least,' said Gemma, laughing. 'I'm not remotely in his league.' She took a sip from her gin and tonic. She wondered what she'd give Ivor for his lunch today. Not that it mattered. He always seemed pleased with whatever she fed him. Relaxed, she peered out at the view. She had already thought of the three rivers that converged at Rye, almost encircling its hill-top site, as fingers of the Romney Marsh reaching inland. Now she thought of the higher ground, the long ridges that ran between them, as fingers of the Weald that stretched towards the sea. Interlocking fingers of land and water – for the Marsh and those river valleys had all been under water just a few centuries before – that symbolised a union of two worlds.

Gemma was right about the task Albert Gutsell would set Ivor the following morning: it was a fiddly repair to the undercarriage of the table from the pub. And Ivor was right to expect that Gutsell would have something to say about the place and the company he'd seen him in. 'Isn't natural and it ain't right,' his boss chided him, raising his voice over the noise of the lathe he was using. 'Lad your age should have a girlfriend his own age, if he thinks he's old enough and rich enough to have a girlfriend at all. And he should be making his own way in the world. Not be kept by some la-di-da bohemian lady with more money than sense.'

'Should be, should be,' Ivor threw the words back at him. 'Might depend how much money the lad's being paid.'

Gutsell managed to drown that last sentence in a whir of equipment and a clatter of chair-legs. 'Old enough to be your mother. Lets you drink beer in a public house for the world to see, when you're still two years off eighteen. What's your own mother thinking of? I'd like to know.'

'Even she's not old enough to be my mother.' Ivor answered, his tone just short of insolent. 'She's off on a world cruise with a man twice her age. Shouldn't think she cares one way or other.'

'If I was her I'd be putting you over my knee and giving you a right good tanning,' Gutsell said, as if reciting something he'd learned long ago.

'Let her try,' said Ivor.

When Norma had written to her son to announce her engagement to Michael Harding Ivor had written back – it seemed weird to be writing to someone on a cruise ship, but people did – with his congratulations expressed as tersely as could be imagined (Well done, Mum) and the information that he was now living with a girlfriend, in no more detail than that. He didn't give much thought to how and when his mother and his girlfriend might meet, or what everyone would say when they did. Gemma did give some thought to this, but wasn't particularly apprehensive about an eventual encounter. When it happened at last, it was oddly low-key.

Gemma drove Ivor to Winchelsea Beach one evening, so that he could pick up his winter duffel-coat. It was something he hadn't needed till now but with November approaching and Gutsell showing no sign that he intended to heat his workshop one degree more than was necessary to keep fingers more or less operational – provided you wore mittens – the coat would soon be a necessary part of Ivor's equipment during his working day.

As Gemma drew up outside the bungalow a taxi coming from the opposite direction did the same. Norma and her grey-haired and grey-suited fiancé stepped out of the taxi at the same moment as Ivor got out of Gemma's car, and then Gemma, who would not otherwise have needed to get out but now saw clearly who these people must be, climbed out too. There was a second of general speechlessness, then Gemma said, 'You must be Norma and Michael. I've heard so much about you. I'm Gemma Palmer.' She held out her hand.

Somehow the others knew who she was. Although her TV and newspaper appearances were rare, she was one of those minor celebrities at whom people would gesture back over their shoulders in Rye after they'd passed in the street and say, 'You know who that was, don't you?' Norma and then Michael found they had shaken her hand before they could come up with any alternative strategy.

'I won't come in,' Gemma assured them. 'Ivor's simply come to get his coat, and you've just got back. I hope it was a lovely cruise.' She let Ivor lead the others through the gate once Michael had paid the taxi driver, then, having assured herself there wasn't going to be any sort of scene in which Ivor might need her help, stood in the open doorway of the car, awaiting his return. She was certain not only that he could handle the situation perfectly capably but that he'd do it better on his own.

He was back in under a minute, clutching the duffel-coat. 'That was quick,' Gemma said. 'Did she have anything to say?'

'Not much,' Ivor said. 'What could she? She got knocked up at fifteen. I'm sixteen already. Pots don't call kettles black. Anyway, she's got this man now. Should suit her very well not to have me around too much.' He added, in a self-mocking way that Gemma hadn't heard before, 'Being needy. Being dependent. Cramping her style.' He had no more to say on the subject. The encounter was over. They got into the car and Gemma drove away.

Ivor was thoughtful during the drive back along Float Lane. His tools were still at the bungalow, in the garden shed. For the moment he hardly needed them. Working all day in Gutsell's workshop, where tools were provided, was enough woodwork for the time being. But one day he would need his grandfather's stuff again. He hadn't broached the subject of installing it in Gemma's studio yet. That might have upset a finely-balanced situation, though one that suited Ivor very well. Gemma had first claim on her studio, but Ivor found there were enough hours when she was out or busy with other things to do his painting there too. She was quite happy about this, and he appreciated that. It was a bit soon, he thought carefully, to clutter the place up with a workbench and a shed-load of tools.

That time might come one day, though, if Norma moved up north with her new bloke, or if they sold the bungalow and bought something else. Then he would need not only the diplomatic skills he was fast learning from Gemma, but some help with transport, too. All that stuff would be too much for Gemma's car. But people he knew from school were beginning to turn seventeen and starting to drive. People like Mark, who lived on farms where there were trucks and vans. He hadn't seen Mark since he'd got him that first job at Reedbed in July. He'd hardly given him a thought. Until, that was, he'd heard Andy tell the extraordinary story of how Mark had had a childhood experience at Welstead House that was similar to his own. Well, maybe. If what both their mothers had said was true. Perhaps he'd get back in touch with Mark some time. When the tools and transport situation looked like becoming urgent. Which it wasn't yet.

ELEVEN

Gemma pointed out to Ivor her Penguin Classics copy of Crime and Punishment in its place among the shelves. 'It's there if you want it,' was all she said, wise enough not to urge her young lover too often to read a difficult book. But with Shakespeare she had necessarily to take a more direct approach. In the space of a few weeks they went up to London twice, first to see the RSC's production of Macbeth at the Barbican, then to Hamlet at the National. Ivor's reaction to both plays was quiet and thoughtful. Gemma was not displeased. She was fairly certain that he would ponder them over time. For now his hearty enjoyment of the suppers she bought him in the City and on the South Bank seemed reward enough.

When Ivor did talk about the plays some time later, it was to ask, 'Did Shakespeare believe in ghosts, you reckon?'

Gemma thought this was a good question, though she had no answer to it. 'I've really no idea,' she said. 'Do you?'

'Not really,' Ivor answered. 'Although...'

Gemma didn't wait for him to continue. She had no reason to suppose he might or could have anything else to say. She said, 'I suppose I'd have to say the same.' The conversation was actually not as abstract as it might have been. They had seen Ian Charleson in the title role in Hamlet. He had taken over the part just a few weeks earlier, following the withdrawal of Daniel Day-Lewis. This had made national news headlines, for the reason that Day-Lewis had been unable to continue in the part when, confronting the Ghost of Hamlet's father on the stage, he heard or seemed to hear his own late father's voice addressing him. This might have provided an opportunity for Ivor to confide in Gemma his own experiences of a vaguely similar kind but, except for letting slip that *'although...'*, whose significance Gemma failed to spot, he didn't take it up. As Mark had warned him after the Lydd experience, tell folk you've seen ghosts and they'll conclude you're a nutter. Which a lot of people, though too polite to say so, probably thought about Day-Lewis at the time.

There were other things than Shakespeare for Ivor to think about anyway. He was fretting because he'd heard nothing from Gemma's agent about the fate of the pictures he had left in her charge, although the weeks since that optimistic meeting had turned into months. Gemma had a hard time convincing him there was nothing necessarily negative, let alone unusual, about that. And then there was Christmas to be sorted out...

Ivor conducted the Christmas negotiations himself, which avoided the awkwardness of Gemma and Norma having to meet again. Ivor would stay at the bungalow over the New Year, whether his mother was there or not, while Gemma played hostess briefly to a couple of American youngsters and then, even more briefly, to her mother, whom she'd neglected to invite down – or been forced by Ivor's presence not to invite – since her father's death. In return for Ivor's agreement to this, Gemma would take him away for a week, over Christmas itself, to Tenerife. Feri would not be visiting during this period: she was travelling with Carlos to New York. Gemma experienced a degree of relief when Feri told her about this. Not huge, sigh-heaving relief: just enough relief to feel slightly ashamed of. She hadn't deliberately prevented Feri and Ivor from meeting; it had just happened that way. It was not as if Feri was any kind of a threat theses days – she now wore Carlos's ring on her finger – but Gemma was conscious, a little guiltily so, of the fact that although she had told Ivor a lot about her friend Feri, the friend with whom she lunched in London and who had often stayed at Gatcombe Farm, she had never found a way to mention that Feri was only eighteen.

Although he had been to Boulogne once on the ferry Ivor had never been in an aeroplane before. He found it a grand and wonderful surprise, as they lifted from the runway at Gatwick, to see the landscape change its form, and the clouds – this was something he had not expected – no longer high up but sliding over the ground, almost touching it, like objects on a table that was covered with a thin sheet of glass. As the clouds shifted their position relative to the aircraft Ivor almost expected their cotton-wool undersides to snag on the roofs and church spires below. Of course, Ivor eventually got tired of the clouds, impenetrable winter cloud that cloaked the vast Atlantic, even when the scene was lit and shadowed by the changing colours of a sunset that went on for hours. But the lights of Tenerife, at last appearing below like necklaces that glittered on the sea, cheered his spirits again.

In the morning they found their bearings by walking down to the ocean, though they hadn't dressed or equipped themselves for a bathe. They stopped at a small breakwater-protected beach where a number of youngsters, some in wet-suits some not, were paddling out to sea on surfboards before turning and riding the waves back, sometimes standing triumphantly all the way, sometimes coming to grief in a quickly unfolding drama of arms and water and legs.

They watched the boys on their boards for some time. At last Ivor found that he couldn't bear to be just a spectator. 'I'm going to have a go,' he said.

'What with?' Gemma asked him with that chink of a laugh in her voice that was like a little bell. 'You haven't got a board.'

'I'll borrow one,' he answered coolly, and began to pull off his shirt.

'You don't have a wet-suit or even trunks,' Gemma protested. 'You can't just...'

But he did. Without saying more or even offering her a smile Ivor, now stripped down to his underpants, handed his clothes to Gemma, who had no words for the occasion herself by now, and walked down the beach to where one of the younger and smaller boys – Ivor wasn't taking his chances with any of the bigger ones – had just landed, following a very showy and professional-looking ride back to the shore. 'Let me have that just five minutes,' he said to the boy, heedless of the probability that the boy was a Spanish-speaking local who wouldn't understand. He pointed back up the beach to where Gemma was standing, looking as awkward and out of place as she felt, watching them. 'She'll give you a hundred pesetas.' But the boy did seem to understand, or at least to have noticed that Gemma looked something like a responsible adult. He handed the board over after only a brief hesitation and then he did a series of mimes, with his hands representing the board and his wiry small body as itself, to show how the board should be used.

Even paddling out, lying on the board, was not as easy, Ivor discovered, as the others made it look. And when the moment came to turn and head for home in the hope of riding the wave that he and the others had spotted advancing towards them – it took much longer for him to get there than he'd expected – Ivor found himself swept off the board and gargling salt water in less time than it took him to blink.

Back on the sand he rather ill-temperedly negotiated a second five minutes from the local kid. Again he paddled painstakingly slowly into the breakers' path and again was knocked mercilessly into and under the wave, which rolled over him with all the weight and inexorability of a giant truck. He struggled back inshore, now told rather than asked the boy that he wanted to have one more try, and headed out to sea again. This time he was knocked into the water even before he'd tried to turn round for the landward run, and this time the board seemed to set about him under the water, whacking his chest and legs with its edges as hard as if someone was attacking him with a tree-branch. And when he at last found his way back to the beach, bruised and for the moment hardly able to stand, he found that a little crowd of youths, some quite a bit bigger than himself, had gathered round the youngster whose board he'd requisitioned, and looked ready to take it back by force. Gemma was in their midst, still clutching Ivor's jeans, T-shirt and shoes, and talking propitiatingly to them in not quite fluent Spanish. It seemed that she was getting ready to act as referee if things hotted up.

Things did not hot up. Without more prompting Ivor returned the board to its owner with a wordless shrug and, reaching into the bundle of his clothes that Gemma was still carrying, jerked a banknote out of the jeans pocket. He handed this to the youngster who, after a moment's puzzling, tucked it into the top of his swimming trunks before walking away up the beach, his board under his arm, in search of a drier spot to store his cash. His supporters took this as the signal for them to disperse and in a second were gone.

So ended Ivor's career as a surfer. Gemma and he continued their walk along the seafront. Ivor's face and his mood were both black with the bruising that he and his self-esteem had received. As she walked alongside her now sullen and silent young man Gemma couldn't help thinking that he really was, still, a rough little tyke and was a little alarmed, almost ashamed, at the quiet thrill that thought sent through her. But there was no denying his physical courage and toughness, his stubborn capacity to endure. He had just given a very public demonstration of those things, and Gemma reassured herself she could at least be proud of him for that.

They stopped for lunch where a row of tables was set, under sunshades, beside the promenade. Opposite, only a line of palm trees and pergolas with bougainvillea trailing over them, crimson, rust and flame, separated them from the dark blue, north-coast sea. Ivor, willing himself to ignore the uncomfortable fact that his underpants, inside his jeans, were still sopping wet, said, 'That book. Did you bring it?' He adopted a truculent tone.

Gemma knew him well enough now to know why. She laughed. 'Which book?'

'The one you're always on at me to read.'

Normally there would have been no reason on earth for Gemma to bring Crime and Punishment on holiday with her, but curiously enough she had. Talking to Ivor about the book a few weeks ago had given her the idea that it was time she read it again herself. 'You're weird sometimes,' she said. 'I don't know why you'd imagine I'd bring a tome like that two thousand miles on the remote off-chance you'd ask to read it. But believe it or not – and you need to realise this is the really weird thing – I have.'

To say that Ivor had never read anything like Crime and Punishment in his life would be understating things very much, given that he'd almost never in his life read a novel, any kind of novel, from choice. When he embarked on it that afternoon, lying beside the hotel pool, clad rather belatedly in swimming-trunks, he did begin to think, during the first few pages, that he'd made a big mistake and that to go on letting himself be battered by the waves while he taught himself to surf might be a better use of his time. But that phase didn't last long. Although he continued to feel that some of the dialogue was awkward, clunky, he discovered that it didn't matter much. He thought back to the previous afternoon, when the scattered clouds had got in the way of his first views of the English countryside from the air, and remembered how that had only been a minor irritation because what was revealed in the gaps between them was so astonishing, so beautiful – and so real.

It was the same with the coincidences that Dostoyevsky had engineered, chapter after chapter, throughout the book. It was hardly to be believed that in a city the size of St Petersburg, the capital of a vast empire, almost everyone should know almost everyone else; that most of the characters seemed to live on the same street corner if not in the same block of flats. Somehow none of that mattered. Dostoyevsky commanded Ivor to believe him, and Ivor did.

At that first sitting he read over a hundred pages, and was astonished at himself for getting that far, and so fast. Characters harangued each other in dense monologues of which a single paragraph might run on over three pages or more. There were unknown words and there was difficult syntax. At times the whole thing seemed clumsy, and ready to collapse under the strain of being written in a feverish hurry – this caused by the author's burning commitment to his subject, or by his burning need to pay his rent, or both. It didn't matter...

Ivor clambered over the text's rocky terrain in a similarly fevered state. As the moment when Rodion Raskolnikov was to murder the old woman drew closer, Ivor found himself at a pitch of thrilled excitement such as he'd only experienced a few times in his life. He associated this most strongly with the feelings he'd had when he was making the arrangements for the accident that befell his grandmother's fish.

He'd never known a book – or a film, or anything on TV – in which characters argued their positions on how to create social justice, or what it was that really made a human being. And if the dialogue was verbose and creaky, if some of the language was opaque...

'You have to remember,' Gemma told him, 'that, first of all, it's a translation out of Russian. It's very difficult to translate both the words and the spirit of a text at the same time. Nobody can get that right every second of the time. Also, the translation was made...' She reached across from her sun-lounger to his, took the book out of his hands and looked inside the front cover. '...Forty years ago. The way people speak does change a bit. And the book itself was written nearly a century before that. Different time, different place.'

It was certainly different from anything in his own experience. But it did more than simply hold his attention as he ploughed through it, surfing its crests, crashing into its troughs, for several hours a day for most of the rest of that holiday. He had never met anyone more scarily like himself than Roddy Raskolnikov. Sometimes Roddy thought and acted so differently from the way Ivor would have done that he wanted to shout to him, no, no, no! like a small child watching a pantomime. At other moments the resemblance between the two of them was so acute as to make him catch his breath, as if he'd come unexpectedly on his reflection in a mirror in a dark place on winding stairs.

'He could have got away with it, you know,' Ivor told Gemma when he'd finally arrived at the end. 'He had only himself to blame for getting caught. Playing mind games with the examining magistrate like that, trying to have fun at the police's expense. That was just asking for it.'

'I know,' said Gemma, 'but I don't think that was quite the point. I think Dostoyevsky was trying to show – his own view, mind – how human nature works. That all actions have consequences, so crime gets punished because people create their own punishments from inside themselves. Well, that's what I think he meant.' She had been surprised by the intensity of Ivor's sudden interest in the book. It had sometimes been difficult to drag him away from it, even to explore Mount Teide, the Orotava Valley, the South coast. He'd had his nose in it even on Christmas Day.

'If I'd killed someone I'd try to keep a tighter grip on myself than that,' Ivor said. 'I'd make sure I controlled my thoughts better than Raskolnikov.' He was about to say more, then realised that he mustn't. Not even to Gemma. It wasn't that he intended ever to kill anyone, or expected that he would ever need to, but you never knew – you never knew anything for certain in this life – and it would be rather rash to give away your thoughts on the subject in advance.

Roddy R. had allowed himself to think that he was killing the old woman for two clearly thought-out reasons. One was to prove some kind of philosophical point – which Ivor didn't quite follow, though this didn't bother him too much – about there being people in the world who were like Napoleon and others who weren't. Or something like that. The other reason was that Roddy intended to do good to others in the aftermath of his crime, using the money he had obtained: he wanted to use the cash he stole from the mean old woman to improve the lot of his genteel-poor mother and sister. This had led to Roddy becoming far too sensitive afterwards, Ivor thought. During the breakdown that he suffered after the murder he felt the goodness of other people towards him like the lash of a whip. He'd been unable to hide that pain, so that those other people had started to ask themselves questions about the cause. Roddy had been far too transparent. He'd been far too good.

There was lots of 'goodness' in the book. Although many minor characters crept into focus from out of the gloom and then slipped back into it like creatures in a nightmare, most of the cast, including R.R. himself, had a remarkable tendency to altruism. People who didn't know where the next meal would be coming from, and who lived in the most dismal conditions, gave away what money did come to them almost on a whim; sometimes to nearly total strangers. Gemma had been right about 'different times, different places'. Ivor thought that people were different today. Nobody these days who had very little would think of giving most of it away. Only the very rich gave things away, and even then usually with strings attached; and they gave very little. While if people committed crime today it was never in order to improve the lot of humanity – even to imagine such a thing would mark you out as halfway to crazy – but always simply to benefit themselves.

Were Ivor ever to commit a major crime, he decided, he would make sure that the only beneficiary would be himself. That way – unlike Mr R. – he might stand a chance of getting away with it.

He could share none of these thoughts with Gemma, of course. He well understood the need to keep a lock on his innermost thoughts. That necessity was demonstrated very clearly in the book, in what Ivor came to think of as 'the Razumikhin moment', a passage he read again and again, until he knew it almost by heart.

It was dark in the corridor; they were standing near the lamp. For a minute they looked at each other in silence. Razumikhin remembered that minute all his life. Raskolnikov's burning and piercing look seemed to become more and more intense every moment. It seemed to penetrate into his soul, into his consciousness. Suddenly Razumikhin gave a start. Something strange seemed to have passed between them. An idea seemed, as it were, to have slipped out, a kind of hint; something hideous and ghastly, something that both of them suddenly understood. Razumikhin turned as white as a sheet.

'Understand now?' Raskolnikov said suddenly, with a painfully contorted face. 'Go back! Go to them!' he added, and turning quickly, went out of the house.

If ever, ever he found himself in Roddy's position he would make sure there was no Razumikhin moment for him. He had been warned (thank you very much indeed) by Roddy's creator himself.

Instead of sharing these thoughts, which even he knew to be baleful and malign, Ivor talked to Gemma about the book, as they sipped an evening cocktail under the palm trees, in more general terms. 'Even the most unlikely, incredible things in it seem so real,' he told her. 'You know, the bit where Mrs Marmalade goes crazy after her husband's funeral and takes the kids outside, making them sing songs in the street, busking, while she beats the rhythm on a frying-pan, it's so...' He groped for a word. One that he'd never used before came to him suddenly. It seemed just right. 'It's so preposterous. It's like Dostoyevsky's challenging you – daring you – not to believe. And of course, you do. It's all so incredibly real.' An image was shaping up in his mind. He worked on it for a moment or two, took a petite slurp of his drink, and then the thought came out like this. 'The whole book's like a house, a castle, a fortress, if you like, built by a giant from granite with his bare hands. It's rough at the edges and some of the joints don't fit snugly, but you can't demolish it – it's too big for that – and you can't laugh it away, it's far too solid. It justifies itself simply by being there.'

Gemma felt very pleased to be hearing this. It seemed to prove that Ivor was not just a good companion, in bed and out of it, not simply a boy possessed of rare qualities of courage and endurance, but was developing in a certain way that indicated that she was having a civilising effect on him. She allowed herself to think that Vince might have talked cleverly about books in this way, had he grown older; had he been real.

When they returned home to Gatcombe they found, among the bills and other depressing envelopes that have greeted returning holidaymakers since holidays were invented, two letters, one to each of them, from the same source. Gemma's agent had written to Ivor – his mother had forwarded this letter from Winchelsea Beach – to inform him that she had sold twelve of his paintings to a publisher of wildlife calendars. Ivor was very excited by this and Gemma had to explain gently to him that *sold* in this particular area of business did not mean he'd be receiving the money any time just yet.

The second letter, Gemma's letter, told her that an approach had been made by a German publisher who had a view to bringing out Nicholas II and the Castle of Rats in a German translation. It shouldn't have been entirely surprising. Most of the story was set in Germany, after all, in a castle on the Rhine. But it hadn't been mooted before. Now it was, and Gemma was as delighted with this news as Ivor was with his. A translator had been found and was ready to start, if Gemma was happy to agree. Gemma found that she was.

TWELVE

By the time Gemma went to London in February to discuss the German translation project with her agent, Feri was back from New York, where she had celebrated her nineteenth birthday. They went to an afternoon screening of The Dead Poets' Society, which neither of them had yet seen, and just had time for a coffee afterwards, before it was time for Gemma to get her train.

'You're a slave to his mealtimes,' Feri told her. 'All men are the same. They promise love between equals, then turn you into a slave at the first opportunity.' But something in Gemma's eyes told Feri that her older friend had no objection in her own particular case.

Gemma had guessed that, as the evenings began to lengthen and the snowdrops and aconites appeared in the long grass beneath the trees, Ivor would discover that his life with her had become cloying and insupportable. He would wake up one morning, look around him in appalled astonishment, flap his wings and take off. But this hadn't happened, and Gemma had allowed herself to feel a renewed feeling of security. Hurrying back from London to cook his supper was a small price to have to pay. Gemma laughed – it was a relaxed and easy laugh born of confidence – as she told Feri she didn't mind at all.

'Well, that's great, I suppose,' Feri said, with a bit of a frown. 'Of course, I haven't met him, so I've really no right to talk, but I can't help wondering what he thinks is in it for him. A boy of sixteen.' She reached across the café table and took Gemma's fingers in her own. 'No disrespect, darling. You're very attractive to any man of your own age and above – when we were at your mother's that time I saw the way your brother-in-law looks at you when he thinks no-one's looking at him – and that's just one example I can think of – but that's not going to be the same as what a normal boy of sixteen wants.'

Gemma did not rise to this. Partly because of her growing confidence in the lasting nature of Ivor's affection for her, and partly because she knew Feri very well. She was fairly certain that her comments this afternoon about men in general and Ivor in particular were rooted in some recent experience of things not going too well in Feri's own love life. 'Boys of sixteen can want a lot of different things,' Gemma said. 'Not only sex. Though even in that department he's still enthusiastic. Hasn't yet moved on to the stage of being merely dutiful.' She smiled, and was surprised to discover it was with a bit of an effort. She continued, 'No, I don't delude myself he really fancies me, but somehow all that part of it really does work.' She paused a moment, sipped her coffee, then looked Feri in the eye. 'On which subject, dare I ask how things are with Carlos?'

Feri laughed. Without trying. 'In bed everything's fine, so yes, you dare ask, but no you needn't, because there's nothing noteworthy to tell.' Gemma nodded her understanding. Feri went on. 'Out of bed's a different matter. Like I said, they start off one thing but then turn into another. Carlos, for all he's Spanish, does all the new man bit, or says it at any rate. The old Spanish macho thing is dead, he'll tell you. No more stopping out doing the bars with his mates till dawn for the modern, enlightened Spanish male. These days they make the beds and clean the bathroom, change the baby – not that that applies in our case, but in principle. Only with him it all is only in principle. The reality is that he's a totally unreconstructed, charming, lovable, lying-through-the-teeth traditional Spanish boy. Nothing changes where men are concerned.' Feri turned her attention to her coffee.

'Are you splitting up?' Gemma had to ask.

'Not yet,' Feri said, giving Gemma a very candid look. 'There's still some mileage to be had. For both of us. But the game is up. He's been seen through. The end will come.'

'Ah well,' said Gemma, doubting that she had been anything like as clear-sighted as Feri when she'd been her age. 'Anyway, boys of sixteen wanting lots of different things. Obviously...' Gemma saw the shimmer of a smile on Feri's cheeks and in her eyes. 'Don't laugh – there's a sense in which I stand in for Ivor's absent mother. He gets fed and looked after...' Instinctively Gemma looked at her watch. 'He has a nice house to live in...'

'That's not something any sixteen-year-old gives a toss about,' Feri interrupted.

Gemma knew better. 'You're quite wrong there. In Ivor's case anyway. He cares very much. You know he's into architecture in a big way. He told me the first time he saw Gatcombe that it's really a medieval hall house in disguise... I couldn't say one way or the other, so I take that with a pinch of salt. But he talks about wanting to take the ground-floor ceiling out in the big living-room, dispense with the bedroom above and the attic bedroom above that, and restore it to what he thinks was its medieval glory, with a huge oak-framed Gothic window, fourteen feet high, in place of the centre section of the front wall.'

'I'm trying to take this in.' Feri's eyes had opened very wide. 'Is he a bit – if you don't mind me saying so – is he a bit mad?'

Gemma laughed. The bell-like one that Ivor liked. 'No. Not in the slightest. But he gets bees in his bonnet about things. This is all because he visited Great Dixter last year, fell in love with the place, and wants Gatcombe to become a sort of copy of it. Though I do tell him Gatcombe is still quite a bit smaller. It would be a pale copy, without quite the same impressive effect. You came to Great Dixter once, didn't you?'

'Of course I did. You make everyone go there. It's the place with medieval woodpeckers' nests in the high beams, and rafters blackened with soot.' A new thought struck Feri. 'He doesn't want to rip the chimney-stack out and have fires in the middle of the floor? Your nice carpet.'

'Mercifully, no. He's not such a purist as that.'

'Hang on,' Feri said. 'You're not actually going to let him do this, I hope.'

'No, of course I'm not. It's just a bit of harmless fantasy. I can reassure you, when you see it again Gatcombe will be looking its usual self. He's very into art, that's all. Like you are. Like I am. Sometimes he gets carried away. Which, in an artist, is as it should be. Remember he first introduced himself to me as a student of art and architecture, self-taught. He's surprisingly studious for a boy with his background and nature. My art books are a sort of treasure trove for him. All this week, in the evenings, he's had his nose in a book of Breughel prints, examining them minutely and making notes.'

'My God,' said Feri. 'He grows more bizarre by the minute. Making notes on Breughel. I had no idea that was the kind of thing that toy-boys did.' This time it was Feri who looked at her watch. 'Isn't it time you went for that train?' But she accompanied Gemma as far as Charing Cross.

At Easter Gemma took Ivor to Morocco, whisking him round Fez and Marrakesh. If he was going to be an artist, or an architect, or a maker of furniture – or whatever else – then let his eyes be opened a little wider. Let inspiration come to him from places that were different from Rye or London. Ivor hadn't asked her in so many words to help him acquire the same level of education as she had, but he had asked her nevertheless, as eloquently as a cat requests its food. And besides, the sun shines more cheerfully in Morocco in March than it does in London or in Rye.

Gemma packed a book for Ivor to read, if he should decide he wanted to read one. It was an old, rather weighty, copy of Civilization by Kenneth Clark. She remembered how he had devoured and digested Crime and Punishment at Christmas – a no less astonishing feat, she thought, than the swallowing by a python of an antelope – and had no doubt that he would make similarly short work of Lord Clark's tome if he decided to embark on it.

For herself she packed something smaller. It was a book that Angela from the chamber choir had lent her a few days before, during one of their increasingly rare coffee conversations in Simon the Pieman's. 'If you've never read this, you should,' Angela had said. 'You can believe it if you want to, or decide it's complete tosh, but you won't be less than intrigued and fascinated. Perfect for a holiday.' Angela took from her handbag and placed in Gemma's hand a faded hardback. Its title was An Adventure, its authors a C.A.E. Moberly and an E.F. Jourdain. The information meant nothing to Gemma. Looking inside, Gemma saw that this was the fifth edition, printed in 1955, of a book originally published before the First World War. 'I won't tell you what it's about,' Angela had said cheerily. 'You can discover that for yourself. While you're enjoying your own adventure in Morocco.'

Neither Gemma nor Ivor read anything much during their first days in Fez. There was too much else to see and assimilate. When they dived, exploring, into the Medina on their first morning, the experience was so intensely foreign and strange for Ivor that he felt the differentness of the place in his nose, on his tongue and in every nerve-ending of his skin. The experience of Fez's streets, the sight of laden donkeys being driven up steep stony stairs, of djellaba-clad craftsmen working at copper and tin behind their open doors, of mourners praying silently in graveyards, reminded him of something else. He remembered being taken to an aquarium when he was small, of seeing the brightly lit tanks where extraordinary things were being done by even more extraordinary creatures. It was a moment of heightened perception: a different world lay just a glass screen's width away, a world whose inhabitants seemed unaware of him: he was a visitor who might have been invisible, he might have come from outer space, or a different time.

It was the same here. Brilliant sunshine lit the scenes Ivor saw, black shadow gave them depth. It was as though... Ivor tried to think. As though he'd stepped into those pictures of Breughel that were scenes from village life five hundred years ago. Here the Middle Ages were in progress, or so it seemed, in front of his eyes. And yet it was as if a glass wall lay between himself and the action and scene around him. He imagined that if he tried to speak to anyone they would not hear. That if he tried to touch an arm or shoulder, the glass plate would be a barrier in his way. It would have been no more possible than to touch a person in a Breughel canvas and step into the action depicted there. It was like ... it was like ... Of course he had to come round to this in the end. It was like his experience in Lydd. There were no people there. Not that he'd seen, anyway. If there had been, would they have been removed from him in this strange way, as the inhabitants of the Medina were, placed behind a glass or gauze, unaware of him? He imagined a gauze, such as theatres use, through which light can seem to pass in one direction but not the other. That night he dreamed, for the first time ever, about his experience at Lydd with Mark.

By the time Gemma got round to opening the book she'd brought with her, and Ivor gingerly flicked open his Kenneth Clark door-stop, they had left Fez for Marrakesh, and Ivor was beginning to get accustomed to Morocco – to the extent that it now seemed just normally strange, no longer quite so weird and surreal. They had come to the end of a day's exploring, and were whiling away an hour on their hotel's roof-top terrace before gathering their energies again and going in search of an evening meal. Below them the dark green plumes of a thousand date palms quivered in the evening breeze. Beyond a sea of pink walls and roofs, beyond a sunset haze, the crests of the Atlas Mountains, almost impossibly distant, were outlined in rose silver as the late sun lit up their snow.

Gemma discovered the book Angela had lent her to be an account of a less exotic journey: a tourist visit to Versailles in 1901. The tourists, the book's authors, were two Edwardian headmistresses, on holiday in Paris at the time. (Gemma found she could see the two ladies, Miss Jourdain and Miss Moberly, extremely clearly in her mind's eye. Their broad-brimmed summer-holiday hats, their skirts that finished an inch or two above the ankle, a fashion they wouldn't have dared to parade in at their schools... She could have done pictures of them easily if she'd wanted to.) These two spinsters had had experiences at Versailles – in the vicinity of the Petit Trianon – that encouraged them to think they were

seeing the place as it was in Marie-Antoinette's time...
Gemma was more than ready to dismiss the story as
better suited to old women at the dottier, more fanciful
end of the spectrum. Yet there was something about it
that appealed to her, or appealed to one part of her mind
at any rate, so she didn't abandon the book at once but
continued to read. She didn't tell Ivor what she was
reading. It wouldn't be at all up his street, she was quite
sure, and he would laugh in her face.

Ivor looked up from Chapter One of Civilization – it
did strike him as slightly perverse to be reading about
the history of western art in the middle of Marrakesh,
but then Tenerife had been a long way, in more respects
than one, from nineteenth-century St Petersburg – and
said to Gemma, 'Why don't you write any more?'

Gemma was now used to Ivor's habit of introducing
unexpected topics, apparently out of nowhere. This was
a question he could have asked at any time in the past six
months but never had.

'Perhaps because I'm not really a writer,' Gemma said,
closing An Adventure but leaving a finger inside to mark
the page. 'I'm a visual artist and always will be. I think
the fact I wrote those two cat books and they were such a
success was a bit of a fluke.'

'Why don't you go on and do a whole series of cat
books – like some children's authors do – and become
fiendishly rich?'

Gemma laughed. She liked 'fiendishly rich'. She liked
the fact that Ivor now talked with a better accent than he
used to, and with reasonable grammar. That he could say
clever, funny things at times. She knew that to some
extent those things reflected her influence on him. She
also knew that they were already latent in him: all she
had done was to draw them out. 'I know what you
mean,' she said. 'But when I finished the second book I
did rather feel I'd exhausted the possibilities of one boy,

one auntie and a cat. Other people's imaginations might have come up with more but mine didn't. I thought last year I might try my hand at something for adults, but it didn't get off the ground.'

'What stopped it?' Ivor asked.

'Death. My father's. It was going to be a murder story. But in the middle of researching it... Well, you know my father died just a couple of months before we met. I was too caught up in a real-life death to want to be involved with a fictional one as well...'

'Tell me about the murder,' Ivor wanted to know, suddenly engaged. 'Did you get as far as a plan?'

'Goodness, I've almost forgotten. Oh yes. I was thinking of it taking place in an oast house. I went up on the hop-storage floor at Gatcombe and had a look with my friend Feri.' Still no hint that Feri was just nineteen. 'My plan was to use the hole in the floor where the hop pocket hangs. Either have someone pushed through the hole, or their dead body dropped into the hop pocket. But I saw it wouldn't have worked.'

'Because the hole is pretty well blocked by the ram of the hop press. I know,' said Ivor. 'You should have had a look at Birdskitchen instead. There they've got a trap-door in the hop floor as well as the pocket hole. They used to use it to haul the pokes up through before someone invented electric elevators.'

'I didn't think it was easy to fall through a trap-door,' Gemma said. 'The whole idea of a trap-door is supposed to be a fail-safe device, isn't it? Used in mills since mills began. You can haul sacks up through them but can't fall down.'

'You could if you took the doors off,' Ivor said.

'Then you'd see the doors were missing, surely,' Gemma objected.

'Not if you were walking backwards or... Oh, I don't know.' Ivor appeared to lose interest in the subject at that point. Though there had come into his mind the image of a gauze: a gauze that let the light through from one side but not the other. But his next question was, 'Why don't you write a ghost story instead?'

This startled Gemma, as it would startle anyone who, unknown to their questioner, was in the middle of reading one. Her hand, the one that was holding the book, jerked involuntarily, so that it looked as if the book itself was making a bid for attention. But the movement was a slight one and Ivor took no notice of it. 'Lots of ghost stories around Rye,' Ivor said breezily, though he wasn't sure why he'd started down this track; it wasn't somewhere he particularly wanted to go; rather the reverse, if anything. But now here he was. He prattled on. 'You know about the ghost of the monk and the nun in Turkey Cock Lane? They were lovers, and got buried alive in a field up Playden Hill. Now their ghosts make gobbling noises.' He laughed lewdly. 'Gobble, gobble, gobble. That's why it's called Turkey Cock Lane.'

'Turkey Cock, poppy-cock,' Gemma said.

'It is all rubbish, of course,' Ivor agreed. 'I never heard them.' Vivid memories came to him suddenly of the two or three times he'd used Turkey Cock Lane as a convenient venue for sex with Meryl. It was good that he didn't have to do that any more. The clean starched sheets of a hotel bedroom were much more his sort of thing these days. 'Hundreds more,' he went on. 'The House of the White Vines. Reyson's Farm... There's whole books about them in Rye library.'

'Then I expect the seam is pretty well mined out,' said Gemma. She too had noticed the sizeable section of library shelf that was devoted to haunted Rye. 'No call for another book on the subject, I'd have thought.'

'Just a suggestion,' Ivor said, without sounding piqued. That was another improvement in him, Gemma thought.

'Funnily, though, I'm reading a ghost story at the moment.' Gemma waved the book in her hand very slightly, but this time intentionally. 'It's not about Rye but in Paris. Or near Paris. Versailles.' She outlined the story as far as she had got.

'Do you believe it?' Ivor asked. Gemma was surprised at how interested he'd become while she was telling him what she'd read. She could always see when he was particularly interested in something she said to him. It was not that he'd say anything necessarily, but you could somehow see it in him. It was the same with her cats.

'It depends what you mean by believe, I suppose.' Safety in clichés, Gemma thought, cross with herself as she said this, and was surprised at the enthusiastic nod with which Ivor greeted her reply. She went on, 'What makes me stop and think, though it's the only thing that does, is that the two women had similar experiences at the same time, but didn't mention them to each other until later in the day, when it came up rather by chance in the conversation. Then they wrote down individual recollections of the event and compared them afterwards. They were academics of a sort, after all, and they were trying to be what academics call rigorous. They found they'd experienced some identical things and some quite different ones. They'd seen buildings that no longer existed, and people in eighteenth-century clothes, but not always the same people and buildings. Sometimes the same, sometimes different. That's... well, in a way it impresses one.'

'So you're more ready to believe something crazy if two different people tell you the same story?' Ivor asked, testing.

'Not necessarily. It's easier for people to collude than they realise. But there are some odd things in their accounts that you wouldn't expect. Listen to this.' Gemma flicked over pages for a few seconds, then read: *Everything suddenly looked unnatural, therefore unpleasant; even the trees behind the building seemed to have become flat and lifeless, like a wood worked in tapestry. There were no effects of light and shade and no wind stirred the trees. It was all intensely still.'*

At the words, *like a wood worked in tapestry*, Ivor gave a small involuntary start, but then was silent for a time after Gemma finished reading. Gemma peered at him, wondering, not for the first time, what words he would break his silence with. Eventually they came. 'Like a tapestry. Like a painting of trees. I've seen that too.'

Gemma had learnt to expect the unexpected where Ivor was concerned, but still she was startled. 'How do you mean? You've been to Versailles?'

'Not there. It was at Lydd. I've never told anyone this. Not a soul. But I wasn't alone. I was with a friend, Mark Harris.'

'What did you see at Lydd?' Gemma closed the book again, firmly this time, with no attempt to use her finger as a bookmark.

'Not very much, really,' Ivor said, which Gemma thought a disappointing beginning, but then he added, 'It was rather what we didn't see that made the whole thing odd. We didn't see any people for a start.' Then he recounted, in great detail, the whole story of his visit with Mark to the towns of New Romney and Lydd and the airfield in between.

Gemma listened in astonishment. There was a world of difference, she discovered, between reading a published tale of inexplicable events, and hearing a similar story told in the first person by someone you knew very well.

And who claimed to have a back-up witness. Well, anyone could claim that. But Gemma was shaken nonetheless. When Ivor had finished she picked up her book again and waved it in his face. 'You're sure you haven't been dipping into this when I've not been looking, and you're trying to wind me up?'

'Course I'm not trying to wind you up. Don't be stupid. I'm not a kid of twelve. What an idiot I'd look. But I knew you'd think I was kidding you if I ever told you. Which is why I didn't. I never told no... anybody. Till you surprised me by reading about the flat-looking trees and the stillness in that book. Because it was exactly the same for us.' He said all this quite fast, sounding peeved, then stopped. More thoughtfully he added, 'And then there was the depression we both felt.'

That was another element in the accounts Gemma had read in An Adventure: the depressed feeling that descended on the 'witnesses'. She hadn't read that information out to Ivor.

'It's not that I don't believe you,' Gemma tried again. 'But I am very curious about this. And sceptical by nature. Which you are too.' Ivor had included in his account of the Lydd experience the details of his conversation with Mark in which they'd both tried to rationalise the thing away. 'Are you quite sure you never picked this book up somewhere else? At your mother's or grandmother's perhaps? Or at the Spraggens?'

'Listen, I said no. Don't go on interrogating me.' Ivor began to feel angry, something which Gemma could see from his face: it was acquiring that dark look. Again he regretted starting down this road. He hadn't wanted to arrive here. But things had crept up on him. He'd lightly suggested ghost stories as a subject Gemma might like to write about. It was almost a joke, made to make her forget his rather too eager interest in her murder scenario. But quite by coincidence she had been reading a story which... Well, that detail about the trees that looked like a tapestry had surprised him into a revelation that he'd never intended making.

Not knowing if this would make the situation better or worse, but suddenly not caring very much, he blurted, 'Anyway, if you want to know, Mark and I both saw ghosts when we were children. Same ghosts. Separate occasions. Years apart. Before we ever met.'

Gemma looked him very seriously in the eye and said, 'Tell me about it.'

Ivor appeared to climb down a little. 'Well, I don't remember anything about it, so I can't say whether it happened or not. It's only that my mum and gran used to go on about it a lot, so it may have been true that I saw something.' As recently as three months ago Ivor had heard Norma retell the story of Welstead House to a politely listening but disbelieving Michael Harding. Now, for the first time in his life, Ivor found himself telling the story in his own voice. He told Gemma about the taped-up doorways, about the lady in a riding-cape and the boy in knickerbockers. Then he told her about Andy's unexpectedly announcing that Mark had had a similar experience. 'As I say, I can't swear to any of it,' he finished. Then, disappointingly again, 'I can't swear to Lydd either. Maybe it was a dream in broad daylight. Only, Mark dreamt it too.'

Gemma looked down. 'I don't know what to say,' she said. 'That's an awful lot of surprises for one evening.'

Ivor said, 'You know those pictures by Breughel in your book at home? That I was looking at? Those little old houses he painted. When I was in Lydd that time the houses looked just like that. A day or two after, I did some sketches of what the houses at Lydd were like. I'd almost forgotten them. When we're back home I'll show you them if you like.'

THIRTEEN

Ivor had been right when he'd said the buildings in his Lydd sketches looked like those in Breughel's paintings. Gemma thought that if the painter had made preliminary sketches for his work they might have looked like these: the outline drawings that Ivor showed her on their return to Gatcombe. The main difference was the total absence of people in Ivor's sketches; in Breughel's canvasses it was the people that were the whole point. Gemma was not surprised by the quality of Ivor's drawings: she knew his work well by now, how accomplished in terms of technique it always was. But there was more than technique here, she thought. Ivor had captured an atmosphere that came not just from the strangeness of the deserted streets. Looking into his drawings you felt a sense of melancholy, of foreboding, almost. You felt that something very bad was about to happen in this place, or perhaps already had.

Gemma knew that her reaction was subjective. She had heard Ivor's story, and had read 'An Adventure'. That coincidence was bound to affect her response to Ivor's sketches, even if she didn't believe a word of either tale. Did she believe the stories? Ivor's? Miss Moberly's and Miss Jourdain's? She didn't know.

As evidence that Ivor had actually seen, or hallucinated, an accurate image of Lydd at some earlier time in its history his pictures were worthless, Gemma knew. Any artist of Ivor's ability would be perfectly capable of drawing a medieval village scene from his imagination. Ivor might claim never to have seen Breughel's paintings until a few months ago – some six months after his own sketches had been made – but that could never be proved. His textbooks at school, even if he had scarcely bothered with them, would have contained images of medieval buildings. Sources of such information were everywhere. His home town of Rye was full of half-timbered houses that had barely changed in five hundred years.

Photographs might have been a different matter. But only might have been. An actual photo, taken by a schoolboy, of a medieval scene would have made headline news. But papers had in the past carried photographs of everything from ghosts to fairies, from the Loch Ness Monster to UFOs. Most such photos had been exposed over the years as fakes and the remainder were widely believed to be so. Anyway, there were no photos in this case. There were just Ivor's sketches, the tale he told and the striking similarity between some of its details and those in the Moberly and Jourdain book.

Gemma relayed all this, the information and her own feelings about it, to Feri, during the course of a phone-call. She did not, for the moment, tell anybody else. Feri's reaction was healthily sceptical, though she was astonished and fascinated all the same. It was she who, jokingly or perhaps only half-jokingly, suggested that since Ivor's revelations had followed his proposal that Gemma should write a ghost story, they should form the material for that very book. Gemma told her she had no intention of doing that. 'Turn myself into a laughing stock, and Ivor too. I can just imagine his reaction if I told him I wanted to get his story into print.'

'Then why did he go to the trouble of making drawings?' was Feri's response.

Apart from the occasion when Ivor showed her the sketches, neither of them had brought the subject up. Gemma felt that something had changed between them, though she couldn't have said what. She was most conscious of it when they were in bed together, especially if Ivor happened to go to sleep first and left her lying awake. She remembered reading, or hearing, an interview with some classical musician, a composer or conductor, in which the musician said he had never wanted to sleep with an opera singer. It would have made him feel uncomfortable, he'd said, the idea of being intimate with all that voice. Now Gemma felt somewhat the same. Inside Ivor slept something extraordinary, like the dormant huge voice of a diva, but she had no words, no ideas to express what it was.

Gemma decided to stop pondering the imponderable, and to deal with Ivor's revelation at a practical level. There were two obvious things to do. One was to take Ivor to Lydd and see what he had to say when he saw the place again. See how he reacted; watch him closely; his reaction might not necessarily be expressed in words. The other was to find the boy called Mark. Ivor had told her that Mark had seen everything that he himself had seen at Lydd, but had said nothing about the oddness of it all to their teacher on their return. Though even if she could find Mark, Gemma was not optimistic about his opening up to her. Driving her young man to Lydd was by far the easier of the two things to accomplish, and she decided to tackle it first.

They went to Lydd the next Sunday. It was a bright and springlike late March day, though it felt noticeably chilly to people recently acclimatised to North African warmth. 'There are cars everywhere,' was Ivor's first, uncomplicated response when they turned into the main street. They parked there and got out. Handsome Georgian houses and cottages lined the street on both sides. Three of them were pubs. The church tower, its four pinnacles like tufted squirrels' ears, reared above, watchful but benign. The tall white poplars and aspen trees were not yet in leaf. 'It looked nothing like this,' Ivor said.

They had brought the pictures with them. Not a building Ivor had sketched was recognizable, even in altered form, in the gently busy scene in front of their eyes. All that could be said to remain was the orientation of the main street, its length, and straightness. It was not possible to work back from where they were and what they saw to the viewpoints where Ivor had mentally placed himself to do those pictures less than a year ago. All he could say for certain was that they'd entered the High Street from the east. They had turned south, then passed an open space on the left – there was no sign of it now – where a muddy pond stagnated and a motionless heron fished. They had crossed the road to see a butcher's shop. Ivor could not say where that had been, only that it was on the right as they walked. After that, he reminded Gemma, he and Mark had both felt so uncomfortable in the place and so strangely depressed that they'd turned back and retraced their steps exactly, leaving the town – more like a village in Ivor's recollection – by the same rough track on which they had arrived. There was no sign among the side-streets of any such track-way now.

A few days later Gemma went back to Lydd on her own. She had a good look round inside the huge church – the cathedral of the Marsh as it was locally known – and browsed the public library, to see if there was anything that would support Ivor's account of a Lydd depopulated and semi-derelict, lacking a church, at any time in the past. She unearthed some interesting things. The area around Lydd – the town had been founded on a shingle-spit island in Roman times – actually had seen depopulation and economic decline in the later Middle Ages. This was due in part to a succession of ferocious storms that battered it during those centuries: they had included the one that destroyed New Romney's harbour and left its church waist-deep in shingle and silt. Other causes were the equally ferocious coastal raids by the French during the Hundred Years' War, and the ravages of the Black Death, which had come along, as if on cue, right in the middle of that.

Another thing was that, although Lydd church had existed since Norman times, its landmark tower had not. This had been added in the Tudor period by its then rector, Thomas Wolsey. Yes, that Thomas Wolsey: later Cardinal of England, and Chancellor to Henry VIII. Before this the church had had a modest wooden belfry, standing on the ground alongside. The books suggested it might have looked like the one that still stood in the nearby village of Brookland. Gemma already knew the folk-legend there. That Brookland's tower had not always had its feet on the ground in the churchyard but was originally sited more normally, astride the church's roof; it was only the unusual event of a virgin presenting herself for marriage – at some point in history wisely left vague – that caused the steeple to jump down and take a closer look. More seriously, Gemma knew that Brookland's steeple only peered a little higher than the ridge-pole of its church's roof. By someone looking for the hundred-and-thirty-foot tower of Lydd, such a structure might well be overlooked.

Gemma didn't discuss these things with Ivor. But she began to wonder whether, after all, there might be something in Feri's idea of making his adventure the subject of a book. It wasn't that she particularly wanted to write such a book. But she felt that if she could interest Ivor in the project and they could work together on it, those feelings of disquiet, that *how could one sleep with such a voice?* feeling that she'd had since he first told her his weird tale, might fade away. But before that could happen she needed to find and talk to Mark.

*

When Gemma saw Feri again it was at the house just off Highgate Hill that she shared with fellow students from St Martin's. Gemma had been there before, though not often, and not since Carlos's arrival. But in the last few days Carlos had vanished from the scene: perhaps that was why Gemma was invited now.

'In the end we had to finish it,' Feri explained matter-of-factly while they drank coffee. 'I told him I'd had enough, and it was time to move on. For both of us.'

'So Goodye Carlos,' Gemma said. There wasn't much else she could say. She was impressed by the steeliness Feri demonstrated in her dealings with the men in her life, but at the same time a little unnnerved, a little dismayed by it.

Gemma told Feri about her visits to Lydd. She had been impressed in spite of herself by Ivor's reaction to seeing the town again. His puzzlement at the discrepancy between the real-life town and the sketches he'd made of it – actually holding those sketches in his hand during the visit – seemed genuine. A big part of Gemma remained sceptical, and would have preferred not to be asked – as Feri of course did ask – if she believed Ivor's story. 'It's not really a question of believing or not believing,' she said. 'In a way, Ivor doesn't even believe it himself. It's just that when somebody says to you that they've seen something which they obviously can't have seen, you have to nod your head and say, ah yes, I see. It's either that or calling the person a liar to their face.'

There was a part of Gemma, though, that had reacted differently. That was the part of her that had created The Cat Who Loved Potatoes, that had turned Ivor into Vince within those pages and now seemed to be carrying out a similar transformation of him in real life; the part of her that had read An Adventure with an open mind. That part of her wanted to say: Yes. Perhaps. What if?

'This boy Mark,' Feri was saying. 'Have you met him yet?'

'No,' said Gemma. 'And although I've asked around among my friends,' she emphasised the word friends, she would not allow herself to use Feri's word for them, 'I haven't found anyone who knows his family. I know his father has a farm on the Isle of Oxney. But that's it. And I can't say I'm looking forward to cold-calling him. According to Ivor he was pretty unforthcoming about it to his teacher, a person he knew well. I'm not too hopeful of his opening up to a total stranger who says she wants to write a book about it – a writer whose only claim to professional status lies in two books about a talking cat.'

'I get the impression,' said Feri, 'that, although you don't want to do the book, at the same time you do. And whatever Ivor says to the contrary, I think if you actually got started on it, and if you could get Mark involved, Ivor would go along.'

'You haven't met Ivor,' Gemma said.

'No. And I haven't met Mark either. But I could.' Feri gave her a look that combined eagerness with challenge.

'How do you mean?' Gemma asked.

'Exactly what I said. I could come down to Gatcombe one weekend and then simply go over to this Mark character's place, if you've got the address. I'm closer to his age than you are. He might talk to me more easily. Of course he might well not, but then there's no harm done. You'd still be free to tackle him yourself, or Ivor would.'

'I think you can count Ivor out,' Gemma said. 'But if you mean that seriously, I won't try to stop you. Come down when you've got a free weekend.'

Gemma had almost got past the stage of worrying that if Feri and Ivor were to meet, something would go horribly wrong. She knew that her relationship with Ivor would not last for ever, she hadn't forgotten the story of Der Rosenkavalier, but she felt pretty sure it could withstand a chance encounter with Feri. After all, it was Mark, or the idea of Mark, that had caught Feri's attention. Gemma didn't remind her how, as a much younger teenager, she had declared her intention to marry a Sussex farmer. Mark lived just over the border into Kent, but that was hardly an issue. It was Mark, the farmer's boy, that she wanted to meet.

Ivor just happened to be away over the weekend of Feri's visit to Gatcombe. Gemma certainly didn't plan it that way. When she discovered that Ivor would be absent she told herself that this wasn't a source of any relief to her, but a quite neutral circumstance. Ivor had undertaken a furniture repair for a neighbour of Gemma's, and needed to use the tools and workbench at Winchelsea Beach. Mr Gutsell was strict to the point of obsession about not letting Ivor use the workshop for jobs of his own at weekends. So on Saturday afternoon Ivor cycled over to his mother's bungalow, with an elegant gate-legged table folded and strapped on behind him, shortly before Gemma set out to meet Feri off the train. Ivor knew Feri was coming to stay the night, but wasn't particularly bothered whether he met her or not: that wasn't his style. Gemma hadn't told him of Feri's plan to make contact with Mark, and the fact that she was very much nearer to his age than she was to Gemma's was still unknown to him.

The next morning Feri set off, on her own, in Gemma's car. They had looked at the map together. There was a route through winding lanes, through the Beckley woods and past Birdskitchen Farm, which would have led eventually to Oxney, but to someone unfamiliar with the way it looked a certain recipe for getting lost. So Feri took the main roads, through Rye, then along the edge of the Marsh by the Military Canal and up the steep hill at Stone Cliff. A little way along the spine of Oxney, Mark Harris's address was announced on a board beside the road. Link Farm.

Feri parked the car in the yard, midway between a brick-built Victorian farmhouse which had a certain charm and a hay-filled Dutch barn of girders and corrugated sheet-metal that did not. Immediately she saw coming towards her a ruddy-faced youth who looked about the right age to be Mark. He was wearing lived-in twill trousers and an old sweater from which the collar of a white shirt, not folded down, stuck up like the wing-collar of a century or two ago. He was not tall, but broad-shouldered and robustly built. Feri, tall and slender in heels which were not absurdly high but not all that sensible for a farmyard either, was dressed simply in flatteringly tight designer jeans and a matching top and scarf which she had created and printed herself as one of her projects at St Martin's.

Feri said, as soon as the youth was near enough for her not to have to shout it, 'Is Mark Harris about?'

'Who wants him?' said the boy, who perhaps watched a little too much television.

'Feri. I'm a friend of someone you know. ...Ivor Wingate? Actually, I'm a friend of his girlfriend.'

'Ivor?' said the youth, unable to keep himself from looking the visitor up and down, as surprised by her appearance – in two senses of the word – as he was by the mention, out of the blue, of Ivor Wingate. 'That's a blast from the past. Never heard what became of him after he left school. Started a job I found for him, then never a word again. Not even a thank you.' He stopped and his eyebrows went up. Rather deliberately, Feri thought. 'So now he's got a girlfriend, has he? He used to be...' But he stopped himself in time, as it occurred to him that a mention of Ivor's boasting of an earlier promiscuity might not be well received by this friend of his girlfriend. He changed course. 'Where's he live now?'

'Over Brede way,' Feri said, keeping it vague. She could have meant the River Brede, or the village that shared its name, a few miles upstream from Gatcombe, where the river is straddled by the Hastings road. Mark said nothing in reply to this, he just mugged an expression that was a blend of mild interest and mild surprise, so Feri went on. 'They're writing a book together.'

The expression became one of genuine astonishment, eyes bulging. 'Ivor writing a book? The Ivor I knew could hardly write a shopping list. A book about what?'

Feri answered calmly, matter-of-factly, smiling, 'Part of it's an account of what happened the day you and Ivor went to Lydd together last year.'

Astonishment became something closer to panic. 'Oh hey!'

Feri would not be derailed. 'They were hoping you might contribute your own story. You know, your own take on what happened and what you saw.'

'Oh no.' Mark now looked thoroughly dismayed. His head shook from side to side. 'There's nothing I'd want to say about that. Anyway,' he challenged, 'if he's so keen to get me involved why hasn't he come to see me himself?'

'He was pretty sure he'd get a dusty answer. And now I see he was right.'

'I'm sorry,' Mark said, softening at once. 'I didn't mean to be...'

'It's OK. Actually it's not Ivor that's all that keen on the idea. It's his girlfriend. She's not anyone you know.' A half second's pause for thought. 'She's shy.' Blatantly untrue, but needs must. 'She was hesitant about contacting you – someone she's never met. So I came instead. As a favour. To help her out. Because I'm neither shy nor hesitant. All right?'

Mark gulped, then tried to look as if he hadn't. 'I see. I see you're not. Shy or hesitant, I mean. But I can't help you out. I don't have a story to tell.'

Gently Feri persisted. 'Ivor said you'd seen the same things he did. The rotting meat in the butcher's shop...'

Mark looked uncomfortable again. 'There *was* something about some meat hanging up in a shop window, that's true. But it's a year ago and I don't remember it all that much. Ivor got in a state, imagining he was looking at Lydd as it used to be in the past. He's got a forceful personality, I suppose you'd say. As well as imagination. He almost made me think I'd seen those things too, but I hadn't. I didn't. That's that, and I can't pretend I did.' He shut his mouth and stood straighter, like someone who has finished a speech and is waiting for applause. He was torn between wanting his visitor to go and wishing the beautiful creature might remain in his company a little while longer. Then he remembered his manners, and manners resolved the impasse. 'Can I get you some coffee? Tea or something?'

Feri considered this a moment. Then, 'I don't think so. Thanks all the same. If you can't tell me what Ivor and Gemma thought you could, well, you can't and that's that.' She smiled puckishly. 'I guess a cup of tea won't make much difference. I'll get on my way. And sorry for pestering you.' She moved to get back into Gemma's car, but then turned back to him, to notice that he was still gazing at her. He seemed rooted to the spot. 'Can I give you my phone number?' she said. She fished in the back pocket of her jeans feeling, for the first and only time this day, a little awkward and needing to explain. 'I'd already written it down. Planning to leave it with someone if you weren't here. Anyway, just in case.'

Then she turned towards the car again, got in and drove off.

'How did it go?' Feri uttered the question before Gemma had time to, as soon as she stepped inside the door at Gatcombe. 'It didn't. Mark's a very nice guy, but that's all. He either doesn't believe any longer that those things happened to him and Ivor, or he doesn't want to believe, or they didn't happen. As I said in London, you're still welcome to try him yourself. He's perfectly charming and sweet. But I rather doubt you'd get very far.'

'I'm sure I wouldn't.' Gemma thanked Feri for going on her voluntary errand – or wild goose chase, as it had turned out. But in her heart she had rather gone off the idea of the book. With neither Ivor nor Mark willing to discuss the subject further, there seemed little point in pursuing it and annoying everybody. Anyway, the idea had been Feri's originally, and seemed to have been overtaken lately by a possibly subconscious urge to meet a new young man. The local farmer of her childhood dreams? Maybe.

'Did you leave Mark your phone number, in case he changes his mind?' Gemma asked. But that was just a postscript. They both knew now that the book idea was dead in the water, if it had ever had any life in it at all.

'As a matter of fact, yes,' said Feri, poker-faced.

Gemma was good enough not to smile. 'Come on,' she said. 'Let's have some lunch.'

After that it was time for Gemma to take Feri to the train. Feri again said how sorry she was, and again Gemma told her it didn't matter in the least. 'Your Ivor may have made the whole thing up,' Feri said. 'Maybe the guy just has too much imagination.'

That made Gemma laugh. 'Oh what rubbish. No-one can have too much imagination. Think of Charles Dickens. Shakespeare...' Which made Feri laugh too.

Gemma wrote a note for Ivor to say where she was going and that she wouldn't be long. People didn't have mobile phones, didn't follow each other's movements minute by minute. She was just putting the note in a prominent position on the kitchen table when the door opened and Ivor walked in.

Feri quickly told herself that she shouldn't have been surprised. A woman like Gemma would not have taken leave of her senses and fallen for just any sixteen-year-old with average good looks. Someone like Mark, for instance, whose appearance had pleased her just a few hours ago. Mark was certainly cute, but this boy was cuter. The lively black curls, the intense blue eyes in their starry haloes of dark lashes... And no doubt he had other attributes, things that went beyond anything that could be discovered by a first glance. Gemma introduced the two surprised teenagers. Feri managed coolly to get out those few polite sentences that are expected in this situation. Ivor, though, could barely manage to mumble his. Ivor was in shock.

'I met a friend of yours earlier,' Feri was telling him. 'Mark Harris.'

'Oh,' said Ivor. The news seemed a pointless detail right now. And he wasn't capable of saying much else.

'Well, lovely to have met you,' Feri said, 'and sorry it couldn't be for longer.' She glanced towards Gemma, then back. 'Sadly we have a train to make.'

Feri and Gemma left by the kitchen door through which Ivor had just come. Ivor sat down at the kitchen table, staring stupidly at the now closed door. A powerful feeling had gripped him with a force he had never known before. And, which was weirder, something told him that he would never, could never, have it again. He just knew that he wanted Feri more than he would ever want anything else. He knew it was more than simply sex, more than lust, or infatuation, or what passed in ordinary people's hearts for love. Had Gemma told him that Wuthering Heights, rather than Crime and Punishment was the one book he had to read he might have been able to recognise the feelings he now had. But she hadn't done, and all Ivor could think was that he wanted to possess Feri in the same way that he wanted to possess Gemma's house. Though a million times more powerfully than that.

FOURTEEN

Ivor had no difficulty finding Feri's contact details. Gemma didn't leave her address book lying about, but she didn't lock it away either. The same went for her bank statements, so that Ivor was quite knowledgeable about her income and savings and, because she didn't lock away her business correspondence either, her investments too. But now that he'd got the information that would enable him to find Feri again he wasn't sure how to proceed. But he knew for absolute certain that whatever next steps he took in her direction he must not, must not, screw up.

Naturally Ivor didn't say anything to Gemma about his feelings for Feri, but he was too clever to draw attention to them by avoiding the subject of her visit altogether. Even so, it was a couple of days before he was in a clear-headed enough state to ask the most obvious of questions. What had Feri been doing, going to call on Mark? Had they met before, perhaps?

'No,' Gemma said. 'And it's all water under the bridge anyway.' She explained that Feri had had a rather silly idea about writing a book based on the Lydd experience. 'And it turned out that Mark no more wanted to get involved in it than you did, so that's an end of the matter.' Gemma was more than happy to let it drop now. She didn't want to go on and voice her suspicion that Feri had actually been on a fishing trip in search of a young farmer. Not to a boy lover who, while not actually a farmer himself, would match the rest of the specification very well.

Ivor decided to phone Mark. He couldn't remember where he'd written his number down nearly a year ago, if he even had done, but he found it easily enough among the numerous Harrises in the local book. When he'd identified himself he heard Mark say, 'Thought I might hear from you. After that bird you sent round. She's a bit tasty. I guess it's your turn now to try and make me say something for your book. But there's really nothing.'

'No. Screw that. The book's not going to happen anyway. It's about the bird I'm phoning. Feri, short for Fermina. Are you and she...?'

'No way. My girl'd kill me. But I've got her phone number if you want it.'

'No. I've got it already. Thanks, though.'

'You got her address? She didn't give me that.'

'It's OK,' said Ivor. 'I've got that too. It's London. Just off Highgate Hill.'

'You don't half talk posh now, mate.' Mark said. 'What kind of company you been keeping?' He sniggered down the line.

'No I don't,' Ivor answered, startled, but reverting quickly to the local burr that had been his way of speaking, as well as Mark's, when last they'd spent time together.

'She said you'd got a girlfriend anyway. That you live over Brede way. You looking to do a bit of two-timing?'

'Sort of girlfriend, yeah,' said Ivor a bit awkwardly. 'Shacked up with... Just say it's worth my while. Leave it there.'

Mark cottoned on at once. 'Shit, man. You're somebody's toy-boy!'

'That's for me to know and you to speculate,' Ivor said, sounding posh again. He wasn't quite sure why he'd phoned Mark. Perhaps it was to check that Feri made the same kind of impact on other boys as she had on him, and that it wasn't simply a case of his own quirky hormones leading him astray.

But it was clear she'd made more than a small impression on Mark, especially when he pulled the conversation round to her again. 'Well, good luck with

Feri, anyway. I'd say she was worth the chase.' Ivor hung up.

It was June now, and Norma and Michael Harding finally got married. Norma had been spending more time in York since Christmas than she had at Winchelsea Beach and Rye, and now she was to move up there for good. Mrs Norma Harding.

Ivor said he wouldn't go to the wedding. It was two hundred and fifty miles away after all. But Gemma asserted herself and told him he must. She made it sound almost as important a thing as seeing Hamlet. She would pay his train fare if his mother did not. She would do more than that. She'd take him into Hastings and get him a nice suit. She told him that if he didn't go he would have less certainty that future help from Norma and her new husband would be forthcoming should he ever need it. Ivor was realistic enough to see that he might not be able to live off Gemma for ever and he was still unsure how to secure himself as the future owner of her house. He saw the point, and went.

Gemma had been right. For all that she had come to like her son less and less as the years passed, Norma was genuinely touched that Ivor took the trouble to make the journey north, handsome in a brand new suit. So was Michael, her greying groom. The evening before the day itself they had dinner together, just the three of them, in a Thai restaurant in the centre of the city. Ivor had quite enjoyed the train journey up, staring out at farmhouses made not of brick and timber but of stone, though he'd been surprised at the flatness of the Vale of York; he'd expected something more mountainous, something more like Morocco or Tenerife. Now, over glass-noodle and stir-fry, Michael made Ivor a very serious speech, placing both forearms on the table and leaning across towards him. 'There's something I need to say to you,' he began. He saw Ivor's face knit into a frown and tried to counter that with a smile. It didn't work so he pressed on. 'You already know my first marriage produced no children. I want you to know that, should I die before your mother does, everything that belongs to me at that time, however little, however much, will go direct to her.' He turned to Norma, who took her cue.

'And just supposing I die first, whatever's mine – that's mainly the bungalow, or the money from it in case it's sold, will go to you, just as it would if I was to die before tomorrow morning.'

For once Ivor found himself unable to complain about his mother's plans. His frown had disappeared. He surprised her with a graceful thank you. It was one of those things he'd learned from Gemma.

Ivor already knew they were planning to let the bungalow, though there was no definite date for this. It wasn't even in the estate agent's hands yet. But his mother had further good news for him, it now appeared. Perhaps this was the result of his little thank-you speech, perhaps of the general warmth of the evening and the particular glow that affects a bride-to-be. 'Until it's let you can have the use of it whenever you want. If you need to. Though you probably won't do, with the comfy billet you've got for yourself – at least for now.'

Ivor, mellow with two glasses of white wine inside him, felt agreeably reassured.

He and his mother stayed the night at the hotel, the Royal York, where the reception would be held the following day. Norma, who had spent the previous night and a couple of hundred others in Michael Harding's bed, nevertheless held to the old-fashioned notion that it wasn't fitting to do so on the eve of her wedding day.

The ceremony was held in the registry office at eleven o'clock. Nobody from the Rye area had made the journey except for Ivor himself. The Spraggens,

Norma's employers at the antique shop, were conspicuously absent. They had been inconvenienced by Norma's repeated and ever longer absences from work in the last year: this was their way of letting her know it. But there was a good turnout of the bridegroom's friends. Michael was conscientious in introducing Ivor to these people, which he did almost proudly, much to Ivor's surprise. In fact, thanks to warm sun and a cloudless sky, and to the fact that the reception spilled out pleasantly into the gardens of the hotel, Ivor found himself enjoying the day. In the evening Norma and Michael would be flying out from Manchester to Nice. Norma was concerned that Ivor might arrive back in London too late for the last train home.

'Don't worry, Mum,' Ivor said. 'I've got friends in London I can doss with.' Coming from a seventeen-year-old boy whom Norma no longer knew very well, if indeed she ever had done, this sounded eminently plausible and left Norma reassured, her conscience salved.

Actually Ivor didn't have friends in London – at least, he didn't have yet – but he had two plans for how and where he might pass the night. Plan B involved sleeping rough in one of the parks, which would be no hardship on a warm June night. But he was determined to give Plan A a go first.

You had to expect the worst, Ivor knew, if you wanted the best outcome. He told himself as he picked up the phone that she wouldn't be there, or wouldn't be free, or wouldn't be prepared to see him if he was. The phone was answered on the fifth ring. He recognised her voice.

'Feri, it's Ivor, Gemma's boyfriend. Sorry to ring so late. I've missed my last train home. I'm in London and I don't have any friends here. I know it's an awful cheek as we've hardly met, but is there any chance you'd have a bit of spare floor that I could crash on?'

Feri hesitated for a second. She wasn't sure whether Ivor, for all his physical charms, was a positive or negative force in her friend's life. His readiness, according to Gemma, to claim that he saw ghosts and then to change his mind on the subject with the alacrity of a weathercock, rang a warning bell that seemed to chime: *too weird by half.* But she reflected that in the time Gemma had known him he hadn't done her any physical harm that Feri was aware of, or stolen the silver spoons. Curiosity overcame caution. 'OK,' she said. 'But where are you? Do you know where I am?'

'Kings Cross. Highgate.' In answering the two questions together so glibly he had given something away, he realised at once. Feri hadn't given him her address, and she'd only given Mark her phone number, so he could only have got the information from Gemma. Who might or might not – he imagined Feri pondering – have volunteered it. He must remember to be more careful. Remember Roddy Raskolnikov.

But she probably hadn't noticed: there was no change in her tone as she said, 'Get the tube – Northern Line...' She gave him further instructions very carefully, as if speaking to someone a few years younger than Ivor was. Half an hour later he was there.

Lazily he had imagined that Feri would be the owner of a large house or flat, expensively furnished, where she lived alone. Like Gemma. And some of Gemma's older friends. But Feri was younger than Gemma by eleven years. She might dress stylishly and smartly too, might have wealthy parents, but she was still a student, in her second year at art school, and she lived like one. Ivor found her address to be a mid-Victorian semi-detached house which Feri shared with five others, four female, one male. Three of them besides Feri were at home when Ivor arrived, including the boy. Although Feri had her reasons for handling Ivor with a certain amount of caution, like a beautiful exotic pet animal that nevertheless might bite, her house-mates had no such inhibition, and were prepared to make much of this cute and youthful visitor so suddenly appearing in their midst.

One of the girls asked him if he'd eaten anything recently and, on hearing that he hadn't done since he'd left the wedding reception about six hours ago, cooked him an omelette, with sliced raw onions as a filling, and gave him bread and butter and a mug of tea. He had his late supper in the living-room, on a tray on his knees, while the others fussed around him and chatted in a general way. Feri sat at a little distance, watchful and a little more discreet. There would be no late-night sharing of confidences with his hostess, Ivor was pretty sure.

But the male member of the household made up for Feri's reticence. His name was David, he told Ivor, who hadn't asked, and he was studying interior design. He had an elder brother, amazingly clever, who was studying to be an architect at the University of Kent. He seemed very interested in everything Ivor volunteered about himself, and in the answers, however inconsequential, to all the questions he put to him. Although he didn't care much, Ivor did notice that David was a very handsome young man, one whose animated facial expressions and physical mannerisms drew attention to his looks. He wasn't quite sure at first what prompted David's more than merely polite interest in him, but some time before he finished his omelette he thought he knew.

Feri offered Ivor the floor of the communal living-room as a parking place for the night, before going up to her own bedroom on – she didn't tell him this – the second floor. Ivor wondered whether a polite goodnight kiss might be a good move but remembered just in time what his omelette had been filled with and abandoned the idea. David was the last of the house-mates to retire to his own room. He seemed to hover rather, even up to the time when Ivor started unselfconsciously to undress, but as Ivor gave him not the smallest hint of a come-on, he got the message and left Ivor to enjoy the solitude of his floor in peace.

In the morning Ivor was not surprised to find that David was the first one up. He was obliged almost to step across Ivor's prone body to get to the kitchen. He was dressed in shorts and a T-shirt. Ivor had to admit that he made an impression: he had a good physique. So had Ivor, but he had no intention of waiting around to be complimented on it as he got dressed. Instead he got up quickly, wrapped himself in the blanket in which he'd spent the night, and took himself off to the bathroom with his overnight bag.

He returned a few minutes later wearing the suit he'd worn the day before – plus the crimson tie that went with it. He was intent on needling David to the maximum by not even showing the unbuttoned triangle of neck and chest that he'd displayed the previous night. (He'd removed the tie for comfort on the train journey down.) By now the other inhabitants of the house were in the kitchen, making tea or burning toast, a very smartly dressed Feri among them. Ivor was in time to hear her say to the shorts-clad David, 'Are you going in like that?' with surprise in her voice. David's answer of, 'Why not?' confirmed what he already suspected: that David did not normally appear at breakfast on a weekday dressed in shorts.

It was only a brief while before everyone, Ivor included, was hastening out of the house. David found a second in which to say to Ivor, 'Call again, any time. Be nice to see you.'

Ivor said, without smiling, 'Yeah. May well be back.' Then he found a second to speak to Feri, before their ways diverged at the front gate. It was now or never, he knew. 'Well thanks,' he said. 'You saved me from the streets. Next time I'm in London,' he went on, only just managing to keep his voice calm, while his heart performed a staccato drum solo in his chest, 'can I buy you dinner?'

Feri was so astonished that for a moment she lost her usual sang-froid. She said, 'Well, maybe,' instead of what she would otherwise have come out with which was, 'Who the hell do you think you are?' Ivor had put the suit and tie on to irritate David, not to impress Feri, but that might just have been a lucky, unintended consequence.

As he sat, forty minutes later, in the train from Charing Cross to Ashford, from where his connection ran to Rye, Ivor thought that, if things had not quite turned out along the lines of his wildest dreams, the progress he'd made was encouraging to a degree.

The money for the sale of Ivor's bird paintings came through from the wildlife calendar company, via Gemma's agent. There also came a commission, from the same source, for a further set of pictures, similar in style and general subject matter, to be used for Christmas cards. And on the same day came news from his mother that a tenant had been found for the bungalow at Winchelsea Beach. If Ivor still had any personal belongings there that he wanted, Norma told him, he would need to get them in the next two weeks. Did he still have his key? Of course he did.

There were a few bits and pieces of his lying around at the bungalow, but not much. Most of his things had migrated to Gatcombe over the past year. But there remained the important question of those workshop tools. For his seventeenth birthday Gemma had bought him driving lessons. He had learned easily, had taken his test after just six sessions, and passed. But Gemma hadn't bought him a car, still less the van that would be required to transport the bulky contents of Violet's shed. As he'd already planned to, knowing this day would one day arrive, he telephoned Mark.

Probably relieved to discover that Ivor hadn't changed his mind and now wanted to badger him about his recollections of the Lydd experience after all, Mark agreed readily to help Ivor out. He too had passed his test easily, as farm boys usually do, and he arranged to meet Mark near Rye station, with his father's Land Rover, on Saturday afternoon.

As it was one of Gemma's Lamb House Saturdays, Ivor cycled into town to keep his appointment, stowing his bike, once Mark showed up, in the back of the Land Rover. On the drive to Winchelsea Beach Ivor told Mark about his mother's wedding and his night in London. 'I didn't actually get to bed with her, but it was still worth going.'

Mark was impressed by the boldness of his tactic. 'What about your – um – girlfriend, though? She OK with that?'

'She doesn't know,' Ivor answered. 'I told her I'd spent a second night in York.'

'Ah,' said Mark. He was a boy who traded in his girlfriends for newer models as regularly as richer boys changed their cars, but he still held to the traditional principle of one at a time.

'She shares with all these other student types,' Ivor volunteered. 'It's not going to be all that easy when I go up again.' There was no question in Ivor's mind but that he would. 'And there's a problem with one of them, who fancies me.'

'Don't seem much of a problem,' Mark said.

'Yeah, but it's a bloke.'

Mark frowned thoughtfully through the windscreen for a second. Then he said, 'You don't swing that way too, do you?'

'Fucking hell, no!' Ivor said, his astonishment that Mark might even have considered asking the question making his voice rise to falsetto height on the *no*.

'Cool it, man. Only asking.'

When they'd arrived at the bungalow Ivor opened up the garden shed and showed Mark what they'd come for. 'You got a ton of stuff here, mate,' Mark said, but then uncomplainingly helped Ivor to carry it across the lawn. The garden had been neglected this spring and they waded back and forth across a seed-waving, pollen-rich hayfield. Carefully arranged, tools and workbench all fitted in the back of the Land Rover with Ivor's bike.

Ivor showed Mark the short way back to Gatcombe, along the Brede valley and Float Lane. It was a route Mark didn't know. Living on the other side of Rye as he did, this wasn't on his normal way to anywhere. 'All open water, this, a few hundred years ago.' Ivor recited what he'd learned from Gemma as they drove along the valley floor. 'An enormous natural harbour, shared by Winchelsea and Rye when they were Cinque Ports.' Mark remembered that a similar harbour had existed back in those days between Romney and Lydd, but wasn't going to bring that up. 'Up there,' Ivor gestured up the sheep-studded hillside towards Cadborough Cliff, 'Edward III's wife watched as he and his ships down here fought off a Spanish raid.' He snorted. 'Good old days.'

'Blimey,' said Mark. 'You've turned yourself into a historian and all. This bird you live with, she a teacher, then?'

'Among other things,' Ivor said, but didn't elaborate. Mark was going to see Gatcombe for himself in a few minutes and would draw plenty of conclusions about the kind of person Ivor lived with then. It wasn't a circumstance Ivor would have wished for but it couldn't be helped: those tools had had to be saved. At least Gemma wouldn't actually be there. There wouldn't have to be social intercourse and tea and cake. Though come to think of it...

Mark was mightily impressed by Gatcombe Farm. 'Pretty fine gaff you got yourself. You planning to stay on here till your woman dies?' He'd meant that as a joke, though realised how tasteless it was as soon as he'd said it and was decent enough to turn a brighter than usual red at once. But Ivor took the question at face value. 'Maybe that's about it,' he said thoughtfully. 'Right now I don't have a much better idea.'

Didn't have a better idea of how to make the house his own, restore it to medieval splendour as a Wealden hall house, as Nathaniel Lloyd had done with Great Dixter. He didn't share this with Mark, he would have sounded addle-brained. He took him, after they'd unloaded their cargo into the garage, on a tour of the house instead.

Gemma had not allowed Ivor to install his tools and workbench in her precious studio, and when Mark saw the studio he understood why. 'Wow,' he said, looking around the big space, with its white walls framed in silvered oak and its polished red brick floor. Examples of both Gemma's and Ivor's work lay or stood about, jostling for space, on all sides. 'I know who your woman is now. You see her work all over Rye. She wrote kids' books about a cat. My little sister had them. She must be worth a quid or two.'

'Come and see upstairs,' Ivor said, perhaps not wanting to dwell further on the question of Gemma's financial worth. Instead he introduced Mark to the four cats, each asleep on a different bed on the first floor, and proudly showed him the medieval king-post in the attic bedroom. Then, 'I'll make us some tea, if you'd like.

There's some chocolate cake in the fridge. Really good one. From Fletcher's or Simon the Pieman. One of those.' That prospect was quite enough to set them on their way downstairs again.

Ivor told Mark, between chocolaty mouthfuls, about his work at Albert Gutsell's. How he disliked his master, despite the invaluable experience he was getting. 'Even the fronts of clock cases and cabinets I repair now, and only a professional can see the joins. I can make tables and chairs in solid oak. Most people can't.' But for every day spent honing his skills he still spent at least two honing an endless stock of chisels. Ivor swore that Albert bought up stocks of useless old blunt ones for the malign pleasure of watching him sweat as he sharpened them.

'Sounds like you're ready for a change,' Mark said. 'Maybe you've learned all you can from What's-his-name. You've got your own tools here now, even if you do have to use them in the garage.'

This chimed with Ivor's thoughts. He knew his craftsmanship was now indistinguishable from his master's. He'd already had thoughts about telling Gutsell what to do with his apprenticeship and setting up in competition with him. He could use the money he'd got from the wildlife calendar paintings to capitalise his first job or two. He said, 'Yeah, I been thinking about that. Looking in the local rag to see the way other local craftsmen word their ads.' Mark showed his approval with a sober nod of the head, then ran a finger round his now empty plate to pick up the last few chocolate crumbs.

FIFTEEN

'When's he coming again?' David asked. He was sitting on the sofa when Feri came in that evening, eating microwaved lasagne from the container. No longer in shorts but jeans.

'Who?' said Feri.

'Don't pretend.' With his fork David rescued a spilt morsel from his chin. 'Your young admirer from darkest Sussex who stayed last night.'

'He's not.'

'Now that's a pity,' said David. 'I thought he was very sweet.'

'So everyone could see. Coming down for breakfast dressed for the beach. Honestly!' Feri thought for a moment, then sat on the sofa beside David. 'He has a girlfriend – my friend and mentor Gemma – as I think he told you last night. He isn't up for grabs. Especially not grabs made by male paws. You're right, though. He is cute. And he has a little friend in Sussex, who I've met, who looks nearly as nice.'

'Spoken for?' David asked.

'For heavens' sake!' Feri laughed. 'I've no idea.'

David put down his lasagne and fork and laid a hand round Feri's shoulder. 'Then why don't you invite both of them up?' he teased her. 'We could have one each.'

'Now stop,' said Feri. She removed David's arm. 'You're being gross.'

Feri might not have remembered that conversation, but then the phone rang a week or two later and surprised her with the melodious voice of Carlos at the other end.

'I didn't think we were doing this,' she told him. 'Calling each other up.'

'We're not calling each other up,' Carlos said. 'This is just me calling you. It's because I've been thinking – couldn't we start over? Give things another try?' There was a second's silence as Feri struggled to find something to say. Really, what could you say to someone who wouldn't be told? Men were just so... Carlos's voice cut in on her thoughts. 'I miss you.'

'It's no good,' Feri heard her own voice say. 'I'm sorry, but we can't go back.' She didn't wait to hear his why or why not. She said, 'I'm seeing someone else.'

Most people dislike telling lies and feel disappointed in themselves when they find they've done so. One of the tactics they sometimes employ in an effort to feel better about themselves is retrospectively to turn the lie into a truth. And so it came about that Feri picked up the phone and called Ivor.

It was a Wednesday evening, a time when people who knew Gemma well would know she was over at Fairlight village with her string quartet. Ivor was alone in the studio, painting a dead pigeon. It wasn't any old dead pigeon. This one had been killed and partly eaten by a sparrowhawk, the tasty breast ripped out, the thorax and belly open, and innards spilling out among the grey and bloody feathers. It was a grisly mess. 'You won't be able to sell that for a Christmas card,' Gemma had told him, giving a shudder that was only partly deliberate.

'It's for experience,' Ivor said seriously. Greater artists than he had painted such gory scenes. He grinned. 'My learning curve.'

Gemma said, 'Rather you than me, then. But try and finish it while I'm out, can you? Then bury the wretched thing. Don't let the cats get hold of it: they'll play with it like a paint brush and daub the whole house with blood.'

When the phone rang Ivor nearly didn't answer it. He had to put his brush and palette down and wipe his hands, then make sure the cats didn't get into the studio while he left it and tear his subject to shreds. But he did answer it. The voice he heard at the other end astonished him, and set his pulse racing, his heart banging, until he really thought it might be audible down the line.

Feri didn't waste time with *how are you*s or anything like that, and since that was Ivor's way of doing things too he appreciated that. 'I've been thinking,' she said, 'that I will let you take me out to dinner some time – that is, if your invitation still stands.'

'Sure it does,' said Ivor. 'So when?'

'When are you going to be in town?'

'Today week,' said Ivor without pausing long enough to blink. 'I have to come up next Wednesday. What time shall I meet you? I'll come to your place and we'll take it from there.' He'd never done anything like this before, never spoken quite like this before, but he'd heard similar dialogue on TV, where it seemed to work.

Feri named a time. 'I have to be straight with you,' she went on. 'It'll be dinner. Just dinner. That OK with you?'

Ivor had heard that on TV too. 'That's just fine,' he said. That Feri's reasons for phoning him were not straightforward would not have bothered him even if he'd known of them. He rarely credited people with straightforward intentions. His reading of other people's motives was based on the knowledge of his own, and Ivor had more insight into those than most.

He thought carefully about what he was going to wear. He needed to look his best for Feri. But if he was going to pick her up from her Highgate home – or perhaps even get back there later – he was likely to run into David, and he didn't want to find himself looking nice for him. Having considered this, though, he concluded it was just something he'd have to accept. A necessary price to pay if he were to present himself to Feri looking great. He eventually decided on a collarless, big-sleeved 'grandfather' shirt, white with a fine grey stripe, and his newest pair of blue denims. He took the very masculine boots he went to work in and polished them till they dimly reflected his determined face.

Other things had to be sorted. Probably Albert Gutsell need only be asked for an unpaid afternoon off, but he had to find for Gemma a plausible reason why he needed to rush up to London on his own the following Wednesday, returning late or, if his luck was in, not till the next day. It took him a day or two to realise that, again, the solution was going to be Mark. He told Gemma that Mark had promised to introduce him to a man in London whom his father knew, and who might want to commission a series of paintings from him. They were going to travel up together. Gemma had never met Mark or his parents and so was unlikely to phone to check, should she have her suspicions about this tissue of untruths. Ivor's plan had two drawbacks, he knew. He would need to have a story to tell, on his return, about what happened at the meeting: whether his work was going to be commissioned or not. Also, he would need to lug a portfolio of his work up to London – a major inconvenience for anyone on a first date. And yet, Ivor thought, even that might not prove a handicap after all.

Gemma would normally have been highly suspicious of Ivor's tale. Perhaps at some level she was suspicious anyway, but she had a preoccupation of her own just then. The German translation of Nicholas II and the Castle of Rats had now been completed and had gone to press. Her German publisher wanted her to make a couple of visits to Germany to promote the book, one just in advance of the launch there, the other a little time after it. She was unsure whether she could, or should, take Ivor with her on these trips – and how she was going to square it with him if she didn't. With her mind distracted by all that, she took his story at face value, or seemed to, and wished him the best of luck with the trip and the negotiations.

Ivor turned up on Feri's doorstep dead on time. He rang the bell and she appeared. looking like someone setting out for a fashion shoot. Before she could ask him if he wanted to come in he said, 'I want to show you an Italian place in Hillgate Street. It's good.'

'Where's Hillgate Street?' Feri wanted to know.

'Off Notting Hill Gate. We could have a drink at the Sun in Splendour first.' It was the only pub in London that he knew. He'd been there with Gemma when she'd taken him to that Italian restaurant in Hillgate Street. He knew no other London restaurants either – except at the Barbican and the South Bank.

'The Gate's miles away,' said Feri, frowning a little. 'Wouldn't you rather go somewhere a bit more local?'

'We'll get a cab,' said Ivor, steely determination masking his nerves, masking the feeling that he was way out of his depth and his league. 'I sold some paintings. I've got money. It's no problem.'

Feri made sense at that moment of the unlikely looking parcel in his hand. Men sometimes arrived with flowers for her, or a bottle – mainly for themselves – but those offerings were never this shape. Ivor's encumbrance was the shape and size of an artist's portfolio. Feri groaned inwardly. It was an artist's portfolio. Dear God. Outwardly she smiled bravely. 'OK then. We'd better go inside while I find a number.'

As they walked through the house Ivor peered about him, while trying not to look as if he was, to see if David was around. He didn't seem to be. Feri showed him the number of a minicab firm on the kitchen wall and handed him the phone. If he was going to open up his portfolio in the middle of a restaurant and make her look through pictures while they ate, she would take her revenge. Invite him back to Highgate on the strict understanding that he'd be sleeping on the floor, then let David loose on him while she retired to bed. Feri never stood any nonsense from men; she certainly wasn't going to put up with any from this kid.

The taxi arrived in minutes. Feri, Ivor and the portfolio clambered in. Only then did Feri ask, 'What brought you up to town today?' Though she thought she knew.

'You did. I didn't have any other reason for coming up.'

Feri was no less pleased with the answer for having guessed it in advance. It was nice of the boy actually to spell it out. 'Then why the portfolio?' she asked him, softening towards it very slightly. 'If that's what it is.'

'I had to get out under the radar,' Ivor said. 'I invented a meeting with a buyer of paintings who, unfortunately, doesn't exist. So I'm lumbered with this. Bit of a bummer. Sorry.'

'You could have left it at the house,' Feri said, without giving herself time to think through the implications of that.

'I'd no reason to think we were going back,' Ivor said, then turned to look her full in the face and grinned, which took Feri rather aback. The taxi pulled up outside the Sun in Splendour.

Feri asked for a tonic water with ice and lemon. This might have dismayed Ivor, but Gemma sometimes went for the same thing if she knew she was going to have a glass of wine later on, so he didn't take it as too bad a sign. He wondered what he should order for himself as he waited at the bar to be served, hoping rather anxiously that the bar staff here were not more eagle-eyed when it came to spotting under-age drinkers than they were in

Sussex. They were not. He felt his chest expand with relief and ordered himself a tonic water with gin in it – though he put the words in their more usual order. It was something he'd never had before.

'I'm not the only one who's brought their portfolio along,' he said, back at the table they had found, and handing Feri her drink.

Feri looked round, but saw no sign of any item similar to the one Ivor had brought, which was now leaning a bit tipsily between their table and the wall. 'Where? Who do you mean?'

'You,' said Ivor earnestly, then broke into a smile. 'You're wearing it.'

Feri might have given him a very frosty answer, but somehow she found she couldn't. 'You're very clever,' she said. 'Cheers. And thanks.'

Ivor at once asked her what she was working on at college, because he knew that's what Gemma would have done next: she'd taught him so much. Feri told him, dresses mainly, this particular term, but, knowing he was deeply into houses in all their aspects, charitably helped him by mentioning that she'd done wallpapers the previous year. He was able then to talk knowledgeably about Pugin and William Morris. Ruskin came next. They got from there to favourite painters. Turner was probably at the top of her list, Feri told him. As for Ivor, he loved the lot. Tintoretto, Monet, Hieronymus Bosch...

If it had to be done, Feri came to the thought at last, it would be less ghastly in a pub than at a restaurant table over the dessert. 'You'd better show me,' she said to him, angling her head and looking towards the brooding thing that he had brought. Gemma had told Feri many times what a brilliant painter Ivor was. Feri hadn't taken much notice. She hadn't met him then, and everyone told you their boyfriend or girlfriend was brilliant, just as they would one day say the same about their kids. So when, one by one, the pictures came out Feri's astonishment left her struggling to find words. 'But they're wonderful,' she said. 'I'd no idea.'

Even the half-eaten wood pigeon drew her praise. 'Though I'm not sure I'd want it on the living-room wall.' Then, last of all came a view of Gatcombe, in full sunshine, hollyhocks in the garden, with oast and barns at side and back. The twin cowls of the oast kiln tops moved like weathercocks in the wind – they were mounted in the same way as anti-aircraft guns, or the turrets of tanks. But one moved more freely than the other, so that a very light breeze might move just one of them, while the other stayed in place. Ivor's picture had caught them in this odd state. 'Oh look,' said Feri. 'I've seen them look like that this last year or two. One of them needs a drop of oil perhaps. They look like...'

'I know,' said Ivor. 'Like two old biddies chin-wagging.'

'Exactly that,' said Feri with a laugh. She'd always had the same thought herself, when one cowl, the bonneted head of the kiln, turned towards the other, its long vane sticking forward like a nose or tongue. It looked as if it had done so in order to pass a remark. And Ivor had had the same thought.

'Sometimes they make me think of witches on broomsticks, or carrying sub-machine guns,' Ivor said.

Feri had thought that too, though she'd been less sure about the exact type of gun. 'How far's this restaurant?' she asked.

'Let's go, then,' said Ivor. 'A two minute walk. Down to the tube station, across the road and there's steps down beside another pub.' Feri helped him return the paintings carefully to their protecting covers.

It was actually a pleasure, Feri found, to exchange ideas, discuss ambitions, over tortelloni and Chianti with this more than usually handsome boy. She thought for a second about Mark, the big-eyed lad who wore his collar turned up. She realised suddenly that he too would have dropped everything and rushed up to London if instead of phoning Ivor she'd called him. It gave her a heady feeling, this discovery that she'd turned the heads of two young men during a single weekend back in the spring. But Ivor was the better-looking of the two, she thought, by the narrowest of margins. Gemma hadn't been mad when she'd fallen for him: it would have been hard for Gemma not to fall for the kid. He was far from being a pussy-cat – Feri did not much care for men who were – but he wasn't a horror either, or a bore.

It wasn't so surprising, she now thought, that her flatmate had behaved so absurdly when Ivor and he had met. She'd been pretty sure then that Ivor had no sexual interest in other men. Now she was more than sure. Even with a restaurant table between them this boy radiated a full-blooded heterosexuality which could be felt like an electric fire. She thought back to her earlier idea of leaving Ivor to sleep on the living-room floor, obliged to fend off the attentions of David. Though she had no doubt Ivor would have managed the situation without the smallest difficulty, she now found the idea grotesque. When they'd finished their meal and Ivor half stood to reach his wallet from the back pocket of his jeans Feri said they absolutely must go halves. But Ivor insisted on paying the whole bill with a wodge of notes and leaving a tip. They stood up, ready to leave. Feri said, looking him straight in the eye, 'Do I remember saying something about you not being asked back to Highgate. Did I say that? Thinking it over, you know, I'm not sure that's quite what I meant.'

Having sex, making love, with Feri, Ivor felt like someone who had found himself, like someone who had for the first time become whole. He had the sense of achieving a longed-for goal, as a climber might feel on conquering a mountain he'd previously gazed at from far off – as he'd seen the High Atlas from Marrakesh. But alongside these feelings ran something else: the idea that all this was his by right. Like the long-awaited coronation of an heir apparent, the capture of Feri had somehow always been his. It was something that had belonged to him from the beginning, and had waited only for its appointed time to come.

David's behaviour at breakfast the next morning caused Ivor some amusement, which he hid. When Feri and he had returned from the restaurant to the Highgate house David had said a perfectly civil hallo to them and then, not much later, a perfectly civil goodnight. But at breakfast, if the general grabbing for toast and coffee in the kitchen could be called that, David's eyes and body had spoken the language of the spurned suitor even though his lips had not. It was as though he felt somehow let down by both of them, by Ivor and by Feri too. But Ivor was hardly going to let that worry him, and forgot it entirely once he'd left the house.

Feri didn't think it necessary to tell Ivor she'd prefer Gemma not to hear about what had taken place. Although even thinking about Gemma this morning, and of what she might have done to that long friendship between them, made her feel uncomfortable, she was able to guess that Ivor would have no difficulty in dreaming up a plausible excuse for staying away all night.

'What the hell do you think you're doing?' Albert Gutscll shouted at Ivor when he walked into the workshop later that day. 'It's twenty past twelve. Twelve twenty!'

'I got held up,' said Ivor.

'Held up for four bloody hours?' It was the first time Ivor had heard Albert swear. 'People who are held up have the basic courtesy to phone in and say they're held up – and why – and what time they expect to be in. But you...? Oh no. How held up? Where?'

'In London,' said Ivor nonchalantly. 'I missed the last train back.'

'Pull the other one,' said Albert. 'You been doing the dance of the sheets, I reckon. Up the Smoke with some tart or bit of fancy stuff.'

'Believe what you want,' said Ivor, moving calmly to his workbench and beginning a mental roll-call of his tools.

'Forgot you'd got a job to go to, did you?' Gutsell had been standing behind his own workbench until now, facing Ivor across it. Now he walked out into the middle of the floor, just a yard from where Ivor stood. 'I'll teach you to forget you've got a job – when there's thousands out there would give their eye-teeth for one.'

Ivor looked at him. He felt his lips curl back. 'Yeah. But probably not this one. And now I think about it I reckon I've done just about as long here as I want.' He looked around him. Not much seemed to have moved forward since the previous afternoon. 'Seems you've survived the morning pretty well without me. Guess you'll manage the afternoon without me too. I'll get on my way now, if that's OK. I'll call in for my wages on Friday. Thanks for whatever.' Ivor laid down the chisel he'd just picked up – it wasn't his after all – and stepped out from behind the workbench. For a second he faced Albert in the centre of the floor, confrontation style. Albert didn't move or back away. But he did look thunderstruck. Ivor turned abruptly and made towards the door. Behind him he heard Albert say, in a voice hoarse with astonishment, 'What? Are you walking out on me?'

Without saying more or turning back, Ivor opened the door and went out through it, banging it hard behind him. He had the odd impression of leaving behind a spurned lover, for the second time that day.

SIXTEEN

Ivor didn't go back to Gatcombe immediately. He repeated his journey of just over a year before, down Hundredhouse Lane and across the broad valley of the Tillingham, up the punishingly steep hill on the other side, then down onto the Rother Levels and Reedbed Farm. Here he had worked, shucking broad beans, exactly a year ago and he wondered what his chances would be of landing the same job a second time round. But as he cycled into the yard he could see a red-haired boy standing on a trailer, just as he had done, emptying the bean sacks down the chute. The boy stared at Ivor with a curiosity that verged on hostility as he dismounted and made his way into the work sheds.

The same familiar band of women, weighing, bagging and making up boxes of beans, greeted him warmly, which was a pleasant surprise: he didn't have any particular memories of them. But when he went to the office to try his luck with the farm manager he was told he was too late. Reedbed had all the staff it needed just then. He was welcome to phone up in a few weeks' time. As Ivor retreated back up the track on his bike he was conscious of the red-headed boy's impassive – or triumphant – stare following him on his way.

He rode back to Peasmarsh, then up Starvecrow Lane. Seeing Birdskitchen again for the first time in nearly a year, he was even more conscious of how like Gatcombe it looked. The twin kilns of the oast peering over the roof of the white-painted farmhouse, the enormous black timber Wealden barn, other red-roofed outhouses and cottages gathered around. He rode up the track and into the yard. There seemed to be nobody about. But, remembering his experience the previous year, he decided against going up and knocking at the house's front door. Then Jack Eason himself appeared from the low shed that was the feed store, wheeling a barrow of what might have been cattle cake or perhaps pig meal.

Ivor dismounted and respectfully pushed his steed towards the farmer. Remembering his embarrassing mishearing, last time round, of *how are you* for *who are you*, he was determined not to let the same thing happen again. 'Ivor Wingate,' he announced himself. 'I worked for you last year.'

'You've a what?' said Eason, looking fierce. He also appeared to have aged far more than the passing of a single year would normally account for.

'It's my name,' said Ivor, feeling wrong-footed a second time. 'My name's Ivor Wingate. I did hops for you last year.' He treated Jack Eason to a smile. He hadn't gone in much for those a year ago, but since then he'd learned from Gemma what a good investment a smile could be.

'I do remember now,' said Eason. 'Didn't you use to ride to the pub with Andy on his tractor, and your bike on the back?'

'The very same,' said Ivor. He patted the saddle beside him. 'Same bike too. Thing is,' he went on without stopping, 'I'm looking for work again. Anything doing here at all?'

Eason thought for a moment. 'Well, there's spuds – and hops again, though not for a month or two. On the other hand – only temporary, mind – my pig man's gone sick...'

'Frank. Yeah.' That was another thing he'd learnt from Gemma.

'Broke his leg, damn fool.' Eason looked down at the barrow he had just stopped trundling. Pig feed was indeed what it contained. 'I'm getting fair sick of doing this all day.' He looked back up at Ivor. 'You worked with pigs?'

'Not a lot,' said Ivor. 'But I could start today.' And so he did.

'Where on earth have you been?' Gemma said when he walked through the kitchen door. 'I've been worried out of my skin.' She did look worried, Ivor had to admit. Pale, drawn, and as if she'd been crying at times.

'I'm sorry,' he said, and took her in his arms. 'Only so much has happened. Most of it bad. The last bit's good, though. But I couldn't face you till I'd got things right.' Once he'd come out with this it seemed to him that it was true. The thing he had invented had become real. He found that his voice shook, and he was afraid he might start to cry himself.

'What are you talking about?' Gemma asked, pulling herself just far enough apart from him to see into his face. 'You didn't even phone.' Her voice trembled too.

'You knew I was with Mark. I thought you'd understand that meant I was OK. Not coming to any harm. But yes, I should have phoned, I guess.' They were still clasping each other's hands.

'The meeting with this man. Didn't it go right, my darling?'

'No, but it was worse than that. I lost my job.'

'You didn't! How?' Gemma's face seemed to flicker in response to surprise upon surprise.

'Old Gutsell said he couldn't afford to keep me on. That was yesterday morning, before I met Mark to go to London. Then this geezer his father knew wasn't interested in anything I had to show him. What a bloody day! I went back with Mark and stayed the night. I knew I had to get a new job today. Before I could come back home. And I did. I went to Birdskitchen this morning and got taken on. I've done a day's work already there. I hope you're proud of me.'

Gemma had to free a sleeve to wipe tears. 'I suppose I must be.' She let go of his other hand. 'I'm just very pleased to see you home. Safe. Please ... next time, just find a moment to phone, that's all.'

'I'm sorry, Gemma,' he said quietly. 'I wasn't thinking straight.'

'You must ask Mark over some time. He sounds like a good friend.' She smiled palely. 'Even so, he should have made you phone. Anyway, have him to dinner some time.' She looked around the kitchen, which had been a dark and horrid place for the past twenty-four hours. Now it seemed bright again with summer evening sun. 'There's a venison casserole. I made it for us yesterday, but couldn't eat any of it myself.'

Ivor said, 'Sorry,' again. He really was sorry that she'd been hurt; it must be horrible to feel so upset. But he didn't quite make the connection between her torn-up state and himself. He was, though, congratulating himself on the success of the little web of lies he'd spun. They had all come out so smoothly, so convincingly. He felt he'd created a little work of art. He had hardly needed to do it, really; it was just for practice. He thought it was a good idea to keep your hand in at that kind of thing. Then, if the day came when you needed to lie as if your life depended on it, you'd be up to the task.

'These things are often even better when you cook them up again the second day,' Gemma said. She was talking about the casserole, which they were now eating: diced venison with shallots and mushrooms in red wine, and parsley stirred in a second or two before it was served.

Ivor stopped spooning up gravy to agree. 'It's great,' he said.

'Now there's something I have to discuss with you,' Gemma said, laying down her own fork. 'I've been asked to make two trips to Germany in the next six weeks. To promote the new translation. Two or three days each time. It means hotels, TV and press interviews, meetings with various people who can do some good. The thing is...'

'The thing is,' said Ivor, nodding his head slowly, 'you're not sure if it's a good idea to have me tagging along.'

'I wasn't going to put it like...'

'No, no. It's OK. I do understand. Meeting the press and all that. Author with child lover in tow... It wouldn't do your reputation there much good. They'd be making a story out of all the wrong things.' Ivor smiled encouragingly across the table. 'I think it's right that you should go without me. I promise not to mind. I'll be quite all right here.'

Gemma had hardly expected that this would go so smoothly. She hadn't forgotten that he'd been well able to take care of himself, living on his own at the bungalow a year ago, when they'd first met, but she hadn't presumed on his being so understanding. So grown up. 'You're wonderful,' she said.

Ivor was thinking how beautifully events were falling into his hands; it was as if he were reeling in a line of silvery, hooked fish. He had been very unsure how and when he could get up to London again to see Feri. He couldn't invent endless meetings that didn't happen but which somehow caused him to be absent overnight. But now the problem had disappeared. 'And maybe we could go and have a holiday in Germany another time,' he said. 'When there's no press to sniff around after us and you're incognito once again.'

'We will,' said Gemma, relief and enthusiasm charging her voice. She laughed that bell-like laugh of hers. 'We'll make that an important date.'

All was right again now in their two separate worlds. And that night he was wonderful with her in bed.

Birdskitchen was no longer quite the farm that used to feature in children's books, where there were pigs and sheep and cows and horses, hens and turkeys and ducks and geese and guinea fowl, all crowding to be fed by the farmer's wife at the kitchen door, and where every crop imaginable was grown. But neither had it progressed to being the unromantic factory affair that Reedbed had become. In terms of livestock it boasted sheep and pigs. There were also a few chickens, but these were not a commercial proposition: they were kept simply to provide eggs for the household. Three empty loose-boxes were the only reminder that Jack and his parents had ridden to hounds and stabled their own hunters in the yard where, a generation before that, Jack's grandfather had kept shire horses for the plough. A sizeable acreage was in use as hop gardens, there was grazing for the sheep – hay was made on the pastures every June – and some barley was grown, along with both winter and spring-sown wheat. There was also an apple orchard. Ivor soon had this information at his finger-tips. The potato crop he didn't need to learn about: he would not forget those back-breaking two weeks of the previous year as long as he might live.

It all came back to him, returning after ten months away. The people too. Though, sadly, not all of them. Jack Eason's wife had died. Ivor remembered her shooing him away from her front door the first time he had called, and although she'd been quite pleasant to him later on, when their paths occasionally crossed, he remembered her only faintly, as if in a few faded snapshots: a plain and demure woman, with little colour in her face, hair or clothes, and strikingly thin. That thinness should have been the give-away, Ivor thought with hindsight now. Cancer had swept her away six months before. Mrs Fuggle – whom Ivor might not have remembered but for her wonderful name – now had the fairly full-time job of housekeeper. She had been widowed for many years but, as she was well over seventy, offended nobody's sense of propriety by living in.

Andy still appeared from time to time when heavy tractor work was required. There were two tractors on the farm, which everybody drove, but Andy's brilliant blue monster was in a different league. Heinz, the German foreman who muddled up his positive and negative sentences, was officially retired now but was pressed into service for odd jobs pretty regularly. Frank the pig man would not return for a few more weeks, but here was Robbie still, with his string vests and curly hair. 'The bad penny returns,' he said to Ivor on his first day back. He didn't say it maliciously, Ivor decided, though he didn't smile. Ivor thought that he too might benefit from Gemma's unconscious lessons in the social graces.

Then there was Jack Eason, his new boss. Farmers came in all shapes and sizes, as Ivor, who had been at school with the children of so many of them, well knew. There were those whose cars were housed in a building that rhymed with barrage, others who rhymed it with the carriage that might have lived there long ago. Some sent their sons to Eton, and had living-rooms full of Dutch marquetry and glass-fronted cabinets containing porcelain from Dresden and Sèvres. Others lived in tumbledown houses that contained furniture of the kind that was most usually to be seen on top of skips. Ivor had never met Mark's father, but could guess him to be somewhere in the posher half of the spectrum. Jack Eason was somewhere nearer the middle of the range.

Last year Ivor had had little to do with Jack, except on those late evenings loading hops into the kilns and going on afterwards to the pub. Back then Jack had been a fifty-something with a forty-something's energy and looks. Now he was still fifty-something, but looked sixty or more. That could happen, Ivor thought, if you lost a wife you loved. It could happen if you simply lost a wife. Jack's head of thick grey curls was even greyer now and his face, always of the craggy kind, had the look that people call noble, or leonine, when it's too late to pay it the kind of compliment they'd give to a younger man's. Ivor thought it unlikely that Jack would be able to attract a new mate at his age, living in this isolated place, two miles from the nearest village, let alone town. Even though his assets in terms of land and buildings were considerable, there were Mark's words to remember: a farmer's only rich when he's dead.

Feeding the pigs and mucking them out did not take all of Ivor's day. He was expected to take his share of the general chores around the farm as well, whether that meant castrating sheep, mixing concrete or carrying out those endless repairs that old farm buildings so endlessly demand. Jack took him one day to the side of the huge black barn and pointed up to a dozen loose and slipping planks. 'Think you can get up a ladder and fix those?' he asked.

'I'm a carpenter, remember,' Ivor told him, grinning. 'Piece of cake.'

'I'll remember you said that,' Jack told him with a very set face, but then he relented and returned Ivor's smile. 'Spare planking's inside if you need.'

Ivor opened one of the two huge doors, each one fifteen feet high and seven wide. The top of it waved about as he pulled it, like theatre scenery. Leaving it open to let the light in he went inside. For some reason or other he had never been in here before. Now he stood

looking around him and especially up, the way people do
when they walk into an ancient church. This barn was
actually built much like a church, though all in wood.
His eyes grew slowly accustomed to the dark. He could
see pinprick light holes between tiles. Beams towered
upon beams. The back of the barn was like the side aisle
of a church, visible through a row of timber pillars. Once
it had housed cattle over winter, but was empty now.
The two ends of the barn had been turned into two floors
of storage space by the addition of plank floors seven
feet above the ground. The vast central space, like a
church's nave, rose uninterrupted to the ridge-pole of the
roof. High in the gloom were the king-posts, mounted on
tie-beams... It was obvious now. Ivor was looking at the
skeleton of a hall house. Not that this barn had ever been
a hall house. It was just made the same way. The
farmhouses of Gatcombe and Birdskitchen would look
like this if floors and ceilings and the in-fillings of the
walls were taken away. Great Dixter would look like this
too. Quite why this discovery was so significant for him
Ivor was unsure. He just knew that it was, or would be
one day.

Ivor collected some planks from inside the barn then
closed it up. He found a long ladder. Then he placed his
tools and nails in a cloth bag that had a butcher's hook
threaded through the handle so that it would hang on the
rung beside him as he worked. Once he'd thought it
through carefully, and made sure to anchor his ladder
securely at the bottom before clambering up, the repair
was indeed a piece of cake. Jack Eason could have seen
what a good job Ivor had done by looking up from the
ground. Nevertheless, he insisted on going up the ladder
afterwards to inspect the work from a distance of less
than a foot.

That was one of the tiresome things about his new
boss, Ivor thought, as he held the bottom of the ladder,

waiting for Jack to descend. He had an obsession about checking every bit of work that any of his employees carried out. Every knot or lashing was checked out, pulled and tugged at, to see if it would come apart. A week earlier Jack had given Ivor the elementary task of replacing two rotting railway sleepers that formed a simple bridge over a drainage ditch with two new ones. It was a job that you could hardly go wrong with: an eight-year-old could have managed it if he'd been strong enough to drag the baulks. Yet Jack had come on a tour of inspection that took him half a mile across his land, in order first to look at the structure and then to bounce and jump up and down on it with great energy and all his weight. As Ivor watched it had gone through his mind that it would have been fun to sabotage his own efforts and watch his boss tumble into the stream. Of course he hadn't done that. But later he'd told Andy about it in the pub. 'Funny you should say that,' Andy said, giving him a mischievous twinkle. 'I've been tempted to do the same thing. Be the end of my job, though.' They both laughed.

This obsessive checking of everything brought back the memory of Gutsell's trying to pull Ivor's first chair to pieces. But Jack was a fairer, kinder boss than Gutsell had been. He might be gruff of manner and short on charm, but he was never cruel or vindictive. To Ivor, who had limited experience of bosses other than Gutsell, this came as an agreeable surprise. He was finding that he could rub along with Jack Eason well enough. The ladder began to shake. Ivor looked up. Jack was coming down now, against the black wall, beneath a blazing blue sky that billowed like a sail. 'Well lad,' he said. 'I'd say that's no bad job.'

It was one thing to listen to your youngest employee boasting of being a brilliant carpenter, another to see evidence of the fact materialising before your eyes day after day. Jack Eason's habit of tirelessly inspecting everything in minute detail turned to Ivor's advantage as time passed. Jack began to realise that, at least in the quality of Ivor's repairs to anything made of wood, he was getting much more than his money's worth from his temporary pig man. When Frank, leg no longer in plaster, returned to work in mid-August it was already time for the potato harvest, and extra labour was needed to cope with that. But unlike at Reedbed the year before, Ivor wasn't to be found scrabbling on hands and knees in the dirt behind the spinner but on one of the tractors instead, hauling the spinner up and down the rows, seated in relative comfort, while the ranks of casual workers behind him crawled, sack-dragging, and breaking their backs. After the spuds would come hop picking again and then apples. Meanwhile Jack was beginning to wonder if a way could be found to keep Ivor on beyond that.

Telephoning Feri was not easy. In those days few people had mobile phones: they were still the size and weight of gold ingots and cost nearly as much. Ivor, like most other people, relied on the land line at home and made use of public call-boxes when out. He couldn't use Gemma's phone to contact Feri, even when Gemma wasn't in: there would be an itemised bill which Gemma might, on a whim, decide to inspect. There were two call-boxes on Ivor's route to and from work. One was in Udimore village, prominently sited, and far too close to Albert Gutsell's workshop for him to use safely. The other was situated, rather improbably, at the meeting point of two narrow lanes in a very remote spot a little way from the main entrance to Peasmarsh Place. Perhaps that was where the mansion's domestic staff had made their private calls in days gone by.

Even here Ivor had to be careful. Nobody is anonymous in country districts and if anyone who was known to have a phone installed at home was spotted making use of a public box more than a couple of times, they would soon find themselves the object of speculation, the subject of many an interesting conversation in the supermarket and the pub. So Ivor took care to stop off here only when no cars or people could be heard approaching, and would hide his bicycle behind convenient bushes before going inside. He flattened his body against the instrument as he dialled, standing very still and facing away from the road. Anyone who saw him in there would have to be on their way to use the phone themselves.

'I can come up again in two weeks,' Ivor told Feri. 'Gemma's going to Germany to promote her books. It's over a weekend, so it all fits.'

'Look, Ivor,' Feri said. 'I don't think we should be doing this. Thinking it over, which I have done, I mean, it's so unfair on Gemma. If you'd made a break with her it would be different, but...'

'Yeah, but look. We already have done it. We can't undo it, ever. Going on seeing each other wouldn't make it worse for Gemma than it is. If she found out. Which she won't.'

'You'd be...' Knowing the female psyche better than Ivor ever could, Feri would have completed her sentence with the word *surprised*, but Ivor didn't give her the chance.

'Anyway, none of that's the point. I need to see you. I can't not see you. Soon. I'm like someone in the desert who's dying of thirst.'

Feri could feel the animal urgency of him even down the phone. She argued a little longer, for the sake of decency, but then gave in and they arranged to meet.

Even with Gemma away Ivor had to be careful about covering his tracks when he made his way to London to spend the night. First there was Gemma herself. She might easily decide to phone Gatcombe on the Saturday evening to see how he was getting on and check he'd fed the cats. So he told her he had some overtime to do at Birdskitchen and that everyone would be going to the pub afterwards, probably till late. He knew that by the time the pubs closed in England it would be past midnight in Germany, and was pretty safe in guessing that Gemma wouldn't call as late as that. If she rang on Sunday morning there would be a message on the answering machine, and he'd deal with that as and when – and if. By Sunday afternoon he would be back.

The cats were another consideration, but easily dealt with. Ivor gave them double rations before he left on the Saturday afternoon. They wouldn't die overnight, and would in any case tell no tales. Finally there was the manner of his leaving. Cycling up the hill and going to Rye station by the main road would take him past the nearest house, which belonged to a Mr and Mrs Broackes. They were a kind couple, who'd fed the cats when Gemma and Ivor had been to Tenerife and Marrakesh. Just the sort of people who, after seeing Ivor ride past on a Saturday and then back again on Sunday, would innocently say to Gemma, 'Next time you're both away, just leave the cats to us.' Then there was the house of Bob Jameson, owner of Gatcombe's fields and farm buildings, to pass, and a dozen other neighbours in between. So Ivor cycled down the hill instead, along Float Lane, where no-one lived, and caught a train from Winchelsea. He took the direction away from Rye, and changed at Hastings onto a London train. Nobody from Rye went to London that long way round, unless the Ashford line was closed, and Ivor was pretty sure he'd manage this unobserved. He did.

Ivor didn't pounce on Feri immediately he came through her front door, as most of her previous boyfriends would have done, insisting on sex at once before doing anything else, before even having a drink. Feri appreciated that. Instead they walked and talked together on Hampstead Heath, had a light supper, and then went to see a film: Postcards from the Edge. It starred Shirley MacLean and Meryl Streep. Ivor remembered the first girl he'd had sex with was called Meryl – whatever had happened to her? – and congratulated himself that what he had now, in terms of sex, in terms of the person to enjoy that with, was so much greater than anything that had gone before, greater to an almost infinite degree, as the stars outnumber earth. That thought came to him again later, when they were back at Highgate, naked together in Feri's bed.

Gemma phoned Gatcombe on Sunday night. Ivor, who had returned in the past hour, unseen by anyone, assured her that he was fine and so were the cats. Everything was going extraordinarily well in Germany, Gemma told him. She'd be back on Tuesday as planned.

When Tuesday came they met at the Plough at Cock Marling for their evening meal. Straight after her minor triumph and journey back Gemma wasn't in the mood to cook. Diners at the Plough were served at tables converted from old-style school desks. They even had inkwells for the pepper and salt. Hanging from the rafters overhead was an assortment of ancient farm equipment that ranged from an entire plough – Ivor dreaded having to sit beneath it in case its chains broke – to pitchforks whittled out of handily dividing branches of ash. Then there were mysterious wooden-handled tools that looked as if they'd been doodled in cast iron by blacksmiths on quiet afternoons, and offered for sale hopefully, in case someone could invent a use for them. But the food was good.

'It was actually great fun,' Gemma said, in answer to Ivor's enquiry about how the German trip had gone. 'I was invited onto an arts programme on ARD – it's one of the main TV channels, their equivalent of BBC1 – and simply given my head and allowed to talk about the books.'

'And your German?' Ivor queried, wondering a bit.

'A bit rough and ready, I should think, but I survived. I met a man, who was also on the programme, who offered me a job. Believe it or not. Oh thank you.' The menu had arrived.

'What kind of a job?' Ivor wanted to know.

'He's the head of an art school in Göttingen...'

'In where?'

'It's a major university town halfway between Hamburg and Frankfurt. It's like Cambridge or Oxford are here, and very pretty, or so he said.'

'And the job?'

Gemma laughed. 'Don't worry. I'm not going to take it. Especially if the books do well over there. But he's starting up a new course in book illustration – especially children's books. He wondered if I'd like to run it.'

'You said no.'

'Ivor, darling. You never say no. Not if you're an artist, of whatever sort. I told him I'd think about it. That is what you have to say. Remember that.' She looked back at the menu. 'Romney Marsh lamb shanks?'

When Gemma went back to Germany a few weeks later, Ivor again employed his successful, cycle-to-Winchelsea-station, tactic for getting away to London undetected. Again he spent a night with Feri, following an evening at a Prom. (Ivor, who had been to the theatre in London twice but never to a big concert venue was shaken by the sheer size of the Albert Hall and by the orchestra's voluminous sound. Shaken in a nice way though.) On his most recent visit to Highgate David hadn't been at home. Neither Ivor nor Feri had mentioned him and by now Ivor had almost forgotten the existence of the man. So finding him in the kitchen when they returned from their concert gave Ivor something of a jolt. But there was no sign of any bad feeling on David's face or in his manner this time; he seemed cheerful and bright. And what he had to say to Ivor was positively cordial.

'Remember I've got a brother down in your part of the world?' he said. 'In his last year at Canterbury.'

'Architecture,' Ivor said flatly. He'd remembered that.

'I'm going down there in a month or two. Thought it might be nice to meet up for a drink. I mean you and me. Do you have a phone number? When I know when I'm coming I could get in touch.'

'Canterbury's not exactly my back yard,' Ivor said. 'It's nearly forty miles away. Long way for a drink.'

'Whatever. A weekend's plenty of time to travel forty miles. Give me your number anyway.'

Ivor didn't particularly want to give David the phone number of Gatcombe but he had no good reason not to, and Feri was a restraining influence, standing at his side. He didn't even try to throw David off by including an incorrect digit or two. If he did decide to phone him up Ivor would be perfectly capable of telling him to take a running jump. So he recited his home number and watched David write it down. Then he gave no more thought to it.

It was two weeks later, and hop-picking time had come again, when David phoned. But it wasn't Ivor he wanted to speak to, it was Gemma. Ivor returned from work to find Gemma standing in the garden, waiting for him, her face clenched like a vice. 'Come inside,' she told him, in a voice he'd never heard her use before. Together with the face it told her that she knew, although he didn't immediately realise how.

Indoors Gemma let rip. There is a standard mental phrase-book for the use of wronged partners with which all people seem to be equipped at birth. Not a sentence from this manual did Gemma omit to fling at her young man. Ivor didn't even attempt to stop her flow. He just stood there facing her, looking into her face quite neutrally from time to time, at other times looking calmly around.

'You've nothing to say?' Gemma had reached the bottom of her handbook's last page and felt she had to comment on his silence.

'It's one of those things, I suppose,' he said laconically. 'Just can't be helped.' He shrugged. 'It isn't that I don't want you, Gemma. Please don't think that. It's simply that if possible I'd like to have you both.'

Gemma stared at him, her eyes bulging. Then she yelled. 'You chump! You utter, blithering idiot! Of all the...! Even a head-case like you must know it doesn't work like that. You don't have that choice. It's almost comical to think you thought you did. You don't have any choice. You've made your choice. Now get out of my house.'

At last she'd said something to startle him. 'What? Now?' He was seriously alarmed.

'I'll call the police if you don't. You'll find your things in the garage with your tools. Fetch them inside a week or they're going to the dump, workbench and all. Now go.'

Ivor thought for a moment. He decided that it would not be impossible to worm his way back into Gemma's heart, but he realised that it couldn't happen today. He said, 'See you around, then,' and without protest walked out of his benefactress's house.

SEVENTEEN

Inspecting Gemma's garage Ivor found his belongings neatly stacked: his clothes in the suitcase with which he'd arrived a year before, other odds and ends in carrier bags. A satchel contained his few papers and, more importantly, his wallet and newly acquired cheque book. He picked the satchel up at once; the rest would have to wait till he had transport bigger than a bicycle. As he stood there, looking at his things and thinking how pathetic they appeared, dumped on a garage floor like this, the urge came to him to burn Gatcombe farmhouse to the ground with Gemma inside it. But he didn't entertain that thought for very long. He knew enough to realise that, however unreasonable her behaviour had been, she had only acted in the way most women would, and did, and always had. He did try, tried very hard, to convince himself that he and not she was the aggrieved party, but even he couldn't quite manage that – although for a second or two he almost did.

The other thing that prevented him from taking such extreme action was the fact that he still wanted to be the owner of Gatcombe one day He had never been quite sure how he would accomplish this, other than by waiting to inherit the place on Gemma's eventual death, waiting patiently for the demise of a woman only thirteen years older than himself. Would he have to marry her perhaps? The prospect of making the property all his seemed now to have receded. But were he to set about the place with matches and petrol-soaked cloths it would disappear for good.

He got back on his bike. There was no point making for Winchelsea Beach: the bungalow's new tenants had already moved in, he knew. Nor were the floors he'd been used to crashing on in the old days still available to him. He had lost touch with that little band of teenage toughs he'd hung out with until a year ago: most of them had grown up and moved on as he had done, either geographically or in personal-evolutionary terms. There were two obvious options left to him. One was to cycle to the station – either Winchelsea or Rye would do, it didn't matter now who saw him go or who did not – and head up to London, to Highgate, to Feri's bed. But if he did that he wouldn't be able to get to work in the morning, and that might just possibly mean the end of his second job in three months. He didn't think the risk of that happening was all that great, but it wasn't a risk he was prepared to take at this particular time. The second option was to go back to Birdskitchen. They would be shovelling the afternoon load of hops into the kiln about now and later Robbie, back in his role of hop drier during these weeks, would be up in the oast looking after them until they were 'cooked'. It would be warm up there, with the burners flaring away below. Ivor would throw himself on Jack Eason's mercy, or on Robbie's, and ask whether, in these exceptional circumstances, he might bed down for the night on the storage floor. He jerked his front wheel towards the left and set off up the hill.

It wasn't much past six o'clock when he rode up the track to the farm. He made straight for the oast. Climbing the rickety stairway to the storage floor he saw Heinz tipping out hop pokes by the door of one of the kilns, while Jack shovelled them inside. The lower half of Robbie was visible through the open hatch: he was using a wooden rake to spread the green load to an even knee-high depth. Hearing Ivor's tread on the stair, and then seeing his head appear followed by the rest of him, Jack and Heinz paused in their work, turned and looked. They appeared faintly surprised, but only faintly. Jack half grinned. 'Fancy woman chucked you out, did she now?'

'After a fashion,' said Ivor, surprised into returning Jack's grin, albeit sheepishly. 'I was wondering if I could stop the night. On the floor here, like. Just for tonight. Till I get myself sorted.'

'Don't see why not,' said Jack. 'Meantime, do you want to give us a hand up here for a bit? Then we can all get to the pub a bit sooner.'

Robbie appeared, framed in the opening of the kiln. 'What's goin' on?' he asked.

Jack jerked his head in Ivor's direction. 'Looks like you got company for the night.'

Robbie couldn't join the others in the pub. A massive proportion of the farm's income derived from the kiln-loads of hops that would be dried in the next two weeks, and while the hops dried Robbie's skill in controlling the temperature of the kilns hour by hour would make the difference between a successful outcome to Birdskitchen's year and financial disaster. Jack promised to bring him back a bottle of pale ale.

Heinz and Ivor rode to the Cock Inn in the passenger seats of Jack's car. On their arrival they found Andy and Frank already there. 'Here's a nice surprise,' said Andy, looking up from his pint and giving Ivor a smile. He'd had a lot of time for Ivor since he had believed his story, or rather Mark's story, about those ghosts.

'It's no ill wind that don't blow nobody no good,' said Heinz, nodding gravely. No-one attempted to ask him what he meant. Heinz asked what everyone wasn't drinking and then walked with a sailor-like roll to the bar to get it. Pints all round. When, twenty minutes later, those pints had been supped to the last drops Jack fished in his pocket for money for the next round. Heinz wasn't staying, he said. It was still light enough for him to get back along the lane to his cottage on foot. He'd take up Jack's offer the next day if that was all right. Frank went too, leaving Andy and Ivor and Jack. Andy would only accept a half this time, because he had his tractor to drive home in the dusk, and Ivor thought it wise to follow his example. He was still a little careful, more careful than most seventeen-year-olds, where alcohol was concerned. Though Jack, who would be responsible for driving him back to Birdskitchen later, had no qualms about ordering himself a pint. Then, when Andy left at last, he bought himself a third. This time Ivor asked for a half of shandy. Were there to be a fourth round, he thought, he'd have to ask for lemonade. It would be a three-mile walk through dark and wooded lanes if it came to it. Ivor guessed he could manage it at a pinch.

Ivor watched as Jack dipped his finger into the foam that capped his pint, then licked it thoughtfully before applying the glass to his lips. It was the first time he'd been alone with his boss outside work and he felt as awkward and tongue-tied as most people in that situation do. But Jack seemed quite at ease with Ivor, seemed almost to be enjoying his company. Perhaps that was to be expected in a man who'd lost his wife and who shared his house now with an elderly housekeeper instead.

'I been thinking,' Jack said slowly. Such a long pause followed this announcement that Ivor wondered whether Jack had already said everything he wanted to say. But then he continued, not looking at Ivor but staring into the middle distance. 'I been thinking, what with you being so handy with chisels and saws and what not, that I could do with a bit of your labour over the winter. Can't offer you a full-time job, mind. There's still Rob and Frank, and Andy and Heinz as and when, to find money for. But part-time I could manage. And we could give you a room to sleep in. No rent to pay. You interested?'

Ivor was more than interested. He could hardly believe his luck. Jack's offer tied in neatly with an idea of his own that had been taking shape in his head over the last hour or so. It was the sort of idea that blossoms, irrigated by a couple of pints of beer, but that can wither sadly under the spotlight of the morning to follow. Ivor thought that this particular moment was perhaps the best time to present it, though it was not a thought he'd had even two minutes before. 'That's a wonderful offer, Mr Eason. I'd like to do that very much...'

'You accept, then,' Jack Eason said, and gave him a calloused hand to shake. 'And call me Jack from now on. Save you a bit of breath each time.'

'Could I...' Ivor's diffidence was genuine, not assumed. 'Could I possibly ask you something else?'

'Well, you could always ask, I suppose,' said Jack, sounding slightly miffed by the implication that his offer had not been quite enough.

'It's that, what with working for you being part time and that, and I'm trying to set up as a furniture maker and repairer in my own right, and having time to do this now but my carpentry tools and workbench are still in my, er, in Gemma Palmer's garage, and I need to find a place where I can keep them and possibly use them too...' Jack began to nod his head, seeing where this was leading and discovering that it was not going to be too bad after all. '...I was wondering if there was an empty corner of a barn somewhere, or even the oast during the winter...'

'I think we can accommodate you,' Jack said. 'Get Andy to help you get the stuff one evening after work. Barn'll be too cold to work in in the winter, and I'm not paying to heat up all that space.' He snorted at the idea.

'But you can clear out the old apple store and move in there.'

Ivor felt so elated by the turn things had taken that his apprehension about being driven back by his well-oiled boss vanished, and he jumped into the passenger seat with a bounce. And to his credit Jack had no problem with the drive home.

Ivor wasn't going to have to spend even one night on the storage floor of the oast. Mrs Fuggle made up a bed for him in one of the attic rooms then set to, cooking sausages for Jack and him, and for Robbie, who was able to take just enough time off from his hop watching to come in and eat, and drink the bottle of beer that Jack had remembered to bring him from the pub. Despite the protests of Mrs Fuggle, who had gone to the trouble of laying plates and cutlery in the dining-room, they all ate the sausages straight from the pan, with their fingers, in the kitchen. Even while Mrs Fuggle had been cooking them Jack had leaned over, feeling their sizzling skins, offering his own opinion on the precise moment at which each of them was fully done. Ivor wondered how Mrs Fuggle put up with it. What would Jack be like if she were cooking a Sunday roast? Perhaps that was something he'd discover in a few days' time.

After the sausages had been despatched, along with chunky bread and butter, Robbie went back to the oast and Jack retired to one of the front rooms, apparently quite happy with a bottle of The Famous Grouse for company. Mrs Fuggle made herself snug in the kitchen with tea and television. Ivor asked Mrs Fuggle if he could, just for once, use the kitchen telephone to tell his girlfriend where he was. It wasn't a very private conversation, with Mrs Fuggle sitting there pretending not to listen, but Ivor was able to explain his new situation to Feri, to let her know that things had turned out very much for the best, and that one of the advantages of the new set-up was that he could get up to London and see her each weekend without having to invent an excuse.

Then he took himself up to his new bedroom at the top of the house. The attic rooms were just like those at Gatcombe, although his bed was cold and the sheets a bit damp from disuse. But he wasn't fazed by this. He felt he'd managed to turn round a desperate situation, and was ready for, and optimistic about, whatever the future might hold. Damp bed-linen was only damp the first night. He knew he would fall asleep almost as soon as the bedside light was off, but for a few moments he lay in bed looking approvingly at the ceiling. Half buried in the wall beside him, running upwards, the bottom-most section of its branching oak crown just visible before it disappeared into the ceiling above, was a medieval king-post.

Gemma didn't leave the house for three days. She didn't eat, she barely slept. She heard the Birdskitchen farm truck arrive to collect Ivor's things and only looked out of the window long enough to check that that was actually what was happening. She saw Ivor, assisted by a man who looked about thirty, a big blond Viking of a fellow, stacking his belongings in the back of it. She turned away feeling giddy. Ivor didn't look in her direction, or if he did, his look didn't coincide with her glance from the kitchen.

She had never known such anguish of the spirit. She wondered if this was how believers felt when they cut their bonds with God. She remembered how she'd imagined herself behaving with the grace and wisdom of the Marschallin in Der Rosenkavalier, yielding the young Octavian to her youthful rival in a trio of voices that was one of the marvels of the operatic canon. Now she realised that Richard Strauss and his librettist

Hofmannsthal knew nothing. Less than nothing. Both men, of course. Between them they had created a monstrous deceit, a travesty of a woman's feelings, concealed serpent-like in a setting of seductive beauty. Those men knew nothing of a woman's capacity to be hurt by loss, of her capacity to be damaged, Gemma thought now, beyond repair.

She wrote to Feri. A terse, dignified letter, reminding her of their long friendship, speaking of her disappointment and sadness at Feri's betrayal of her trust. No answer came. What possible answer could there be?

At last a phone-call came from Jane, her sculptress friend. Not seeing her about the place, Jane wanted to know if Gemma was all right. Gemma said, no, she was not.

'It's that boy, isn't it?' Jane homed in at once. 'I know.' Gemma could imagine the corners of her mouth turning down at the other end of the phone.

'We've split,' Gemma said. She could as well have said, I've split, because it really felt like that. 'I'm afraid I haven't taken it well.'

'I'm coming over,' Jane said. 'Right away.'

Talking about it all with Jane when she arrived didn't make Gemma feel a great deal better all round, and yet in one or two particulars it did. She learnt that she could discuss the matter calmly, at least with Jane, and when Jane insisted they go out for lunch together the following day, and Gemma did go, she discovered she could do that too. That evening she telephoned Angela and spoke to her. It was like going back to the time, a year ago, when she'd had to announce to all her friends that she had a sixteen-year-old lover in tow: difficult, but once you'd managed the first conversation on the subject the next ones got slightly easier. The day after that she phoned her sister Sarah, to whom she hadn't spoken in a month.

If Jack decided on something, and on a method of doing it, then that was how it was going to be done. Even if, in putting a plan into action, it was found that there was an easier or a cheaper way to go, the better alternative was never adopted. You were stuck with Plan A, even when it had been demonstrated to be inefficient. Ivor was to discover this in the course of the business with the alder trees.

At the bottom of the farm, where the Eggs Hole Brook ran out of Eggs Hole to join the Tillingham in its broad valley, a spinney of ash and alder saplings grew near the boundary where the pasture came to an end. A local log merchant had had his eye on these trees for some time: they had reached about thirty feet in height and their trunks were nearly as thick as telegraph poles. Hops were long finished and now, in mid-October, the apples too. Over morning tea at the beginning of the week when autumn ploughing was due to begin Jack told Robbie and Frank and Ivor, 'Roger's made me an offer for them trees. Too good to say no to.'

Robbie nodded approvingly. 'Bit of good news, that. When's he coming to fell them?'

'It's not that good an offer,' Jack said, looking him in the eye. 'We're doing that bit.'

'We and whose army, Jack?' Robbie said, suddenly frowning.

'Come on, man. There's four of us. Two chain saws. The two Fergies with buck-rakes... We'll be done in no time.'

'You're having a laugh,' said Robbie boldly. 'The Fergies will never handle the climb out, not unless we go one log at a time.' Then, reflecting that he was talking to the man who paid him, he withdrew to a fall-back position. 'At least let's get Andy in on it. With a proper tractor.'

'There's nothing wrong with our Fergies,' Jack protested.

'Nothing wrong with 'em fifteen year ago,' put in Frank quietly.

Jack ignored him. 'If I have to pay Andy, bang goes the whole profit. May as well leave them for the woodpeckers.'

'What about Heinz?' Ivor asked innocently. They all looked at him.

'Heinz is seventy,' Robbie told Ivor severely. 'Can you see him hauling timber through thick briar?'

Ivor tried to visualise that particular scene. 'No, you're right,' he was forced to say, and that irked him because every time he had to say that Robbie was right about something he felt he was losing some kind of battle. Robbie hadn't shown any resentment of Ivor when he'd first arrived, but it had been building up as the weeks passed.

They began the following day, after the pigs had had their morning feed. It had rained in the night and the bottom of Eggs Hole was even more of a swamp than usual. Jack and Robbie drove the two small Fergusons down through the meadows, Frank and Ivor walking in their wake, with Jack's two sheep dogs gambolling along beside them, excited at the prospect of a day out.

Ivor's experience in working with wood did not extend to felling the actual trees. But he'd seen it done on TV and now he could watch how Robbie did it, while pretending not to, like a cat. You cut a wedge out of one side of the trunk, then sawed through from the other side an inch or two higher up; then you shouted, 'Timber,' and watched it crash. The first tree took no time at all to bring down. But then there were the side branches to saw off – dozens of the things. And then there was the next tree to deal with, and the next. Leaf-fall hadn't really begun yet, but the disturbance created by each collapsing tree triggered a mini-blizzard of half-dried foliage which caught in people's hair and clothes and at moments made it difficult for them to see. Meanwhile the brushwood had to be dragged to a bonfire in the clearing, which needed regularly to be splashed with paraffin to help the rain-wet sticks along. Once or twice Ivor's cry of 'Timber' rang out against Robbie's, their two falling trunks collided halfway down and swung sideways, sending everyone running and hopping through the brambles as they tried to get out of harm's way. The idea of safety helmets had crossed no-one's mind. Finally the trunks had to be hauled on ropes to where the tractors waited like patient donkeys, and rolled onto the buck-rakes that were coupled on behind.

By lunchtime the loads on the backs of the tractors looked quite big, though the spinney looked almost unaffected by the morning's work: there seemed as many trees still standing as before. They tied the loads on to the buck-rakes to stop them bouncing off, then set off up the hill.

It wasn't easy on the muddy surface. The two Fergies crawled optimistically up the hill, in bottom gear, throttles open to the full, and roaring till the whole Tillingham valley echoed with their din, and the noise sent the autumn lapwing flocks cartwheeling into the air. They had got nearly halfway up the steepest part of the climb when the front wheels of Jack's tractor rode up on a little lip of ground, no higher than a kerb-stone, where the soil had eroded away below. The tractor's centre of gravity, already dangerously far to the rear, now shifted still further back. Like a temperamental horse the tractor reared up on its hind wheels. Worse might have followed had not the cord that secured the load of tree-trunks to the buck-rake snapped under the strain, sending the logs rolling, bouncing and somersaulting downhill, higgledy-piggledy, towards the boggy edge of the stream. At least the tractor was back on its four wheels, and Jack, whose composure had been shaken for half a second, back firmly in his seat.

It took the rest of that day to collect the escaped logs. It took four more days to fell the remaining timber and to transport it, in minuscule loads, up to the farmyard for Roger the logger to collect with his lorry at the weekend. At no point were Andy and his magnificent machine summoned to save the enterprise. Heinz only got involved to the point of handing out a good deal of advice every evening about what they shouldn't do. And autumn ploughing was set back by a week.

'Of course you know what all that was about,' said Robbie to Ivor in the pub a few days afterwards. Jack had gone to the bar to order another drink, briefly leaving the two of them alone. It was a situation that Ivor never much liked.

'No,' said Ivor. He looked warily into Robbie's coal-sharp eyes. 'What was it all about?'

'About your fucking salary, that's what.' Robbie nodded his head two or three times to reinforce the point.

'What about yours then?' Ivor asked. 'He has to pay you too.'

'Let's get this straight,' Robbie said, leaning a little way over the table towards Ivor. 'I've been Jack's right hand here for fifteen years. It's going to stay that way. You may be his flavour of the month right now, doing everything he tells you – yes Jack, no Jack, lick your arse Jack – but that won't go on for long. Don't worry, mate. I'll make sure of that.' Robbie looked away for a moment, then back again. 'Andy losing out on work because you have to be paid.'

'Come on, man,' Ivor said. 'I'm just part time. If Jack can't afford me let him say so and give me the sack.'

'It'll happen sooner than you think.'

'Then let it. But it'll come from Jack, not you.' Ivor took a slow swallow of beer, rolling it round inside his mouth like a professional taster, to show Robbie that he wasn't intimidated.

'Letting you run your own cowboy business from the old apple store. Jesus...' Robbie shook his head in a what-is-the-world-coming-to sort of way and finished the last of his pint in silence. Then he got up and, without another word, left the bar.

Clearing out what had once been an apple store to create his workshop had not been a small task, and it made Ivor remember the story Gemma had told him about Hercules and the Augean Stables. But he needed to get it right. His workshop would also be his showroom, where his customers, once he had any, could come and see the work he had on display: its interest would be further enhanced by attractive surroundings. Perhaps in the future his paintings could go on display there too. But for the moment, with autumn coming on and heating arrangements not yet negotiated, paints and canvasses were safer in his bedroom.

Something that did have to be negotiated was the use of the farm phone for incoming calls. This had to include the services of Mrs Fuggle in answering them when he was not in the house. He reassured her that he wouldn't be expecting that many. He placed advertisements in Rye and District Fixtures, in the Wealden Advertiser and the Friday Ad. He chose the wording carefully to indicate that no carpentry job was beneath him, but that nothing was beyond him either: that he was up to undertaking high-end jobs, restoring and copying antique furniture and fulfilling commissions for expensive new items in solid oak. No job too small, no job too big. He thought for a moment about that choice of wording. Gemma would have told him to change big to great. He did.

His first customer – Mrs Fuggle wrote down the phone message – had a stripped pine chest of drawers whose drawer bottoms were damaged, and the runners warped with damp. It was an unappealing job, fraught with a multitude of tiny problems, and one for which he couldn't charge very much given the damaged article's limited worth. But he did it anyway, his customer went away satisfied, and he waited for better things.

Ivor was happy with his attic room. The dampness had disappeared after his first night. He was happy with the whole house, which he now had the run of. He didn't in fact use the first floor, of which Jack's bedroom made up one end and Mrs Fuggle's the other, with two more between them and the bathroom at the back. But the ground floor was a match for Gatcombe's in most respects. Where Gemma had converted the parlour into a study for herself, at Birdskitchen the parlour still remained: unvisited except by Ivor, and full of family photographs four generations old. The central room was just like Gemma's, handsomely beamed and with an inglenook: officially the dining-room, with table and oak chairs to prove it. The third front room, where Gatcombe's kitchen was, had become Jack's den, with guns and old newspapers and dogs snoozing around it. Furniture throughout the house appeared to have got mixed up in recent years. In every room cheap and cheerful kitchen chairs of deal and beech were randomly mixed in with finer things: a Dutch marquetry long-case clock from the seventeenth century, an out-of-tune square piano whose maker's label announced, *John*

Broadwood and Sons 1796; it had been played when Beethoven was still a young man.

The pictures on the walls were mostly portraits of frock-coated men from long ago. Some were ancestors of Jack's; he wasn't sure which. Ivor couldn't imagine what anybody would want with frock-coated old men who weren't their ancestors, in pictures whose varnish had darkened to the colour of pitch. He wondered about asking to put some of his own work on the walls instead. Perhaps after Christmas. Perhaps after Feri had seen the place.

Ivor had an idea for a new picture, though it probably wouldn't do to hang it in Jack's house. He wanted to capture the moment during the alder-trees disaster when the tractor had got up on its back wheels, Jack had risen from his seat and leaned forward across the steering-wheel in a desperate attempt to make it go back down, and the tree-trunks had leaped into the air behind, just before making their spirited dash for freedom down the hill. Disasters and accidents made great subjects for artists, he already knew. He thought of Breughel's Icarus. And his own picture of his grandmother's dying fish. Then there were all the depictions by medieval and Renaissance Christian artists of what they considered the biggest catastrophe since the cosmos began, the Crucifixion of Jesus of Nazareth, the killing of God himself by mankind.

Violet had told him when he was a child that Christ had died to redeem the world, though he'd long ago stopped trying to get his head round that. But he wondered, did the art that sprang up as a response to that death, and to all those other catastrophes – mythic like Icarus's or real – in some way redeem the disaster? Did it to some extent make things all right?

EIGHTEEN

Gemma had expected that of all the people she knew the most likely to say 'I told you so' would be her sister. So it was a real, if minor, consolation to find that she did not. 'You poor darling,' she said instead, and then startled Gemma by behaving completely unlike the person Gemma had known for thirty years. 'You need to get away. I'll come with you. We'll do it in the morning. Get hold of that woman who looks after the cats, then get your passport and a toothbrush. We'll meet at Gatwick at twelve o'clock. Pick a destination and just go.'

'But what about Jeremy? The kids?' The idea had caught Gemma's fancy straight-away, but she could think of a dozen obstacles that would have to be demolished first.

'Mum'll come over and cook. You know how she loves being granny. Don't say no, Gemma. Say you'll come.'

Gemma said yes. When she'd put the phone down it occurred to her that her sister might have dreamed for years of carrying out this madcap idea but until now had had no suitable pretext.

Gemma summoned Mrs Broackes to feed the cats for a few days, then phoned the American School and told them she couldn't come up to town that week. She packed a small hold-all and next day at noon met Sarah in Departures at the South Terminal.

A flight was leaving for Barcelona at two o'clock. There were seats available, though the woman on the ticket desk didn't manage to hide her surprise at being asked. A few hours later they had joined the evening *paseo* along the Ramblas.

'What about getting right away,' Sarah said. 'I don't just mean like this, a weekend in Spain. I mean selling up your country pad and making a new start somewhere else.'

'Are you sure it's not you who wants to do that?' Gemma said, looking at her closely. 'And you're projecting your idea for escape onto me?' Sarah's marriage with Jeremy always seemed as solid as cement, and her contentment with life too, but people outside a marriage could never know exactly what was going on within – and sometimes that went for the people inside too.

Sarah assured her that she was not thinking about escaping from anything herself. Her concern was entirely for her sister. They stopped where chairs and tables were set out along the wide pavement, sat and ordered a juice each, and watched the other people walking bare-armed in the dusk and the street-lamps coming on. Autumn, already making the Brede valley melancholy with mists, would not come to Barcelona for a few weeks yet. Gemma told her sister about the offer she'd had in Germany to teach at an art school there.

'You must take it, of course,' said Sarah. 'It couldn't have come at a better time. These things are meant.'

'I did say I'd think about it,' Gemma admitted, 'though that was mainly to shut him up. But that was weeks ago. It'd be too late now.'

'You must phone the man as soon as we get back,' Sarah said. 'See if the offer stands. Promise me.'

They spent three days in Barcelona and its environs: Sitges one day, Tarragona the next. Gemma found her emotions had arranged a kind of cease-fire, a truce with her during these few days. It was as though she'd stopped feeling the hurt of things. As with a local anaesthetic, you still knew what had happened to you and what was going on, but there was no real pain. She wondered how long this would last, and what she would feel like when it wore off.

Back at Gatcombe Gemma checked the cats and turned the heating up, then looked at her post. One letter bore a German stamp on its computer-addressed envelope. Inside the address read: Kunst Akademie Göttingen. Her contact of a few weeks earlier was writing to ask if she would honour his school by accepting the offer he'd already informally made. He hoped she would have no objection to his telephoning her to discuss it further in the next few days.

He didn't have to telephone. Gemma phoned him first.

Ivor spent some time wondering if anything could be salvaged out of the wreckage of his relationship with Gemma. Despite the fact that he now lived in a farmhouse that was almost identical to Gatcombe, if a little less elegantly furnished, he would still have liked to get his hands on Gemma's house. It wasn't as if he was the owner of Birdskitchen; he was just someone who lived under the roof. At least at Gatcombe he'd lived as Gemma's equal, even if she hadn't agreed to let him restore it to its medieval splendour as a hall house. But he couldn't see any way to get Gatcombe back without prostrating himself in front of Gemma – possibly literally – and begging her to take him back. And he didn't see how he could do that without losing Feri, which he was not prepared to do, since she was by a million times the most important thing in his life. No solution came to him. He made no attempt to contact Gemma and, as far as he knew, she didn't try to contact him either. They had not even run into each other by chance in Rye, and Feri had heard no more from her since that letter.

One day in December Ivor was startled to catch sight of a photograph of Gatcombe in the window of the estate agent's in Cinque Ports Street. He peered closely. The house was not for sale but to let. A couple of days later he cycled over to Float Lane and called on Mrs Broackes. He was greeted at the door by M'pusscat and Tiramisu, who twined themselves, purring, around his legs, and that pretty well answered his question before he asked it. Nevertheless Mrs Broackes was able to sketch in some details which the cats could not. Gemma had moved to Germany to start a part-time job teaching in an art school. Mrs Broakes called it a very prestidigious one. She thought she might stay in Germany for several years, though not for ever – which accounted for the house being to let rather than up for sale. There was already someone interested in taking Gatcombe; they were hoping to move in in the New Year. In the meantime she, Mrs Broakes, had been awarded custody of the cats.

'Funny, Gemma wanting to move so far away all of a sudden,' Ivor said. 'She told me about that job in Germany. Said she wasn't going to take it. And she did love Gatcombe very much.'

Mrs Broakes gave Ivor a look that he didn't want even to try to interpret.

Feri paid one of her rare visits to her parents in America over Christmas. Since they were now divorced that actually meant a separate visit to each of them, but that was modern living, Feri said. Ivor was left to choose between the company of Norma and Michael in York and that of Jack and Mrs Fuggle at Birdskitchen. He looked forward to neither prospect, as he had been hoping for a Christmas alone with Feri in Highgate. But since that was not to be, he opted to join his mother and her husband, though he made his getaway afterwards as soon as he reasonably could. On his return to Sussex he found Jack looking as though he had done nothing but drink since he'd been away, and the disapproving look on Mrs Fuggle's face suggested strongly that this had been the case. But they both looked a bit pleased, or simply relieved, to see him back, which cheered him a little bit.

There wasn't that much work for Ivor on the farm in January and February. But by now he had a commission for a set of dining-room chairs in oak which kept him busy in his own workshop. From time to time Robbie would look round the door, grunt unattractively and disappear again. Ivor took no notice. He'd managed to keep Robbie's hostility in check by being scrupulously polite, though not over familiar, with his wife, and friendly to his three children: the family lived in one of the cottages adjoining the farm.

Ivor spent some of his spare time in the big barn, staring round its cavernous interior and thinking about the potential that it held. After a while he took to going inside with a sketchpad and making progressively more detailed drawings. Then he took a massive tape-measure in and started to collect its vital statistics. An idea was shaping up.

Lambs came, and spring sowing, and the women were drafted in to re-string the hop gardens: attaching thick sisal to the metal hooks embedded in the ground beside each dormant hop root – called a hill – and threading it up to the overhead wires that criss-crossed the gardens, supported by sixteen-foot poles. The apple trees were pruned and sprayed, and the pigs grew fat and went to market. The lambs grew up and followed in their turn.

You could remove the barn doors, Ivor realised, and fill the space with a huge window, like the one at Dixter, in the great hall. Cut dormer windows in the glorious ski-run of the back roof – the catslide, it was called – and make any number of bedrooms. Leave most of the skeleton on view, including the mighty king-posts that braced the ridge-pole, but in-fill the walls with modern materials that kept in the heat. He was undecided about whether you'd have to build a chimney stack in the side wall of the great hall or whether you could simply make a fire in the centre and cut louvres in the tiles above to let the smoke out as in the old days. He guessed there would be something about that in Building Regs.

He told Feri about his idea. She listened politely, but a little wearily. She had heard from Gemma how he'd wanted to tear the ceilings out of Gatcombe and create a medieval hall house there, and had thought back then that he must be barking mad. She hadn't been in love with him then, but now she was, which made a difference. Even so.

She still hadn't been invited down to see Ivor's new home, not even to see his workshop, which was something in which she could take a professional interest. She would be graduating from St Martin's in a year's time, and didn't know what she would do then. It was nice to have Ivor's company at weekends – well, more than just nice – but things didn't seem to be progressing very far. Ivor kept telling her he'd choose the right moment and invite her down to Birdskitchen soon, yet he never did. She made him take her camera down and take photos of the place. When she saw them, especially the pictures of his ongoing woodwork projects in the converted apple store, she was impressed and, unconsciously, metaphorically speaking, renewed his lease.

Ivor had been at Birdskitchen a little over a year when, on his return from London one Sunday evening, Jack invited him to drink a pint or two with him at the Cock Inn. 'Just you and me for once,' he said. This was unusual. If Ivor and Jack were at the pub together it was generally with other members of staff. Also, it wasn't Jack's habit to go out on a Sunday night. Unusual, Ivor thought, but hardly something to be worried about, even though he knew that most people worried automatically if they were invited for a drink by their boss.

Ivor said, 'Why not? Thank you. And why don't you let me drive?' Ivor wasn't sure whether Jack had drunk quite so heavily during his wife's lifetime, or whether it had come on since. He wasn't sure even whether Jack drank more now than he'd done when Ivor first moved in, or whether he was simply noticing it more. But having been employed previously by the teetotal Albert Gutsell it seemed to Ivor that he was now dealing with the opposite end of the spectrum.

Jack ordered two pints at the bar, then joined Ivor at a table near the fire. 'I been thinking,' he said. Ivor remembered how Jack had said exactly that, in exactly this spot, when he'd offered him his present part-time job. Mixed feelings arose in him. With his furniture business taking off so well now, would he have time – should this be Jack's intention – to work for him full time?

Ivor waited, his heart speeding up just enough for him to notice, while Jack took a deep breath, then a swallow of beer, then another deep breath. At last he said, 'You know I got no-one to hand Birdskitchen on to when I pass on. No kids. Not even a younger brother. The wife's family were never close...'

Ivor commanded himself to think of nothing. Jack Eason was surely not about to announce that he intended to leave the whole works to him. Then he was startled to hear his own voice say, 'Mrs Fuggle. You're going to leave it to Mrs F.'

'Mrs Fuggle?' Jack sounded really surprised. 'Nah. What would she be wanting with a farm and a big house and all? At her age. She'd only go and hand it on to her

idle oaf of a son. Great layabout. Good-for-nothing.'
Ivor's eyebrows went up. He'd never heard anything
about Mrs Fuggle's son, didn't know she had one.
'Down at Brighton, working the fairs that come in from
time to time. Drawing the dole year after year. No,
there's no way I'd be letting him get his hands on
Birdskitchen and drive it to rack and ruin. No, I got a
better idea.' He turned towards Ivor, opened his blue
eyes wider than Ivor had ever seen him do before, and
smiled at him. 'I'm thinking I might leave it to someone
who cares about the place, who works harder than
anyone I ever met, makes a good fist of every job he
puts his hand to, and has a bit of business sense. Now I
wonder where I might lay my hands on such a person.
Any idea?'

Ivor's relatively new ability – learned from Gemma –
to handle difficult conversations deserted him then. He
couldn't find any words at all. His heart was flapping
away so violently inside his rib-cage that he could
imagine it would fly out of his mouth. Hoarsely he got a
word out. 'Robbie?' Then, mouth and eyes wide open,
he stared at Jack in an agony of uncertainty as to what
would come next.

'Oh, Robbie'd like to get his hands on a farm of his
own, I don't doubt. Him and his wife and brood. But, for
all he's a good enough worker, it ain't him I had in
mind. There's a mean streak there somewhere, I always
reckoned, though I couldn't put a finger...' Then Jack
laughed out loud, in appreciation of his own cleverness
and Ivor's slowness to catch on. 'It's you, you great
lummox. Yes, you. I want you to run the place after I
retire, and then have the place to do as you will with
after I'm dead. What do you say?' Jack gave him another
smile, which was intended to be encouraging but
actually looked quite alarming.

'Jesus, Jack! What can I say? I mean...' Ivor paused and the shadow of a thought fell across his face. 'I mean, you could be winding me up.' As he spoke the words Ivor felt increasingly sure that this was the case. 'Guess you must be.' Now he was certain. He added, 'Good joke, though.' He didn't mean that. If it had been a joke, then it was the cruellest one anybody had played on him in his life. 'Gosh, Jack. You nearly had me there.'

Jack looked at him gravely. 'It ain't no joke. It ain't a leg-pull. What do you youngsters call it theses days...? It's no wind-up. A joke's a joke, but I'm a fair man. I'd not say what I said just now for a joke. Not to you. Not to no-one. Tomorrow I'll go to the lawyer fellow in Rye and make a will. You shall see me do it. That I promise. Now what do you say?'

Again Ivor found himself bereft of words. 'Wow. Oh wow. Whatever can I say? Except the obvious. I mean, if you are serious, that is, I'd have to say thank you. Thank you very much.' Ivor felt very choked up and, curiously, close to tears. It hadn't been easy to get those last words out. Even so, they sounded less than adequate. He said, 'I guess thank you doesn't sound like quite enough, does it?'

'Then let's just drink to the new situation instead, shall we?' Jack raised his glass and, wordlessly, Ivor did the same.

Ivor didn't phone Feri with the news that night. He didn't know how he'd find the words to explain the extraordinary event that had taken place. He was afraid he might cry down the phone. Besides, for all that Jack had sounded genuine enough, he hadn't actually written the will. Nothing was down on paper yet. And Ivor had heard Gemma use an expression which, while it amused him, he felt expressed a very important truth: the opera isn't over till the fat lady sings.

All the next day Ivor kept his eyes on Jack and Jack's car, as far as he was able to. By the end of the day there was no sign that Jack had been to Rye. After supper, and after much indecision, he knocked on the door of the room where Jack kept company in the evenings with The Famous Grouse, watching TV football with the sound turned down, and said, 'I'm sorry to sound... I don't know... I mean, I just wanted to ask you if you'd gone to Rye today. You know, that business we discussed last night.'

'Yes,' said Jack. Then he looked uncomfortable. 'Well, I mean, yes and no. You can't just walk in and see a solicitor, which I wasn't thinking when we spoke last night. You have to make an appointment.'

'And...?'

'No. Not yet. Must do that tomorrow. Haven't forgotten, though. And don't you worry, Ivor. I haven't changed my mind. Nor I will.'

'Would you like me to phone up and make the appointment?' Ivor offered.

Jack sat forward in his chair and placed his hands on the arms as though he was about to stand up. 'Good God, man, no! What do you think I am? Some senile old... Look. Put your mind at rest. Get a good night's sleep. Tomorrow without fail.' He sank back into his previous attitude, comfortably slumped, and gestured towards the bottle at his side. 'Want a low-flier before you go?'

'No thank you,' Ivor said. 'Thanks for the offer.' He withdrew backwards from the room, like someone in the presence of royalty, and closed the door behind him.

The next day again nothing happened, as far as Ivor knew. He didn't tackle Jack a second time, but he did cycle to the call-box in the lane and from there telephoned Feri. 'Something's happening,' he told her. 'I really can't tell you what it is, because it's at a stage where it still might not come off, and I don't want to put a curse on it. All I can say is that if it does happen it'll be very big indeed for me. Actually, for us.' It was the first time he'd spoken to Feri like this. It was the first time he hadn't felt that she held all the cards. Feri was curious, but didn't try to wring any more out of him. He said he'd be able to tell her more when they met at the weekend. When Feri put the phone down she felt a sense of suppressed excitement, but it was somehow tinged with fear; she didn't know why.

In the morning Ivor did something he'd never done before to anyone. He gave Jack a look. He'd practised the look in the bathroom mirror and had a pretty good idea of how it might work. It was the look of a spaniel that wants to go for an especially long walk but fears such a treat to be unlikely. Later in the morning Jack came to see him in his apple-store workshop. 'Look, Ivor,' he said. 'I been thinking. Those solicitor boys cost. Usually unnecessarily. That's why I didn't have my will done before. Well, not since Nell died. My father wrote his will on a piece of paper with his own hand. He wrote it clear, and signed it and had it witnessed by two folk. Nothing wrong with it, there wasn't, and everything came to me.'

'You were his son, though,' Ivor said. 'I'm not yours.'

'You don't worry now,' said Jack. 'I'll write it now, you'll see it, and you'll see me get it signed this evening in the pub.' Then he turned and walked out of the workshop.

Ivor had never seen a will before. He studied Jack's carefully. And to his credit Jack seemed to have written it carefully too. The entirety of Jack's estate – with the exception of seven thousand pounds which was left to Robbie, and another two for Mrs Fuggle – would go to Ivor, who was also to be Jack's executor. Ivor had a rough idea what being an executor meant, though none at all of what it might entail in practice. Jack had taken Ivor to a different pub, choosing one where Robbie and Andy and the rest were unlikely to be: the Peace and Plenty, on the way to Rye. A farmer whom Jack knew, in the way that farmers know each other, only slightly but since the year dot, was asked to sign and date the now folded-over document, and the landlord obliged with the second signature, standing behind the bar beneath the record-breaking pike that kept a lugubrious eye on the proceedings from within a glass case. Ivor, trying not to look too interested and keeping a certain distance, nevertheless was careful to watch the proceedings too. Was everybody writing legibly? Had they remembered to put their addresses? Later he saw that they had.

It was with a massive sense of relief that Ivor finished his first pint and offered to buy Jack his second. There lingered at the back of his mind a nagging feeling that all this should have been done at the solicitor's office, whatever the cost. Things had changed since Jack's father's day. A farm was a business. Shouldn't there be systems in place to deal with the running of it in the event of Jack's decease? This had all seemed too simple. Yet, as Jack had said, a will was a will. Even Ivor knew that. It had to stand, unless someone found a reason why it shouldn't. (For some reason the thought of cousins in Australia jumped nastily out at him.) Or unless Jack one day wrote a new one on a whim.

At least he was confident enough to phone Feri – though not to use the phone at Birdskitchen, again he cycled along the lane – and tell her the good news.

It made a difference. Feri was ashamed of the fact, but it did. She was still besotted by the beautiful teenager who had so romantically come in search of her: she thought of him as someone like the miller boy in Die

Schöne Müllerin. Yet, like the miller's daughter, she was conscious of his lack of substance in worldly terms. Even if he had managed to sell a few pictures for a Christmas calendar he was still very much a farm labourer. He might manage to sell a few more oak chairs but there seemed little possibility that he'd ever amount to anything else. And although Gemma had done a lot for his manners and education, there was a lot of the country bumpkin about him even now. To say nothing of the more unsettling things. The ghost things – not that they ever mentioned those now – and his general obsessiveness. Going to the same art galleries every weekend in winter, for instance, endlessly studying the same paintings. Sketching the same old buildings again and again. Painting dead animals that were in ever greater stages of decay. Although she would have hated to admit it even to herself, the more calculating side of Feri had begun to wonder if it was time to move on from him.

And now suddenly he was the heir to a sizeable chunk of Sussex countryside and a beautiful house. His tenure of the workshop where he made his furniture was secure for ever. It shouldn't have made a difference but it did. He'd been her toy-boy in a way, just as he'd been Gemma's, even if the age difference was much less great; he'd been her exquisite exotic pet. Now he was transformed in her mind from a talented but rather ineffectual artist into a serious craftsman, an entrepreneur with solid prospects, sure of both commercial and artistic success.

Feri congratulated Ivor. 'And now can I come down and see the place?' she asked.

'I guess you'd better,' Ivor said. 'I'll sort it out.'

'I don't see that there's anything to sort,' Feri answered, puzzled. 'If Jack's taken such a shine to you as that, I don't see you need "sort it out" with him before I come down one weekend.'

'Leave it with me,' said Ivor and rang off.

Thinking about it later, Feri realised that Ivor's news was a bit difficult to swallow. Farmers didn't usually take it into their heads to nominate their most junior employee as their heir. Could Ivor have invented the whole thing? Yet he'd shared with her his disquiet at the fact that Jack's will was merely handwritten, and told her about its being witnessed in a pub, even told her the witnesses' names, and about the watchful pike in the glass case. If he had invented the story, wouldn't he have invented a watertight document drawn up by solicitors? She took the leap of faith and decided to believe. She was still puzzled by Jack's action in leaving Ivor his farm, but then there was no end to the puzzling things that people did.

In a few months Feri would be leaving St Martin's and would need to harness her talent and training to the need to earn a living. That would be easier if her partnership with Ivor grew beyond the matter of the heart which it was, and became a business partnership as well. She found herself imagining the burgeoning of a country crafts enterprise that would be Ivor's and hers. If you put it all together, his furniture making and antique repairs, her scarves and curtains, dresses and fabrics for upholstery, his paintings, maybe also hers... There were the makings of a serious business venture, using premises that were in effect already theirs. Ivor's news might be bewildering but it was also positive. Feri was determined to make sure that was the way it stayed.

NINETEEN

Ivor had good reason to be wary of Jack where Feri was concerned, though it wasn't a reason that he intended to divulge. He was not surprised to find there was a quid pro quo in being left Jack's entire estate in his will. He knew that was what life was like. He was only a little bit surprised at the nature of this particular quid pro quo, which he discovered among the warm straw bales in the barn one autumn afternoon. And that limited degree of surprise was due mainly to the fact that Jack had been married until a couple of years before. Ivor had never been much troubled by the knowledge that some men enjoyed sex with other men (each to his own) but he'd thought that such men usually drifted into the bigger towns and became hairdressers, or students of interior design like David. But then he realised that if you were born with the prospect of inheriting a farm ahead of you, you were hardly going to up sticks and become a hairdresser in Brighton.

The sex itself was no big deal. Ivor knew that sex created all kinds of problems for some people. Perhaps for most people. But that only happened if you made a big issue out of it: if you told yourself, for instance, that it could only happen between yourself and such-and-such a person, or with a certain kind of person – gender-specific, or in special circumstances such as marriage. If you thought like that you were simply bound to get yourself into an unholy mess: that had been the case with Gemma, who had made an assumption about exclusivity between Ivor and herself that she'd never taken the trouble to mention to him. So long as it didn't involve any physical discomfort to himself – and he was well able to take care of himself in that kind of negotiation –

Ivor was not particularly troubled by the idea of sex with Jack, despite his maleness and advancing years. But he was not sorry that Jack felt the farm's outbuildings were the appropriate place for it. He remembered how he'd felt about Meryl: that she wasn't special enough for him to take her to bed at the bungalow at Winchelsea Beach. So he was pleased that Jack – probably out of fear of discovery by Mrs Fuggle – never forced his attentions on him inside the house, and that his attic bedroom could remain his private sanctuary still.

Despite his own relaxed views about sex Ivor knew that they were not held by everyone, and certainly not by most women. He knew better than to share the news of this half-expected development with his girlfriend. And without his telling her there was no way she could find out. At eighteen he had enough sexual drive and energy to keep a dozen people happy, not just two. But when it came to getting Feri down to Birdskitchen he knew he'd have to tread carefully. Somehow that was a thing he'd known all along.

In the kitchen one morning he showed Jack his drawings of the big barn re-imagined as a hall house. 'It's hardly used for anything right now,' he explained, intending no irony. 'Just a few straw bales when the Dutch barn's full. Stacks of wood. Nobody's kept an entire potato harvest over winter in a wooden barn since your father's time. Converted, it'd sell for a mint.'

Jack studied the drawings, frowning. He looked at each of them in turn, then looked through them again, then handed them back. 'What do I want to go and sell it for? Time'll come when I need that barn again. When things change. As they will. And what'll I do if you've gone and sold it to some troglodytes or hippies? They're the only sorts of folk'll want to live in a barn, converted or not. Fire in middle of living-room floor? Come off it,

Ivor. If I didn't know you better I'd say you was off your head.'

'Fair enough, Jack,' Ivor said, stowing the drawings away in the old music case in which he kept them. 'There's one other thing I meant to ask you. Could I bring my girlfriend down one weekend? Show her the place. Let you meet her. Would you have any objection?'

Jack looked taken aback for a second, but quickly concealed his reaction with a smile. 'Objection? No. What objection could I possibly have? But just to see the place, mind. I'm not for having her stopping over, sleeping the night with you. Not because of me, you understand. It's just Mrs F.' He nodded in the direction of the old dairy, now a utility room, from which could be heard the creak, squeak and soft thumps of the washing machine being unloaded. 'She wouldn't be happy with it, and we can't afford to upset her. Neither of us. Also...' He gave Ivor a man-to-man look. 'You get a woman into a place like this, you never get them out. Next thing, you'd probably be asking to move her in for good. So let the lass come and see the place, she's more than welcome, but let her buy a day return.'

It was more or less the answer Ivor had expected. Though when he thought about it afterwards he realised it was rather more negative than that. Jack had not only answered his immediate question but also the more long-term one which he'd been saving up to ask in a few months' time, once Jack had got used to the idea of Feri and seen what a wonderful girl she was. It was curious, he thought slightly bitterly, how people who had no qualms about enjoying physical intimacies with their staff in outhouses became squeamish at the thought of what those staff might want to do in their beds.

In the months since Jack had made his will, a time when he had been loth to drive into Rye to see his solicitor, he had got into the habit of driving there around lunchtime for a more relaxing purpose. He would take himself to the Standard Inn – it was another of those five-hundred-year-old buildings that Ivor would have liked to get his hands on if he could – and pass the midday hour with a pint or two of Harvey's ale. As time passed, his daily shift at the bar lengthened imperceptibly until it involved a pint or three, or a pint or six. The moon waxes just as imperceptibly, but always to a limited extent, over its allotted period of time, and then shrinks back again. In the case of Jack's pub visits there seemed to be no such constraint. Not now that pubs opened for twelve consecutive hours each day. Ivor wondered where this was going to lead.

It led to an accident. Jack was coming out of the pub at three o'clock in the afternoon. There was an awkward step up into the street from the doorway, which was dark just inside but, when the door opened, was flooded with light. Quite enough to blind you for an instant if you'd drunk as much as Jack had that lunchtime. The street outside was very narrow, just the width of a car, and Jack fell into the path of one. It was travelling at no more than five miles an hour and did little more than give Jack a shove as he stumbled across the pavement. But it was enough to roll him onto his back, and to cause a passer-by with a mobile phone to call the ambulance and the police.

By the time they arrived Jack had been helped into a chair that someone brought out onto the pavement from the pub. The shaken driver told the policeman who questioned him, 'He just jumped out under my wheels.' The other policeman, leaning rather more closely over Jack than Jack thought was polite, noticed the smell of his breath, as well as a slurriness of speech that might or might not have been caused by the fall. But the ambulance crew, once they had given him a general look over, pronounced him fit enough to go home. The police let the motorist go on his way, fully accepting the accident was no fault of his, but they had not quite finished with Jack. They told him quite sternly not to drive himself home, either that day or on any other occasion when he'd had a drink. Then they got him into the back seat of their squad car and took him round the one-way system to the taxi-rank, watching him carefully until he was safely inside one of the cabs that waited there outside the station and had been driven off. When Jack arrived back at Birdskitchen Mrs Fuggle took charge of him while Ivor rode back to Rye in the taxi to retrieve the car.

When Feri came to Birdskitchen the day was beautiful. The hedge-banks in Starvecrow Lane and its tributaries were starry with primroses and violets, white wood anemones and butter-yellow celandines; they made a mosaic of colour so bright that in the sunshine it dazzled the eyes and made them almost hurt. Hawthorn hedges were patched with gem-clean new leaf. The farmhouse shone white in the April brilliance, the cowls of its oast kilns proud as two white flags, aligned by the breeze, above the roofs. 'It's like Gatcombe all over again,' Feri said. It struck her more forcefully than it had done in the photographs she'd seen. 'But better in a way. Because everything around it still belongs. It's still part of a working farm.'

'To state the obvious,' said Ivor, slowing Jack's car over the pot-holes in the track. But he was pleased with Feri's reaction just the same. As they got out of the car Jack emerged from the hen-house with a basket of eggs. It made a bucolic picture. He walked up to Feri, smiled at her and gave her his hand. Ivor almost purred. This moment couldn't have been better choreographed. He had chosen the time – a little after eleven o'clock –

deliberately. It was the time of day when Jack was at his best, his hangover dispelled by a morning's work, the new day's drinking not yet under way.

Jack took them into the kitchen, and Mrs Fuggle made coffee for everyone, including Robbie and Frank, both of whom had seen the smartly-dressed girl step out of the car and at once found themselves more interested to meet her than they'd expected to be. Jack invited Feri to stay to lunch, although he'd already been told, along with Mrs Fuggle, that they wouldn't need providing for. Ivor would take Feri to one of the local pubs. Now that Jack's lunches were becoming increasingly liquid affairs this seemed a prudent plan to make.

Ivor gave Feri a tour of the house. Though its interior was shabby in comparison to Gatcombe's, Feri could see as clearly as Ivor that only a little effort would be needed to transform it into something equally lovely. She tried not to feel proprietorial as she walked through the rooms, but couldn't help running a finger over the nicer items of furniture – the oak dining-table, the Dutch clock, the square piano – that shared the rooms with discarded gum-boots, kitchen chairs and cardboard boxes full of who knew what. Over everything the spring sun threw undiscriminating folds of light. She touched a few of the square piano's keys and pulled a face. 'Couldn't you get it tuned?'

'For who to play?' Ivor asked practically.

'It's just the principle, isn't it?' Feri said. 'One day. Someone.'

In Ivor's workshop Feri inspected his current project: a copy of a Charles II chair, with barley-sugar-twist legs and hand-carved crown and scrolls at the top of its tall back. It was intended to complete a set of six, one of the originals having been broken beyond repair. One of the remaining five stood in the workshop to serve as a model. 'It's just about as close a copy as you could have,' Feri told him. She had only seen very small examples of his woodwork till now: things he could easily take up and show off to her in London. Seeing his large-scale work she was more than ever impressed.

'Got to pay someone else to do the cane-work,' Ivor said. 'That's one thing I can't do myself.'

'It'd be nice if I could help,' Feri said. Cane-work was one among her many skills. 'But it's not a practical option. Me in London and the chair down here.' They didn't try to take the idea further.

Ivor took Feri to the Cock Inn for a ploughman's lunch. He was well-known there by now, a regular visitor though still a cautious drinker. But, apart from his workmates at Birdskitchen, people were still wary of him. Some had been at school with him and either knew the reputation he'd had there for being rough, not to say a bully, or had direct experience of that side of him. Most people knew he had a girlfriend in London, but no-one had seen her yet. Ivor was pretty sure that once they had, his standing would change overnight – though this was not a thought that he wanted to share with Feri or anyone else.

Later that afternoon they went by taxi to Rye station and caught the London train. Ivor spent his Saturday night at Highgate as he always did. Together they ran over the day that had just passed. Both felt it had been a success. 'I don't know what all your fuss about Jack was for,' Feri said. 'He seemed perfectly OK. A gentleman. A bit gruff and woolly perhaps, like one of his own sheepdogs, but friendly as anything underneath.'

'You may be right,' said Ivor, still a little surprised by Jack's good behaviour that morning. 'I was probably worrying for nothing.' They began to talk with something like confidence about the possibility of Feri moving in with him at Birdskitchen once she'd graduated in the summer, and joining him in business in his workshop. It would be Ivor's job gradually to bring Jack round to the idea. He still couldn't share with Feri his reasons for thinking this would be a hard task. But he'd been buoyed by seeing Jack and Feri together and getting on so well. Jack had clearly found her attractive, everybody did, and Ivor had perhaps, though for understandable reasons, lost sight of the fact that Jack had spent most of his adult life married, and that good-looking women appealed to him as much as to anyone else.

But when he returned to Birdskitchen on Sunday evening Ivor was again reminded of the tough road ahead. His entry through the back door coincided with Jack's emergence from the kitchen with a tray on which had been set a plate of pork pie and salad, and a bottle of ale, en route for his TV and whisky room. 'Nice bit of skirt you got yourself, man,' Jack said to him, pausing on his short journey. 'American, is she?'

Ivor fine-tuned that. 'South American. Her parents anyway. But she's spent most of her life in New York'

'Bring her down again any time you want. Pretty girl like that's always welcome. Even Mrs Fuggle took to her. But I'm not having her moving in with you, so don't get your hopes up in that direction.' Ivor opened his mouth to say something but Jack carried on, compelled by the thought of a possible protest to get his answer in first. 'I have in mind for you to have this place after I'm gone. And you can do what you like when it comes to women then, but till that day comes, just let's do things my way, shall we?' He gave a wink that Ivor thought looked truly dreadful.

'Yes, I understand that,' Ivor said, trying to achieve a reasonable tone, 'but you wouldn't expect me to live as a bachelor for... I mean, you might live another forty years, fifty even, the way things are going – I mean medical advances and all that. You wouldn't want me not to have children in all that time – children to hand the place on to when my turn came – or to have them brought up in a poky London flat and I'd only get to see them at weekends. Would you?'

Jack did a pantomime of reeling backwards – though perhaps it wasn't entirely an act – so that his beer bottle skidded sideways along the tray he was carrying, and only just avoided disappearing over the edge. 'There, you see. I was right all along. You are serious about that lass. Looks like I'm going to have to watch you carefully.' Jack chuckled, then turned towards his sitting-room and disappeared inside, shutting the door behind him.

Ivor felt that stomach-tightening, breath-squeezing feeling that comes after spending any length of time trying to hold a rational conversation with someone in the early stages of dementia. Was it the drink that was doing this to Jack? he wondered. Or was it just another example of his extraordinary obstinacy, his refusal to go down the obvious path once he had made his mind up to take another one? Memories came back to him of the time, nearly two years ago, when they'd all spent a week cutting timber and hauling it up out of the spinney in Eggs Hole, instead of calling in Andy and his state-of-the-art machines. But whatever the cause of Jack's dog-in-the-manger position, Ivor was obliged to report back to Feri that for now at any rate no progress had been made.

Ivor thought again about the Eggs Hole episode. At the time he had wanted to do a painting of that moment in which disaster to Jack and the tractor had only been averted by the snapping of the cords that tied the tree-trunks to the buck-rake. He had made a series of preliminary sketches of the subject, but then other things had happened and the painting had not gone ahead. Now he found his interest in it reawakened. He searched out the sketches, studied them carefully, and then began to create the picture he'd envisaged all that time ago. It crossed his mind to replace the humble grey Ferguson tractor with a bigger Fordson Major, on the artistic-licence principle. With its bright blue paintwork and scarlet wheels such a machine would leap more energetically out of the canvas, in an echo of its energetic upward bound, like a racehorse commencing its rise to a high fence. But in the end he decided to let real memory be his guide: the small grey pony that was the Ferguson would be more truthful to the scene.

Also, the actual Ferguson was still on the farm, available to be painted in all its intimate detail: Ivor wouldn't have to scour the surrounding farms in search of a Fordson to model for him. He chose a cheekily big canvass, four feet by two and a half in height, and set to work in oils. He did most of the work in the apple store, from time to time working in the yard to capture the likeness of the Fergie. One afternoon he walked, with his easel, all the way down to Eggs Hole, and painted the background: the steep hillside, the spinney at the bottom beside the Eggs Hole Brook, and the view beyond it of the Tillingham valley meandering towards Rye. At this time of year there were no lapwing flocks to carve the sky, making the air plaintive with their *whee-whits*, but he brushed them in from memory. Later, back in the apple store, he painted Jack, caught in that straining attitude, instinctively searching for equilibrium, that is common to men and all animals when the container or vehicle they are occupying begins to capsize. He felt he'd captured Jack very well, actually restoring to him some of the youthful quality he'd had when Ivor first knew him, but which he'd lost on the death of his wife. The only liberty he took with his memory of the occasion was to add in a few whirling autumn leaves.

There had not been many flying around on the actual hillside that day, though there had been plenty down in the spinney; but Ivor felt justified in moving them those few hundred yards uphill.

When the painting was finished Ivor felt very pleased with it. With airborne leaves and lapwings, the rearing tractor, Jack halfway to leaping, or falling, off, and the logs tumbling and somersaulting off the back in frenzied disarray, it contained as much kinetic energy as anyone could want. Even Robbie, putting his head round the door and glancing at it, chortled and said, 'You got that moment to the life, mate. Hats off to you. What Jack's going to say, though...'

'He's not going to see it,' said Ivor without turning round. 'I'm taking it into Rye in the morning to be sold.'

Ivor drove into Rye with the painting, smartly framed in plain bare wood, on the seat behind him. He parked outside the door of the art shop in Market Street, causing all other traffic to mount the opposite pavement as it squeezed uncomfortably past, and took the painting into the shop. 'I'd like you to sell this for me,' he told the person inside. An insight honed over years of living above an antique shop had told him this was the boss.

'Pretty striking, I must say,' the man said, peering through spectacles. 'What sort of price were you hoping to get?'

'Four hundred pounds,' Ivor said straight away. 'Before you add your commission on, that is.'

'Four hundred?' The shop owner rocked back an inch. 'That's as much as most people earn in a month. If you want a sale I'd suggest something nearer two-fifty.'

'Took me a month and more to do the picture,' Ivor said calmly. He put the painting down on the floor, leaving it propped against the only available supports, which were the shop owner's legs. 'Won't be a tick,' he said, and walked out to the car, reached in through the passenger-side window and brought out a calendar and a Christmas card which with some forethought he'd placed on the front seat. 'Saw you had these for sale at Christmas,' he said, indicating the calendar, 'and these.' He flourished the Christmas card. 'And the year before. Sold a few of those, I bet.'

The shop owner got the message at that point. 'OK then. Didn't realise who you were. So point taken. Four hundred it is, plus my commission.' He smiled cautiously. 'In the window for four weeks, mind, then you collect it if unsold.' They shook hands and Ivor left the shop.

When Jack went into Rye he always parked in the High Street if he could, though year by year that was growing more difficult. When it was impossible he would look for a space down in Cinque Ports Street or, failing that, by the station at the bottom end of town. From none of these places did he need to pass the art shop on his way to the Standard or his other haunt, the Union Inn. But Ivor had forgotten Jack's trips to the bank. When Jack was forced to park at the bottom of the town his walk back up to the High Street took him straight up Market Road. Ivor remembered this only when Jack came bursting into the apple store one afternoon the following week.

'You want to make me a laughing stock?' he said. It wasn't quite a shout, but somewhere on the way to being one. 'Picture of me failing to control a fucking Fergie in a shop window for everyone in Rye to see! What was you thinking of?'

'It's nothing personal, Jack,' Ivor answered, momentarily taken aback but quickly recovering. 'No disrespect. It isn't you any more, you see. It's a piece of art. You need to realise that. I mean, it's you, of course it's you, but you transfigured by art.' He grinned involuntarily as a new thought struck him. 'It's immortality, Jack. You're immortalised on canvas, like the Laughing Cavalier or Henry VIII.'

'Henry VIII, my arse,' said Jack. 'And four hundred and sixty bloody pounds!'

Having achieved a friendly bantering tone Ivor stuck with it. 'I'll buy you a pint in the Cock tonight. And if the painting sells, I'll stand you a bottle of low-flier. Though it's only four hundred for me, the sixty's the shop's commission. Sure you don't want to buy the thing yourself?'

'My arse,' said Jack again, but he sounded mollified. The offer of a drink, perhaps, or the comparison with royalty, had softened him. With a grunt, but in a better humour than he'd shown when he came through the door, he left Ivor to his work.

Parking in Cinque Ports Street had one disadvantage for Jack in addition to the necessity of walking up the hill. He discovered it a few days later when, following a lengthy stay at the Union, he found himself trying to unlock his car opposite the police station. The officer who came out and stopped him was one of those who had attended the scene a few months earlier when he'd fallen out of the pub doorway. 'I really would advise you most seriously to get a taxi again,' he told him. Fortunately Jack was not so drunk as to argue the point. The policeman added, 'Very nice likeness of you, sir, in the window in Market Road.' Jack looked at him, uncertain whether to say something, then decided not to and walked, a little unsteadily, down to the station and the taxi rank.

Ivor was getting used to this now. He went back with the taxi to Rye to pick up Jack's car before its allotted span of parking time ran out. 'One of these days,' he said to the taxi driver, whom he had got to know quite well by now, 'he'll have an accident that's serious. A farm's not a good place to be working if you go getting yourself in that condition too often.'

'Too right,' said the driver. 'Farm's the kind of workplace where there's an accident waiting to happen around every corner.' As he pronounced the word corner he was forced into a violent swerve to avoid a woman who was using her child's pushchair, snow-plough fashion, to clear her path across Tower Street. He wrenched the taxi back on course. 'Same with this job.'

If Jack did meet with a sudden accident, Ivor thought, whether in traffic or on the farm, then Birdskitchen would become his much sooner than would otherwise be the case. Then he'd be able to do as he liked with the property. Move Feri in. Convert the barn into a hall house. Rip the ground- and first-floor ceilings out of the farmhouse if he still felt inclined to and make a second hall house. But how soon was sooner? If Jack suffered some fatal accident in ten years' time, say, Ivor would still be a youthful twenty-eight. But would Feri have consented to wait for him for all that time? In his heart Ivor knew that she would not. And if Jack turned out to have the survival capabilities of the proverbial cat, well, as Ivor had once said to him, he might live a further forty or fifty years – though the latter eventuality would see him still around at nearly a hundred and ten. On the other hand the way he was drinking at present suggested that scenario was not as probable as all that. Ivor didn't actively wish an early death on his benefactor. It was only the consequences of his death that were desirable.

A few days later Ivor came across Robbie near the pig pens, shovelling up the contents of two fertiliser sacks that had split and spilled. What had split them was the front wheel of the tractor, still parked where Robbie had stopped it, having just driven it round the corner of the big shed unaware of what was lying in its path. He looked up when he heard Ivor's footsteps. 'Look at this,' he said, sounding more than fed up. 'Jack just goes and leaves these here for anyone to crash into, forgets all about them and goes off to the pub. What are we going to do about him? I mean, Christ's sake! Drinking away the profits. Putting his health and life at risk. Not to mention bloody us.'

'Us? Do about him? ' Ivor queried. 'What can we do? Us.'

Robbie shook his head, looking exasperated, though whether with Jack or with Ivor it was hard to tell. He bent down again to his shovelling. Ivor also shook his head as he walked away. When he'd gone a little distance he turned and looked back at Robbie, who had his back to Ivor now but was still shovelling up. A thoughtful frown came and settled on Ivor's face. What could they do? Though in his mind Robbie and he did not constitute any kind of *us*.

TWENTY

Gemma put her unsold paintings and sketches into a sale in London. She took some of her more precious books and papers to her mother's house. Ursula helped her stash them in the loft, tight-lipped and uncomprehending. When you hadn't told your mother you were in a relationship with a young boy, you couldn't very easily explain that the reason you were taking up work abroad was because you were not. Sarah, honouring her promise to Gemma of two years before, did not enlighten their mother either. Back at Gatcombe other valuable small items were locked in the attic. The furniture and crockery remained where they were, for the use of the tenants.

Gemma set off for Germany by ferry and train with two suitcases and a small portfolio of drawings. She wondered if the whole of her life would be like this. Crashing out of one disastrous relationship after another. Fleeing with a suitcase to begin life again in a different country.

She was lucky, she soon realised, in the place she had come to, and in the person who had invited her there, the art school head, Gerhardt Ritter. Gerhardt was happily married, Gemma had already ascertained, and that was reassuring. She was in no state of mind or heart to deal with complicated relations with any man, let alone a new colleague. Happily, he proved easy to work with when, together, they began to plan the course that Gemma would be delivering, starting in the Spring Term. The city of Göttingen, which Gemma had known only as a name up to now, turned out to be an architectural gem, undamaged by Allied action in the Second World War:a place where the natives were friendly, and the streets of half-timbered houses begged, as much as those of Rye, to be painted, lived in, and explored. Even before her arrival Gerhardt had found a flat for her. It was on the third floor of a residential block on the southern edge of town. At the bottom of the garden the countryside took over: woodpeckers drummed and fieldfares made their clacking cries. And yet, from her front door it was a mere twenty minutes' walk into the centre of town. Only ten minutes if you had a bike.

In some ways it was like being a student again. Students were what Göttingen was all about, its university huge in proportion to the town. The older people who shared it with the youthful hordes were there, for the most part, because of them. They ran the shops and bars the students used, they manned the hotels their parents stayed in when they visited, or they were there for the same reason as Gemma was: to teach.

Though Göttingen, five times as big as Rye, was easily as picturesque it lacked Rye's hilltop setting; its streets were nearly flat. So, as at Cambridge and Oxford, the students rode bicycles. Many of the university teachers too. It was always said that contact with the young kept you young yourself. In the light of what had happened to her, Gemma was not intending to make those contacts any closer than the demands of teaching required. But she did buy herself a bicycle – before she'd been in the town a week.

Her bicycle gave her wings, or so it seemed. She felt that she flew around the town as it prepared for winter. She saw parents escorting their very young children along the streets at dusk as they, the children, carried paper lanterns and softly sang a song to propitiate the winter dark. How lovely this was, she thought. How different from the trick-or-treating, with its thinly veiled suggestion of menace, that had escaped like a virus from America and was taking over Britain's November streets. She examined the massively carved half-timbered houses by the town wall and in the old city centre that it wrapped itself around. It was too cold by now to set up her easel and paint them, but she made mental notes of where she would do that in the spring.

The course that she began to teach in January was only one of many options from which students at the Kunst Akademie could choose. All the same, Gemma approached it with a seriousness and a respect for her students that bordered on trepidation. But very early on she realised that she was making an impression. Her students loved her course, they loved the way she taught them. They seemed to feel that she herself was *OK*. She'd passed the test. The following term, and throughout the year that followed, their numbers swelled.

Gemma had worried that her German might not be up to the task of teaching. That it would have a damaging effect on her lessons by making her students laugh. But again she found her anxiety misplaced. Not only did her command of the language improve rapidly in response to the challenge but, when it occasionally happened that she lacked the necessary words to get a point over and she was forced to switch to English it seemed to make little difference: her students always understood. And of course the principal language of her teaching was articulated in lines or brush-strokes on paper or canvas, and those were universally understood.

It helped that Nicholas II and the Castle of Rats was becoming a major success in Germany. Not that her students read it, but they all knew people of an age to have children, they had nieces and nephews who had the book at home, and enjoyed telling those nieces and nephews they knew the lady who wrote it and had done the pictures. The German setting of *Niklaus II und das Rattenschloss* spurred the book's upward progress. It became the more successful of the two books in Germany, just as The Cat Who Loved Potatoes, *Die Katze, die Kartoffeln liebte*, had always been the more popular in Britain.

She had no trouble finding a social life. Her new milieu of artists and academics was international not only in outlook but in its make-up as well. No-one here was puzzled, let alone affronted, by her foreignness. She made friends with a Russian painter, female, and an Italian lecturer in Renaissance art, male but gay, as well as the German crowd. Where men were concerned she remained cautious, at least for now. She was well aware that, still in her early thirties, with a certain amount of reputation and the funds to go with it, she would be seen by many as a catch. Where students still in their teens were concerned she didn't even need to be cautious. She knew she would never again burn her wings on one of those.

With the coming of spring Gemma began to paint Göttingen. She did views of its streets, its handsome old buildings, in her familiar, trademark medium of Biro. She did the same views in oil and in water colour. By midsummer she had enough canvasses for an exhibition. It was held in the town's largest art gallery, in Prinzen Strasse. A television crew turned up for the opening. It was just the local news channel, but it pleased Gemma all the same. A few days later, perhaps because of a shortage of material, a fragment of this item, including a few words to camera from Gemma in her idiosyncratic German, was aired on national TV, on the same arts programme as she'd appeared on the year before.

It was the first time Gemma had had an exhibition devoted entirely to herself. While it was on she tried to resist the temptation to pop in every day to count the red stickers that announced a sale. She restricted herself to one visit per forty-eight hours. Sometimes a picture had been sold since her last visit, sometimes not. Sometimes there were one or two viewers in the gallery, sometimes just the owner or her assistant. On the first Friday of her exhibition Gemma looked in at the end of the afternoon. And there he was.

'Dieter!' They stood and looked at each other across what seemed an immoveable block of space. 'What are you doing here?'

'I came in the hope of finding you. And I have,' her former lover said.

'Came from where?'

'Still in Koblenz,' he said.

'You came halfway across Germany to look for me? How did you know I'm here?'

'You were on TV, though you may have forgotten that. I thought what a stupid idea it would be to write to you, or try to contact you by phone. When I woke up next day I knew for certain it was a mad idea.' He smiled at her, although a bit diffidently. 'I decided to come and look for you instead.'

Gemma wasn't sure if she was pleased to hear that or not. She wasn't sure if she was pleased to see Dieter or not. 'I don't think I'd have driven across Germany to see you.'

'I didn't drive,' Dieter said, wanting, as Gemma remembered he always did, to be precise. 'I came by train.'

Gemma hadn't meant to smile at him but now she did. The six years in which she hadn't seen him had aged his face a lot. Without chemical assistance few men can be called blond after forty, and Dieter's hair and his now full beard were the colour of old rope; a few fibres of white offered a preview of what was yet to come. But his eyes had lost none of their light.

'I'm very flattered,' Gemma said. 'What else can I say?'

'Later this evening,' Dieter said. He switched to German. *'Hast du etwas vor?'*

'Nothing that can't wait, I suppose.' She was supposed to be meeting her Italian lecturer friend later, but that could be rescheduled with a phone-call. It would have been worse than rude to cold-shoulder Dieter now that he'd so quixotically travelled two hundred miles, and to send him on his way without even having a drink.

They were just round the corner from the Ratskeller, the vaulted underground hangout of many of Gemma's students on a Friday night. Gemma was too grown up, she now decided, to care who saw them together or what anybody thought. They walked side by side, Gemma steering her bicycle with one hand as they went.

'Shouldn't you be married or something?' Gemma asked.

'Should I? Shouldn't you?'

They went into this over a glass of cold Pilsner beer. Dieter had been in a relationship during the last few years. They had got as far as getting engaged. But as the countdown towards nuptial zero-hour accelerated they had both felt less and less like spending the rest of their lives together. One day they'd found the honesty and courage to tell each other this. They'd managed to part company with dignity and mutual respect intact. At a distance now – the woman lived in Hamburg – they were still friends.

Gemma told her own story. They had moved on now, round two more street corners, to the Schwarzen Bären for a meal. Gemma could see that Dieter was startled by what she told him about Ivor and herself, but somehow it was easy to talk to him, even about this. It was more than easy, it was nice. 'You must think I've been an awful idiot,' she told him.

'I think you're an artist,' Dieter said. 'As opposed to someone who learnt to paint in the army. Real artists are allowed to do these things. Different rules apply.'

Gemma smiled. 'I'm sorry about the army thing. If I could, I'd take it back.'

'My mother died,' said Dieter next.

'I'm sorry,' Gemma said.

'That's not what I meant,' said Dieter. 'I've also changed a bit. As you would see if we...' He didn't, or couldn't finish that thought.

'I'm not sure men do much changing,' said Gemma. 'Not after the age of about four and a half.'

'Then maybe I'm the exception that tests the rule. I'm not sure women change, though.' Dieter gave her a smile that took her back in time as abruptly as if she'd fallen down a well. 'But then I wouldn't want that.'

'Dieter...' Gemma said, in what was meant to be a warning tone of voice.

He began, 'I was just wondering if, by some chance...' But then the waiter arrived with loaves of bread.

TWENTY-ONE

Jack asked Ivor to do a repair to the hop press in the oast in advance of the season. It was hardly a repair at all: the frame had been made of solid oak some century and a half before. A few screws needed tightening, that was all. Ivor said that while he was up there he'd put new battens on the trap-door that was set in the floor beside it. It was only as he was saying this that everything seemed to swim into place.

He remembered boys at school making flying model aeroplanes out of balsa wood. Their wings and fuselages were covered with the finest imaginable tissue paper which was strengthened by brushing on a coat of something called dope. He made enquiries. Not in Rye or Hastings, where people might know him or at least remember him if they were asked later. He found a model shop in London, not far from Charing Cross station, in one of those passageways that link St Martin's Lane with the Charing Cross Road. Yes, they sold the paper. The finest one was called Esaki tissue. Most people bought it coloured, but there was a transparent kind, if that was what Ivor really wanted. The assistant fetched it in from a back room and showed it to Ivor with a frown. Ivor did want it. It was like very thin, very fragile, tracing paper. He bought the dope to go with it, and put both items carefully into the overnight bag he used when he came up to spend his weekends with Feri. Then he took the underground to Highgate. Sometimes he pulled things out of his bag to show off to Feri: a miniature carved wooden object or a small painting. This weekend he had a tiny water colour to show off. But he didn't show Feri what he'd bought in the model shop.

There were dozens of dry fragments of hop tendrils lying around on the storage floor of the oast, very light and very fine. Ivor spread and pegged the Esaki paper on his workbench in the old apple store, brushed it with the dope and laid the hop tendrils on top of it to form a semi-rigid frame around the edges, and a rather irregular grid, like in a stained-glass window, across the rest of it. He had previously measured and cut the paper so that it exactly matched the dimensions of the trap-door.

When it was dry Ivor turned the panel over very carefully. It weighed next to nothing but, provided you were exceedingly gentle with it, remained just about rigid. Then in water colour he painted the top side the yellow-ochre, greyish tone of old wood, with two stripes across it in a brighter tint of beige in imitation of battens of new wood. When he left the workshop he covered it neatly with a dust-sheet, something he regularly did to most of his ongoing work.

The oast house, hectically busy during three weeks every September, was virtually unused through the rest of the year, except as an equipment store. The ground floor housed the hop trailers, whose detachable crows' nests, tall frameworks of tubular steel, lay flat on the ground beside them. Nobody came in here much, but even so Ivor took the precaution of laying a couple of planks over the hole in the floor that was created when he took the trap-doors off their hinges to repair them. He took the further precaution of painting a notice which read, *Danger – Trap-Doors Missing*, and placed it at the top of the steps.

The repairs to the hop press and the doors took very little time to accomplish: just a part of a Friday evening. Ivor told Jack at breakfast the next morning that he'd have the trap-doors back in service that Saturday afternoon, before he left to catch his train to London. But before any of that could happen Jack had to be driven to

Rye for his liquid Saturday lunch. He had taken the warnings of the police quite seriously and now got either Robbie or Ivor to drive him into town whenever he was going drinking, and took a taxi home. This Saturday it was Ivor's turn for chauffeur duty. Robbie was not around: a circumstance which fitted well with Ivor's other plans.

He waited till Mrs Fuggle was in the garden on the other side of the house, pegging out washing, before collecting his paper-and-sticks creation from the apple store and carrying it gingerly into the oast and up the steps. He had already removed the planks that covered the hole; all he had to do was gently to lower his gauze into the aperture. It fitted perfectly, resting on the rim that normally supported the edges of the doors. Then he picked up the notice he'd written and laid it face-down on the floor. The windows on both floors of the oast were small and, being cleaned only rarely, let in very little light. But the upstairs electric light, which Ivor had used while working on the press, was still switched on. He angled it slightly, so that it lit the trap-door area, and examined the result. The spotlight effect made his featherweight little work of art appear quite solid, viewed from up here, the water-paint reflecting back the light like the scales on a butterfly's wing. Certainly no light from below was making its way through the paper. But when Ivor went back down the steps the light from upstairs streamed down through the trap-hatch. Unless you stood right under it and looked up you'd never guess that a semi-transparent membrane lay stretched across. He turned off the upstairs light from the switch halfway up the steps and left the oast. Mrs Fuggle was obligingly still hanging out the clothes: she had seen neither his entrance into the building nor his exit from it.

It was a work of art, Ivor told himself. Not just his ingenious little gauze effect, but the whole thing that he was in the middle of. Even the contemplation of the idea of it was setting his whole body tingling; a physical thrill was running through the centre of him, like the thrill he'd observed in cats when they were catching, letting go, and catching mice. This was art. As Crime and Punishment was art, as Roddy Raskolnikov's crime was art, as Hamlet and Macbeth were art. Feri had told him about two men in London, called Gilbert and George, who had made their whole lives a work of art: they themselves were both its content and its form. Ivor hadn't quite seen the point of that before, but now he thought he did. A work of art, every work of art that was true to its creator's ideal and imagination and was executed perfectly, was the justification of itself.

Ivor looked out for Jack's taxi, bringing him back, making its way up the drive. It came a little after three o'clock. Ivor waited till Jack had bumblingly got out and the driver had turned round and disappeared from view, then he emerged from the apple store, crossing the yard in the direction of the house, but managing to intercept Jack's weaving path to nowhere in particular when he'd got halfway across. 'Trap-door's back,' he said, and carried on his way. He was taking the biggest gamble of his life. It was loaded with the most enormous risk. Everything, literally everything in Ivor's life, depended on his having read Jack's character right, and on Jack now behaving in accordance with what Ivor thought he'd learnt.

Ivor went into the house through the back door and into the kitchen where Mrs Fuggle was. Looking through the window he saw Jack open the door to the oast and go inside. Carefully he'd positioned himself further away than Mrs Fuggle stood from the back door. 'Oh Christ!' he called to her. 'Jack's gone into the oast, there's no lights on and the trap-door's still off. We've got to...'

Mrs Fuggle took her cue. She ran – it was a sight Ivor had never seen before – out of the house and across the yard. Ivor followed a yard or two behind, managing a goodish impression of not being quite able to catch her up. Mrs Fuggle reached the open door of the oast. The ground floor was in darkness but the upstairs light was now on again – Jack must have pressed the switch on his way up the steps – and was flooding down through the trap-hatch, which looked as open as could be. There was less than a second before something moved into that overhead light-beam, causing a narrowing of its shaft. Then there was a yell of terror, and Jack appeared like a falling, well-filled, hop sack. His body appeared almost to unroll downwards through the hatch, like a roller-blind in silhouette. When his arms appeared they at once spread wide so that just for an instant he was the crucified Christ. A broken halo or crown of something seemed to fall with him: bits of hop tendril, as you'd expect, and sheets of what might have been cobweb. It was over almost before it began, but it was a nanosecond of beauty, a blink-and-you-miss-it, unrepeatable but abiding and indissoluble work of art.

Mrs Fuggle's scream began before Jack's finished, and went on long after he stopped falling, and was lying lifeless across the tubular steel frames of the two crows' nests on the floor. Ivor ran past Mrs Fuggle, grabbed Jack's hand and felt his pulse. He shouted to Mrs Fuggle, 'Run and phone the ambulance... But he has no pulse... But run.' Ivor wasn't sure if he was making sense, or if he was getting this part of the thing right. However, Mrs Fuggle did what she was told and rushed out of the door and back towards the house.

Ivor ran up the steps more quickly than he'd known he could move, and put his warning notice back on its feet. No part of his gauze had remained in the hole or on the floor nearby, it had all fallen through. He rushed back down again, speedy as a cat, and picked up all the bits of his web of sticks and tissue that had fallen around Jack. He was careful to find every last one. He scrunched them in his fist and stuffed them in the pockets of his jeans. He'd be OK now, unless anybody asked him to turn his pockets out.

On her return from the telephone Mrs Fuggle found Ivor sitting on the bottom step of the stairway that had taken Jack on the last tour of inspection of his employees' handiwork he would ever make. Ivor was in floods of tears now. Tears of fear, of shock, or of relief, he didn't know which. Mrs Fuggle sat down beside him, laid an arm around his shoulder and tried, like a grandmother, to comfort him. They were still sitting like this when, a few minutes later, the ambulance arrived, so that for a moment the crew, appearing like silhouette puppets in the doorway, took them for a real grandmother and grandchild.

One paramedic, feeling for pulses and signs of breathing, confirmed Ivor's conclusion that nothing more could be done for Jack. The other asked Ivor and Mrs Fuggle what had happened. Ivor had conquered his tears by now, and was alert enough to be pleased that Mrs Fuggle took it on herself to answer. 'Blind drunk, he was. Poor, poor man. Went up into the oast and just walked through the hole. Trap-doors was off for repair.' Her voice stalled on a sob.

Ivor put in, 'Doors were only off for five minutes. I told him they'd be fixed this afternoon. I meant the end of the afternoon. How'd I know he was going to go up and inspect them straight after lunch, soon as he got back from the pub?'

Mrs Fuggle regained control of her voice. 'There's been no accounting for his behaviour these last months,' she said, which Ivor found helpful.

'He must have been pretty drunk to walk into a hole in the floor,' said the ambulance man. 'Mind you, it's pretty dark down here.' He looked up. 'You wouldn't see much light coming up to warn you.'

'I put a warning notice at the top of the stairs,' Ivor said. 'Not that I thought anyone would go up there, but you can't be too careful.'

'No, you can't,' said the ambulance man. Whether there was any irony in his remark Ivor couldn't tell. Then, 'Has anyone contacted the police?'

Ivor was a bit startled and it showed on his face. He hadn't realised that anyone would have to. The man smiled to reassure him. 'It's just standard procedure. A workplace accident, leading to a fatality. I'll do it, if you like.' He walked out and across to the ambulance and leaned in through the door, twisted the knobs of a radio. Ivor was able to hear him report the incident in very precise detail, almost in the exact words that Mrs Fuggle and he had given him. There was nothing in his tone to suggest he thought it was anything other than an accident. Returning to the two witnesses he explained they would have to wait for the police to arrive and clear the scene, then they would take Jack's body away to Hastings. 'And then?' Ivor asked.

'You'll be hearing.' He'd brought back from the ambulance a clipboard with papers flapping from it. Now he started to take down Ivor's details, and Jack's. Was Ivor Jack's next of kin? Ivor realised there would be a lot of this over the coming days.

The police arrived with unnerving despatch. There were three of them. One went to look at Jack, escorted by one of the paramedics, the other two interviewed Mrs Fuggle and Ivor separately, having manoeuvred them out of each other's earshot first. Ivor repeated the story he'd told the ambulance man. It had been swallowed that time, so Ivor was able to see that now as a dress rehearsal for the real thing. He hoped Mrs Fuggle would tell the same story too. He hoped she wouldn't suddenly remember the puzzling detail of the gossamer fragments that had appeared, falling around Jack as he plunged, but he knew she was neither an imaginative nor a particularly observant woman: there was a good chance she would not. Anyway, there was no trace of Ivor's contraption to be found at the scene, it was all screwed up inside his pockets. He was a little worried, as he wound up his account, to see the third policeman emerge from the oast and take a walk around the outside of the building, looking up, down and around, like someone illustrating the adjective *observant* in a charade.

'Why did you remove the protecting planks before going to get the doors that would replace them?' his policeman was asking.

During the few fast-thinking minutes between the paramedic's calling the police and their arrival Ivor had prepared an answer to this. 'It would have been difficult to handle four heavy bits of wood at once. The trap-doors are solid oak. I thought about it. I know I could have taken the doors up the stairs, laid them on the floor and then removed the planks, but I decided not to. It was only going to be for two minutes, there was a warning notice, and I'd no idea someone was going to go up there all of a sudden.' Tears had misted his eyes, and his voice had cracked, several times during the course of his statement. Now they did so again. The tears were unforced, he'd had no need to fake them. But the bit of him that was still doing rapid calculations about how he should act now took another big gamble. He turned his wet face up at the officer, looked him in the eye like a lost little boy and said, 'It seems I thought wrong. Will I be in trouble?'

The policeman thought for a moment. Then he said, 'If the lady's statement confirms your own, and the post-mortem findings are consistent with them both, then maybe not. The maybe, of course, is because the dead man's family might want to bring an action for negligence against you.' Ivor tried not to let the policeman see the shudder of relief that went through him. Negligence, and a civil suit at that. If that was the greatest risk he ran, it was something he could live with. The policeman said, 'Who comes in for the place now? Do you know that?'

'I can't really say I do,' said Ivor. He made a noise that was somewhere between a wistful chuckle and a sniff. 'He once told me, a long time ago, that he'd leave the place to me, but I'm sure he was joking. He was pretty drunk at the time, and he never mentioned it again.'

The policeman seemed interested, even surprised by this. 'Well, perhaps one of your next moves should be to try and find out.' He gave Ivor a searching look. 'Perhaps you could include any results of your researches in the statement we'd like you to make at the police station in a few days' time.'

Relief fled away. Ivor went back to feeling alarmed again. 'I thought this was my statement.'

'It is, but we require people to go over things again in a more formal setting, after they've had a chance to think about things, and then put a signature to what they've said.' He saw Ivor's apprehension and said, quite kindly, 'It isn't meant as a trap. If people are telling the truth in this kind of situation they usually have no difficulty in remembering the details again perfectly accurately a second time.'

'If...?' Ivor couldn't help himself.

'Like I said,' the policeman rehearsed it smoothly. 'They have no difficulty.'

Saturday afternoon is a bad time to die, from the point of view of those left behind. Not much of a practical nature can be accomplished before Monday and the only thing left to do is think. Ivor knew he would have to keep a careful rein on his thoughts if they were not to gallop off wildly and overturn his sanity – perhaps his life itself. He remembered the cautionary example of Roddy in Crime and Punishment. Step by step he would need to focus on the realities, and the choices he must make in dealing with them, if he were not to go mad. The first thing to keep hold of was the fact that Jack's death was simply a tragic accident. True, Ivor had been remiss in leaving the trap-hatch unguarded by planks and by prematurely laying the danger notice down on its face. But as for the clever trompe l'oeuil he'd executed with the Esaki tissue and hop tendrils, that had been in the nature of a teasing joke. Jack would have seen through it in the normal run of things, if only he hadn't been so drunk. He'd have prodded at it with his foot, as he always did with new repairs, but would have realised in time what he was dealing with; he wouldn't have put his whole weight on it, or stumbled onto it, whichever it was that he'd actually done. Of course Ivor would not go into all this when he made his statement at the police station. They wouldn't understand. Nor would they get the point about this accident being also a work of art, just as Hamlet was a work of art, just as Gilbert and George were a work of art – or possibly two.

The other thing to focus on was the fact that Jack had obviously loved him. In a rather odd way, perhaps, but he had. Almost like a father. And he in return had loved Jack, almost like a son. Why else would he have worked so hard for him, in exchange for an ill-furnished, unheated room and a rent-free but draughty workshop? Thinking about this made him cry again, as he sat with Mrs Fuggle at the kitchen table, with untouched cups of tea in front of them. It also made him remember that other evidence of Jack's love for him, his will. And then there was Feri.

He made an effort, stopped his tears, wrenched his mind back to the here and now. Looking up at Mrs Fuggle he said, 'I won't be going up to London tonight. But I need to talk to Feri. I was wondering if you'd mind if I asked her to come down. Just for the one night, of course.'

Mrs Fuggle shot him a rather beady look but, before he could register it, replaced it with a smile. 'It's no skin off my nose, you know. Jack might not have wanted it, but I'd have no objection. Anyway, you could do with company tonight, I reckon, and I'm not – well I was just about to tell you this – I don't want to spend tonight here if I can help it. I'll go home, if you don't mind taking me in the car.' Mrs Fuggle did have a cottage of her own, on the Iden road, but since she'd moved in to Birdskitchen it had been taken over by her daughter and son-in-law. But that was where she intended to stay the night. 'Back tomorrow, bright and early, of course.'

'There's another thing,' Ivor said a bit cautiously. 'Did the police say anything to you about Jack's will?'

Mrs Fuggle nodded vigorously, surprised into remembering. 'They did, you know. It went straight out of my head.'

'Nearly went out of mine,' Ivor told her. 'The police asked me to look for it. Will you help me? Now?'

She looked a bit surprised at the suddenness of this but said, 'Suppose there's no time like the present, Ivor.' There were occasions when she used his name when talking to him, and Ivor recognised those as moments of affection, though they didn't occur every day; perhaps not every week. Like most people who came into regular contact with him Mrs Fuggle found herself approaching Ivor with an instinctive wariness. There was something about him – though she couldn't have said what. But he had always behaved well towards her and treated her with almost exaggerated politeness and respect. She hadn't found anything, ever, on which to hang any sense of dislike.

Ivor knew he had to be more careful than ever of Mrs Fuggle's feelings now. Especially if in the next few minutes they found Jack's will, as he hoped they would. He might have to be deferential to her for the rest of his life, or at any rate hers. She would forever have the power to review her impressions of how the accident had happened and draw new and potentially damaging conclusions. Never would this be more dangerously the case than in the next few days, between her discovery of Jack's testatory intentions and her visit to the police station during the coming week.

Together they left the kitchen and made their way along the brick-floored rear hall to what Ivor in his mind called Jack's TV and whisky room. Ivor reflected as they opened the door that it would now require a new, if still unspoken, name.

Mrs Fuggle pulled open the drop-top writing desk that had come from Waring and Gillow in Jack's grandfather's day. Without any show of hesitation she started to leaf through the compost heap of papers that occupied the interior. And surprisingly quickly she drew out the paper that Ivor had seen once before, in the Peace and Plenty, beneath the all-seeing eye of the stuffed pike. 'It's here,' Mrs Fuggle said, then, perhaps aware that she'd been leading the operation up till now, handed it stiffly to Ivor, giving him with it an unintended little poke in the ribs.

Ivor took the paper and unfolded it. He read it aloud, but at the same time held it out so that Mrs Fuggle could see the words too, as if they were sharing a hymn-book in church.

'How's that, then?' Mrs Fuggle said in a voice hoarse with astonishment. 'The whole place to you? Oh lordy, lordy, my head's going round like a top. Let me sit down.'

At that moment Ivor realised how lucky it was that Robbie wasn't here, but had taken his wife and children to Camber Sands for the day. They wouldn't be back till late. Robbie, had he been here now, would have been quite capable of tearing the paper in shreds, Ivor knew. Frank would be coming up the drive in an hour to feed the pigs. Heinz would be at home in his cottage watching Grandstand on TV. How very necessary it was going to be for Ivor to be able to deal with them all one at a time. And for the moment that meant Mrs Fuggle.

Sitting in a low-backed armchair Mrs Fuggle looked even greyer than Ivor had seen her look before. Grey stockings, grey skirt and cardigan, grey face, grey hair. He sat down opposite her and said, 'Well, it's as big a surprise to me as it is to you. Who did you think would come in for the place?'

'I didn't,' said Mrs Fuggle, now sounding quite collected again. 'You don't think that when people are younger than you are. You don't expect to be around when they die.' She shook her head involuntarily.

Ivor saw the point. He said, 'It's just something written by hand on a piece of paper. The lawyers may pick all sorts of holes in it. Best if we don't think too much about it yet, reckon?'

Mrs Fuggle nodded. Ivor was careful to keep the paper in his hand when, for want of anything else to do, they walked silently back to the kitchen and their cold un-tasted tea.

Ivor met Feri off the train at a quarter to eight. Neither of them was able to say very much. Ivor had had a tricky afternoon. He'd called on Frank and Heinz and exploded his grenade of news into their peaceful weekends. He told them about Jack's accident, the ambulance and the police, but not about the will. They'd get that from Mrs Fuggle soon enough. It wasn't that she would make a point of telling them in the morning. It would just come out. Robbie still hadn't returned when Ivor went to call on him. He'd left a note on the door, asking him to call round urgently. Then, on the way to the station, he'd dropped Mrs Fuggle off at her cottage near Iden. This gave him the opportunity to continue on to Rye through Iden village; it was a route he never normally used, through a village where he was hardly known. He'd stopped the car by the bus shelter there and, while pretending to consult the timetable on the wall of the shelter, emptied his pockets nonchalantly into the litter bin beside it. Nobody was looking for fragments of Esaki tissue paper and dried-up hop tendrils. If they ever did they wouldn't start looking here in Iden, and anyway, the bin would be emptied long before that.

Feri had spent the afternoon in a bewildered state of mind. Of course it was a wonderful thing that Ivor should have come into his inheritance so soon. On the other hand it had involved a tragedy for Jack. And it was – she couldn't not frame this thought – worryingly soon. Little more than a year had passed since Jack had made that will. If even she was going to be troubled by that thought, it occurred to her, how much more wounding would be the suppositions of everyone else.

Together they prepared the supper of lamb stew that had originally been intended for Mrs Fuggle and Jack. They were just finishing it when, without a knock at either the back or the kitchen door, Robbie arrived with the suddenness of a cannonball. He was momentarily startled to see Feri sitting at the table with Ivor and mumbled an awkward sounding, 'Evening Miss'. But his attention quickly went to Ivor. 'So I'm summoned into the presence.'

'You don't have a mobile phone,' Ivor said, looking him in the eye. 'There was no other... Look, do you know what's happened?'

'Oh, I've heard, all right. Heard from Heinz. Come out of his door when he heard me pull up.' He looked around the kitchen. 'Where's Mrs F? She dead and all, now?' He turned towards Feri and attempted a disarming smile. It was not pretty.

'She's gone home,' Ivor said. 'I took her. She asked me to. Back tomorrow. Look, Robbie...'

Feri broke in. 'Please sit down. There's something else you need to hear.'

Robbie folded himself stiffly onto a bentwood chair. Ivor said, 'This may not mean very much. But Mrs F. found a will of Jack's. It leaves pretty well everything to me. I have no idea why it should. Mrs F.'s taking it into Rye on Monday. No doubt they'll have a better one that, what's the word...?'

'Supersedes it,' Feri provided.

'But...'

Robbie gave Ivor no time for whatever proviso he was about to utter. 'Tell me you're winding me up.'

'Wish I was,' said Ivor, assuming a poker face.

'Even if you're not,' Robbie told him, 'nothing'd come of it. People turn up out of the blue in these situations. You'll have people marching in here by tomorrow afternoon... Unknown cousins from Australia or what not.'

'They'll have had to book their plane tickets pretty sharpish to get here from Australia,' Ivor said. 'But I take your point. I'd been imagining cousins from Australia myself.' Feri shot him a surprised look.

'We both knew it was only a matter of time, of course,' Ivor went on to Robbie. 'The way he drank.'

That idea triggered the next one. 'Look, mate, want a whisky? Calm us all down?'

'No thanks.' Robbie's glance went quickly round the kitchen. 'Settled in already, like you own the place.' He aimed this at Ivor but he couldn't help darting a significant little look at Feri afterwards.

'I'm just down for tonight,' Feri told him sharply. 'Today's been a shock for everyone. You'd expect me to be at my boyfriend's side if I possibly could.'

'Enjoy it while you can,' Robbie told Ivor. He made a studied effort not to implicate Feri with a second look. 'It'll be marching orders for you in no time, me lad. Maybe also for the rest of us.' He waved a finger towards Ivor's chest. 'But you'll go first.' He turned abruptly and left.

For a second time Feri explored the empty rooms of Birdskitchen with Ivor as her guide. How different her state of mind from her last visit, her first, her only visit, three months before! Her connection with those living-rooms, those bedrooms, had been tenuous back then: it had been like visiting your parents in a new house, one which might in theory be yours one day but about which you didn't bother to think much in those terms. But now Birdskitchen was a place which might possibly belong to Ivor – and to herself? – at the end of the time it took to test a will. A year? She'd vaguely heard that was the usual case. Might possibly belong to Ivor. Or possibly might not. The thought of Gemma came unexpectedly to her mind. As Feri was exploring Birdskitchen now, so must Gemma have walked round Gatcombe when it first became hers, peopling in her imagination the empty rooms. She'd filled them in the end with teenagers from the American School, Feri among them. Would Feri be peopling Birdskitchen one day? With whom?

Their conversation veered between the upbeat and the fearful, at times full of the awed marvelling that is experienced in the immediate wake of death, at times plunging, weighted with doubt. What if the will had been a joke after all? How would other 'stakeholders' as they were beginning to be called these days react to the news? As Robbie had? Or more angrily still? The other staff; owners of neighbouring farms... What was everybody going to think? There was no reason why distant cousins of Jack's or his wife's shouldn't emerge from nowhere to contest the thing. Several times during the evening Ivor broke down again in tears and Feri, who had never seen any emotional weakness in him before today found herself strangely touched by this evidence of his vulnerability. She took his hands as they sat side by side on the whisky-room sofa and said, 'I love you.'

There had always been a businesslike atmosphere to their conversations up to now. Each knew they loved the other and was loved in return, but till now neither of them had voiced it in those words. Ivor would have said his passion to possess Feri went far above and beyond love: that everyday prosaic trap that most of the human race fell into at some point or other. What he felt was vastly more violent and powerful than that. Were there words in the English language to express it? Not in Ivor's vocabulary, there weren't. Had he read Wuthering Heights rather than Crime and Punishment he might have had a stab at paraphrasing one of Heathcliff's more grandiloquent avowals off the cuff. But he hadn't and so he didn't. He did what most people do in this situation and answered, 'I love you too.' But later, when they were uncomfortably tucked together in Ivor's single bed beneath the crown-post that reached away into the ceiling, Ivor found himself unable, for the first time in his life, to muster the physical proof.

TWENTY-TWO

Ivor hadn't seen Jack's face as he fell. Only, of course he had. It had been turned towards him. It was just that his conscious mind had blocked it out in the immediate aftermath, it being a sight too awful to be borne in memory. But his unconscious was a different matter. The vision appeared in his dreams that night, or rather, early morning, just as the midsummer sun rose. Jack's eyes and mouth had melted together, it seemed: coalesced into a single, agonised, orifice. Ivor's cry of terror woke Feri in a fright. She thought it was as well they were alone together. Ivor had yelled loudly enough to wake the whole house. As it was she could hear the sheep-dogs barking two floors below. 'You had a dream,' she told him. 'People do when people close to them die. It's all OK.' But she couldn't bring herself to ask him what the dream had been about.

Feri wasn't happy about leaving Ivor that Sunday evening. But her finals exams at college began the next morning. Ivor told her firmly that she had no choice, and that he would be fine. He put her on the train just before six. At least Feri had the comfort of knowing he wouldn't be alone in the house that night. Mrs Fuggle was back. She had even – to Feri's astonishment – set to and cooked them all Sunday lunch.

Ivor phoned Jack's solicitors' chambers on Monday morning, dead on nine o'clock. He'd barely been able to contain himself as the minutes leading up to this time clicked past. He would have got up and called the solicitors' at four a.m. if there had been any chance of someone picking up the phone.

A woman's voice answered and Ivor gave his name. 'You handle the affairs of Mr Jack Eason of Birdskitchen Farm, I think,' he said. 'I need to tell you Mr Eason's dead. Also that I'm holding in my hand a will of his. I'd like to bring it to you if I may.' He had had hours to rehearse this speech and had used them well. He was asked to wait a moment. It was a longish one. Then it was a male voice that spoke. It asked Ivor his address, and if he'd mind repeating the information he'd just given, with one or two additional details. Then the voice offered him an appointment at two o'clock that day, with a Mr Lyle.

Robbie perhaps hadn't remembered, or hadn't taken in, Ivor's announcement that Mrs Fuggle would take the will into Rye on Monday – a statement that allowed the assumption that the precious document was in her keeping and not his. At any rate Robbie didn't refer to it. He had been in a state of sulk all the previous day, even his catch-up with Mrs Fuggle in the kitchen had been brief and terse, and Monday brought with it no change in his general mood. Ivor told himself this was a normal thing to expect and anyway, Robbie's silence was better than a harangue or cascades of abuse. Silence could be answered with silence. Ivor was in no mood for a fencing match with words.

He left early for his appointment, dressed in the suit he'd worn to his mother's wedding two years before, even though the day was ticklingly hot. He used the extra time to call in at the Peace and Plenty on the way. Half a dozen customers sat at tables or at the bar as he went in. He paid them no attention. That was focused on the man serving behind the counter who, Ivor noted with relief, was the same landlord who had witnessed Jack's signature on the paper he now had in his pocket. Ivor remembered him vividly; the details of that evening were branded on his brain. The landlord, though, had no reason to remember Ivor. Ivor approached the bar, unable to stop himself glancing up for a second at the stuffed pike, glowering from its glass case. Another familiar face.

'Does Mr Tennant still come in here?' Ivor asked. 'Martin Tennant.' The name of the second witness was another detail that had burned into his brain. He had not needed to look at the will to check it. In response to the landlord's circumspect nod Ivor went on, 'Does he still live at Furnace?'

The landlord laughed, though in a friendly enough way. ''Course he does. When did you ever hear of a farmer moving houses? Well, not until they move to the big one in the sky.'

'The one with many mansions,' Ivor was surprised to hear himself say. He must have heard the phrase from Violet when he was a child. 'Well, thank you,' Ivor said. 'I'll be on my way.' He turned to the door. As he closed it behind him he heard, 'I'll tell him you...' and then the click and shudder of the catch and jamb.

The chambers was a handsome double-fronted Georgian house, stuccoed and painted primrose, in one of the cobbled streets. Inside, a dark oak staircase wound its way upward from the thick-carpeted hallway. Ivor was shown into one of the two front rooms.

In such a building, with its immediately sensed atmosphere of propriety and respect for tradition, Ivor had expected to find himself shaking hands with someone of at least fifty, nobly bald perhaps, or with a head of hair that was 'a sable silvered'. But Mr Lyle – 'Please call me Stephen,' – looked little more than twenty-five, just a few years older than Ivor. He was blond, wore beige chinos and a very crisply ironed white shirt with a silver tie. He shook Ivor's hand and made a sit-down gesture, indicating a chair pulled up opposite his own, facing him across the leather-topped mahogany desk. Ivor wondered if he hadn't over-prepared for the occasion rather, by putting on a suit.

'First of all,' said Stephen Lyle, 'my condolences. I never met Mr Eason but the partners here knew him well in earlier years.' He leaned forward a little with an encouraging smile. 'I believe you're not a family member. Or have I got that wrong?'

'No,' said Ivor. 'I'm not family. Just an employee.'

'Fine, fine,' said Stephen, his tone indicating subtly that there was no need for Ivor's 'just'. 'Now I think you've got a piece of paper you'd like me to see.'

Without saying anything, but giving away his state of agitation by his face, which was a mask of tension, Ivor reached into the inside pocket of his jacket, pulled out the will, a folded sheet of paper unprotected by any kind of envelope, and handed it across the desk. The solicitor, his face now also a mask, though one of a different nature, sat looking at the document for a good two minutes, even though the writing on it, leaving aside names and addresses, ran to no more than a dozen lines. Then he looked across at Ivor. 'You are Mr Ivor Wingate,' he said. He made a polite affirmative of it, rather than a question.

'I am,' Ivor answered. From an outside pocket he produced his passport and slid it across to Stephen.

The solicitor glanced at the passport but didn't pick it up. He continued to hold the will in both hands. 'Then I can see why you wanted to come and see us so urgently,' he said. 'What is written on this piece of paper – as you no doubt already know – is that Mr Eason wanted to leave almost the entirety of his estate to you.'

'Yes,' said Ivor. His voice sounded frozen somehow, as if he'd just taken it out of the fridge.

'Hmm,' said Stephen. 'I have to warn you, though you may have an idea of this already, that these things are sometimes not that simple. Were you aware of that?'

'Yes,' said Ivor.

Stephen smiled faintly. 'We've all seen films and read books where handwritten wills get read out to everybody in the library following a family funeral. But those days are gone.' Seeing that Ivor's mask of a face now looked positively ashen, he added, 'I'm not saying this will isn't a genuine document; it may well prove to be. Only that it may take a little time to find out.'

'Mr Eason showed it to me himself and let me read it,' Ivor protested. 'I was there when it was signed and witnessed. I saw all that with my own eyes.' He was cross with himself for sounding suddenly like a child.

'I'm sure that's true,' Stephen said. 'But I'm also sure you can see the reason why you can't be a witness in your own case.'

Ivor was silent for a second. Then he said, 'How long is a little time?'

Stephen didn't answer. He picked up Ivor's passport now, looking carefully at Ivor's photo, then back at the living breathing original sitting opposite, then he read the details in the passport with equal care. He handed the passport back and picked up the will again. 'These two witnesses,' he said, pointing at the signatures but without touching them. 'Are they still alive, do you happen to know? Still resident at these addresses?'

'Yes they are,' said Ivor, feeling hope enter him again like a sharp intake of breath. 'I saw one of them this morning, and he confirmed for the other one too.'

Stephen laughed. 'You're a quick worker and very thorough,' he said. 'We could probably use you here. Anyway, what you've told me is good news. We should be able to clear up that particular issue quite quickly. One thing less to stand in the way and cause delay.'

'The thing is,' Ivor said, 'when you talk about delay, what happens when Friday comes and everyone needs to be paid?'

'They might have to be – you might have to be – patient for another week. Look, let me help you with an idea of how it works. By the end of next week there's a good chance we'll have satisfied ourselves as to whether we can consider this a genuine will or not. If the situation is positive, from your point of view, then we can begin to do the work that will result in a grant of probate – subject to no more recent wills turning up. To prove the will in the legal sense.'

'And that takes...?'

'It might be only a year. It depends what happens, and how complicated the affairs of the estate turn out to be. With a document like this one,' he paused for a fraction of a second, 'well, it can take several years.'

'But what...?'

'Don't worry. There are mechanisms for dealing with the farm's finances in the interim. As you say, letting everyone get paid. We can discuss that when we meet again.' Stephen began to get to his feet.

'When will that be?' Ivor asked, and an echo of the children's rhyme tolled bleakly across his memory. Light you to bed. Chop off your head. 'The sheep-shearers.' He'd remembered the casual labour that would be required in the coming week. 'They'll need cash.'

'With any luck it should be one day next week.' He smiled again, and this time Ivor just about managed to smile back. 'We'll try not to overrun too many pay-dates. We'll call you.' The solicitor gave Ivor his hand to shake, then walked with him to the door.

When Ivor got back to Birdskitchen he found that Robbie's sulk had passed off. If he wasn't quite able to be agreeable he was at least prepared to discuss the practicalities of the new situation, the need to make funeral and other arrangements concerning Jack's death; also the day to day business of the farm, apportioning what had remained of Jack's workload between themselves and Frank. Ivor's visit to the solicitor seemed to have concentrated Robbie's mind. If there was even the smallest chance that Ivor would, in time, become the new owner of the farm then it would not be a brilliant move to make an enemy of him right now. Perhaps Robbie's wife had had a word with him over lunch.

They had a businesslike discussion in the kitchen. Ivor explained the time-frame the solicitor had set out, and Robbie seemed to accept it as something that couldn't really be altered or challenged. 'Perhaps we should try and get stock paid for in cash for a bit,' he suggested. Right now, that meant pigs and lambs. 'That way we can pay the shearers at least, even if we can't pay ourselves.' Ivor thought this was a good idea; he even wished he'd thought of it himself. The present crisis had coincided with a bit of a lull in the Birdskitchen year. Haymaking was over, wheat and barley wouldn't be harvested for another few weeks and, as they grew no early summer fruit or vegetables, there was really only sheep-shearing to be organised in addition to the daily routines. 'Reckon we could get cash for the fleeces?' Ivor asked, but Robbie pulled a not too optimistic face.

Other things, arrangements for the funeral, the contacting of scores of people in connection with Jack's death, combined to make the next few days a hectic time for Ivor. He was dimly aware that this was good for his state of mind, preventing him from dwelling too much on *that*. Nevertheless, a feeling of nightmare still hovered over Birdskitchen and could not be dispelled, no matter how hard Ivor applied himself to work. Mrs Fuggle and Robbie did join forces with him but, with the knowledge that Ivor might be recognised as sole executor as well as Jack's heir in only a few days' time, there was a general, unvoiced feeling that most of the extra burden should fall on him. Ivor could think of another reason why that should be the case but it wasn't one he meant to share.

Mrs Fuggle put the question that Robbie's self-importance had prevented him from asking. 'What happens to all of us now?'

'Nothing changes,' Ivor said. 'If that will is accepted and I turn out to be the executor, nothing changes then either. Nobody will be asked to move out – it's probably not even permitted, for all I know. And if, in years to come, the farm really turns out to be mine, then I wouldn't intend any changes then either. Of course, if cousins pop up from Australia,' – the mythical Australian cousins came in for regular mention these days, by all of them – 'I can't answer. I guess we'd all be out on our ears. But short of that happening I'd want you to stay as long as you liked.'

A look on Mrs Fuggle's face hinted that she'd believe that only when the time came. But she turned the look into a pragmatic half smile and said, 'Thank you.' She had reacted to post-solicitor Ivor in rather the opposite way from Robbie, perhaps guessing that once Feri was installed as mistress of the house there would be no further need for her. The spontaneous display of grand-maternal feelings that had manifested itself immediately after Jack's death had not been repeated in the days since. Ivor offered to drive her into Rye to make her official statement at the police station. They'd go together... But no, it seemed that Mrs Fuggle had other plans. Her daughter always took her in to Rye on market day. She would go to the police station then.

Ivor found this rather disconcerting. He would have liked to keep Mrs F. under very close watch around the time of her statement making. A further opportunity to discuss what she'd seen with her daughter, and perhaps to remember things differently – the mysterious bits of gauze that fell alongside Jack, for instance – was a chilling prospect. But there was nothing he could do about this. Insisting that he accompanied her to the police station would set even Mrs Fuggle's unimaginative mind on a journey that Ivor didn't want it to make.

He telephoned the police and told them he'd like to make his own statement the following morning. They asked if he could make it the day after that instead, and he of course said yes. No reason was given for this minor delay and, as Ivor couldn't imagine an innocent one, this gave him additional cause to be anxious. But preparation conquers fear – had he once heard someone say that? – and he now had two days in which to rehearse his story, to make sure he could get it right, watertight, and without risk of contradicting himself. He played devil's advocate with himself: posed all the tricky questions the police might face him with, and made the wise assumption that he'd be given a much tougher grilling than he'd had on the day itself.

He didn't put on his suit when the time for his interview came but, remembering Stephen Lyle's choice of business wear, chose spotless chinos and a crisp pressed shirt. At the desk inside the entrance door the duty officer listened to his name and business, then told him to go upstairs to the sergeant's room, indicating the way with his left hand while picking up the internal phone with his right.

As if life were holding up a reverse image of his visit to the solicitor's office, Ivor found himself entering a room that was bare in the extreme, and confronting across a plain wood desk a very large man, with iron-grey curly hair and a weather-tanned face. A mud-coloured tie set off his charcoal suit. The man did not get up. He did not look like a sergeant. Ivor was about to excuse himself for having come to the wrong room when the man said, 'Good morning, Mr Wingate. I'm

Detective Inspector Tart. Thank you for coming in. Please sit down.'

A plastic chair this time, and not drawn right up to the desk. The detective said, 'I just happened to be passing through this morning,' and he pressed a button in front of him. A sergeant appeared magically with a clipboard. The detective took no notice of him but continued to scrutinise Ivor's face. 'Now,' he said, 'if you wouldn't mind, we'd like you to tell us again in your own words what you remember about the accident last Saturday afternoon.'

Thanks to his rigorous preparation and rehearsal Ivor was able to give a clear account, matching his previous statement almost word for word, of what he was almost beginning to believe had taken place. The sergeant, standing at the side of the room, wrote it down, then took it away to be typed. D. I. Tart continued to sit at the sergeant's desk, seeming to overflow it, as senior people often appear to overpower the surroundings of their subordinates when they temporarily inhabit them. He had been leaning back a little while Ivor spoke, saying nothing, but listening attentively. Now he leaned forward slightly. 'Just one more thing,' he said. 'Did you manage to find out who, if anyone, Mr Eason left his property to?'

Ivor nodded. 'Mrs Fuggle discovered a will, dated last October, that apparently leaves almost everything to me.' The detective looked dismayingly unsurprised. 'It's with the solicitors at the moment,' Ivor went on. 'They're trying to establish if it's genuine, or if a later one supersedes it, or something like that.'

'So it wasn't just a joke when he told you he wanted to leave you his estate. Sounds like he may have meant it. And curious that he did intend that, when you'd only been in his employment for a year.'

'I'd worked for him before,' Ivor said.

'Bit of a tragedy him dying so soon after making his will, wasn't it?' Tart gave Ivor a very hard look at that point.

'Bit of a tragedy him dying at all,' Ivor said. Don't get smart with him, he cautioned himself. But don't grovel. Keep it ordinary. He tried to remember how Roddy had behaved at this point. Roddy had really lost it, winding up the examining magistrate Porfiry Petrovich; playing mind games with the man. Ivor would not do that.

Tart was speaking again. 'Leaving you a person of some consequence at the age of, uh, not quite twenty. A big leap for the boy who used to get cautioned for vandalising bus shelters not so many years ago.' His face was neutral, watchful.

'I hope I've changed a bit since then,' Ivor said in a demure voice. 'Grown up a bit at least.' This man was like a doctor who has your file out in advance of your appointment with him and now knows more about your medical history than you do. Ivor wished the sergeant would return with his statement so that he could sign it and then go home. But the detective had a look on his face that indicated he hadn't finished with Ivor yet. Ivor felt unpleasantly like a mouse that is being gently biffed by the paws of the cat that has caught it, before things really hot up.

In a voice so unconcerned and casual as to sound almost dreamy, Tart asked, 'I wonder what it was that made him leave the property to you.'

Fortunately Ivor, in role-playing this interview in his head in the small hours of the last few nights, had anticipated this one. 'I think there might have been an element of sexual attraction,' he said calmly. 'I mean, on his part.'

The policeman, who was not himself attracted by other members of his own sex, now looked searchingly at Ivor's face. He saw the point at once. There was no denying Ivor's fresh-faced, late-teen good looks. He moved smoothly to his next point. 'Was there any actual manifestation of this attraction? I mean, did Mr Eason make any unwanted advances towards you, for instance? Any suggestions that would have struck you as lewd or improper?'

'No,' said Ivor. He'd expected this too. 'I'd have remembered.'

D. I. Tart adopted the air of a college teacher in tutorial mode. 'A very interesting thing. There exists in law a concept known as homosexual panic – identified by psychologists in the twenties, I think. A sexual advance causes such a violent reaction in the person to whom the advance is made that they end up killing the person who made it. It's been used from time to time by defence lawyers – they call it the Portsmouth defence – in the same way they can invoke the idea of provocation.'

Ivor had not known about this. He adopted the role of eager student. 'And did the people get off?'

'Hmm. Murder reduced to manslaughter, I think, usually. Though it's not run as a defence very often. Usually in the case of violent deaths in prison, or in army barracks, that kind of thing. Anyway,' he waved his hand to put an end to his own digression, 'we're not talking about murder today. I don't remember any cases that involved disputes on farms, or pushing people through trap-doors.' The detective smiled broadly at Ivor as though he'd made a particularly clever joke which he was sure Ivor would enjoy and laugh at.

Ivor was stung, but avoided the trap. 'Are you suggesting...?' was a phrase he'd schooled himself not to use in the course of this interview. Not under any circumstances. He had got one more little speech ready, though he didn't have much in reserve for after that. He put his head a little on one side and said, 'In many ways I think he wanted to be like a father to me. And I suppose I began to respond to him a bit like a son.' He caused a wistful little smile to hover about his lips. 'Not a very good son, I'd have to admit.'

'He wasn't too happy about your having a girlfriend come to stay, was he? That must have got up your nose a bit.'

Where had Tart got that from, for heaven's sake? Ivor wondered. Then he realised Mrs Fuggle must have told the police this during her initial statement. The statement she was going to repeat to them in this very room tomorrow. He felt a tiny cold stab near his diaphragm. He hoped his breathing didn't give it away.

'It did get up my nose,' Ivor said. 'But that particular argument happens a lot between fathers and sons. It's almost universal, I'd have thought. It doesn't normally result in a terrible revenge. You might say everyone who expects to inherit something from their parents has a motive for getting rid of them, but people don't.' Ivor heard himself say this and was appalled. It was one thing for the detective to drag the conversation round to murder, even if the possible reasons for this were quite terrifying to imagine; but now here was he, gratuitously bringing up the subject himself!

Tart actually laughed. 'Quite the young philosopher, you are,' he said. 'I thought we'd stopped talking about such unpleasant things. Anyway, you'd have to be a very clever chap – clever in a certain sort of way, I mean – to persuade a man to climb stairs and then to jump through an open hatch in front of witnesses. Very clever indeed.'

'It's a horrible thought,' said Ivor meekly.

The detective gave a nod expressive of wisdom. 'The thing is about people who get clever in that rather special way, you know what happens?' He nodded again. 'They get a bit too clever eventually. Then they get caught. That's my experience anyway.'

The sergeant reappeared – not before time, Ivor thought; he'd seldom been more relieved to see anyone – and placed the typed statement in front of Ivor for him to read and sign. While Ivor was attentively reading the detective spoke again. 'By the way, you may be interested to know we got the result of the post-mortem examination this morning. Would you like to know what it said?'

'Of course,' said Ivor, keeping his voice steady, though his heart had started to behave like an engine that is about to stall, like a plane about to fall out of the sky. But a burst of adrenalin, like a fuel injection, came to the rescue.

The examining magistrate in Crime and Punishment had talked at Roddy while walking, almost running, about the room, so that Roddy had imagined Porfiry as a ball, rolling, and rebounding from every wall and corner. D. I. Tart was quite the reverse. Except for the occasional movement of a hand or a forward lean to emphasise a point, he had stayed unnervingly still throughout the interview. He might have been glued to his chair and the chair nailed to the floor. Now he said, 'According to the report, the injuries to Mr Eason were consistent with a fall through a trap-door from the height given. No sign of any struggle. It seems he'd tried to save himself by clutching at the sides of the hatch as he fell through. Only he was too late. His reactions were slowed by his recent excessive consumption of alcohol, something which the post-mortem also confirmed. Anyway, you'll be pleased to know the coroner's office accepts Mr Eason's death as accidental. They're satisfied that a full inquest will not be needed.' He stopped and looked at Ivor, who looked back at him but said nothing. He went on, in a lighter tone of voice, 'So it appears that your account of events, and the other witness's – she's due to come in tomorrow to put it on record, isn't she?

Mrs Fuggle, isn't it? – it seems you both got it about right. Unless of course the lady comes in tomorrow and tells us something quite different.' Tart's expression became suddenly stony; for a moment he actually glared at Ivor. Then his expression changed again. He smiled and got to his feet, like a bank manager ending a discussion with a customer. 'I'm sorry to have taken up so much of your time. Anyway, that's all we needed from you. Thank you for coming in. It's unlikely we'll be troubling you again.'

Ivor said a polite, slightly breathless, thank you and turned towards the door. The detective had known before Ivor arrived that the post-mortem results appeared to leave him in the clear. Nevertheless, he had still pursued his menacing line of questions, and steered the conversation easily towards the subject of murder. Ivor was aware – eyes in back of head aware – that the policeman continued to watch him closely as he left his presence. He also realised that the police would not stop watching him now. They would go on, following every remotely suspicious step he might make, for years and years. Perhaps for as long as he would live.

TWENTY-THREE

What D. I. Tart had said – that criminals who were too clever by half eventually became too clever for their own good – returned often to Ivor's mind during the days that followed. Not that he classed himself with those people. At times he thought of Jack's death as an accident, at others as a work of art, sometimes both. He refused to give mind-space to the idea that it had been cold-blooded murder, the elimination of a fellow human's life for personal gain. When that idea did insinuate itself into his consciousness he made an effort of will and imagination and shooed it straight out again. But those others – that class of clever killers in which he did not place himself – the things they did! They returned to the scene of their crime, many of them: the fools. Roddy Raskolnikov had done it in the book. Gone back to see if he'd described the doorbell correctly to the police. He'd even rung the bloody thing! Clang, clang! Had been spotted by no end of people as a result. Nice chap, Roddy, but crazy, crazy mad. Ivor couldn't not revisit the scene of Jack's accident in one sense, because he lived there. Birdskitchen was his home. But he could resist the temptation – though it was uncommonly strong, he hadn't expected that – to go into the oast and stand and stare. He went up once, to re-hang the trap-doors, but not again. At hop-picking time, yes, when work would require, but till then, no.

The other thing these people did was kill a second time. Even dear old Roddy had done this. He'd killed the innocent Lisaveta simply because she'd walked into the old woman's flat, seen her newly dead and bloody corpse on the floor, and then seen Roddy come in from the bedroom with the hatchet in his bloodstained hands.

He'd split her poor skull with the hatchet, feeling he'd had no choice, though that had never been part of his plan. Poor man.

Then there was Macbeth. After Duncan was dead he'd killed his two bedchamber gents – easier to pin the king's death on them after they were dead and in no position to argue back. Then he'd gone on to kill Banquo, because the witches who had prophesied that Mackers would be king had also said that Banquo's children, not his own, would eventually inherit the crown. Then killing after killing had followed, each one making a necessity of the next, justifying it in fact. This sort of thing happened in real life too, Ivor knew, and not just in the cases of those who were termed serial killers. It was reflected in the detective stories and police series that Ivor sometimes saw on TV. In fact, so great was the viewing public's expectation of a second murder that it had become a necessary element of almost every plot. This second murder would occur at the mid-point of the story. If you knew the start and the end time of the programme you could practically use the second murder to tell the time by, and had no need to look at your watch.

Ivor imagined – an absurd example, this, but you had to follow the logic of your thoughts – what would have happened had Mrs F. met with an accident before she was able to make her formal statement to the police. They would immediately have wanted to talk to him again, but this time much more aggressively and with less openness of mind. Whereas what had in fact happened achieved a far more satisfactory result.

Mrs Fuggle's daughter had arrived with her car, as she usually did on Thursdays, and taken her mother into Rye for the market there. Only this time they'd had to call at the police station in Cinque Ports Street on the way. Mrs Fuggle had returned to Birdskitchen later that day, with a face that radiated quiet smiles and much relief. 'So good to get the whole thing over with at last,' she'd said to Ivor, breaking precedent by going to look for him in his workshop – a place where he hadn't been able to spend a lot of time during the past few days – the moment she came home. She found him meditatively polishing a mahogany chest of drawers. She told him how the interview had gone and, almost incidentally, pretty much everything she had said. Which sounded just great, as far as Ivor was concerned. Clearly no doubts as to what she'd witnessed had entered her mind in the week since, nor had any puzzling memories of falling tissue-paper fragments swum up into the light.

Ivor had asked her, 'Did they chat to you while your statement was away being typed?'

Mrs Fuggle frowned mildly for a moment. 'Nothing went away to be typed. The sergeant stood and listened, while a woman – so clever, so quick she was – typed all the while I spoke. I didn't go on too long. Tried to be considerate, think of her. I signed it there and then, the sergeant told me that was all, thanked me for coming and let me go. They showed no sign of wanting to chat, neither of them. Come to that, neither did I very much.'

'You said, the sergeant?' Ivor queried.

'Oh, I knew he was a sergeant all right. Had the three stripes on his uniform sleeve.'

Ivor had said, 'Yes, of course.'

No. This work of art of Ivor's would have no successors. It would stand for ever alone. Unique, like a Titian, or a Henry Moore. That way suspicion could never again alight on him. There would be nowhere for it to land. This artwork was a very private one. Carried out by himself without help from anybody else, and for no-one's benefit but his own. Mrs Fuggle had been the only witness to it, but even she had not understood its full significance; its unique beauty had been savoured by himself alone. Now, by virtue of Ivor's resolution never to create a copy of it, or anything remotely similar to it, nobody else would ever know of it. Nobody would want to. Nobody would need to. Nobody ever could.

For the second weekend running Ivor did not go up to London. Sunday was Frank's day off, so that feeding the animals on that day of the week had usually been Jack's concern. Now the obvious person to do it would be Heinz, but no-one quite felt they were in a position to ask him to step in. Who would pay him if he did? There was nobody actually in charge of Birdskitchen just now. Not until something was heard from the solicitor. Ivor thought it a sensible idea to take on the care of pigs, chickens and sheep for the day himself. Feri came down to spend the Saturday night. Her exams were going OK, she thought. But there were more to come in the week ahead. She wouldn't be able to get down for Jack's funeral which, now that the body had been released by the coroner, had been fixed for the following Wednesday at Peasmarsh church.

Mrs Fuggle didn't leave Birdskitchen that Saturday, but stayed the night. There was a feeling of awkwardness between the three of them, which went unvoiced in an atmosphere of politeness that seemed a little forced. Ivor, who might or might not be the heir to the house – his position was ambiguous – slept with his girlfriend in an attic room while Mrs F., whose position as housekeeper was not ambiguous at all, occupied one of the best bedrooms on the first floor at the front. It was not the time for turning out Jack's room, and certainly not for contemplating sleeping in his bed.

Feri felt uncomfortably as though she were joining Ivor in a state of siege. Robbie had been polite but distant when their paths had crossed in the yard during the afternoon. Mrs Fuggle created endless jobs for herself to do – jobs that Feri could clearly see didn't need doing. Again she wasn't happy about leaving Ivor alone at Birdskitchen after she returned to London on Sunday afternoon. With any luck, she hoped, the uncertainty over Ivor's status would be resolved within the next few days. She had an idea about the future after that, but knew that it was too soon, for a number of reasons, to air it yet.

It had been a relief to Ivor when Stephen Lyle had said to him, just before they parted at the front door after their first meeting, 'Don't worry about the funeral costs. They're paid for out of the estate directly, no matter who comes to inherit it.' Would that include money for beer and sandwiches somewhere afterwards? Ivor had wanted to know, but Stephen had told him, sadly, not. At least, Ivor thought as he crossed the cobbles, hearing the door of the solicitors' chambers close behind him, beer and sandwiches would be a relatively minor expense. He couldn't imagine many people turning up. Whereas he'd heard that funerals cost literally thousands of pounds. And when he'd gone to meet the funeral directors later that day he was able to confirm that as a fact.

This morning, Monday of the second week post-Jack, with two days to go before the funeral, it was again with relief that he heard the solicitor's voice, this time on the phone. Stephen asked him if he could call in at the chambers that afternoon. The news was about as good as Ivor could expect in the circumstances. Would he mind bringing his passport in again? Also, if he could lay his hands on them, his birth certificate, and Jack's?

It was only his second visit to Stephen Lyle's office, but even so Ivor had a feeling, as the heavy panelled door was opened for him, that he was coming back to a place that he not only knew well but also inhabited, albeit infrequently and briefly, by right. He guessed this was because he was in a much stronger position than he'd been in a week before. After bidding him sit down Stephen Lyle took the documents Ivor had brought with him and went out briefly to give them to someone to have copies made. Returning, he took his own seat opposite Ivor and, laying his palms flat on the table, announced, 'You'll be pleased to know we've concluded that the will you brought us is indeed genuine, and we can proceed towards probate on that basis.' He paused and gave Ivor a professionally cautious look. 'That's not a guarantee that we'll get there, of course. A more recent will could still come to light, and there's always the chance someone might try to challenge it – at any stage.'

'Cousins in Australia, you mean?' Ivor said.

Stephen gave him an appreciative smile. 'I'm afraid there are more cousins in Australia than either of us might wish. On the other hand, in most cases where people jump out of the woodwork they do it quicker than you can say knife. Nine days have gone by and no-one's popped up yet. I think you stand a fighting chance.' The smile became a grin. 'Don't worry too much.' Stephen went on to talk about his firm's charges and gave him the cheering news that they could be paid relatively painlessly, out of Jack's estate, at a later date. Then he told him how things would proceed, step by step. Wages, this week's and the last's, could be paid on Friday. There were special, interim bank accounts to be set up: cheques would need Stephen's counter-signature in addition to Ivor's own, which was a bit of a nuisance, Stephen appreciated that, but at least it meant the farm's business could go on.

Ivor broke in. 'There's something else I want to ask. There's a great barn on the farm that I want to convert into a house. A medieval hall house in fact. And then to sell it off. Will I be able to make a start on that?'

Stephen looked at him in some surprise. 'That does seem an odd priority for someone who's just taken over a farm. Actually, I'm afraid you won't be able to do that just yet. You can't sell off a major asset before probate's granted. And you wouldn't be able to get planning permission to alter a building whose ownership isn't yet established in law. I'm afraid that project may have to wait.' Stephen saw Ivor's mouth turn down at the corners. He pressed on. He had to impart one more piece of news that Ivor might find unwelcome. 'It also wouldn't be a good idea to make changes of personnel just yet. Sacking people and so on. Just in case you were thinking of it. Other people might not feel you had that right, and if by some chance the inheritance turned out not to be yours after all, any such decision might prove costly to unpick.'

'I wasn't thinking of sacking anyone,' Ivor said. He had already worked out that any sudden spate of dismissals – Mrs Fuggle's? Robbie's? – would draw almost as much attention to him as if he should decide, Macbeth-like, to start bumping the difficult people off.

'That's good,' said Stephen, visibly brightening. 'Now to the positive. Have you ever come across Malcolm Saunders, Mr Eason's accountant? His office is just down the hill, in the Landgate. I'll get the two of you in touch.' He picked up the phone on his desk and a minute later was saying to Ivor, receiver still in hand, 'He can see you for a few minutes as soon as we're done here. If you've got the time. Shall I say in a quarter of an hour?'

Ivor had a strange feeling of comfort as he made the short walk in the sunshine, down from the cobbled streets to the lower end of the town. It was as though he was strolling along in bedroom slippers, perfectly at home. And the accountant, when Ivor met him, had good news for him. Although Birdskitchen was not a goldmine by any means, the estate was not encumbered with any mortgages or long-term debts. This would help speed the journey towards probate. And Ivor would be able to start with a clean sheet.

It gave Ivor a good feeling to be told this. Yet there was a kind of unreality about it. There was a sense of unreality about everything that happened now. To the whole of his life since Jack had had his accident. It was unsettling. Ivor wondered how long this feeling would last. But when he tried to see forward to the end of it a problem loomed. Because there was no possibility of reversing the events that had led to Jack's death, no possible way to bring him back, Ivor couldn't see any reason why this sense of strangeness, of unreality, this – he hated to admit it to himself, but in the end he had to – this downright awfulness, should ever end.

Ivor stood in the little church at Peasmarsh. It wasn't really little. It only appeared so from outside, in its setting of open pasture, with woods nearby and, in the grassy churchyard, two miles outside the village it served, enormous spreading trees: oaks and yew trees and one radiant copper beech. Inside, the nave was oddly divided from the chancel. In the place where you expected a carved or traceried rood screen was a massive Norman stone wall. The wall was pierced by an original arch, though its typically rounded top looked as if it had been somehow flattened by the weight of wall and oak-framed roof above, and it seemed almost to want to spread itself even wider, into the keyhole shape beloved of the Moors.

Through the arch Ivor had a view of Jack's coffin, laid on its trestle bier.

Ivor was wearing his one and only suit. Although he'd seen the inside of countless churches now – it went with the territory of architectural research – it was the first time, he was fairly sure of this, that he'd ever attended a religious service. Certainly, he'd never been to a funeral before. He was in the front row – the deceased man's heir. Next to him was Mrs Fuggle, then Robbie and his wife. Their brood of three was of necessity divided by the aisle, the eldest sharing a pew with Frank and Heinz and Heinz's English wife.

Nobody had come to challenge their right to occupy the front row. No cousins had come from Australia or anywhere else. No distant relatives of Jack's dead wife, Nell. Or if they had, they hadn't yet made themselves known. Which Ivor took as permission for a little cautious relief, a little optimism about that inheritance of his which, like a landed fish, still seemed to have within it the alarming capability of slipping suddenly away again with a wriggle and a jerk.

The detective who had interviewed him, D. I. Tart, wasn't there. This was another thing that helped Ivor to feel hope. In TV stories the police always attended the funerals of people who'd died in what they, the police, considered to be suspicious circumstances, to get a feel for the grass-roots of the case. Ivor held his fragile flowers of optimism closely to him, as a small child clutches a nosegay to its chest.

But if he was pleasantly relieved by the absence of those persons, real or imaginary, who hadn't turned up, Ivor was astonished at the enormous number of people who actually had. He had never before today thought of Jack as someone who had friends. But he'd reckoned without the fact that farmers, who of necessity live miles apart from their neighbours, do form a social network of their own kind, wide-meshed and widely cast. He thought there must be two hundred people here. They packed and overflowed the pews. They stood in the side aisles and crowded the bell-ringers' domain, the square ground floor of the tower right at the back. They filled the porch and some stood on the outside, craning through the door. Ivor wondered apprehensively if they were all going to come back to the Cock Inn afterwards, to drink beer and eat sandwiches at his expense. At the expense, rather, of the overdraft the bank had considerately arranged for him with this event or eventuality in mind. It was true that he had recently sold his painting of Jack astride the rearing tractor among the plunging logs. He'd got the four hundred pounds he'd wanted for it. But the cheque – this was something he was quickly learning about the art world – was still in the post.

Ivor was surprised to find his old boss Albert Gutsell among those who'd come to pay their respects. Albert shouldered his way towards Ivor at the graveside and said sourly, 'Well, you've come into your own all right. No more mucking out of pigs for you from now on, I'll bet. Seems like you've a great knack for getting away from jobs you no longer like.'

Ivor only half turned to look at him. 'You owe me three days' pay,' he said, and Albert sidled away. He didn't show up at the Cock Inn afterwards, to Ivor's relief. He was further relieved that most of that enormous congregation had not made the tortuous journey through the lanes. Even so, about sixty people had. They were relaxed and friendly with Robbie and Mrs Fuggle but Ivor sensed a wariness in them when they politely shook his own hand. Some of them remembered him from school, of course, or had heard of him and his bullying ways back then. But throughout the gathering ran an atmosphere of thoughts unvoiced, at least not in his hearing. Ivor sensed in the buzz of conversation an undertone: a sense of puzzled wonderment at how Ivor had come to inherit Jack's estate. He might have knocked about the Rye area all his life but he was no farmer. No farmer's son. His connection with Birdskitchen was tenuous and his arrival recent when measured along the slow-moving time-scales of farms. He was a cuckoo in the nest. The word interloper seemed to have been designed for his special case.

Among the gathering were Gemma's old neighbours the Jamesons, who owned the land and buildings of Gatcombe Farm. Bob Jameson spoke to Ivor, as almost everyone there did, but he alone came close to voicing the general feeling of disquiet. 'Awful, Jack going the way he did. But, you know, it reminded me of something. When Gemma was living at Gatcombe, I think it was before your time, she told me she was thinking of writing a murder story set in an oast. She and that young friend of hers ... what was her name?'

'Feri,' Ivor said.

'Feri, that's right. They came around and examined the kilns and the hoists. Of course there's no trap-door in Gatcombe's oast – you know that, of course. Don't know if she ever wrote the story up.' He looked at Ivor rather searchingly. 'Did she ever tell you about that?'

'Don't think she did,' Ivor brushed the subject away. 'I never knew she was thinking of writing anything like that. Cuddly little kittens was more her sort of thing.'

Something about Ivor's answer obviously struck Bob as amusing, because he had to suppress a smile. Ivor thought that if Bob Jameson were to go trumpeting his knowledge of this coincidence around the neighbourhood his days of freedom would be numbered, but something told him that Bob would not. Just as, two years before, he hadn't notified the News of the World of the well-known children's author's liaison with a sixteen-year-old boy.

Robbie, all traces of chest hair for once obliterated by shirt and tie and suit, said to Ivor, 'Well, I suppose you're going to give us all the sack now.' It was a joke, but a joke with a challenge hidden in it, like a pebble in a snowball. The subtext was: *just you try and you'll see what.*

'No, of course not,' Ivor said. 'I know you're joking, but obviously, of course I'm not. First I'm not allowed to, as the solicitor told me, and second I wouldn't want to even if I could. I'll need all the help you can give me. And I'll find a way to reward that help as soon as I can.' He managed a bright smile for Robbie, who might or might not have guessed the effort that it cost.

Robbie put his drink down on the nearest table and stuck both hands in his trouser pockets to indicate that he had something more, and more interesting, to say. ''Course I do know how you came to end up in Jack's will. In his good books and more.'

Ivor frowned. 'What do you mean?' He was sure that Robbie didn't know all the things that he himself did, so he wondered what he could possibly be going to say.

'Private things. You know what I'm talking about. Two men together in a barn or oast.'

Ivor was genuinely startled and it showed. 'Bloody hell, mate! What are you suggesting?'

Robbie grunted, and grinned momentarily in reaction to Ivor's outrage. 'All right. Keep your hair on. Only he used to try it on with me when I were your age. I said no, of course.' He snorted. 'Maybe if I'd a known...'

'Well, you can forget it. I hear what you're saying now. The answer's absolutely not. I'm not like that. Never have been, never will. Excuse me, there's someone I need to see.' Ivor moved away.

There really was someone he wanted to see. It was Mark Harris, here with a man of about Jack's age who was presumably his father Trevor. 'Thanks for coming,' he told them both. 'Thank you very much.' He really meant it. He hadn't seen Mark for two years, not since the time Mark had helped him move the tools from

Winchelsea Beach to Gatcombe and they'd eaten Gemma's chocolate cake.

Now Mark steered Ivor slightly away from his father, who was talking to another man. 'Not an easy situation you're in right now,' he said. 'I know, from the outside it looks like you've had all the luck in the world. Fallen on your feet. But I know it doesn't go like that. People won't forgive Jack for leaving the place to you – though fuck knows what else he was going to do with it. Give it to Robbie? Not. And people won't forgive you for being left it either. Not yet. But they will with time.' He paused after dispensing this bit of wisdom, with quite a satisfied look on his face. Then a slight frown replaced it as he added, 'At least, that's what my dad says.'

Ivor wasn't used to needing support from people. He'd never appreciated efforts people had made to comfort him when he was a child, so that most of them had given up. Nor did he usually care what people thought of him, at least not in the abstract. He did care, of course, about the practical consequences of what people thought: what their opinions of him might lead them to give him or withhold from him in terms of opportunity or cash. But this indifference seemed to have lessened since Jack's death. He was dealing with this day all on his own, since Feri was in London, sitting an exam, and he was very conscious of his vulnerable state. He was moved by Mark's moment of kindness in this potentially hostile environment, and found himself unexpectedly, once again, on the verge of tears. He said, 'Thank you. You're very kind, mate,' and heard – as Mark did too – the huskiness in his voice.

In the evening Feri phoned Ivor, apologising yet again for not having been at his side – 'not being there for you,' as she put it – during the day. He stopped her, told her it had all gone very well, despite the horrific bill he now expected to receive from the Cock Inn in view of the number of people who'd turned out. Would Feri be coming down at the weekend, he asked her, or should he come up? Someone else could be found to feed the pigs.

Feri said, 'We're not going to go on like this, surely, now? Seeing each other just at weekends?' Since Jack's death this hadn't been discussed. 'Aren't we going to run the place together, like we always said?'

'You mean, you'd come down and we'd live together here?' Of course they'd always dreamt of this. Now for the first time Ivor saw obstacles. Never having been frightened of Mrs Fuggle before, he suddenly and unexpectedly found himself caring what she might say or think. Would the solicitor kick up a fuss? Robbie...?

'There's living together and there's living together,' Feri said, rather softly, so that Ivor had to ask her to repeat it. Then suddenly he saw what she meant. It was as if the idea she'd had for some days now but had not yet stated, had suddenly become his.

'OK,' he said slowly. 'I hear you. Are blokes supposed to go down on one knee, telephone in hand, when they do this?'

Later in the evening Ivor phoned Mark. 'Feri and I are getting married,' he told him. 'Would you do me a favour – I mean do me the honour – of being my best man?'

TWENTY-FOUR

It wasn't that Ivor was a particular fan of the institution, but he understood the symbolic significance of it. It was a way of showing to the world that you – meaning Feri and you – were one person, not two. As far as Ivor was concerned they always had been one person; it was just that they hadn't discovered this until they met. The idea of a wedding, on the other hand, interested him much less. He imagined a cavernous huge church somewhere in London, or even New York, full of wealthy overdressed Colombians who were about to become his in-laws. He still had the memory of his mother's wedding in York to draw on – admittedly he had enjoyed that day – but now he saw nothing but billowing gowns that inevitably clashed, and morning coats, and people, businessmen from New York and Bogota, who would imagine they were more important than he was.

Over the next few days he talked a lot to Feri on the phone. He saw the need to avoid saying rude things about her mother and father but maybe, if he phrased his concerns carefully enough, she would come to feel things as he felt them, and save him the trouble. He said, 'Won't it have to be a very big affair, with your family? South American Catholics and all that.'

It was the first time Ivor had mentioned religion to Feri in the two years since they'd met. That had made him, in her eyes, refreshingly different from all her previous boyfriends. Those others had all wanted to know about the Catholic Church in Colombia. They'd wanted to hear about the country's politics too, and about the dependence of its economy on the drugs trade. (Lots of people said this was the case, but was it really true? they'd all asked.) They'd wanted Feri to be a mine of information on all these things, and to have strong opinions on them of her own. Feri did have strong opinions, as it happened, but not on religion, politics or economics, or even drugs. She regarded the dismaying tendency of other people to poke these questions at her as a symptom of something else she disliked: their view of her as a tropical exotic, someone to be treated differently simply because of the soil in which her family had its roots.

But Ivor, unlike the others, took her exactly as she was. He always had done. He was interested in her opinions about art, architecture, furniture and design. He had never tried to talk politics with her, or ask about religion or the drugs trade, simply because he had no opinions on these subjects himself. All this suited Feri very well, the more so now that she was going to share her dreams with him – the dreams of being a Sussex farmer's wife, while running a country crafts and furniture business with him on the side.

'No,' she said, in answer to his question. 'It doesn't have to be a big Catholic religious thing. Traditionally, South American women are devout, the men are mostly atheists. Except for the priests, of course, though I'm not even sure about some of those. But in my family we're non-believers on both sides.' She paused for a moment, and Ivor had a sense of her trying to peer at him down the phone. 'Do you want to involve your mother? And her man?'

'Not really,' Ivor said. 'I know they invited me to theirs but...' He'd only spoken a couple of times to his mother, and on the phone at that, in the two years since that wedding day. Birthday and Christmas presents had been exchanged by post, but that was that. 'It's a different generation.'

'Then why,' said Feri, 'don't we just go ahead and do it? A couple of witnesses is all we need.'

'I've told you about Mark,' Ivor said.

'And that's just fine. We can tell everyone else afterwards. My parents. Your mum. Tell them when it's a fait accompli, and there's nothing anyone can say, let alone do.'

They discussed things further when Feri came down to Birdskitchen that weekend. Ivor invited Mark to join them for a drink at the Bell at Iden – a pub that was not only a convenient halfway point between their two farms, but was also not frequented, as far as they were aware, by anyone they knew. Ivor introduced Mark to his fiancée, forgetting they had already met: forgetting that Mark had had the pleasure of a bewildering conversation about the Lydd experience with Feri a whole twenty-four hours before Ivor had set eyes on her. They pointed this out to him with a laugh, then Feri said to Mark, 'You're taller now,' as though this should be surprising in a boy who'd grown from sixteen to nearly twenty since she'd last seen him, and had swapped his schoolboy status for that of a student at the Royal Agricultural College at Wye. Then the two of them sat down with Ivor, once they'd all got a drink, and discussed the business of the day with him in the easy way of people who have known each other all their lives.

The first idea they had was to arrange to be married at Chelsea registry office, in emulation of a slew of celebrities. But there was a problem with that. The people who most needed to have their noses rubbed in the fact of Mark and Feri's new status in law, as opposed to simply in each other's hearts, the Mrs Fuggles and the Robbies, would be the least amenable to being dragged up to London for a day. Ivor thought that Mrs Fuggle would probably only consent to travel to a wedding in the capital if it were to be held at Westminster Abbey or St Paul's, and the invitation sent by the Queen. In the end logic pointed to a simple ceremony at the local registry office, in Hastings. There could be a bottle or two of champagne afterwards in a nearby sea-front bar, and that would be that. They were all sensitive enough to see that a big party at Birdskitchen Farm itself, within a month or two of Jack's death there, would be frowned upon by those people whose goodwill, for the present, mattered most.

Ivor and Feri made their announcement to the Birdskitchen staff the next morning. And Ivor took advantage of the startled moment to make a more private announcement to Robbie a few seconds afterwards. They each held a glass of champagne in their hand as Ivor walked Robbie across to the window of the big kitchen and said to him, 'I've been talking to the lawyer and the accountant.' He'd done so the previous Friday afternoon. 'I can offer you the job of farm manager, with the salary to go with it. I hope you're interested.'

Robbie gave him a look that was both wary and searching. 'I thought you couldn't do that. Touch the salaries, I mean. Change people's jobs.'

'I can't sack people, and I can't create a bigger wages bill. But they'll let me do a bit of juggling things around within the bill as a whole, if you get me. There's the wages Jack paid himself, I mean. And I don't want to appropriate those, because I don't want to do Jack's work. I'm not a farmer. I don't have the experience or the expertise, and it's not what I want to do. I need to concentrate on the furniture business – Feri too. So there's money to give you a bit more...' he named a figure that he thought would win Robbie's approval, and saw from the look on his face that it had, 'and we hire a kid from one of the villages to do some of the donkey work at the youngsters' rate.'

'And you?' Robbie asked, trying to sound as though he hadn't just been bought.

'I go on drawing my part-time wage just as before. I do the same part-time hours as before. But effectively you're in charge.'

'And when your precious probate comes through, then what?'

Ivor made a show of taking a sip from his champagne, which pretty well forced Robbie to do the same. Ivor said, 'Nothing changes. Certainly not in the short term. If I don't get probate, if it turns out that somebody else owns the place after all, then everything's up shit creek, for me as well as you and everybody else. But if that happens it won't be through my fault, and there'll be nothing I can do about it. You going to accept?'

Robbie nodded his head.

'We'll talk details another time,' said Ivor. Together they walked back across the room and joined in the others' small talk. The announcement of Robbie's new status could wait.

The bride wore a black trouser-suit with wide, star-pointed lapels, which she had designed herself and then had had made by a St Martin's friend. Her concession to the idea of white was to be found in the ruff-fronted shirt that gleamed out from beneath the jacket. Her groom and his best man were almost identically colour-themed. They wore dark suits, white shirts and matching dove-grey ties. It was a small but very carefully chosen gathering that witnessed the occasion at Hastings registry office. Almost the entire population of Birdskitchen was there; even Frank had felt able to manage a few hours away from his pigs. The only other guests were half a dozen of Feri's London and college friends who had driven down or come by train. As Ivor and Feri had both planned, there was a conspicuous absence, which the elderly Frank and Mrs Fuggle found bewildering, of family from either side. Mrs Fuggle tried not to be too upset about the non-appearance of a white bridal dress, then found to her surprise, after three glasses of champagne at the Yelton Hotel, that in the end she didn't mind the novelty of Feri's outfit quite so much.

Brief and businesslike though it was, the guests enjoyed the little reception more than they'd thought they would. As soon as it was over Mark and his current girlfriend, the two official witnesses to the signing of the register, drove the newly-weds to the station. They were going to Gatwick, to catch the evening Naples flight.

Ivor and Feri spent their short honeymoon in Sorrento where, in autumn sunshine, they enjoyed the sights of the Bay of Naples and the Amalfi coast. But for all that they enjoyed themselves, Feri was conscious of something worryingly different about her new husband. She guessed he was suffering from stress or anxiety or some other kind of emotional upset. She wasn't unduly troubled by it though: she was pretty certain of its source. It was the uncertainty about his future that hung over him, that nagging doubt that the lawyers' slow trail towards probate might fail, that Birdskitchen, in which he had so much at stake, might in the end turn out not to be his. This anxiety didn't manifest itself in his frequent bouts of sullenness, she was used to those. But it did quite noticeably affect his performance in bed. Not that she'd married him for that alone. Even so, it had been part of the package of his desirability. Now it all too seldom was.

It was not until their return from Sorrento that Feri officially moved out of the flat in Highgate and into Birdskitchen. A short time before the wedding Mrs Fuggle had astonished Feri by doing something gracious.

She announced that she wanted to cut down her hours and would therefore no longer require to live in. She would return to her own house on the Iden road, where her daughter lived with her husband and family. If it suited everyone she would cycle over to Birdskitchen every morning, and back in the afternoon. Perhaps occasionally, when the weather was bad in winter... Feri promised that she could expect a lift.

By now Jack's bedroom had been cleared and cleaned out. A new carpet had been laid. Some of the furniture was heavily Edwardian and would, Ivor and Feri agreed, be replaced in due course. A priority, though, was the bed. Ivor favoured an original Elizabethan or Jacobean four-poster with brocaded silk curtains all around. Feri did not. She would accept a traditional design, even imitation antique or lacquered brass, but the frame had to be new – and the mattress too, of course. Ivor had compromised. A new mattress, well, that had gone without saying, but he wasn't too happy with lacquered brass. Instead he'd set to in the workshop with posts and planks of seasoned yew the colour of glowing saffron, and built a new bed-frame for his wife. Where her bed was concerned he'd do the best he could.

As for the rest of the house, they agreed that they wanted it to look as much as possible like the smart interior that Gemma had created at Gatcombe. There was a limit to what could be done for the time being. But a marked improvement could be effected simply by moving unsuitable things like kitchen chairs and teetering stacks of egg-boxes from the front rooms. With some of the clutter gone, the star items – the square piano, the Dutch long-case clock with marquetry inlay, the oak dining-table and chairs – were able to shine more brightly, like flowers in a garden that had been stripped of weeds.

They contacted their parents in the end. Feri telephoned hers at their separate addresses in New York. They were only momentarily stunned by the news, and at the end of the conversation in each case wished their daughter well. A few days later wedding presents arrived in the form of two generous cheques. At least they had heard of Ivor, knew his name and their daughter's new address. They'd heard that he'd recently inherited the farm...

Ivor conveyed his news to his mother by letter.

Dear Mum

I can't remember if I told you this but Jack – the owner of Birdskitchen, my boss – died suddenly back in the summer and left the farm to me. This has made it easier for me and my girlfriend to tie the knot. We got married a few weeks ago. Sorry we didn't tell you or invite you down, but we didn't tell anyone very much. Now we're going to run the farm together and build up a business with furniture and antiques. When we're sorted come and see us. In a year or two. Hope things are good with you.

As always.

Ivor would not have been surprised to receive a phone-call in response to that but he didn't. A letter came back a few days later instead. It was from Michael. He read it while he and Feri were breakfasting in the kitchen.

Your mother has asked me to write this. If you have really got married she is really happy for you. (Both of us are.) But she's a bit surprised you've said so little about any of this before. (It's a bit difficult for her to take in the idea of you being left a farm, then getting married to someone she's never heard of, all in the space of a few weeks.) We can't help wondering if this is all one of your jokes. Your mother would be very happy if you'd phone her and let her know what's really going on, if different from the above.

Meanwhile we have a bit of news of our own to impart.
You know, of course, that some people who are very
religious in early life lose their religion later, while with
others it can be the other way round. Well, it looks like
your mother and I have joined the second lot. As a result
of talking with certain friends of ours we know from
work, we became interested in the Quakers and have
decided to join the Society of Friends. It's still very
recent (that's why you haven't heard from us on the
subject yet). It's another thing your mother would like to
tell you more about when you phone...

'What exactly are the Quakers?' Ivor asked Feri across
the coffee mugs when he'd finished reading this. 'The
Society of Friends?'

Feri dealt with the last corner of a piece of toast.
'They're a sort of Christian denomination, I think,' she
said. 'For people who want to be Christian but without a
denomination, without a Church. Does that make sense?'
Ivor thought it sort of did.

They both worked hard, right from the beginning, to
build up their business. Adapting to the move from town
to country Feri knew better than to limit herself to
scarves and other fashion accessories. She made designs
for fire-guards, which she had a local blacksmith realise
for her in wrought-iron. She also came up with a novel
idea in this connection, which she didn't think anyone
else had thought of. She remembered how at Gatcombe,
years before, glowing embers would all too often topple
out of the fire and singe the hearth-rug. Hearth-rugs were
always getting singed, that was their function, and ended
up mottled with unsightly small black blister marks, but
Feri found a pragmatic remedy to this. She designed
patterned hearth-rugs and, to go with them, a number of
star-like metal studs whose outlines matched the spirit of
the rug's design. A soft metal stalk lay behind each stud.

In the event of a burn you simply pushed this through the burn mark, folded the stalk flat on the underside, and your unsightly black blister was transformed into a decoration. Feri would supply a dozen with every hearth-rug sold. The customer could always come back for more. She was working on one such design one dark day in December when Ivor – at the other end of the apple store, dealing with a gashed moulding on a Jacobean court cupboard – said suddenly, 'Remember David?'

'Of course I remember David,' Feri said. 'I shared a house with him till three months ago.' She had seen quite a lot of him until that time, though only during the mid-weeks. David had been careful to be absent from the Highgate house during Ivor's weekend visits for the previous two years. Both Feri and Ivor were fairly certain that he was the source of Gemma's information about the start of their relationship, but Feri had thought it beneath her dignity to confront him with this and Ivor hadn't had the chance.

'Did you know he had a brother who was studying to be an architect?' Ivor asked.

'I did. And he did become an architect. Richard. I met him. He lives not far from here.'

'I want to get in touch.'

'With David? I didn't think you liked him.'

'No. With his brother. I want him to help me convert the barn.'

Feri's face acquired the look it always did when her husband said something more than usually off the wall. This tended to happen when he got onto the subject of the barn, or else – something he mercifully hadn't mooted for some time – of ripping the centre out of Birdskitchen farmhouse and reconstructing it as a medieval hall. 'You know you can't convert it before probate. Don't run ahead of things.'

'Yeah, but it doesn't hurt to plan ahead, does it?' Ivor told her. 'And when I say plan, plan's what I mean. Plan in the sense of architectural drawings and that.'

'Oh, those,' Feri said. She had already seen the future he had outlined for the barn.

'Plans with someone's name on them, printed underneath, with RIBA after.'

'I don't know that he's as qualified as that,' said Feri doubtfully.

'Well, he must have some letters after his name if he's passed his exams,' Ivor said. 'Let's get him over here at least. Especially if he lives locally. You can get in touch with him through David. Who, as you say, I don't like.'

'I won't even need to go through David,' Feri answered. 'When we met and I told him about this place he gave me his very, very new business card. He works in Ashford.'

Richard came over to Birdskitchen the next weekend. Like his younger brother he was a handsome and athletic-looking man. He had the disconcerting quality that all siblings who are not twins share – that is, of looking at one and the same time both alike and totally different from each other. Ivor was relieved to find that Richard did not share his brother's compulsion to flirt with him.

Richard liked the look of the barn, whistling approvingly and nodding his head as they walked round the outside and then the interior, peering upward at the massive skeleton of beams. His reaction pleased Ivor more than he had dared to hope it would. 'Sometimes an idea meets with a moment in history,' Richard said, as he continued to walk round inside the barn with Ivor and Feri. 'You're not quite the first person to come up with the idea of turning these old Wealden barns into homes, but you're among the first. There's a few barns like this one already being converted, dotted about Kent and Sussex. People will see them and in a few years there's going to be an explosion in demand for them. Then for a few years there'll be a gold rush – my bosses think this and I believe them – until eventually the supply of old barns runs dry. But while the supply lasts – for the next few years that'll be – you can cash in.'

'Yeah,' said Ivor, 'but I've only got the one barn.'

'Convert it, sell it – it is yours to sell, isn't it? – and with the money you make you could buy up six more. Or use the skills you've learned to convert other people's barns for them – for a good fat fee.'

'It is my barn,' Ivor said slowly, 'but...' He explained how the need to wait for the grant of probate was holding everything up.

'You'll get that in a year, surely,' Richard said comfortingly. 'The boom won't be over as soon as that. You'll still be in time to get your share of it.'

'That's good to hear,' Ivor told him. 'But even then I'll need some expert help.'

Richard turned to Feri. 'Isn't that why you sent for me?' He turned back to Ivor. 'I wouldn't mind getting involved, you know. Find some businesslike arrangement that would work. And I don't mean my firm. They'd see you as a customer and charge the earth. It'd just be me, on my own.'

Ivor said, 'Do you have letters after your name?'

Richard laughed. 'Yes, I suppose I do. BArch.'

'Not RIBA?' Ivor sounded disappointed, like a child.

'Not yet,' Richard said, smiling. He clearly thought Ivor was a bit of a character. 'Otherwise you'd have to pay *me* the earth.'

'I suppose it'll do,' said Ivor, and Feri hoped that Richard would mistake this for a joke.

At least Richard didn't seem to be put out. He went on blithely, 'There used to be what seemed an endless supply of un-modernised old farmhouses and cottages round here. But that's all gone. Right now the only hope for the successful tycoon types who want a big country pad tailored to their wants is to convert a barn. Or move to France. You only have to imagine in a bit of detail the kind of house you could create from this to realise the price it would fetch.'

'I already have,' said Ivor. 'I'll show you.' They walked back to the farmhouse and Ivor fetched his plans. When he examined them Richard was more than impressed. 'Blimey,' he said. 'Where did you learn to do architectural drawings as good as this?'

'Taught myself,' said Ivor coolly. 'Anybody can.'

'Some of us might disagree about the last bit,' Richard said, with a bit of a smile. 'But you'll save yourself some money by doing this yourself. Less for me to have to do. If you decide you want me involved, that is.' He handed the plans back to their author. 'On the other hand, these particular ideas won't wash.'

'What do you mean,' Ivor asked, his expression switching suddenly from smile to frown.

'Nothing to do with the quality of your draughtsmanship, I promise. It's just that... Well, this medieval thing...' Richard went on to explain that modern people did not want to inhabit a great hall that was open to the rafters, with what would effectively be a bonfire burning in the middle of the room. Nor did they really want to occupy rooms that were called bowers and solars, rooms which were lit by teensy lancet windows and were accessed by staircases that were little more than ladders, fitted through holes in the floors.

Ivor was not pleased to be told this. He was very much in love with his original medieval-dream plans and hated the thought that he would have to change them. It wasn't the work that would be involved in re-planning everything: he never minded work. It was simply that he hated to compromise the integrity of his artistic vision. But he knew very well what Feri would say if he refused. And he was realistic enough to know that money would in the end carry the day. 'All right,' he said, 'I'll have another think.' Glumly he confronted the idea that before probate was granted, if it ever would be, he'd have all too much time for that.

TWENTY-FIVE

In the days that followed Jack's funeral Ivor had the whole time expected that the police would drive up to the farm and, in response to some tip-off they'd had (from whom? Robbie? Mrs Fuggle? Bob Jameson?) arrest him on suspicion of murder or some differently worded crime that amounted to the same thing. But the days had turned into weeks, then months. He had expected that hand on his shoulder even during his wedding ceremony and at the reception that followed. He had even half wondered if he would be stopped at the airport and prevented from flying off on his honeymoon. But the months continued to pass and no police car came rolling up the track.

When, in the normal course of casual greeting, people asked Ivor how he was, he would answer, Fine, or, All right, or, Not too bad, depending on the weather, the season, or whether or not he had a cold. (It would still be a few years before British people began to answer the trite enquiry with the startling announcement that they were good.) But he wasn't fine. If he had told the truth he would have said he felt permanently ill. Physically, he felt as if he had swallowed something while it was still alive. Something like a starfish perhaps. Something that would from time to time stretch out a tentacle or two, as if seeking a way out. Sometimes it would convulse inside him, tying its slippery members into knots. Sometimes it would lie still for whole days at a time, but he always knew that it hadn't gone away. He grew to understand that it never would.

He believed he'd learned the good lesson from Raskolnikov: to keep an iron grip on his mental processes; not to let his feelings take control – as had happened so disastrously in Roddy's case, to the point where they gave him completely away. But he wasn't quite as successful at putting into practice what he'd learnt from Roddy's failure to control his emotions as he'd expected to be. He almost managed it: he'd done nothing to give himself away to other people, he was pretty sure of that; but he knew his efforts had not quite worked inside himself, where the internal discourse of his psyche was concerned. There was the bedtime thing. Sometimes everything worked just fine, but very often not. He'd apologise to Feri then, and say he had things on his mind. And fortunately she knew he did: she knew he was worried about the probate uncertainty, and in a hurry to get on with converting the barn. But it was difficult to be relaxed about sex when you were in bed and knew that presently you would be dropping off to sleep, and knew what would happen just the moment before you did. That the sight of Jack falling through the trap, arms outspread as if in crucifixion, a gaping hole of terror in replacement for a face, would appear before him as if the image had been branded permanently on his retina, and needed only the semi-lapse of consciousness that precedes sleep to reveal itself like a photograph in a dark-room. It came again in the mornings. Not every day, but often enough. And making love on those mornings, in the aftermath of those harrowing optical tricks, was as impossible as it often was at night. How could you live when you were too frightened to go to sleep? *Macbeth hath murdered sleep.* And Ivor, it appeared, had murdered sex.

He felt depressed. He knew that a visit to the doctor could result in a prescription for something that would deal with that. But depressions had causes, or most depressions had. A doctor had a responsibility to probe with questions about those things. Ivor's depression was not endogenous; it had a simple, easily identifiable cause. Ivor knew exactly what it was. But no doctor ever might.

Ivor prescribed for himself the only remedy that he could think of. Dizzyingly high, punishingly hard, doses of work. As the winter dark and cold reduced the labour of the farm to a trickle of jobs – always excepting the never-ending routine of feeding and caring for the livestock – Ivor plunged himself into his cabinet making. He was lucky: orders were coming thick and fast. Commissions for new-built oak furniture, repairs to fine antiques, even picture frames that needed to be patched. And if there was a lull, the slightest slowdown in the procession of jobs arriving for him to do, then he stayed out in the workshop and built things for the house. His house. His and Feri's. He built a nest of tables in solid walnut for the room that had once been Jack's whisky room, and for what had been Mrs Fuggle's bedroom a smart mahogany chest of drawers. The old stripped pine number that had been there previously made a few pounds at the auction rooms in Rye.

By taking this medicine constantly, by never letting up, Ivor managed to keep himself from falling apart. He could tell himself he led a normal life. Whatever normal meant. There was a drawback, though. The trouble with any painkiller, he reflected, even with one that was as healthy an option as hard physical and mental graft, was that as time passed you needed a higher and higher dose in order for it to work at all.

Feri was also an impressively hard worker, and as keen to build the business up as Ivor was, but even she was conscious of something manic in the way Ivor ploughed through his tasks. She learnt to say to him things like, 'Time to call a halt now.' Or, 'Down tools, Ivor, we're going out for a drink.' If she hadn't done, they would probably never have gone anywhere except where work took them, which usually meant Rye, to get cheques countersigned by Stephen Lyle, or to go to the bank. For shopping they avoided the supermarket giants of Rye and Peasmarsh, preferring their trusted local grocer's shop in Northiam instead. Feri made a point of inviting people over for a meal from time to time. Stephen Lyle and his wife came once. Mark was invited several times, plus his girlfriend of the season, and they were in turn invited to his parents' house. Richard the architect came over more than once, so that Ivor could pick his brains about the barn project and show him his developing plans.

They would eat out too, either in Rye or in one of the local pubs or, as in old and calmer times, simply go out for a drink at the Cock Inn. In the aftermath of Jack's funeral Ivor had been conscious of a chill descending upon the atmosphere of that pub whenever he walked in. But as the months had passed, and winter blackness had given way to spring's evening light, he noticed a gradual thaw. The bar of the Cock Inn still didn't exactly light up when he walked in, but he felt his existence was beginning to be accepted more and more. This was what Mark, quoting his father, had said would happen, when he'd been kind to Ivor that grim funeral day. But Ivor was aware that the gradual acceptance of him as owner of Birdskitchen had less to do with himself than with the vibrant, extrovert presence of his beautiful and hard-working wife.

The gauzy greens of spring gave way to the darker, thicker textures of midsummer. The apples were grape-sized on the trees and the hop bines began their corkscrew clamber up the poles. In the middle of one hot cuckoo-calling June morning Mrs Fuggle came into the apple store workshop with the post. Generally letters waited in the kitchen until people came in, at coffee time or lunchtime and collected their letters from there. So

Mrs F.'s arrival today marked a departure from normal routine. Feri was at the far end of the workshop, checking samples of a batch of place-mats she'd had made to her design. Ivor, nearer the entrance, was using a spokeshave to give an authentic rusticity to a set of kitchen chairs. It was to Ivor that Mrs F. now came, waving a long white envelope. 'I thought this might be important,' she said. 'And that you'd want me to bring it across.'

When Ivor looked at the envelope he too thought it might be important. It bore the name and address of his solicitors' chambers. Taking it, he tore it open in silence while Mrs Fuggle, also silent, waited, watching him with the expectant look of a dog that is about to be thrown a chocolate drop.

Ivor read: *I write to inform you that the Grant of Probate has been issued by the Probate Registry. I enclose a photocopy of the same for your records. Sealed copies of the Grant will be available to you at...*

Ivor stared at it. There was no doubt about it any longer. Birdskitchen – every brick and every stone of it – belonged to him. He was the owner of everything he could see, except the sky and the sun in it, as Robbie had so memorably said of Jack when Ivor had first come here. Now he looked at Mrs Fuggle. 'I've got probate,' he said hoarsely, then he caught hold of her and distractedly gave her a kiss on each cheek, while Feri walked slowly towards them, wondering but not yet guessing, what was up.

One of the first people Ivor shared his good news with was Richard. The conversion of the barn could at last go ahead. The great central hall concept had remained, but the plans for the surrounding rooms, on ground, first and attic floors, had been greatly altered, to meet modern tastes and needs. Large dormer windows would pierce the orange-tiled catslide at the back; other windows, double-glazed but in the vernacular style, would light the front and sides. The front wall of the great hall – where the barn doors had been – would be almost entirely glass: a series of vertical lights like the west window of a Tudor church. The front door would be formed in the centre of this arrangement, itself shaped pleasingly in the Tudor tradition, topped with the nearly flat, late Gothic arch.

A damp-proof membrane would be laid beneath new floors of reclaimed brick. Also of brick would be the chimney-stack, a massive affair that would house the open hearth in the hall, a wood-burning stove in the adjacent front room, and an Aga for the kitchen at the back. The Aga, gas-fired, would also provide central heating throughout the house.

Within a week of finding himself the undisputed owner of everything he surveyed bar sun and sky, Ivor had negotiated a contract for Richard's services as consultant to the project and, at least as important, a hefty loan from the bank. Some parts of the project required the involvement of specialist firms, but Ivor was careful to see that such contracts would be few. Hammering and sawing, brick-laying, plumbing... There were plenty of people in the neighbourhood who could help Ivor do those things, and who could be winkled out easily enough by asking around in pubs and shops. And Feri, who had already shown her skill in finding local craftsmen to realise her designs and local outlets for her finished products, would be good at this.

It took nearly a year, and a second bank loan, but eventually the barn conversion was complete. Black wood, orange tiles, standing tall in a newly hedged plot of land no longer required for growing hops, and which could be made into a garden and a small paddock for a pony or two, it looked mightily impressive in Ivor's eyes. When it was put up for sale, although there was a worrying month in which nothing much seemed to happen, it realised Ivor's rather cheeky asking price of something over half a million pounds. The bank got its money back and Richard got his fee. There was a substantial profit. Only a small proportion of this was needed for the purchase, from farmers at Wittersham and Rolvenden Layne, of two more barns.

It was Richard who advised Ivor to buy those next two buildings. Once these two had been converted – in, say, another year's time – the moment would be right, Richard believed, to set up a specialist barn conversion business, using the expertise they'd gained; their three highly visible achievements would be be their advertisement and quality guarantee. Other people were doing the same thing now; it was a real growth area; they only had to look at the contractors' boards standing by old black wooden barns as they drove around. The old apple store, already housing Ivor's workshop as well as the showroom for his and Feri's wares, was pressed into additional service as an office – which Ivor and Feri between them manned part-time: it was now the headquarters of Wingate Barn Conversions Ltd., as well as of Hop Bine Oak Furniture and Country Crafts.

Ivor, coming out of the farmhouse one morning en route for the apple store, was astonished to see Heinz's elderly wife May arriving from the direction of their cottage at a run. Even before she'd reached him she was calling out, 'Oh, come quickly,' her voice and facial expression a double proclamation of distress. 'I can't find Robbie and it's Heinz.'

Ivor didn't wait but set off towards her at a run, and continued with her back the way she'd come; they ran together towards her front door, at the far end of the track, open as she'd left it in her haste a half minute ago. Ivor asked his questions as they ran. 'What happened?'

'He's had a heart attack – or else a stroke. He fell on the floor. After breakfast. I heard the noise – and went to...'

'Have you called an ambulance?' Ivor asked.

'Yes, I have. But...'

'It's OK. I understand. Of course.' Two years earlier Ivor would not have understood. He'd been a different person then. Before Jack's death he hadn't known the need that human beings have for comfort and companionship in moments of distress. Now he knew almost too well.

They reached Heinz and May's cottage, the nearest of the three. The thought went through Ivor's head – crazy and inappropriate though it was at this moment – I own these cottages: this home of Heinz's, these bricks, this mortar, actually all mine... Up the path between beds of sweet William, flowering pinks and Canterbury bells. The old woman dived in through the open door with Ivor just an inch or two behind. The door opened directly into the living-room and there lay Heinz, on his side, in the middle of the floor. May and Ivor both dropped to their knees beside him. Ivor noticed that Heinz's shirt was buttoned tightly, right up to his neck. 'We must loosen his collar,' Ivor said and, seeing May make no move, leaned over Heinz to do it himself. Heinz's eyes were closed but at the touch of Ivor's fingers on his neck they opened suddenly and looked fiercely into Ivor's face. Heinz's lips moved once or twice without making a sound. Then suddenly some words came out. 'I don't know what you didn't,' he seemed to say. 'What you didn't done to Jack.'

Ivor recoiled in shock, rocking back on his heels, leaving the tight top button still done up. What had Heinz just said? Had he said anything at all in fact?

Perhaps Ivor's haunted imagination was playing a trick. But if Heinz actually had spoken, then had his wife heard? She was presumably better practised at unscrambling his cryptic utterances than anybody else. Ivor needed to find out. He turned to May. 'Did he just say something?' he asked.

May shook her head. 'I don't know. Perhaps he did. I didn't catch it if he did.'

That granted Ivor some relief at least. He reached out a second time to try and unfasten the button at Heinz's neck. This time, at the moment when his fingers made contact with the pearly little object, a spasm passed through the whole of Heinz's body. Ivor experienced it like a trembling of all the earth. In Heinz's throat a choking cough welled up, which dissolved into a sigh and then cut off. Immediately came the sounds of a vehicle drawing up outside, and then the slams of doors. Two paramedics, one carrying oxygen cylinders and a mask, came through the door. Ivor turned and looked at them, dimly remembered that one of them had two years earlier attended the scene of Jack's death. Ivor did not get up. 'I think he just died,' he said.

The following day one of Ivor's worst nightmares at last came true. A police car came up the track, slowly but purposefully, like a hunting shark. Ivor came out of the apple store where he was working and walked up to it. There was no point in doing anything else. There was nowhere to run to, nowhere for him to hide. 'Can I help you?' he said to the uniformed male officer who was just stepping out of the car. A woman in uniform was getting out on the other side.

'Mr Ivor Wingate?' the policeman asked, and Ivor said that was who he was. 'Just a little question for you – a routine thing, that's all – in connection with the death of Mr Heinz Müller yesterday.'

'Oh yes,' said Ivor politely. 'I was a witness to his death. I'll tell you anything I can. What would you like to know?'

'Perhaps you'd like to tell us, in your own words, what happened exactly.' It was the police woman talking this time. By now all three of them were standing together on the same side of the car. 'What you saw, and what you did.' She paused a second. 'Just remember carefully, and take your time.'

Ivor felt that thing that lay inside him, that starfish or private Kraken, wake and writhe and tie a tentacle or two into a knot. What could have happened to bring the police out here to question him? Heinz had died of a series of strokes, the ambulance crew had been pretty sure, and later in the day the hospital doctors had confirmed that. There was no earthly reason for the police to doubt this, to imagine anything other than a natural cause of death. Or was it that May had heard her dying husband's final words after all? Perhaps those words had made no sense to her at the time, or else she'd hardly been aware of them in her state of grief and shock, but on reflection afterwards the words had come back to her, the meaning of them suddenly leaping into place. Had that given her grounds for suspicion, sufficient grounds to pick up the phone to the police? Ivor had been to see her earlier in the day; she was staying for the immediate present in Peasmarsh, at the house of her eldest son. She'd been shocked and grief-stricken still, but hadn't seemed displeased to see Ivor – and certainly not frightened of him in any way. But that had been this morning. The revelation, if there had been one, might have come to her after his visit, might have been triggered by it for all he knew. He would need to be careful what he said when he came to describe that part of yesterday's event. As he began to tell his story he was aware that Feri had come to the workshop doorway and was standing watching him in puzzlement from there, while across the yard the front door of the farmhouse had opened and Mrs Fuggle stood looking out.

Ivor described May's precipitate arrival in the farmyard. Told how they had set off, running side by side along the track. That he'd asked May if an ambulance had been called, and understood that it had. He noticed how attentively both officers were watching his face, as though they expected that at any moment some involuntary twitch of a muscle might catch him out, a nanosecond's side-slip of the eyes betray an untruth. But there was no need for any untruth, was there? He was telling the story exactly as it had happened. If May Müller were asked to, she could confirm the lot.

'His shirt was very tightly buttoned. I thought if it was a heart attack or stroke he'd had it should be loose. Undone. May – Mrs Müller – didn't make a move to do it. Too shocked, I think. So I tried. As soon as I touched him he opened his eyes and made a sound. It startled me and I pulled my hand back.' Ivor thought this needed explaining. He went on, 'You see, I thought he said a few words. But if he did, the words were unclear. Mrs Müller didn't seem to hear them at all. 'Least, that's what she said. I leaned forward again to reach his shirt button and then he died. Like that. The ambulance crew arrived exactly then. They took over at once, of course.'

Ivor stopped. He'd done the best he could. But if May had heard what her husband had said, if she'd made sense of it either at the time or later and had then gone to the police, now was the moment he would find out. He waited, while the thing inside him heaved again and the two police officers looked at each other and exchanged barely perceptible nods.

The male officer turned back to Ivor. 'I think you've told us what we need to know,' he said. 'That all makes perfect sense. It was simply that one of the ambulance crew saw your hand on the dead man's neck and was dutiful enough – a bit over-zealous perhaps – to pass it on to us. Perhaps – I don't know why – it was the coincidence of there being two deaths on the premises in the space of two years and you a witness to them both. Anyway, we seem to have cleared that little mystery up. You didn't think to tell the paramedics what you were doing and they didn't think to ask. Often happens. Thank you for your time. We won't take up any more of it.'

The police woman spoke. 'Mr Wingate, thank you very much.' A brief smile and a nod. They got back into their car and by the time Feri had reached Ivor's side a few seconds later had turned round and driven off.

Ivor felt dizzy suddenly. May hadn't called the police. She hadn't heard her dying husband speak. Surely, married to someone, you'd be all ears to catch their parting words. She hadn't heard. In that case perhaps Ivor hadn't either. His imagination had done the whole thing. He'd hallucinated words and the movement of Heinz's lips. Perhaps. There was no way he could ever know. There was nobody he could ask.

'What was all that about?' Feri was asking him. And now Ivor found it even more difficult to explain things satisfactorily to his wife than it had been to explain them to the police.

TWENTY-SIX

No two Wealden barns were exactly alike. They were built to the same general plan and constructed in the same way: timber frame, tarred weatherboard cladding, big doors at the front and long sloping catslide at the back, orange-tiled or thatched. But the dimensions of each were different, the arrangement of the internal structural timbers never quite the same. There was no question of Ivor's using the same plans that he'd used for his Birdskitchen barn for the ones at Wittersham and Rolvenden Layne. The varying sizes of the structural bays inside the buildings meant planning for different-sized rooms and therefore imagining a different layout and disposition of those rooms in each case. Also, while the Birdskitchen barn faced south-west, the one at Wittersham had a south-eastern aspect and the Rolvenden Layne barn looked almost due north. This meant taking a new approach each time to the arrangement of the windows, and imaginative decisions – subject to the stipulations of English Heritage and UK Building Regs – as to where the walls and roofs could be pierced for natural light.

Perversely perhaps, Ivor enjoyed having to do all this, working late into the nights, doing drawing after drawing, re-checking his measurements on site by day, running his ideas past Richard at every stage. It was another layer of armour-cladding, another dose of the medicine of keeping busy, an extra way of protecting him from himself. The police car hadn't come back again, but that didn't mean it never would. And he sensed a wariness in Feri now: it was as though she had tried to satisfy herself that there was nothing troubling about that police car's visit on the day that followed

Heinz's death, but somehow hadn't quite managed to. As for the thing inside him, that tentacled hideousness that seemed to have a mind, a will and a timetable of its own, that would never leave him now. He was sure of that.

One evening, returning from a day on site at the two new projects – Wittersham and Rolvenden Layne were handily just miles apart – Ivor called at the Swan in Wittersham for a thirst-quenching pint of Spitfire. As his eyes adjusted from the outdoor brightness to the duller light within, he was surprised to see Mark Harris and his father Trevor standing at the bar. Ivor didn't visit the Swan often and hadn't known that Mark or his father ever did, but now he thought about it he realised that of course the Swan was one of the nearer pubs to where they lived. It crossed Ivor's mind as he walked up to them and they greeted one another that Mark was one of the few human beings he actually liked. He'd become aware of that on the day of Jack's funeral, and had gone on liking him since.

Mark was just as surprised to see Ivor. He knew about the conversion of the Birdskitchen barn, had been invited to see over it before it was sold, but he'd had no contact with Ivor in several months and knew nothing of the new projects nearer to his home turf. Ivor brought him up to date while Trevor ordered him a drink.

'Don't know how you find time to manage the farm these days,' Mark said. 'Carpentry, antique repairs, hand-printed scarves – or should that be hand-painted – and now converting barns. God, you've taken on a lot.'

'The hand-painted scarves as you call them and the other what-have-yous are Feri's thing,' said Ivor, 'but you're right. I don't have much time for the farm. Robbie does the whole thing and makes a pretty good job of it. Old Heinz's daughter comes in and does the book-keeping. Mind you, I keep an eye on that myself.

Once people know they couldn't fiddle things even if they wanted to they're not tempted to try.'

'Quite right,' said Trevor. 'You're a good little businessman, son.' He turned to his real son beside him. 'You want to take a leaf out of Ivor's book.'

'Ah, come on, Dad. That's not fair. You know I'm pretty sharp.' Mark, now twenty-one like Ivor, had left Wye College some months ago and now managed Link Farm jointly with his father.

'Well, all right, but you've only got one business to run, and that one with me, not three like Ivor here, doing it all himself.' Presumably Trevor wasn't thinking of Feri's input as amounting to much. 'I'd like to see you handling as much as that.'

Mark grinned at his father cheerfully. 'You'll just have to wait and see, once I'm given that chance.'

'Anyway,' said Ivor, displeased to find himself sidelined in the banter between father and son and wanting to edge back in again, 'farming was never something I expected to be doing. Not really in the blood.' He wondered, as he said that, what really was in his blood. His grandfather Peter Wingate had been a builder, and now Ivor was a builder too. Wingate Barn Conversions Ltd. But his mother had been adopted by Peter and Violet: there was no connection by blood. He wondered what his own father had done for a living, if anything. In Mark's case everything was clear-cut. His father farmed his own land and one day Mark would too. Ivor had become a farmer by mere chance, if you didn't include Jack Eason's death among the things that had brought the unexpected career change about. He had wanted a beautiful farmhouse, a beautiful woman in his life, a work life that involved painting, furniture making and architecture, and he had all these things. Owning an extensive acreage and a cluster of buildings that needed endless repair had never been part of his long-term plan.

'Sometimes,' he said, looking at both Trevor and Mark, 'just recently, with the turn things have taken, I've thought about selling off most of the Birdskitchen land, getting shot of that side of things and building up the building... I mean building up the other side of things.'

'Building up the building business,' said Mark, pouncing on Ivor's unintended pun. 'Building up the...'

'Enough,' said his father, then, turning to Ivor, 'Send them to college and they drive you bloody mad.'

'Trouble is,' Ivor said, ignoring all that, 'who's buying up land at the moment? You show me anyone round here who is.'

Mark and his father exchanged a look. 'Do we tell him?' said Trevor. 'Let your young friend in on it?'

'Yeah, OK,' said Mark. To Ivor he said, 'Funny, you saying what you just did. You see, Dad's been thinking of doing just that. Adding a couple of dozen acres...'

'I've got a lot more than that,' said Ivor, sounding more boastful than he'd meant to.

'Well,' said Trevor, 'I might be considering more than that. Quite a lot more, as it happens. It'd depend on the price, of course. Tell you what.' He gave Ivor a smile but his eyes said that he was also weighing the youngster up. 'Suppose you got the land valued – if you're serious about selling, that is – and you let me send someone round to value it for my side – then maybe have a talk. No need to say yes or no to that right away. But something to think about?'

'Blimey,' said Ivor who, cool cucumber though he usually was, found himself momentarily at a loss. 'This is all a bit sudden. I'd have to talk it over with Feri first.'

A few weeks later Ivor asked everyone to come to the farmhouse kitchen one lunchtime. Everyone meant Robbie and his wife, Frank, who was a widower, Alec the sixteen-year-old lad of all work, Mrs Fuggle, Andy the tractor man, and Heinz's daughter, who did the accounts. Heinz's widow no longer featured. She had moved permanently into her son's house and her tied cottage stood empty. Even without the glasses of cider that Feri handed around the kitchen everyone was pretty sure they knew what Ivor was going to say. Two sets of valuers had come peering round the buildings with clipboards and tape-measures and had driven in their Land Rovers through the fields. Robbie hadn't been slow to confront Ivor over this. 'So now you're selling the place, right?' he'd said to him. He'd come swaggering into the old apple store to do so.

'Maybe yes, maybe no,' Ivor had told him coolly. 'It hasn't happened until it's happened and even then it's only if. If it does, you'll be the first to hear of it. From me. And nobody's jobs are going to go.' He'd turned back to the computer, a very new piece of kit that he was having to come to terms with, and to his struggles with that week's payroll. Robbie had given one of his pony-loud snorts and left.

Now Ivor broke the news officially. He named the new owner: Trevor Harris of Link Farm, Stone-cum-Ebony. Frank nodded; he knew who Trevor was. Robbie said, 'Your mate's dad.' Though he didn't seem too displeased. Then, 'Job for young Mark an' all, is there?'

'Maybe,' said Ivor. 'Maybe not. I thought we might have a quiet word about that. Just you and me.'

In some circles this would have been taken as a signal to the others to finish their cider and make themselves scarce, but with Mrs F. and Frank and Alec it was never quite like that. With a jerk of his head in the direction of the door Ivor said to Robbie, 'Come through,' and led him along the back hall to what had once been Jack's TV and whisky room. It was still the TV room, not that Ivor and Feri watched TV that much; and whisky no longer played such a big part in the life of the room as before.

But it remained a comfortable living space, furnished now with a bit more elegance and taste. Here Ivor sat Robbie down in one of the big armchairs and offered him a new job. What would Robbie say to becoming project manager for the barn conversion company – at twenty percent more in terms of salary than he was getting at the moment – and bidding farewell to farm work? Robbie already knew he wouldn't be required to fulfil his traditional function of hop drier after this year's season was done. It was already beyond arguing over that Kent and East Sussex hops were no longer viable economically. Imported pellets from Germany and the Far East were what the brewers wanted now, what with the market for lager beers far bigger than the demand for traditional English ales, and with the added benefit that the imported varieties came cheap. Within two years the traditional hop gardens of the region would nearly all be gone. Robbie pondered all this in silence for a moment. Then he said, 'You did say twenty percent more?'

'I did,' said Ivor, and he spelled the difference out in pounds per week just in case Robbie hadn't yet managed it in his head.

'What do you say to making it twenty-five percent?' Robbie asked him with a sharp little light in his eyes.

'Wow,' said Ivor. Then, 'All right. OK.'

Robbie stood up, said, 'You're on, mate,' and they shook hands. Ivor privately congratulated himself on the ease with which he'd handled Robbie in a potentially explosive situation. The contract he'd signed with Trevor had stipulated that Mark would be the manager at Birdskitchen and that Robbie would go. Of course, the fact that he had quite a bit of leeway with the money had given Ivor an advantage. He just wished that he could be as smart when it came to managing his own inner turmoil. In that old business money had no power to do anything at all. And in the interpretation of what had

341

happened to Jack – the idea that his death was an accident or a work of art having long ceased to serve its purpose in Ivor's mind – there was no leeway at all.

Heinz's empty cottage was cleared out. Mark had it fumigated for woodworm and death-watch, covered the scuffed brown wallpaper with clean magnolia paint and, a month or two after the purchase of the land was completed, moved in. He only planned to be there during the week. His status at this time was, unusually for him, that of a bachelor. As he put it himself he was, 'between girls.' The cottage became his on-site bachelor residence, but he returned at weekends to the comforts of Link Farm: to his mother's washing-machine and ironing, and her wonderful home-cooked food.

Now that Mark was a close neighbour of Ivor and Feri's during the week, their paths crossed often, both by accident and by design. There was a rather bizarre welcome dinner for him at Birdskitchen, at which Mrs Fuggle cooked, as well as sitting down to table alongside Ivor, Feri, Robbie plus his wife, and Alec and Frank. In the weeks that followed that memorable meal Mark sometimes joined Ivor and Feri in a visit to the Cock Inn. Or else they made their separate ways there and met up by chance.

One such occasion occurred about two months after Mark moved in. Feri was out late, meeting one of the local artisans – a wrought-iron specialist this evening – who made items for Hop Bine Country Crafts to sell, according to Feri's specifications and designs, so Ivor paid a visit to the Cock by himself. It occurred to him as he walked from the car-park up to the door that he could have called on Mark at his cottage and asked him if he wanted to come too. Of course it was too late for that now. However, once he opened the door and stepped inside he saw Mark at the bar already, chatting to the barmaid obviously, but otherwise on his own.

'Should have called on you. Seen if you wanted to come out,' Ivor said as he joined him.

'And I was just thinking I should have done the same.' They grinned at each other and Ivor ordered himself a pint. Ivor realised it was the first time they'd been on their own together for years. He guessed the last time must have been the afternoon they'd moved Ivor's tools and workbench from Winchelsea Beach to Gatcombe. They had ended up putting the world to rights over chocolate cake from one of the tea-shops in town. They'd both been seventeen.

They took their drinks away to a table, sat down and began to talk about the day each of them had had in his different sphere, Mark's at Birdskitchen Farm and Ivor with his barns. 'How's Robbie shaping up as project manager?' Mark asked.

'Not bad at all,' Ivor told him. 'I use him as my eyes and ears. He checks on the progress at the two sites, and spends a lot of his time on the road. It's quite a relief, actually, not having him over my shoulder at Birdskitchen all the time.'

Mark sniggered. 'I've sometimes thought the same,' and Ivor laughed too.

'Yeah,' Ivor went on. 'It was a good move. Project co-ordinator, he's called now. Like having your own rottweiler. He's brilliant at handling the men. Better to have the camel inside the tent, pissing out, than ouside the tent, pissing in.'

Mark nodded in agreement. Then he said, 'Could have used him early today, though.' And after a pause, 'Or you. Two wild boar were in among the winter wheat, rooting up like Christmas had come.' A fair number of wild boar had escaped from specialist breeding farms all over the region during the '87 hurricane; they had been doing low-level but chronic damage to local farms ever since, as Ivor well knew. 'Chased them off with the sheepdogs in the end, but I could have done with an extra body. Robbie's or yours. One with a brain attached to it at least. Frank's past it and as for that kid...'

'I know,' said Ivor. 'Alec's OK when it's only brawn you need... But Robbie or I would have come if you'd asked, you know.'

'Thank you,' said Mark, 'but you'd both already left. And Feri'd gone out too. There was only Mrs F. about the place.'

'Well, sorry,' said Ivor. 'But in principle, any time.' There was silence for a moment as they bathed in the warm shared glow that follows the offer of a small kindness between two friends. Then Ivor said, 'You know, I was sitting here once with the old Birdskitchen crew, years ago – I think at hopping time. There was a fire.' Ivor pointed towards the inglenook, empty now in midsummer, except for extravagant tall sprays of blue delphiniums and red tobacco flowers. 'We got talking about... Well, Andy told me something about you.'

Mark looked up, frowning. 'Oh, did he?' He sounded unsure whether he was going to like this or not. 'And what might that have been?'

Ivor smiled reassuringly. 'Nothing bad. Just something interesting. Especially to me. It was about Welstead House.'

Mark grimaced in a rather exaggerated way. 'Oh no,' he said. 'Not that.'

Ivor leaned towards him. 'It was interesting,' he pressed on, 'because what you saw...'

'I don't know what I saw.' Mark sounded annoyed that Ivor had brought this up. 'It was all...'

'Hang on a mo, mate. I haven't finished yet. You may not remember it but your mother did. It was the same for me.'

'Hey, hey,' said Mark, the frown returning. 'What are you...?'

'My mum used to tell me I'd seen something at Welstead House when I was four. That I'd described it to her at the time but had no memory of it when I got older. I don't know if I'd told her something I thought I'd seen or if I'd made the whole lot up. It was a woman in a hooded riding-cape or something, and a boy in... What are those...?'

'Christ Almighty!' Mark said. 'That's what my mum still swears blind I saw. To a T.' Then his expression changed. 'Uh-oh. OK, I get you. You're having a laugh. Andy told you that and now...'

'I swear I'm not.' It seemed terribly important to Ivor now that Mark believe him. 'I swear it. Ask my mum.'

'I've never met your mum.'

'You can phone her in York...'

Mark shook his head. 'Still won't work. You and she could easily have...'

'Oh for fuck's sake, Mark, Why would I want to go to all that trouble just to a wind you up? OK, come on. Forget it. Let it go.'

There was another silence as Ivor found himself once again thinking that he did like Mark. He liked being with him now. Thinking that made his lower lip suddenly tremble, astonishingly, and took him back in time to the first time that had ever happened to him, when he'd read the last sentence of Crime and Punishment, the line that let a little chink of hope appear, like a gleam of sunlight at the end of a winter afternoon. He said, so softly that Mark could hardly hear him, and had to ask him to repeat, 'What about the Lydd thing, then?'

'What?'

'That day in Lydd. There were the two of us. What was that all about?'

Mark was silent for a while. Then he said, 'It happened, didn't it? I didn't want to believe it. Not then, not afterwards. I don't want to believe it now.'

'Nor me,' said Ivor. 'But we saw what we saw. I drew sketches. From memory.'

'That isn't evidence,' said Mark.

Ivor thought for a second. 'Why don't we want to believe it?' He was putting the question to himself as much as to Mark.

Mark also thought for a moment, then said, 'Because people would think we were mad. Two nutters. The lads at school would have teased us without mercy. And it'd be the same now. Every time I walked into a pub people would be thinking, even if they didn't say it: Here comes Mark, the young farmer who sees fairies at the bottom of his garden. Think what would happen at the stock auction when I was trying to sell sheep. It'd be the same for you. You've got properties you'll be ready to sell in three or four months for over half a million each. Who's going to hand over sums like that to someone...?'

Ivor cut him off. 'You're not mad, Mark. You're the sanest man I know. It's only me that's mad.' Not just the sanest, Ivor thought, but also the nicest. The nicest in the best possible sense of the word. Then he felt his lip quivering again and to his mortification and to Mark's utter astonishment tears spilled suddenly down his cheeks.

Mark said softly, 'Hey, hey. Forget this. Talk about something else.' There was a look of friendly concern on his face but he made no physical movement towards Ivor.

It took a moment or two, but at last Ivor did manage to pull himself together enough to talk about something else. They talked about the winding down of the hop industry. Reminded each other that this September's would be the last hop picking that Birdskitchen would ever see.

'When the root-hills are grubbed up,' Mark said, 'Dad's going to put the old gardens down to grazing. Sow in the autumn, buy a herd of cattle in, overwinter under cover, out to pasture in the spring.'

'You're buying a barn?' Ivor queried. 'A whole new cow barn?'

Mark laughed. 'Not one of your million pound jobs. Cheap-as-chips sheet-metal. Milking parlour and dairy all included.'

Ivor frowned. 'You sure about this?' He was alarmed for his friend. 'With all the stories about you know what?'

Mark reassured him. 'It's all up north. Dad's done his homework. He's buying from round here. Sussex cattle. A herd from down Lewes way. Safe as... If our friends in the north are having to be careful – well, that's bad luck – I wouldn't wish it on them – but it does mean a bigger share for us down here. You're a businessman. You know. You have to be a realist about these things.'

A realist, thought Ivor. A man who sees ghosts and a deserted medieval village and then goes on to murder his benefactor in cold blood to get his hands on his farm. A realist. Is that what I am?

TWENTY-SEVEN

It was a marriage of convenience, they said. Though only in private. It was a joke between themselves. When Gemma and Dieter married in the spring that followed their re-encounter they knew it was a marriage that would stand the test of jokes like that. They had a registry office ceremony in Koblenz, to which Gemma's now fragile mother came, accompanied by Sarah. There was a party afterwards, followed by another one a fortnight later in Göttingen for the people who hadn't made it to Koblenz. The convenience of the marriage was that it was not only the wedding celebrations that were a tale of two cities – the rest of their lives would be. Dieter maintained his house and studio and reputation in Koblenz, while Gemma kept her roomy third floor flat on Akazienweg, continued to paint Göttingen's characterful streetscape and to teach, two days a week, her ever more popular course at the Kunst Akademie.

Gemma's mother had worried about the wisdom of this arrangement, and had fretted to her elder daughter about it during the plane journey to Germany. It was so different from the way things had been in her own day. Living together day in, day out was, for her, one of the things that made a marriage. When circumstances arose in which that could not be managed – circumstances such as war, or the necessity in individual cases for the man to earn his living abroad while his children stayed behind in the home country for the sake of their education, and needing their mother's care – those situations were a kind of personal tragedy, which required effort and good fortune to overcome. Even allowing for certain careers, like the navy...

Sarah had cut her off. 'They're not going to live apart for ages, like in the war. They'll be together each weekend. It's just that they've got separate careers. Women don't abandon everything they've made of their professional lives just because they've got married. Not these days. Anyway, don't you think Gemma's old enough at thirty-three to decide what she wants and to have some idea of what's in her best interest? Why do we all have to be the same? It's not one size fits all, like it was with your generation. All of us are different from one another. Why should we have to force ourselves into exactly the same strait-jacket? And Gemma does have some experience of cohabiting with men, so presumably she has some idea of what works for her and what doesn't.'

'Presumably,' said the mother, investing the word with a battleship's weight of significance.

'I say presumably,' her younger daughter went on undeterred, 'because I honestly don't know. Because I haven't asked her, and because it actually isn't any of my business in the end.'

Her mother said, 'Hmm,' but added nothing more. They were being told to fasten seatbelts in readiness for landing at Köln-Bonn.

For all her mother's misgivings the arrangement worked well. Both Gemma and Dieter were self-employed and reasonably well-off, so that travelling between Koblenz and Göttingen did not have to mean Sunday afternoon goodbyes or dealing with the Friday afternoon rush. They had the luxury of being able to make their weekends together roughly the same length as their working weeks apart. They didn't bother with the strain of a weekly round trip of some five hundred miles by car but took the train. In general they alternated between the two towns for their weekends, though without being obsessive about the turn-and-turn-about principle, and would each meet the other at the station with the car. One car for Göttingen, one for Koblenz. There was no need for two in the same town.

They were no longer the competitive twenty-something and thirty-something they had been during their earlier two years together; Dieter was forty-something now. They no longer needed to bicker about everything; they found to their surprise that they agreed about most things and, where they found they didn't, had learnt not to bring those particular subjects up. One thing they had decided at the outset: they would not be looking to start a family. Gemma, playing host to American teenage waifs and strays for years at Gatcombe, felt she'd already paid her dues. And as the years passed it grew less and less likely that they'd change their minds.

They had social lives in both towns. Gemma still had her Göttingen friends, the Russian painter lady and the Italian lecturer in Renaissance art among others, and Dieter, because he taught at Koblenz University once a week, counted a sprinkling of academics among his friends – who were otherwise mostly artists.

Among the academics were a married medical couple. The husband, Lothar, taught anatomy at Koblenz's medical school while his wife Gaby worked as a clinical psychologist. They lived in a rather wonderful house, high in the old town, that overlooked the confluence of the Mosel river with the Rhine. It had a terrace from which both Dieter and Gemma had at different times begged to paint the view – and been rewarded with a yes – and which also served as a peaceful spot for early evening drinks.

Discussing the great painters in her adopted language over a glass of Mosel presented few problems for Gemma; at a pinch she could even rise to trends in modern German art: it was when the conversation came round to her hosts' special subjects that the use of English became essential. She would not have been able to deal with the intricacies of modern surgical techniques, let alone the byways of neurotic or delusional personality disorders. It was during one of these mercifully English-based conversations with Gaby that Dieter happened to say, a propos of something he'd read in a newspaper, 'It's curious that we never hear the word psychopath these days.' Turning to Gaby he asked, 'Do you still use the term? Or has the condition stopped to exist?'

'Oh dear,' said Gaby. 'That is a quite big question,' while her husband gave a half smile of relief, glad that it had not fallen to him to have to try to answer it.

Gaby decided to have a go. 'The fact is that medical conditions, yes, they change their names from time to time. Example, at one time the words dementia praecox were a usual description for a condition that would have been described by most people along the centuries quite brutally as madness. Later that condition became known as schizophrenia...' Here Gemma and Dieter both nodded their heads vigorously, glad to have captured a word they thought they understood. 'While manic depression has more recently come to be known as bipolar disorder.' The last words drew rather blank looks. 'There is an element of buzzwords in this, of course, or of wanting a more new, more shiny, word to describe a thing. Also, even, it is young researchers who want to make a name for themselves – if you will excuse the play on words. But also – perhaps more honourably – it is because we know more and more, as time passes, about the different conditions, physical as well as mental.' She gave an inclusive nod towards her physically-specializing husband. 'And so we want to name them a little bit more accurately too.'

Stirring himself, perhaps in response to his wife's nod, Lothar added his own pfennigsworth. 'Also is there the fact that conditions which we once thought of as single entities have been discovered to consist of several separate – ah – strands, may I say. For instance, the names of different types of cancer have proliferated along the years, as intensive research into these conditions shows there to be more and more different types.'

Gaby picked up the reins again. 'You were talking about the word psychopath, Dieter. I can say, there is a case in point. People began to make a distinction between the psychopath – clever, manipulative, brilliant at concealing himself in society, even in the middle of an own family – and the withdrawn sociopath, whose inabilty to empathise with others, or to function socially, like not being able to hold down a job, draws much more attention to itself. Then later, a new term was created. APD.' Gemma and Dieter nodded slowly, both hoping the initials would be decrypted for them. They were in luck. 'Antisocial personality disorder. That is especially a convenient term because it admits of a plural. Antisocial personality disorders.' Gaby smiled mischievously. 'It lets you go on and discover as many of those as you want.'

'But that could go on for ever,' Gemma objected. 'Surely, eventually, by dividing and subdividing medical conditions you end up at a point where you say, well, everybody's different, and have done with all those names.'

Lothar laughed. 'You are absolute right, of course. We all are different. But in practical terms it is real useful, helpful, to have some system of pigeon-holes. Example: if Herr Schmidt comes to his doctor with the symptoms of kidney stones, it is enormously useful when the doctor can apply the tried and tested treatments for kidney stones. Not to have to consider that these kidney stones are Herr Schmidt's unique and individual kidney stones, which require a unique and individual remedy just for him, and force the doctor to reinvent the wheel just for Herr Schmidt and start from scratch.'

'I see what you mean,' said Dieter, though he was beginning to wish he hadn't started this. He elbowed his way back to his original question. 'The other thing about psychopaths – or sociopaths, or whatever you call them now – the thing that puzzles me is, they are always young people. When you hear about them in news stories, or crime stories, in films or books, they are always young. You never hear of an elderly one.'

Gemma came in before Gaby could answer. 'Isn't that because they live such dangerous lives, taking the sort of risks most people don't, that they don't weigh up the risks in situations that are dangerous for themselves and so they come to sticky ends?'

Gaby smiled at her as if rewarding a bright student. 'There is truth in that,' she said. 'You are very right. But there is another thing also. And this can perhaps sound – uh – silly. Especially because for many generations psychiatrists have tried to cure these sort of conditions without great success. But the fact is that in many cases, though of course not all, when these APD people, these psychopaths and sociopaths and others ... when these people mature into adulthood they quite simply grow out of their condition. Little by little they can develop, in some cases, into reasonable well adjusted human beings.'

At this point Lothar stood up and went in search of the bottle of Mosel in order to refill everybody's glass. When he came back the conversation had turned to lighter things. It was not until many years later that Gemma thought back to that conversation, and when she did it was with some surprise at the fact that during the course of it memories of Ivor had never entered her head.

Ivor had to admire the new arrivals at Birdskitchen Farm. Mark showed them to him with understandable pride. They were sixteen rough-coated Sussex cows, the colour of rich dark ginger cakes. Their winter quarters, a prefab affair of shiny sheet-metal on a steel girder frame, was erected expertly by the company that supplied it, in the space of a couple of days. Ivor couldn't help comparing that rate of progress with the painstaking business of restoring and converting his own ancient, timber-framed barns. But then, the cows' accommodation was not going to be sold for half a million pounds.

Trevor and Mark employed a dairyman to deal with the cows' day to day needs. Frank was tacitly considered to be beyond the learning of such new tricks. The cows had arrived already impregnated – that was guaranteed: pregnant or your money back – and would be calving in the spring. In the meantime Ivor and Feri got used to the daily arrival, past their front door, of the tanker coming to collect the milk.

Spring arrived and, with the first primroses, the red-furred, big-eyed calves. If you dipped your fingers in a pail of milk they would ticklingly suck it from your finger-ends. And then in March came the news that everyone had privately been dreading –   though few had spoken openly of it: the implications would be so terrible. The government announced that you-know-what had jumped the species barrier. You-know-what stood for bovine spongiform encephalopathy, which mouthful was quickly shortened for the benefit of the public to BSE, though the public preferred to call it mad cow disease. The government's announcement confirmed the existence of a human version of the sickness, which was called – another mouthful, this – new variant Kreuzfeldt-Jacob disease, or vCJD for short. The European Union promptly banned imports into all other member states of British beef, while demand plummeted at home. Trevor's herd of red Sussex cattle and their beautiful calves became worthless overnight.

In the period which followed, the trading accounts of British farms went into free fall. The industry plunged through crisis after crisis, as if a stricken jet-plane were having the ill-luck to encounter patch after patch of turbulence on its way down. As you drove round the countryside now you saw, wherever you looked, hand-painted notices advising of woodland and pasture offered for sale. The price of agricultural land went on down, while the notices stayed up for years. Once more Ivor could feel the hostility of neighbouring farmers, like a film of ice forming over everything, whenever he entered a local pub. It had taken years of effort, his own and Feri's, to break down the distrust of him that had sprung up after he'd inherited Jack's farm. Now that distrust had grown back, like the night hoar-frost, when it was realised that he'd got out of farming in the nick of time, and used the proceeds to set up in one of the few lines of business in the region that was capable of making an absolute mint. Sometimes Ivor thought that it was only the existence of his attractive and popular wife that saved him from being set on outside some village pub one dark evening and beaten to a pulp.

Surprisingly, the very person who had most cause to hate him, Mark Harris, never did. He never complained to Ivor, or to anyone else as far as Ivor knew, that in the deal between Ivor and Mark's father, Trevor and Mark had very much had the worst of it while Ivor had come out very much on top. More than that, Mark remained friendly towards Ivor and had no qualms about showing his friendship publicly, happy to be seen with him in the

Cock Inn or anywhere else. Ivor was grateful for Mark's continuing friendship. Richard was a business associate rather than a real friend, and the same went for most other people too. Other than Feri, Ivor sometimes thought, Mark was the only friend he'd got.

Feri's parents came to Birdskitchen, though not together, of course. Neither of them had much experience of rural life and their first plunge into the English countryside was a headier experience than they had expected, while their daughter was almost as keen to show it off to them as she was to parade her handsome young man. During both their visits – a few weeks apart during the same mid-summer – she and Ivor drove their guests up to the highest point in the neighbourhood, the sea cliff above Fairlight Glen. They climbed the steps inside the church tower that topped the cliff, the tower that could be seen from thirty miles around, and reaped the reward that comes to those who go up there on a fine, clear day. To the west, twenty miles off, lay the South Downs and Beachy Head, like the back and nose of a basking whale, in a bath of silver. In the other direction the Marsh and the shingle spit of Dungeness streamed towards France, and far beyond the Marsh the white cliffs of Dover and the South Foreland, minutely visible forty miles away, stood guard over the Strait. Viewed from the church tower's height the sea, which swept the compass from east through south to west, appeared to climb to infinity through the sky. The blue expanse was studded with white dots which came and went and which, if peered at carefully enough, turned into the superstructures of ships, which were not in the sky at all but in the sky-est, most distant part of the sea. On the day they took Feri's mother up those winding church-tower stairs, France astonishingly presented itself, mirage-like: the continent's rim, like the edge of a brown saucer, on the vertiginously high horizon. And Feri's mother actually said it, declaiming the New-York-accented words from the battlements of the tower: 'This precious stone, set in a silver sea.' To Ivor's astonishment her daughter finished off the quote. 'This earth, this realm, this England.' Ivor hadn't known his wife knew such things. He guessed at once that it was Shakespeare even though, since it didn't come from Hamlet or Macbeth, it was something new to him.

To landward the sun was lighting the woods and fields in vivid shades of green: from near-black olive to sharp apple, bright mustard, lime, and palest lemon. Tiny oast houses dotted the view, their masthead weather-vanes all streamed out in the south-west wind. Beauty that seemed inviolate for mile beyond mile encircled them. Neither Feri nor Ivor could bring themselves to tell their visitors from overseas about the deadly thing, the awful folded thing, that was eating out that beauty's heart. The crisis that was tearing the countryside apart. The cause of it, the thing that made the cows go mad, that bankrupted the land around, was called a prion, or so they said. A piece of protein gone awry, a molecule that had a defective fold, that transmitted its twisted nature to other molecules till bit by bit it infected everything and everyone. Ivor saw it as a reaching, tentacled thing. It was the thing inside him, the thing that ate him up, the thing that writhed. The thing that could not be killed. Even boiling it alive, laboratory sterilization at an unimaginable number of degrees, could not damage a prion, but left it to go on and do its terrible work. There weren't words in the English language to describe such a thing, Ivor thought. There were, in alphabetical order, *awful, dreadful*, and *terrible*. Those words were pathetic in their failure to convey anything of what Ivor felt. Nothing could. Sometimes he felt it was the thing inside him, the tentacled starfish prion, that had caused all this mess. Mad cow disease, the Kreuzfeldt-Jacob strain in humans, the devastation of the bucolic landscape, invisible from high up here in the brilliant afternoon. All this had been caused by the harm he'd done to Jack. All this was his own fault. He stood on the top of the tower of Fairlight church in the glorious sunshine and, to his wifc's consternation, wept.

Other than that incident the visits of both of Feri's parents passed very successfully. Her mother did inevitably broach the subject of grandchildren. Married for three years but with no sign of children: such a state of affairs was unusual, the older woman thought. Feri protested that it wasn't unusual at all. She, unlike her mother, had not married a Colombian. She and Ivor both had careers to manage, children would come later, that was the usual way of things. Besides, they had married very young. She was able to say all this with conviction. Fortunately she had nothing to hide. The situation during the first year of her marriage, during which Ivor had scarcely managed to make love to her at all, had slowly and gradually improved even if, Feri couldn't help noticing privately, they had never quite recaptured the abandon and sheer energy with which they'd made love at first. But that was what happened in marriage, Feri guessed. She could only guess: she had never been married before.

Mark met both parents. He was invited to dinner during each of their visits, though not alone. Mark was no longer a lonely boy these days: he brought his latest girlfriend, Melanie, along. He was British enough not to bore the visitors with his and his father's farming woes: they talked of other things. As for Feri, although she had married a Sussex farmer in fulfilment of her childish dream, her husband was no longer a farmer, which was more than fortunate – a fact which none of the people gathered around the oak dining-table had the bad taste to point out.

Having survived these whirlwind visits Feri felt confident enough to suggest to Ivor that he should invite his parent too. Ivor still hadn't seen his mother since her wedding, and in the years since they had exchanged their surprise announcements – Ivor's that he'd married Feri, Norma's that she'd joined the Society of Friends – they had barely spoken half a dozen times on the phone. To Feri's surprise Ivor agreed to ask Norma to come to Birdskitchen. Except for the embarrassment of the crying incident (although Roddy would have understood) Ivor had been as relieved by the success of the last two visits as Feri was. He'd got on better than he'd expected to with both his parents-in-law: the father formally suited, and braceleted with mini-ingot chunks of gold; the mother attired even at informal mealtimes in a way that Ivor had previously associated only with weddings and – though this in imagination only – Buckingham Palace garden dos. It was still high summer, a good time for having guests in the countryside. You could be outdoors with them, or send them off to places on their own for hours. It wasn't like the wintertime, when there would have been nothing to do but sit indoors while the landscape beyond the windows teemed with dark and rain. He telephoned Norma that evening and a fortnight later Norma and Michael, Mr and Mrs Harding, drove down.

His mother seemed a different person. Like someone he had never met. There was a calmness about her – not something Ivor had associated with her in the past – and she looked older. That was less to be wondered at: she looked older because she was. But she treated her son as if he were someone *she* had never met. Treated him with the friendly courtesy she might have used in dealing with one of her son's friends rather than with the son himself. Treated him in fact much as she treated Mark. Ivor wasn't surprised to find that his mother took a liking to Mark: most people did. He was more surprised to find that she took to Feri, and Feri to her. The three-day visit passed very smoothly. Norma didn't even bring up the subject of grandchildren.

Thanks to the happy uneventfulness of those three days Feri would probably have remembered them only in a vague, though generally pleasant way. Had it not been for one conversation that took place between Norma and herself one evening in the kitchen, when they were alone together and loading the dishwasher after supper. Norma had her back to Feri when she said, 'I need your advice.'

'I'm sure you don't,' Feri said, almost with a laugh. 'But anyway, what about?'

Norma turned away from the dishwasher and faced Feri. It struck Feri for the first time that Norma's pale blue eyes were unusually far apart. Perhaps it was simply an impression they gave just then, for they were open very wide. 'The thing is,' Norma said, 'that now we've joined the Quakers, well, there's a sort of understanding – nobody puts it more strongly than that – that we're supposed to be straight with people...'

'Isn't everybody?' Feri said. 'Quaker or not?'

Norma nodded. 'Precisely. But very few people manage it. To not have secrets from people we're close to. You only have to think about it for a moment to realise how hard that is. But as Quakers we're supposed to try that little bit harder. And that brings me to it.'

Feri got there in a sudden rush. 'It's about Ivor's father, isn't it? It's about whether you should tell him who his father was.' She stopped, then added, 'Or is.'

Norma sighed, then smiled. 'Well done. But it's more complicated than that. You see, even I don't know who his father is, or was.'

Feri laughed, she couldn't not do, but apologised at once. 'I'm sorry. But it did sound peculiar. How could you not know – sorry if this sounds crude – but how could you not have known the father of your child?' Then she thought again and quickly put out her hand to touch Norma's arm. 'Oh no. I'm being dreadfully stupid. Please forgive me. You mean rape, of course.'

'No,' said Norma quietly. 'It wasn't rape. I wanted it. But aged fifteen... I suppose I was rather taken advantage of. By a man old enough to be my father – at least, in biological terms. It was dark, it was an alleyway near a pub – sorry, I don't mean to shock you – so squalid – and I didn't even see his face properly.'

'He didn't tell you his name?' Feri's voice too had dropped to a near-whisper.

'He said his name was Jay. It might have been just his initial. He was a farmer, a married man. He lived somewhere over this way.'

'He told you that?' Feri was astonished. 'Didn't give you his name but told you where he lived?'

'Not quite. He meant to be vague. He said something like, 'I got a farm hereabouts.' But he pointed his arm without thinking. Later I worked the direction out. It was roughly this way. Now here I am in my son's farmhouse. A house that was left to him, pretty unbelievably, by a farmer named Jack. You see, I can't help wondering...'

'Jack with a J,' Feri said.

'You see the difficulty. About whether to tell him or not. With Jack being dead, he might be terribly upset.'

'Yes,' said Feri. 'I do see.' She closed the dishwasher door and switched the machine on. A thought struck her and she said, 'But maybe you've struck your blow for openness simply by telling me.' She looked Norma in the eye. 'Suppose you left it with me now. I mean, for me to tell him. Not that there's anything to tell exactly. It's only a possibility we're talking about. But I could tell him, if I decided to tell him at all, when and if the moment seemed right. Would you be happy with that?'

Norma looked wonderfully relieved all of a sudden. She said she would be happy with that. It seemed the best and most comfortable solution.

Then Feri found she had a question to ask. 'Norma, did Ivor cry a lot when he was a child?'

Norma frowned as she thought back. Then the frown disappeared and she said, 'No, he didn't. Once he'd left babyhood behind, no, he never cried. He was unusual in that. Went on wetting the bed a few years after most children stop but crying, no. Thinking about it, I think I never knew a child who cried less.' Behind her the dishwasher clattered and shook.

TWENTY-EIGHT

Wednesday was one of Gemma's two teaching days. She didn't have a heavy schedule even then, and it was the more relaxed for the fact that Gemma taught now as much for the fun of it as out of financial necessity. She taught one class in the middle of the morning and another in the early afternoon. In between there was lunch in the college canteen which, since she didn't have to experience it five days a week, could also be a reasonably enjoyable occasion. It depended on the people you found yourself sitting next to. On this particular Wednesday, a June day some seven years after she had come to Germany, there was pasta with meatballs among the offerings behind the glass of the service counter. It was one of those utterly inconsequential details of the day that, for some reason Gemma would never forget. The dish looked appetising and Gemma felt a moment's envy for the youth of those around her who could ingest such a meal in the middle of the day without either having to battle against sleep during their afternoon classes or, apparently, gaining any weight. She slid her tray along the counter and, catching the eye of the aproned woman behind it, gestured instead towards the grilled river fish.

Peering round the large room Gemma saw an empty seat at a small table. Next to the empty place was sitting the young woman who, this year, taught the life-drawing class. Gemma rather liked her and so made her way towards the vacant seat and began to unload her tray onto the table. 'Have you heard ?' her neighbour said to her at once.

'No,' said Gemma, settling into her chair. 'Heard what?'

'The ICE has crashed.'

'Crashed where?' Gemma asked. They lived in a world of acronyms now, but the ICE was an easy one. It was Germany's high-speed train, the Inter-City Express. It called at Göttingen on its arrow-quick passage between Munich and Hamburg.

'Just north of here. Near Hanover. They've declared the Celle district a disaster zone. It's a total wreck.'

'My God,' said Gemma. She felt the dizzying surge of feelings that all frequent train travellers experience when they hear of a rail catastrophe on their home patch: a sense of unreality mixed in with horror and, squeezing in alongside those, the shaming but unavoidable *There but for the Grace of God...* Her next thought was for her husband. On a Wednesday he would be in Koblenz. They would talk on the phone this evening, as they talked every evening, but recently, now that everyone had a *Handy*, there had grown the habit, which had become ingrained, of calling up your nearest and dearest whenever a national or international emergency occurred. You knew it wouldn't have affected them directly but you didn't know for certain in this interconnected world whether someone close to them might not have been touched. Gemma reached instinctively into her shoulder-bag, drew out her phone and dialled the number of the Koblenz flat. She heard the long solemn *toops* of the German ring-tone and then, after a little while, the dispassionate voice of the message service. Gemma said the usual things – It's me, give me a ring – and ended the call. Wednesday was not Dieter's teaching day but of course he didn't have to be in his studio or the flat. Or he might be simply in the *Klo*. She'd try his mobile when she'd finished her fish.

Now everybody seemed to have the same idea. Gemma, like almost everyone else, ate quickly then took her coffee, following the crowd, down to the common room where a television was on. Hardly anybody was sitting down, most stood in a great crush, and it was hard to peer between the mass of heads to see the screen. When Gemma at last established an uninterrupted line of sight she found herself looking at scenes of railway carnage such as she hadn't seen on TV since she was a child. As stretcher-bearers and firemen with cutting tools bestrode the screen the commentary spoke of Germany's worst train disaster for twenty-seven years. More than half the people who stood near Gemma had phones clapped to their ears, but nobody was actually speaking to anyone else in the room. The way we live these days, Gemma thought. And how we tut-tut at the people who stop their cars and gawp at accidents, so hampering the emergency service workers, while we do exactly the same as them through the cold intermediary of television radio waves. But Gemma made no attempt to behave differently from the rest. She went on watching the TV in a state of frozen shock. She fetched her own *Handy* out of her bag again and pressed the button that would dial Dieter's automatically. She heard the digits peep and then the ringing tone. It rang out and went on ringing. For some reason the voice of the answering service did not cut in. There was just the ringing tone, which went on ringing out. *Toop … toop … toop …*

The conversions of the barns at Wittersham and Rolvenden Layne were long completed. They had sold at such a profit that Ivor briefly forgot the raging of his inner pain. He took Feri on a luxury trip to see the Pyramids and the Nile. They took a cabin on a river boat, which Feri said was very Agatha Christie, though in the nicest possible way; but that was a reminder that Ivor thought he could have done without. On their return Ivor bought three more barns. Two were in Kent, at Snargate and Midley, two hamlets on the great flatness of the Marsh, in the general direction of Lydd. The third one lay in quite the opposite direction, tucked away among the folding hillsides near the source of the Tillingham at Cripps Corner. When these in their turn were sold he bought a couple more. At the same time he did conversions, in return for man-sized fees, for barn owners who did not want to sell their buildings to him. These people usually had some idea of how their barns should look when completed, and then Ivor would have to argue them out of their impractical or unaesthetic specifications and convince them of the superiority of his own.

Richard had quit his junior post at the architects' firm he'd worked for in Ashford. In return for a share in the substantial profits of Wingate Barn Conversions he had joined Ivor as a full-time business partner while continuing in his existing role as consultant architect. Of necessity the labour force had grown considerably. An office extension had been added to the old apple store and here Mark's younger sister Anne now worked alongside Heinz's stalwart daughter and Mark's latest girlfriend Stephanie.

(Ivor had once told Mark he was amazed at his luck in never having got any of his string of girlfriends pregnant. To which Mark had replied, 'I'm like the Irishman, me. Always wear two condoms, to be sure, to be sure. No, seriously, they sort that side of things out for themselves these days.' He had given Ivor a mischievous look. 'As you may have noticed yourself. Haven't seen you pushing a buggy around the place...')

Feri continued to design and market her country-craft wares but Ivor had little time for making or repairing furniture now. Ivor had found two very keen young brothers who had just completed apprenticeships and they carried on with the furniture under his – or more often Feri's – careful eye.

The conversion and sale of the very first barn, at Birdskitchen, had altered the dynamic as well as the look of the farm. Birdskitchen Barn was occupied by a wealthy couple of about sixty, the MacFadyens. They had sons and daughters in their twenties who, along with girlfriends and boyfriends, visited often at weekends. Each year the MacFadyens gave a no-expense-spared party on New Year's Eve, to which all the denizens of Birdskitchen were invited. Even the now retired Frank came, and was habitually shaken awake to hear the midnight chimes in the armchair into which he'd gratefully sunk at around ten o'clock. Ivor savoured the experience of these occasions. To stand in the great hall, inside the vision he'd first had, and then realised in timber and brick, amidst a crowd of people, temporarily carefree, to look up into the great roof space and see the branching crown-posts springing through the gloom above the wood-hoop chandeliers – an idea he had pinched from Lutyens's designs for Dixter – these were fulfilling things. Ivor joined the dancing in the great central space. (The open hearth he'd first envisaged at the centre of the hall would have made this impossible. Richard had been right to make him change his plans.) He danced with Feri, with Anne and Stephanie, with Richard's wife and Robbie's. One year, just for half a minute and to everyone's amusement, he even danced with Mark for a joke.

At times like this Birdskitchen gave all the appearance of a lively, thriving place and so it was, provided you didn't look too closely at the part of it that Mark dealt with, the green expanse that was his father's nearly bankrupt farm. Somehow Mark kept things going. That's what people in his situation do. The BSE catastrophe continued to unfold, though now in a more contained and managed way. There began to be a feeling of guarded optimism; initial panic had been replaced by a dogged determination somehow to get through. When you heard of the wives of ruined herdsmen in the West Country going on the game to pay for their children's clothes you dished them out some silent applause, impressed by their grim determination to survive. Then, gradually, the market for cattle had started up again. Each year now Trevor could sell his calves, even if it was usually at a small loss each time. The same now went for pigs and sheep. You looked on the bright side of this; you had to; a small loss was better than a big one. At least the wheat and barley did all right; the dairy too. People still needed bread and beer and milk.

Ivor was not surprised when Mark wanted to talk to him about the oast. His father too. The three of them discussed it over civilised pints of Harvey's in the Cock Inn. 'Well, Ivor,' Trevor introduced the subject as he slid the pint he'd bought him across the table, 'I can't help noticing companies like yours are branching into oast conversions now.' As Ivor knew, the Birdskitchen oast had stood empty for several years: since hop-growing in Kent and Sussex had come to an end. Only a few odds and ends of rusting machinery lay inside. And he already knew that other barn conversion companies were turning their attention to the brick-built redundant oast houses that crowded the region, their towering kilns, now pierced for light, offering their purchasers the novelty of circular rooms. 'And what we'd like to know is if you're thinking of going down the same road.' Trevor went on very candidly to make his position clear. If Ivor's company would like to make him a cash offer for the oast it would be an opportunity from which Ivor could not fail to profit handsomely. Otherwise Trevor could engage Ivor to convert it for him, he and Mark would sell it on and, albeit a long way into the future, reap the profit themselves. This would not be their favourite option – Trevor was open about this – as they'd need to borrow the money for Ivor's fee.

As Trevor spoke Ivor noticed how haggard his face looked and how gaunt his frame had become. When you see someone very often, slow changes in their appearance pass you by and so it happened that only this evening did the changes in Trevor strike Ivor with force. Ivor recognised them for what they were: the war wounds Trevor had suffered in his struggle to survive. Ivor would have liked to help – what a different Ivor from the Ivor of ten years ago – but Trevor's proposal was not one with which he could easily deal. He gave the following reasons for this. He had stretched his company's resources as far as he prudently could in his most recent purchase of a barn just over the Kent border at Kenardington. His accountant Malcolm had advised him not to buy another building until the next one in the pipeline had been completed and sold. 'And when's that likely to be?' Trevor asked him, though as his son and Ivor regularly exchanged news of their dealings and plans, he probably already knew.

'Six months at the earliest,' Ivor said. 'But when you're selling a house, well...' He shrugged his shoulders to underline his inability to control that particular element of the thing.

Trevor and Mark exchanged looks. Trevor turned back to Ivor. A tightness about his lips at that moment enhanced the impression of strain. 'I suppose we could wait six months.'

Ivor tried to be encouraging. 'I think that's the better way to go. I mean, going the other way, having me convert it for you – well, you'd make more money in the end but it wouldn't be for a couple of years. And the other thing with that, well, we're a bit stretched at the moment. In terms of having the staff, I mean. We're going pretty flat out.' He took a swallow of beer.

'You're welcome to approach another company. One of our competitors, I mean. In the circumstances I could hardly mind.'

'Well, we'd need to think about that,' Trevor said. 'Though we'd obviously prefer to deal with someone we know.'

'And trust,' said Mark, giving Ivor a sweet and artless smile that cut him like a knife.

Ivor would have preferred them to get in contact with a different company. The real reason for his reluctance to get involved with the conversion of the Birdskitchen oast house – a reason which was impossible for him to reveal to anyone – was the same one that had kept him from setting foot inside the building, except when absolutely essential, since Jack's death in there all those years ago. The memory of that, quite simply, was still too strong for him. It was as though it had singed his brain. Although his 'tween-sleep-and-awake visions of the falling, dying Jack, arms outspread as though crucified, came less often now he was very afraid that if he spent time in the oast, as he would inevitably have to, discussing things with Richard, measuring up and drawing plans, those early terrors would return, their frightful power renewed. 'I see where you're coming from,' Ivor said. It was a phrase he'd heard a lot recently and liked to use himself when the opportunity arose. 'I need to think about it. See what Malcolm says.'

As autumn began to heel over into winter there came a rain that made people say they'd never seen its like. Not for a generation, they said. People in towns made jokes about Noah and his flood, his animals, his ark. Those who lived on farms did not. Looking down from any hilltop vantage point towards the Romney Marsh or along its branching fingers, the valleys of the Rother, Tillingham and Brede, you saw sheets of water that were almost indistinguishable from the sea, grey with winter, that prowled, growling, beyond. You might imagine you were looking at the landscape as it had been in medieval times, when fighting ships lay anchored in the great harbour between Winchelsea and Rye, and tied up against the wall of Romney church; when ships rode up the valleys as far inland as Udimore and Brede, and could navigate right round the Isle of Oxney, past Wittersham and Stone, to land their cargoes in the port of Tenterden at Smallhythe.

Christmas came, then the New Year was celebrated, thanks to the hospitality of the MacFadyens, at Birdskitchen Barn. It was either the second or the third year of the new century, depending on your point of view. It was, all agreed, 2002. Because of the rain farm work, except for the essential feeding of animals, had become almost impossible. Men and machinery floundered helplessly in black seas of mud. Milk tankers became hopelessly bogged down on remote farms and then would arrive late for their other calls or not at all, in which case the precious hundreds of white gallons that were almost the only product the farmers could sell were poured wastefully down the drains. Even the barn conversion sites were unworkable for days on end at times, despite the manic energy invested in them by Ivor and Robbie, as the rains fell and went on falling, and landslips cut the railways and the roads.

What came next was Britain's worst epidemic of foot and mouth disease in years. TV screens were lit nightly by footage of beef carcases burning, hooves pointing upwards out of flames, like scenes from medieval frescos that represented the suffering of hell. In some regions farmers were effectively imprisoned on their farms. Livestock markets closed. The stuttering recovery from BSE went into reverse again. For the second time in a few short years farmers were going out of business in their hundreds every week. Once again Ivor found himself contemplating a scene of desolation and disaster with the feeling that all of it had somehow been caused by him.

One night the herd of sheep that grazed the Rother levels below Link Farm, the only animals Trevor still had left, lost their way in the unfamiliar surroundings of the valley floods, panicked in the deepening water in the dark, attempted to swim for it and drowned. Every last one. Trevor found their floating corpses, winter fleeces waterlogged and weighty, in the morning. Trevor was alone, except for his twelve-bore. He pushed its barrel into his mouth and without further reflection – or so people had to suppose, since there was no-one there to see him – pulled the trigger.

Ivor left early that morning, well before dawn, to drive to the newest conversion site, a few miles west, at Sedlescombe. From the apple store Feri watched his tail lights disappear into the rain and mist before he was even halfway up the drive. Robbie's car followed Ivor's just yards behind. She had an idea he was going to the other site, across the county boundary, at Kenardington. It was a very normal beginning to a working day. Less usual was the sight of Mark's car, less than a minute later, also disappearing up the drive, crashing over the pot-holes at axle-breaking speed and throwing up great water splashes like a power-boat. She wondered what kind of emergency had demanded his exit from Birdskitchen at such an hour and such a speed. No doubt it was nothing he couldn't handle on his own. Had he needed help he would have come and asked. He sometimes did, just as Ivor and she sometimes asked for help from him.

Twenty-five minutes later a car appeared in the drive again, but this one was arriving, its headlights staring through the endless downrush of the rain. It splashed to a stop outside the door of the apple store. Feri recognised the car as Mark's. She ran out into the pelting waterfall. Mark was climbing out. He seemed barely able to stand. Although the sound of the rain was crashing in the air all around, Feri could hear above it the enormous sound that was coming from Mark's throat: the terrible, roaring, choking noise of a grown man's scream.

Feri and Mark met halfway between the apple store and the car. Feri caught hold of Mark's flailing arms, held them fiercely and forced them to be still. 'What's wrong?' She was practically shouting herself. 'Oh God! What's wrong?'

'My father. My father's dead. Shot himself. In the water. Among dead sheep.'

'He shot himself?'

'They'll think it was me. Think it was me. Mum... Mummy...'

'Mark, Mark, go steady. They will think? They do think? Which? And who are they? Have you called the police? Does your mum know?'

'The police don't know. I haven't told. And Mum, she doesn't know. I can't... She phoned when he didn't come up for breakfast. I went straight there. I can't tell her. They'll think... They'll say... No witnesses, you see.'

'Mark, it's OK. It'll all be OK. But get a grip. No-one'll think it was you. No-one at all. We'll go to the police right now and explain.'

'You...'

'We'll take your car. I'll drive. Your mother after that.' She released his arms. 'I'll do that if you like.'

'Stephanie. She'll wonder...'

'All in good time. And Anne's not due in for another hour. Get things in the right order.' Feri saw Mark's right hand fumbling in a pocket. 'Don't try phoning people now. Not in the state you're in.'

Feri behaved as if this were the moment she'd been born to live. She drove calmly but quickly through the rain, along Starvecrow Lane and the Peasmarsh road to Rye. Inside the police station Feri spoke, while Mark sat shaking. A car was despatched to the flooded pasture by the Rother where Trevor's body and those of his sheep still lay. Another car, driven by a police woman and with Feri as a passenger, set off for the farmhouse, where Mark's mother sat pale-faced in her kitchen, among the stone-cold ruins of a breakfast laid for two. For the moment Mark remained at the police station, drinking sweet tea, until the time should come when he was calm enough to make a statement of his own.

When Feri got back to the police station, following a few minutes with Mark's mother that were among the most harrowing of Feri's life, she was led upstairs, before she could speak to Mark again, into a private office. From behind the desk an urbane-sounding plain-clothes officer invited her to take a seat. He introduced himself as Detective Superintendent Tart. 'Sorry to waylay you like this,' he said, 'but I promise not to keep you long. You are married to Mr Ivor Wingate, are you not? Correct me if I'm wrong.'

'You're right,' said Feri, setting her voice and jaw to confrontational mode.

The detective ground himself into his chair with a little wriggle, like a limpet screwing itself to its rock. 'May I ask you if you know where your husband was between six o'clock and nine o'clock this morning?'

Feri felt herself flushing, responding to a mix of sudden emotions of which anger was only one ingredient. 'What on earth makes you ask me that?' she said. 'In connection with this business we're just going through? Good God!'

'I'm sorry to upset you at a time that's already upsetting for you,' said Tart smoothly. 'Believe me, we do understand these things. Perhaps... If you could just answer the question, then I won't need to put you through anything more. OK?'

Feri said, more quietly, 'He was at home with me until seven thirty. Then he drove off to one of his building sites: the one at Sedlescombe. I'm sure you don't need me to tell you about that. It sounds as though you know all about his business already.'

D. S. Tart smiled without warmth. 'We don't know very much about it at all. And I'm sure it's most unlikely that we'll need to. Is there a site office perhaps at Sedlescombe with a phone number we could use?'

Feri took her phone from a pocket and handed it to Tart with an out-thrust arm. 'You'll find the number in there. You'd probably arrest me if I touched the thing in here.'

'Unlikely in the extreme,' said Tart, handing her back the phone. 'In fact I give you my word. But you'll find the number more easily than I will. If you'll kindly tell me it I'll write it down, I'll promise not to lose the piece of paper, and I'll never trouble you over the matter again. Deal?'

Feri half-smiled in spite of a gallant attempt not to, and did as she'd been asked. Tart wrote the number down, then looked at her and said, 'I assure you it's just a matter of routine. There's nothing you have to worry about at all. I won't keep you any longer. Look after Mr Harris now. If you won't think me impertinent I'd like to suggest you take him to see his mother. I think that may be where he's needed most – and where he most needs to be.'

To say there was a site office at Sedlescombe was an exaggeration. There was a well-lit corner of the barn in which a trestle table was set up, with papers and safety-helmets crowding it in company with a couple of mobile phones. The nearest bits of wall were pinned with memos and lists of phone numbers and plans. Here the site foreman took the phone-call from the police and went at once to Ivor to tell him they were on their way.

'To talk about what?' Ivor couldn't conceal his irritation about being disturbed in this way when work on the site was so far behind. Other feelings lay deeper down, though, and needed to be concealed, not to say stamped on hard.

The foreman shook his head. 'They wouldn't say. Except it was a matter of routine. They did ask me what time I got in this morning, mind. And what time you did.'

'You said...?'

The foreman shrugged his surprise. 'Just said what was true. I got here seven thirty or thereabouts and you come twenty minutes behind.' That second detail was the truth; Ivor couldn't disagree. But why were the police concerned? Even when they arrived a half hour later and, eyeball to eyeball, were given the information a second time, they gave no indication of the reason for their sudden interest in Ivor's movements. It wasn't until a few minutes after Feri had telephoned him later in the morning with the news of Trevor's suicide that it all fell into place with a sickening jar, which left Ivor nauseous and unable to concentrate for the rest of the day.

'But why?' Feri asked him that evening. They were eating cold pork and pickle in the kitchen because nobody had had time to shop and there was nothing else. 'Why should the police go hounding you?'

'Well, they were fine about it in the end,' Ivor said. 'Robbie confirmed my time of leaving, just as you did, and everyone at Sedlescombe saw me arrive twenty minutes later. There was no possible way I could get to the Rother levels and back in that time.'

'That's not the point,' said Feri. 'Why on earth should they want to question you about it in the first place? You don't have any sort of criminal record. You've never even stolen an apple from a tree. Well, not since you were a kid, maybe. They might have thought of Mark, of course, since he's presumably Trevor's heir, but they didn't. Once they'd heard what he had to say they let him go. They could have questioned Robbie. He drove off to Kenardington, right past the spot, around that time. But of course they didn't question Robbie. They had as much reason to suspect any man, woman or child in the whole of Sussex or Kent as they had to wonder about you.' She pressed her lips tightly together and shook her head involuntarily. 'It makes no sense.'

Ivor thought it made perfect sense from the promoted Mr Tart's point of view, but had no intention of saying so to his wife. Instead he said, 'I feel bad about it. You know, the thing about the oast. Suppose I'd said, yes, let's go ahead. Buy it off him. Do the conversion. Do you think...?'

'Don't be silly,' Feri said. 'You're not responsible. It was the bloody BSE, the weather, and the foot and mouth that put the skids under things.'

That didn't help. It might have been the foot and mouth, and BSE, or even the three months of incessant rain, but Ivor – or at least the thing inside him, whatever it was – had been responsible for those. He said, 'In some ways Trevor was like a father to me.' He paused. Then, 'I still don't know who my father was. My mother gave me the impression even she didn't know. It could have been anyone from roundabouts. Could have been Trevor for all I know.'

This was the moment when Feri, quite without meaning to, dropped the equivalent of an atom bomb upon her already fragile spouse. 'It wasn't Trevor,' she said. 'I've been trying to find the right time to tell you

377

this. I promised your mother – the only time I met her, that I'd tell you.' During the five years since, Norma's vague suspicions had turned into a certainty in her daughter-in-law's mind. 'Your father was Jack.'

Mark stayed with his mother for the rest of that day. Feri baby-sat the farm and rooted out Frank to help. In the evening Ivor and Robbie had done the final rounds with her, while Mark stayed at Link Farm overnight. But in the morning, soon after Ivor's departure for Sedlescombe, Mark's car came bumping up the track. He was back at work. Feri went out to him and took him into the house. Mrs Taylor, who was Mrs Fuggle's successor, delivered stuttering condolences in the kitchen, then Feri took him along the back hall and into the privacy of the first sitting-room. Mark spoke. 'I'm sorry about yesterday. I've never gone to pieces like that in my life. I never thought I would. I imagined, if I imagined anything, that I'd be ice-cool and keep my nerve. Instead...' His mouth clamped shut and his head shook slightly from side to side.

'We don't know ourselves as well as we think we do,' Feri said quietly. Then, though she seemed to address the afterthought principally to herself, 'We know others even less.'

'The worst thing,' Mark set off again, 'was not so much looking pathetic in front of you, it was how selfish my feelings were. Instead of thinking about Dad and poor Mum I went out of my mind thinking about how I'd look – what people would think about me.' He shook his head again, more deliberately this time. 'That was bad.'

'Mark,' said Feri gently, 'don't beat yourself up. Anybody can go to pieces for a moment in a crisis. You behaved irrationally just for a moment. There was nobody with you to help. You couldn't do anything for your father. If you could have done you would. I know you. And you went to give your mother the support she needed the moment you were strong enough. You couldn't have done better than you did.'

Mark chose not to answer that. He said what he'd been preparing in the car as he drove along. 'I have you to thank for yesterday. You saved me. I don't know what from. From me perhaps. So, thank you for being brilliant.'

'It's OK,' said Feri. 'No thanks needed. No apologies either.' She looked at him. 'Do something for me.'

Mark frowned. 'What do you mean?'

'Turn your shirt collar up.'

'What?' His eyes did their hallmark surprised thing.

'Just do it.' Puzzled, Mark obeyed. 'That's how you were wearing your collar when I first saw you. The fashions of seventeen-year-olds in those days, I suppose.' They were both silent, both mentally counting back the years. Feri made it eleven, Mark twelve. 'Now you look seventeen again,' Feri said. 'Which is nice just once in a while.'

Mark's surprise made him laugh. Then the thought of doing that, laughing, just twenty-four hours after his father's death made him start to cry. He quickly stopped himself. Feri got up out of her chair and walked towards him. He stood up too. Their fingers found each other's and then their lips. It was not a wild or passionate kiss: it was meditative, like the kisses of those who have loved for a long time. But it wasn't an extended business. After a few seconds they quietly stood back half a pace and let their fingers relax and unclasp. They looked at each other a few moments longer. Then Mark said, 'Better get to work, I suppose.'

TWENTY-NINE

Trevor's funeral service was held in the church at Stone: the square-towered church that perches on the scarp edge of the Isle of Oxney and watches over the outspread Marsh below. In summer it would be a bucolic scene but in this winter of disease and rain the view looked grim and threatening. The Marsh was a series of interlocking lakes around which the white-pepper sheep trod warily if they were wise. In the far distance the sea wall at Dymchurch seemed unsure of its role: between two sheets of water, one fresh, one salt, it seemed to be doing as much to retain the flood-water on the land as to keep the English Channel out.

Following the burial in the family plot on the steep hillside most of the mourners drove, or were driven, to Link Farm a mile away. Ivor drove Feri, Heinz's daughter and old Frank. There was some conversation in the car, although not much, and Ivor didn't join in at all. Feri had found him more than usually withdrawn and silent since Trevor's death, and was sure this had as much to do with his run-in with the police as with the suicide of the father of a friend. That the police should have wanted to talk to him about his whereabouts that morning still seemed to her outrageous as well as inexplicable. What on earth had the police been thinking of? That, because he'd been on the scene when Heinz had breathed his last, and had had the misfortune to have witnessed the death of Jack, he might as well have been present when Trevor took his own life? When she tried to make sense of it she came across something strange in her own mind, something she had never experienced before; at least, she thought she hadn't. It was as if a kind of road-block, or a series of road-blocks, were stretched across the pathways of her thoughts, preventing her from going beyond them and, stranger than that, warning her somehow that she mustn't even try. Some deep-seated instinct for self-preservation then backed those warnings up, and she made herself think of other things.

Arriving at Link Farm they walked beneath umbrellas to the house's front door. In this very yard, although in sunshine then, Feri had first seen Mark, with his shirt collar so memorably upturned. Shaking streams and showers from their umbrellas they now trooped inside. A couple of dozen people were already in the big living-room and were being offered the traditional choice between tea or coffee and stronger stuff. As they walked towards this huddle of men and women Ivor saw one man – it was a person he didn't know – turn to look at them, then turn back to his little group. He then said to them, 'Here come the Macbeths.'

Hearing this, Ivor found himself suddenly enraged and furious, maddened like a goaded bull. He lunged towards the stranger and caught him by the rain-wet lapels of his dark suit. 'What did you just say?' he said. His jaws seemed to have locked themselves together and it was an effort to pull them enough apart to get the words out.

'Hey, lay off me,' said the startled man. 'What the...?!'

Ivor's jaws had loosened now. 'You said, "Here come the Macbeths,"' he almost roared.

'He said no such thing,' said the woman next to him robustly.

Feri had her hand on her husband's sleeve. 'What the hell's the matter with you? Have you gone crazy or something?'

Ivor wouldn't leave it. He tugged roughly at the man's lapels. The man was Trevor's age but very solid and strong, and gave no sign that he was likely to topple or lose his purchase on the floor. Instead the two of them rocked gently towards each other and back again. 'You said Macbeths,' Ivor said again.

'Why would I say Macbeth?' the man said, sounding quite angry now. 'Is your name Macbeth? Perhaps it is. I don't know who the hell you are. Macbeth's a play by Shakespeare, I do know that. But why would I be talking about that? Here. Now.'

'What he said was, "More in out of the rain,"' a younger man said icily. 'That's if you must know. But he wasn't talking to you.'

'For God's sake, Ivor,' Feri was saying. 'Let the man go.' She turned to the older man. 'I'm terribly sorry. I don't understand... Look, I think my husband's been a bit upset.' In the corner of her eye she could see Andy, awkward and huge in a black suit, begin to shoulder his supportive way through the room towards them.

Then Mark arrived. He was newly the master of the house in which he stood and it showed. Immediately he was in command. He laid one hand on Ivor's shoulder and the other on the older man's and said gravely, 'Please.' He looked at them both in turn and repeated it, slowly and clearly. 'Please. Please.'

Ivor let the man go. 'I'm very sorry,' he mumbled to him. 'I must have misheard.' To Mark then, 'Sorry, mate.' He turned away and Feri followed him, though turning once to share with the little group a look of apology and bafflement. The group were looking in equal bafflement at Mark, who now found himself apologising for his friend.

'Why the Macbeths?' Mark asked Feri as soon as he could. He had found a moment to beckon her into his mother's kitchen while Ivor was busy being talked at by somebody else. 'I don't get it.'

'No,' said Feri. 'I asked him and he said he doesn't want to talk about it. I know that's not what the man actually said. So why Macbeth? Everybody knows Macbeth but I've never heard Ivor mention it before.'

'Is it the one where he kills his uncle?' Mark asked. 'I mix them up.'

'No, that's Hamlet. Look, I'm sorry. Your guests. Your father's friends... I really don't understand. But you've known him longer than I have. You know how strange he can get.'

'He was upset about Dad dying,' Mark said. 'I know that. It may have made him go … I don't know … out of character somehow.'

'Yes, but you're upset about your father's death. Far more than Ivor can possibly be. But you haven't gone berserk. Ready to punch someone at a funeral over something you've stupidly misheard.' Feri stopped, looked down for a second, then back at Mark. 'I'm a bit afraid it might be something I've done. Or said.'

'How do you mean?' Mark asked.

'I told him something he didn't want to hear, or it was the wrong time to tell him, or it was something I should never have told him; I should have treated it as a secret I was meant to keep.'

'Tell me,' Mark said. He wanted to take hold of Feri at that moment but resisted the urge. Anyone could have walked in.

'We were just talking about fathers and sons. OK.' Feri had to take a breath. 'When his mother came down that time she told me something she wasn't sure if she wanted Ivor to know. I said I'd find the right moment and tell him myself. The other day I let it slip. I don't think it was the right moment. Now I don't think there would ever have been a right moment. Norma told me she thought Ivor's father was Jack.'

'Bloody hell,' said Mark, his eyes bulging in their sockets as he digested this. 'That's a thought that's got some mileage. That could explain a lot.' He stopped, realising that he didn't know quite what he meant by that last remark. He thought for a moment and decided it was just one of those things you said. They looked at each other for a second longer, then went out of the kitchen to rejoin the gathering in the big room. They were both fiercely conscious of the fact that they hadn't kissed.

There was a dinner party at Birdskitchen Farmhouse a few days later. Although convention dictated that you didn't do such things in the aftermath of a funeral – in the wake of a wake – Feri had never been someone to allow convention to dictate to her: she was obedient to it when it suited her but otherwise not. She felt that this was exactly the time when everyone needed cheering up. Whether by everyone she actually meant Mark, or whether she was looking for a reason to have him under her roof for a few hours, were not questions into which she cared to delve too deeply.

There were eight around the table. Besides Feri and Ivor there were Mark and Stephanie, Richard and his wife, and one of the younger generation MacFadyens, Daniel, with his new girlfriend Isabelle.

For all her defiance of convention Feri was not insensitive in the matter of what she served. There was no beef on the menu nor, for equally obvious reasons, mutton or lamb. Instead she casseroled a brace of guinea-fowl with mushrooms, shallots, grapes and white wine and defied her guests to find anything politically incorrect in that. And since none of them was vegetarian, nobody did.

As they were getting up to move into the dining-room Daniel's girlfriend caught sight of a familiar title among the shelves of Feri's books. 'Oh, The Cat Who Loved Potatoes,' she said. 'I used to love that as a child.' She turned to her boyfriend. 'About a wonderful cat that talked if it was fed on potatoes, a discovery that was made by accident. And a boy called Vince, and his Aunt

Hattie, always wearing a different hat in each picture. The illustrations were wonderfully funny.'

'By Gemma Palmer,' Feri said. 'She used to live near here.' And Ivor added, surprisingly, 'She was a good friend of ours.'

'A bit upstaged by Harry Potter these days, I should think,' said Mark.

'She lives in Germany now,' Feri said. Then, loyally, 'but her books still sell.'

'Oh, could I borrow it?' Isabelle asked. 'I'd love to see those pictures again.' Ivor happened to be nearest to the bookshelf on which the volume sat. He pulled it out and handed it to Isabelle. Then they all resumed their journey towards the dining-room.

For Isabelle life in the depths of the countryside was a very new experience and she approached it with the same wide-eyed wonder as the teenage Feri had, more than a dozen years before. Casting those wide eyes at Mark and Ivor in turn Isabelle asked them, 'Did you shoot the guinea-fowls yourselves?'

Both men chuckled but it was Mark who answered her. 'You don't shoot guinea-fowl. And it's always guinea-fowl, by the way, not guinea-fowls. You find them in the supermarket near the poussins and the ducks. They're all farmed.' But he noticed a crushed look appear on Isabelle's face and saw that he needed to put things right. 'Although, come to think of it, why not? We shoot pheasants, after all. We might have been having pheasant tonight, only nobody's done any shooting this last couple of weeks.'

'Do you hunt and that stuff as well?' Isabelle asked, coming un-crushed and bouncing back.

'Lots of farmers round here do,' Mark said. 'Our family never went in for it.' He thought back for a second. 'Had a pony as a kid.'

'Unlike some,' said Ivor, and forced a smile to show this was a joke.

'Ivor's never been on a horse,' Feri said. It was one of those things they'd teased each other about over the years. Feri had ridden, back in the Gatcombe days, though rarely since.

What happened next was one of those random convergences of tiny events that go on to have consequences out of all proportion to their initial cause. The butterfly and hurricane effect. Mark and Ivor noticed simultaneously that the wine bottles on the table were all empty and at exactly the same moment got up with the intention of fetching the next one. It stood patiently awaiting its turn on the Georgian sideboard just a yard or two away. And at exactly that moment Richard's wife was heard to say, 'What a pity. I think they'd both look rather nice in hunting pink.'

This made everyone focus their attention closely on the two young men. By now they had both taken the single pace needed to reach the sideboard and were rather comically looking at each other and then the wine, unsure which of them was going to pick the bottle up. You had to agree, Feri thought, they made a handsome pair. They were both a little less than average height, although equally so: you'd have needed a spirit-level to argue anything else. They both had thick dark hair and deep blue eyes. They differed in their build. Mark was broader in the shoulder and almost stocky, while Ivor still kept the slender figure he'd had when Feri had first known him. But he was no less strong than Mark, Feri knew that, having seen them both engaged in the same physical work over the years. But while Mark's strength was evident to anyone who looked at him, Ivor's was a more deceptive thing. It was like a panther's, Feri thought: hidden in a frame that was lithe and lean. She looked at their mouths. They had quite full lips, both of them. She would never have thought of doing a compare-and-contrast of those two pairs of lips until a few days ago. Their noses were a little different, though... Feri was startled to hear Isabelle, who must have been thinking along the same lines, though she had no business to be, say, 'Aren't they cute, the pair of them? They ought to give each other a kiss.'

The suggestion produced an eruption of surprised laughter. Stephanie said, 'No way!' in a high-pitched giggle of a voice that suggested she was fascinated as well as appalled. Mark looked at Ivor and laughed, which made Ivor laugh too, and now that they had turned to face each other it looked to the others, still at the table, as though they were squaring up actually to carry the suggestion out. Daniel MacFadyen and Richard spoke at the same time. One said, 'Spare us, please!' and the other, 'Go for it, guys,' but nobody remembered afterwards which remark was whose.

By now the atmosphere of tension and expectation in the room had permeated the two young men. Mark said to Ivor, 'Well, are we up for it?' as if challenging him to a dare and Ivor shrugged his shoulders and said, 'Why not?' They leaned in towards each other and, without making physical contact at any other point, and to a background noise of whoops of encouragement and squawks of protest from the others, kissed each other on the lips.

A lot can happen in the course of a kiss. Right now a lot did. Mark found himself shocked – it was almost like an electric shock – to realise that this was a very intense experience for him. The shock, the naughty thrill of it, lay in the discovery that he was enjoying it very much. Ivor found himself experiencing exactly the same thing, though with memories of certain long-past experiences to draw on, as well as a somewhat shrewder understanding than Mark's of how these things worked, he was marginally less surprised. Then, for a second, they both thought the identical thought: that it was OK to enjoy this just the once, without needing or wanting ever to do it again. Then they released each other's lips, but still stood close enough to read their identical conclusions in each other's eyes.

And then, as they stood looking at each other, something else happened. *Something strange seemed to have passed between them. An idea seemed, as it were, to have slipped out, a kind of hint; something hideous and ghastly, something that both of them suddenly understood...* It was the Razumikhin moment, the very accident that Ivor had drilled his psyche into making sure would never occur. He had striven to make sure that, unlike Rodion Raskolnikov, he would never betray his secret in some dark corridor beneath a lamp. But he had. Now Mark knew. Ivor had betrayed himself with a kiss.

Their two faces crumpled with the sickening shock of it. From both their throats escaped a little sound, a little breathy sound that was something between a gasp and a groan. In silence they turned from each other and returned to their seats. Mercifully – they both thought this – those seats were neither adjacent nor directly opposite; they would not have to sit looking into each other's eyes. It had registered with everyone around the table that something odd, something strange and very powerful had just occurred, that a kiss had not been just a kiss, a sigh not just a sigh, but nobody could imagine what that odd thing might be. There was silence for a second, then Daniel MacFadyen said, 'Hey, love-birds. You forgot the wine.'

That night Ivor barely slept. When, some time in the small hours, he did briefly drop off it was only to wake with a shout of terror that woke up Feri too, leaving her perplexed and anxious as she tried to stroke him back to sleep. Something had clearly happened to her husband in the last few days – Trevor's death, perhaps, or her ill-timed unveiling of Norma's theory about who his father was. Maybe it was something that had happened tonight, something connected with that silly kiss, that had set Ivor back to where he'd been around the time of Jack's death and their marriage, which had followed hard upon. Those night terrors, his difficulties with sex, had taken years to fade yet fade they had. Now it seemed that they were back again. Feri decided she would be patient. If it again took years, this second time, for Ivor to heal himself then she was prepared to wait again. They still loved each other; they would manage this. She would talk to him. She wondered as she lay still now in the darkness if it might be the right time to start trying for a baby at long last. If Ivor had things in his past that weighed heavily on him – though what those things might be she decided she wouldn't care to know – then he needed a future big enough to weigh in as a counterbalance, and what bigger future could there be than the making of the next generation? There was nothing to be done about this just for now. She would need to discuss it with Ivor when the time seemed right. She would also have to come off the pill.

On a slightly different matter she would like to talk to Mark. Perhaps he'd be able to give her some idea of what had taken place. She would find a time to speak to him in the morning.

But Ivor got there first. Before even a first cup of tea he was throwing on coat and wellingtons and off down the track in the grey of dawn and the drizzling rain, then knocking on Mark's front door. The cottage once inhabited by Heinz. Lights were on, of course. Mark was a farmer. He was up.

Stephanie answered the door. She was dressed in a filmy, flimsy gown. 'Is Mark about?' Ivor asked.

Stephanie gave him an odd look. 'Have you come to wake him with a kiss?' she asked.

'Look,' said Ivor, 'would you mind if we just draw a line under that?'

'Sorry, boss,' Stephanie said, ushering him indoors out of the wet. She called her husband, then turned back to Ivor. 'He hardly slept a wink last night. Which meant I didn't either. I'd better go up now and get dressed.' She started up the stairs by the front door while Mark, fully clothed except for his bare feet, appeared in the doorway to the kitchen and came into the room When he saw who his visitor was he looked at him in bug-eyed horror as if expecting Ivor to reach a hatchet out from under his coat.

'It's OK, Mark,' Ivor had to say to him. 'I want to talk to you about the oast.'

'About the oast?!' Mark sounded terrified and after a moment's reflection Ivor realised why.

'I mean, about buying the oast. I should have done this before. Christ, I'm so stupid. If I'd done this sooner maybe Trevor... Look... Sorry.' Ivor shook his head as energetically as if a wasp had landed on it. 'Too fucking late, mate, but, you know...' A new thought struck him. 'Oh shit, man. I'm far too late. There'll be that probate thing. You won't be able to...'

Mark cut him off. 'It's not an issue. Dad turned us into a limited company years ago. You did know that, though there's no reason why you should remember. He did it mainly in order for me to avoid having to go through what you had to after Jack...' He stopped, struggling to keep the conversation grounded and safe. 'It means,' he resumed, 'that money can come in and go out without waiting for probate or anything like that.' He stopped again and looked warily into Ivor's face. 'Are you serious? You really want to buy the oast?'

'I'll go to Malcolm today. And the bank. Cash on the table. Just ask your price.'

Mark said to him, 'You don't have to do this.'

Ivor said, 'I do.' It came out as a sort of growl.

'Oh, mate,' Mark said quietly. 'I sort of know. I understand why you wouldn't want to get involved with the oast house. I don't want to know but somehow I do. Somehow, perhaps because of the Lydd thing and what we went through together, perhaps because of Welstead House... Matey, I don't know much. I certainly don't – and never want to – know how. ...Don't look at me like that... I'll see the agent today. Quote you a price for the oast house.' Then Mark tapped the bottom of his chest a couple of times, very solemnly, in the region of his diaphragm. 'Everything else stays here. Right here. But we must never talk about it again.'

Ivor wasn't tempted to kiss Mark. But he would have liked to give him a big hug just then. To have rough-cuddled him like one of the big sheep-dogs. But he knew that it couldn't be done. Not now.

Ivor made no secret of where he'd gone before breakfast. As they drank coffee and ate toast at the kitchen table Feri contented herself with saying, 'Everything all right with Stephanie and Mark?' and with Ivor's grunted, 'Yes,' in reply. She didn't rush off to talk to Mark herself immediately afterwards; she was confident their paths would cross later in the day. Which they did. Mark went strolling into the office annexe of the apple store with a query for Stephanie about an invoice. When he was about to go out again Feri came in from the workshop end and they walked together out into the rain. In better weather they might have stopped and chatted in the yard. Instead Feri asked him into the farmhouse for a coffee. Mrs Taylor could be heard vacuuming a couple of rooms away, so they had the kitchen to themselves. Feri said at once, 'What happened with Ivor last night? He had a dreadful night and woke up shouting at three o'clock. It was back to the bad old days.' But as she spoke a thought crossed her mind. She was cross with herself for not thinking this before: she wouldn't have put Mark on the spot in this way if she had. Was it possible that Mark and her husband had had some sort of a fling, or a thing, whatever one called it, when they were in their teens? You never quite knew with boys. Where they'd been before you got to them. Perhaps last night's kiss had brought back troubling memories for both of them. Of course it hardly mattered. And it would have been a very long time ago. Even so, Feri found that she didn't want to be told about it, didn't want to hear Mark come out with some stumbling and bedraggled history of adolescent experiment now.

Mark was looking at Feri with an expression of great discomfort on his face. He too was wishing the question unasked. But the question had been asked and now he had to come up with some plausible story to explain his and Ivor's odd behaviour the night before. He realised that it was not the kiss itself that troubled Feri but the way the two of them had reacted afterwards that had disconcerted her, and puzzled everyone else: the reaction that neither he nor Ivor had managed to hide.

'Ivor's going to buy the oast,' Mark blurted. 'He suddenly made up his mind. That's what he came to tell me earlier. I don't mind telling you, it's a big weight off my mind. But about last night...'

Feri said quickly, 'You don't need to tell me, Mark. If it's something...'

But Mark thought he did need to tell Feri. Since what he was going to tell her would not be the whole truth, but rather a little fragment of another truth that would serve as a fig leaf to cover the real brute thing, Mark was determined to put it on display. He said, 'I lied to you all those years ago.' Feri looked suddenly baffled, uncomprehending. Mark went on. 'When you asked me about what happened to Ivor and me at Lydd. The thing is, what Ivor said at the time, and then told Gemma, was true.' He spoke rapidly, urgently, almost jabbering. 'Like it or not, we both saw a medieval village street. With Ivor last night... It sort of brought things back.' Mark stopped and looked carefully into Feri's face, searching for signs that his ploy had worked.

It seemed to have. Feri was so relieved not to be hearing what only a moment earlier she had feared she would that she was in no mood to question Mark's grafted-on bit of truth or to try peeling it away. 'I'd been thinking,' she said slowly, another preoccupation surfacing in response to Mark's admission. 'Thinking I'd try and get in touch with Gemma. I don't know if I could put things right with her. But now so much time has passed. I wonder if what you've told me... If it might give me a way in.'

They looked at each other with a relief that neither of them could hide. For reasons which were totally different and impossible to share, they had each found a conversation whose conclusion they'd dreaded had come to a safe and reassuring end. The sound of the distant vacuum cleaner filled the silence as they leaned towards each other, embraced, and kissed a second time.

Feri drove down Float Lane and knocked at Mrs Broackes's door. It seemed the obvious place to start. Promisingly the door opened and Mrs Broackes stood there and smiled. Mrs Broackes had been elderly when Feri had last seen her and elderly she remained now. In contrast Feri had matured from teenage student to married thirty-one-year-old. But Mrs Broackes welcomed her indoors as though she'd been coming to call every day in the meantime. The cats too. They couldn't be the same ones, surely. But two of them were. Mrs Broackes proudly showed her Debussy and No Knickers, curled beside the Rayburn in senile doze, both nearly sixteen years of age.

Gemma visited England quite regularly, Feri learnt to her surprise. She came about twice a year. She would check up on her house, make much of the cats, see the estate agent in Rye and visit her aged mother and her sister at Tunbridge Wells. Mrs Broackes was surprised Feri had never run into her in the town.

'Rye's a big place,' Feri said deadpan and was gratified to see Mrs Broackes smile.

The old woman fetched her address book and Feri copied Gemma's down. There was no email address and in a way Feri was relieved by that. The old-style solemnity of a letter would be more appropriate in the circumstances and after all this time.

'She married, of course,' Mrs Broakes said. 'A German chap. But her husband died.'

'Oh dear,' said Feri trying to take in simultaneously these two juxtaposed big bits of news. 'How dreadfully sad.'

Dearest Gemma

I hope you won't be too displeased to hear from me after such a long time. Mrs Broackes gave me your address. Also the sad news that your husband died. Feri thought for a moment. She couldn't use the stiff word condolences. Not to Gemma. She wrote instead, *I was so sorry to hear that. I hope – if you won't think me impertinent for saying so – that you are able to keep memories of a lovely man.*

Ivor and I have been married for nine years. We have our ups and downs. Remember Mark? The lad who didn't back up Ivor's story about their visit to Lydd that time. Well – and this has been the spur to make me write you now – he suddenly does. So if ever you thought again of turning that story into a book, you'd find me willing to get involved, and probably the two boys as well.

Feri looked at what she'd just written. The letter was a terrible muddle. And she seriously doubted that Mark and Ivor would sit down together and collaborate on writing a book. She hadn't broached it with either of them. But everything was a muddle at the moment, and the letter simply reflected that. Anyway, this book thing wasn't the real reason she was writing, just the pretext.

Gemma, I know I can't undo things that happened years ago. But I miss your friendship terribly. This year I find I need your wisdom, and your advice, more than I've ever done. If you could find it in your heart to talk to me I'd love to see you next time you're in the UK.

What Feri most needed to say were the things she couldn't put in the letter. They needed discussing face to face. The first was that she was desperately worried about what was happening inside Ivor: not just worried but fearful too. The second was the heart-bursting realisation that she now loved two men.

She decided not to try rewriting the thing. Her phone number and email address were at the top of the page. Gemma either would or would not reply. Feri wrote, *With Love,* and signed her name. Later that day she dropped the envelope into the small post-box near Peasmarsh Place.

THIRTY

Mark found it difficult to believe that, within a fortnight of losing his father in circumstances which would previously have been unimaginable, and seeing his mother ship-wrecked and broken by grief, he was embarking on an affair with his best friend's wife. He hadn't thought he was a person who would do such a thing. But he hadn't thought he was the sort of person who would go to pieces when faced with a death in his family. He hadn't thought he was someone who would be sharing that same best friend's appalling secret: that the man to whom he was close enough to kiss for a joke, with whom he felt comfortable enough to dance with at a party, had killed a man in cold blood.

But what had Mark done, actually? Falling in love was not something you did. It just happened to people, with the suddenness and finality of falling through a trap-door. You didn't do anything but then the thing was done, and you lay in a mangled heap at the bottom. The image of that event in the oast house kept coming to Mark now, although he hadn't been there at the time. Mrs Fuggle had. She, one of the least imaginative people Mark had ever met, had seen nothing except an accident: a drunken man stumbling through a hole in the floor. She had told the same story for years to everyone, including Mark, again and again until she had finally retired. Mark didn't want to know how Ivor had made Jack walk to his death. He just knew that he had. Mark had seen a film in which alien-spawned children caused people who'd crossed them to bring accidents upon themselves just by giving them an intense look. Ivor had seen ghosts: did Ivor have that power also? Mark thought not. He too had seen ghosts, but his looks were incapable of killing anyone. He knew that because he'd tried it. On Miss Sutton at school. There had been no result of any kind, unless you counted the detention Mark had been given for being rude.

Mark wasn't sure how he knew the thing he knew. There was Ivor's odd behaviour since Trevor's death. Other odd things in the past, some of which had been told him by Feri. There was the Macbeth thing. But other people knew those things, and Feri better than anyone. Yet nobody else, not even Feri, had seen how everything fitted into place.

What was he supposed to do with his secret knowledge now? Shop Ivor to the police? He couldn't see what would be gained by that. Ivor had shown no sign of wanting to go on and kill anybody else. He wasn't a danger to anyone. He hadn't made any move to shut Mark's mouth. Well, yes, he had. He'd made that crack-of-dawn visit and offered to buy the oast. Mark was quite clear about this: in that offer lay a massive bribe. But Mark thought that, in those circumstances, he would have done the same. Also in the offer lay an element of real friendship, Mark was sure, and some sacrifice: it was obvious that Ivor didn't want to set foot in the building; that was why he'd refused to buy it sooner. If Ivor went to prison the offer would be gone. What else could Mark possibly sell to realise cash? Nothing. Everybody around had tens of acres up for sale, but no-one bought.

Mark could not even tell Feri what he had learned. Certainly no-one else. He had pressed his hand against his heart and gut and told Ivor that his secret would stay buried there for ever. Nothing had happened in the few days since to make him change his mind.

It was the kiss that had started everything. A social kiss between friends, such as he and Feri had exchanged often and innocently enough, in front of Ivor as often as not, and no-one had given it a thought. But that kiss he'd given Feri when he'd gone to apologise for going to pieces on the day his father died, and to thank her for her cool-headedness and support, that had unlocked everything. The power kisses had to unlock things! Mark thought he'd learned more about kissing in the last few days than he'd done in the rest of his life.

A few days after Ivor had accidentally burdened Mark with his grim secret, Mark and Feri had made love for the first time. Not in the matrimonial bed that Ivor had built for his bride. Out of a delicate concern for Ivor's feelings, a shared concern they had no need to voice, they went up to one of the attic bedrooms that were hardly ever used. Feri, who had had sex with nobody except Ivor for nine years, had almost forgotten, but now remembered with an agreeable tingle of shock, that some men could be gentler in bed than her husband usually was. Mark for his part was making the discovery – and this went way beyond the physical experience of sex – that Feri was the woman for whom that series of girlfriends of his teens and twenties, including the still current Stephanie, had been mere rehearsals, precursors. He was vividly aware of where he stood right now but, like most men in his particular situation, couldn't begin to imagine how the future would deal with him. With them. Or, as he thought of Feri and himself now, with *us*.

When Daniel MacFadyen's girlfriend Isabelle came to Birdskitchen to return the copy of The Cat Who Loved Potatoes the following Sunday afternoon Ivor was, unusually, alone in the house. He thanked her for returning the book and after she had gone went to the bookshelves meaning to find a space and squeeze it in. But the book fell half open in his hands and one of the pictures in it caught his eye. He noticed something that hadn't struck him when, back in Gatcombe days, he'd riffled through Gemma's illustrations and praised their charm and her skill. What he now saw was how uncannily the eight- or nine-year-old Vince resembled himself at a similar age. It could only be coincidence, of course. Gemma and he had met when Ivor was sixteen, and the book had been written some six years before that. But now his curiosity was whetted and, instead of returning the book to the shelf, he sat down and did something he'd never done before. He began to read the text.

Ivor experienced that mild surprise that all adults who haven't looked at a children's book since they were children themselves discover: how quickly it can be read. He read it through from beginning to end. In it he found all those silly jokes of Gemma's about food that had delighted him years ago. The tanglioline and the tinned puma chunks. Others he didn't remember: someone said they had eaten *an elephant sufficiency*, on one occasion Mumberland sausages were served with custard, and on another, Aunt Hattie announced that her winter woollies had been *ravaged by Goths*. Ivor was surprised to find the story entertaining, even for someone as old and unhappy as he was, and good fun. He enjoyed reading it more than anything he'd read in years. Though as his reading matter had consisted for years of weekend newspapers, tomes on architecture and updates to standing UK Building Regs, that could hardly have been a surprise. Yet the thing that struck him most forcefully was the mismatch between the character of Vince, who looked so much like his younger self in the pictures, and his own.

It was not that Vince was some pallid goody-goody. He mischievously drove someone's parked car a hundred yards down the road and then re-parked it, for the fun of seeing its owner's puzzled face when she returned. He dug potatoes out of a neighbour's vegetable plot by torchlight once when he thought Nicholas II had something important to say to him and his aunt's vegetable box was empty. And he was forever ignoring his aunt's wishes and disobeying her instructions. But he was not the sort of boy who would ever have poisoned his grandmother's goldfish, let alone arranged for his benefactor to die in a terrifying accident. This boy Vince, this creation of Gemma's, this piece of fantasy, seemed to Ivor to be almost impossibly *nice*.

Perhaps that was precisely because Vince was a piece of fiction. It was a convention of fiction, Ivor supposed, especially of children's fiction, that people could behave like that. *Nice*. Or was it that Gemma, dear old deluded Gemma, was like that herself? Innocent in some deep way that was so much a part of her that she foolishly believed other people could be like that too? Then a new thought came to him. Could it be that some people really were like Vince, and that Gemma had got it right?

Ivor started to think about Mark. Mark was no paragon. He had lied to their history teacher that day after their visit to Lydd. Out of sheer cowardice, and for the other reason that most lies are told: to avoid complications in the life of the teller. He had dumped a whole string of girlfriends as soon as they began to bore him, and that couldn't have been pleasant for the girls. But he had never done anything worse than that. He had never caused anyone's death for his own advantage. He hadn't killed his own father. Something which it now seemed Ivor very possibly had done. Ivor knew absolutely that Mark had not killed Trevor. How could he know for sure? He hadn't been there. Yet he knew, because Mark was Mark. The police knew that too. They hadn't suspected him for an instant. Instead they had actually come and questioned Ivor. Dear Mark. Ivor felt very close to him sometimes, but then he had got too close. So close that his secret had escaped him in the course of a facetious kiss. But that couldn't be undone now. And anyway, what had Mark done afterwards? Struck himself solemnly where his heart and innards were and said that his new knowledge of who and what Ivor was would stay buried there. Ivor did not disbelieve or doubt him. Because Mark was nice. Ivor was Ivor, but Mark was Mark.

How good it must feel to be Mark and to know yourself, as Mark knew himself, to be nice. Whereas if you were Ivor that possibility was forever out of reach. The memory of what he had done to Jack had never left him alone. Even with the passing of years it remained, like the sustained pedal-note in an organ solo, the background to all his thoughts. It was like the endless drip-dripping note in the Chopin piece that Gemma had made him listen to sometimes: the Raindrop Prelude. It would crescendo sometimes to a terrifying fortissimo, then fade again. But unlike in Chopin's music it would never fade to stillness with the return of the sun. For Ivor the sun would never return. How could it? Especially now that it seemed Jack might well have been his dad. There was something else that was terrible now. Ivor had had had sex with Jack. With his own father? Easygoing about sex Ivor might be, but even he would wake shivering in the night at the thought of that.

Ivor was driving back from Kenardington, along the low-lying lanes on the far side of the Isle of Oxney. After months of rain it often happened that, rounding a corner, you were faced with a sudden expanse of deep water ahead of you instead of road. This happened to Ivor now, in the hamlet of Reading Street, on a particular route back from Kenardington that he hadn't taken for some time. You had to overcome the reflex that told you to brake and instead change down and accelerate through. At least the Marsh lanes were reasonably flat and these floods, though they might be a hundred yards or more long, were seldom more than six inches deep. Keeping up a reasonable pace as you powered through them was usually enough to prevent water from getting into the exhaust and bringing you to a stop.

'Don't accelerate.' The voice spoke from the passenger seat beside Ivor, where no-one was.

The hairs on every part of Ivor's body rose as if he'd had an electric shock. Even though he knew no-one could possibly be sitting beside him he automatically turned his head to look. The other reflex that kicked in was to stamp on the brake. Hard. The car slid crab-wise to a stop in the water and the engine died. 'Oh fucking shit,' Ivor said.

He knew the voice, how could he not? Although it could have come only from his own imagination that gruff, German-accented delivery belonged to Heinz. Heinz dead for more than six years now but whose dying words, real or imagined, still tortured Ivor when he lay awake at night. That voice, shockingly loud and clear in Ivor's mind had said, 'Don't accelerate.' Well, that was Heinz. Negatives and positives so mixed up that you had to sort them out. 'Don't accelerate,' in Heinz-speak would have meant more like, 'Power your way through the flood.' But of course Ivor hadn't. He'd been startled out of his wits and, either because of that or because he'd taken the instruction at face value, had not accelerated, had hit the foot-brake like a panicking schoolboy, and was now stuck in water that, when he stepped out into it, came up over his ankles, soaked his trouser-legs and icily filled his boots.

Grunting and swearing he managed to push the car to where the water was no more than puddle deep. Here, after a few minutes of spraying WD40 around the engine compartment and waiting for it to take effect, he managed to re-start the car. At first the engine fluttered feebly like a damaged butterfly but then it came back to full life. As he drove out of the water and back onto dry road he remembered what you were supposed to do now. He more than expected to hear Heinz's disembodied voice giving him further misleading instructions, like, 'Now, don't try your brakes.' But no voice spoke and Ivor cautiously did try the brakes, one foot on the middle pedal, the other gently accelerating, in order to dry them out.

When Ivor got back to Birdskitchen he saw Mark coming out of the front door of the farmhouse. This might have surprised him in ordinary circumstances and made him wonder what Mark had been doing in his and Feri's house, but he was still in such a state of mental shock and physical discomfort that the oddness of it passed him by. Mark found himself blushing hotly, but as he had a ruddy face anyway and the evening was already dark with the promise of yet more rain he hoped it wouldn't show. And he was relieved to notice, as Ivor stepped out of the car, that he looked pretty preoccupied with other things. For a start, Mark noticed, his trousers were drenched all the way up to his knees. Mark used this as a convenient decoy to lure Ivor's attention away from his having just come out of his door. 'Hey there. What happened to you?'

'Got stuck in a flood at Reading Street,' Ivor said, shutting the car door a bit aggressively. He walked towards Mark.

'What? Forgot to put your foot down?'

Mark's bullseye guess surprised Ivor into saying what he'd already decided he would tell no-one, not even Mark. 'You could say that. It was like I heard a voice in my head saying, "Don't accelerate." You know, like

Heinz used to. Give instructions and you never knew if he meant do or don't.'

Mark's eyes bulged. 'Really? A voice?' Ivor nodded silently. Mark was torn between astonishment and the need to keep Ivor's attention away from himself. He said, 'Remember, I never knew Heinz. I just live in his cottage during the week. Mind you, I remember you telling me that story: "What didn't you do with those wellingtons," or something.' To Mark's surprise Ivor looked suddenly ready to burst into tears. Mark closed the gap between them and put a hand on each of Ivor's upper arms. 'Hey, hey.' He looked into Ivor's eyes, thinking suddenly that because of what he'd just been doing, and who with, he had forfeited the right to look there, and saw the lower lids brim with wet. He said, 'It's OK, Ivor, it's OK. You're with me.'

Ivor made no move to wriggle away but consented to leave his biceps in Mark's grip. 'Sometimes,' Ivor said, 'I think you're the only friend I've ever had.' A proviso occurred to him. 'Except for Roddy.' He had been thinking about Roddy in the car. He couldn't remember if Rodion Raskolnikov had suffered hallucinations like the one he'd just experienced. It was a long time since he'd read the book and many details had got blurred. But he remembered the thrust of the story, and the atmosphere, and the kind of person Roddy was.

'Roddy? Don't you mean Robbie?' Mark queried, though he would still have been surprised had Mark said yes.

Ivor laughed in a humourless, croaky way. 'No,' he said. 'Not Robbie. No way. Roddy's the man for me' Then he shook himself free from Mark's restraining, comforting hold, pushed past him and disappeared into the farmhouse.

*

By the time he next saw Feri, in the apple store the following day, Mark had recovered from the shock and embarrassment of walking into Ivor in such a compromising place. He gave her an edited account of the conversation they'd had and Feri told him how difficult, silent and withdrawn Ivor had been for the rest of the evening – something which did not surprise Mark at all. He asked her, 'Does he have an imaginary friend?'

Feri looked at him in as much surprise as if he'd said he was the king of Portugal. 'A what? He's twenty-nine. Of course he doesn't,' she told him curtly.

'Then who is Roddy?' Mark had to ask.

'Roddy? Robbie, he must have meant. Though I'd hardly...'

Mark interrupted. 'I asked him if Robbie was who he meant. He said no. He laughed and shook me off – I think I was trying to hold onto him. Said Roddy was the man for him.'

Feri shook her head, astonishment having temporarily taken away her words.

'He said he'd heard a voice,' Mark pressed on. 'Did he tell you that? Telling him to slow down as he drove through the flood at Reading Street. He said it sounded like Heinz.'

'He's told you he's hearing voices?' Feri's own voice was little more than breath. 'Is he going...?' She stopped abruptly and changed course. 'Does he know about us?'

'No,' said Mark very seriously. 'I don't think he does. I think he's got bigger fish to fry.'

Feri reached out and caught at Mark's sleeve. 'Please talk to him. Find out what is going on. For me. You know him better than anyone...' She stopped and her head shook again, 'I don't know why I'm saying that.'

'I'll do my best,' Mark said. He looked steadily into Feri's eyes. 'It might mean we'd have to end... Well, you know.'

'Is that possible?' Feri said. 'I mean, do you really think it is?'

'I don't know,' said Mark. 'I think...' But Heinz's daughter walked in from the office annexe just then and the conversation had to stop.

Ivor had not forgotten the stories of Macbeth and Hamlet, had not forgotten the messages they delivered on the subject of guilty consciences: the way that those afflicted by them fell apart as fortune turned against them with time. He also remembered his devoutly Catholic grandmother trying vainly to sow the seeds of her religion in him when Norma wasn't around to hear. Among other things, Violet had told him about a magical thing called Confession. Apparently, if you told a Catholic priest what you had done and then recited a particular set of words, and then the priest recited another formula, you were released unconditionally from the spell created by your bad deeds. Violet had called bad deeds Sin. It was a concept that Ivor guessed must have gone out of fashion in recent years, as he couldn't recall hearing the word since, except perhaps in those two plays of Shakespeare's that Gemma had taken him to see. According to Violet, Confession literally cancelled Sin out.

Ivor thought carefully about this. He didn't believe in ghosts, he told himself, despite those things that had happened to him in the past, but he had been seriously spooked by hearing the voice of Heinz beside him in his car and, although he knew it had been a trick of his own brain, he rather dreaded hearing Jack Eason's voice in similar circumstances. The fright those words of Heinz's had given him had been enough to make him to stamp on his brake and stall the engine while driving through six inches of water. What effect might a similar remark in the accents of Jack Eason have?

Perhaps he was going crazy. Crazy people heard voices in their heads. So was he going crazy, as Roddy had done, as Lady Macbeth had done, as a direct consequence of his guilt in arranging Jack's death? His father's death perhaps. Hamlet's uncle, Ivor remembered, had tried praying to God to put things right between his conscience and himself. He hadn't got very far. Perhaps Ivor could do better. Claudius, after all, hadn't actually gone to see a priest.

The next time he was in Rye Ivor walked along the cobbles of Watchbell Street, towards the cliff-top view at the street's end over the flooded valley of the Brede. But he didn't walk right to the end. He stopped outside St Anthony of Padua's, the church that Violet had attended so assiduously – Ivor put the building down as a modern example, far from displeasing, of the Spanish Romanesque style – and looked at the notice by the door that gave the times of services there. He noticed there was a Mass on Saturday at seven pm. For some reason which he didn't understand this was included among the Masses for Sunday, but that was neither here nor there. Tomorrow was Saturday and seven in the evening would do fine.

He told Feri that he had arranged a meeting with a potential client at the Union Inn, and although she thought it an odd time and place for such a meeting she agreed to have their evening meal later than usual, when he got back. It would give her an hour, she thought, to spend with Mark. Mark had talked of ending their affair, but he hadn't talked of ending it just yet. Meanwhile it occurred to Ivor that he might be the first man of the neighbourhood to tell his wife that he was going to spend an hour in the Union Inn while actually going to St Anthony's to hear Mass, instead of the other way round.

*

407

Ivor arrived fifteen minutes early but there were already a few people in the front rows, kneeling in the semi-dark. There was also a little line of people in the back row and rather than drawing attention to himself by walking down the aisle he added himself to these. Looking about in the gloom he was pretty certain that none of those present knew him or had even been at school with him. Some of them indeed looked as though they might have been at school with Violet. A door opened behind him suddenly and a woman came out, leaving it ajar. The person on the other end of his row immediately got up, genuflected in the side aisle and went in through the door, closing it behind him. The other people in the row then shuffled their bottoms along the pew to fill the gap he'd left and to create space at Ivor's end. With an awful start Ivor realised that he'd joined the queue for confessions by mistake. That hadn't been his intention – not tonight at least. He was only here to have a look around and get a general feel for things. He stumbled to his feet, apologised to the woman who had just come into the row after him and blundered past her, re-installing himself in another pew two rows in front, where he hoped he would be reasonably safe. As he went he became aware of an unintelligible murmur emanating from the closed confession box as one more parishioner unloaded his sins.

By the time the line of penitents had come to an end the church had filled up a lot. Ivor saw the priest emerge from the other door of the confession box: a tall, grey-haired man in a grey habit that was belted with a knotted white cord. He made his way towards the altar, then disappeared through a door at the side. About a minute later lights went on and a man in a black cassock came out of the same door; he carried a long pole on whose end a taper was fixed. He walked towards the altar and lit four huge candles that sat enthroned in bronze sconces atop a tall structure behind it. There was a lot of ornate brass in that vicinity, and a lot of polished marble, cut to symmetrical patterns in Italian Renaissance style.

Another set of lights came on suddenly, illuminating the high beamed spaces of the roof. Involuntarily Ivor looked up. He gasped so loudly that people actually turned round. Above him, suspended from a high tie-beam was a vast representation of Christ in Majesty, a more than life-size figure in carved wood, in robes of bronze and with a crown of fire, arms outstretched on a massive cross whose edges were also decorated with something that shone like fire or molten gold. Only the ivory face, the hands and feet of the huge figure protruded from the robe. The face was handsome but strangely calm and expressionless: it was a face that had gone beyond all pain. The white hands and feet were transfixed with big square nails. Crucifixes that Ivor had seen before, in Canterbury cathedral or St Paul's perhaps, might have been bigger. But they hadn't had the shocking power that this one had. Partly because this was how, except in the matter of the tranquil face, Jack had looked as he fell through the trap-hatch. Partly because Ivor realised as soon as he looked up that he had also seen this crucifix before. Violet must have brought him here once long ago and, until now, the memory had been blocked out.

Then the priest re-emerged, himself transfigured now by gold and purple robes, and Mass began. Ivor had difficulty in concentrating on the spectacle or the words, let alone on what, if anything, it all might mean. There was a sermon at one point, but Ivor could take none of it in. Instead his gaze kept returning upwards to where Christ, having suffered every imaginable pain on his physical cross of wood, was now returning on a mystical cross of fire, impartially to deal with the human race that out of its own wickedness had encompassed His death:

on the final day, to judge the living and the dead. How did Ivor know that was what it meant? From where had that come back to him? Only one person could have told him all of that. He'd remembered it from Violet's words, heard and then forgotten, when he was a child.

When the time came for Communion and those who wanted to receive it began to line up in the aisle a few people took the opportunity to leave the church early, under cover of the general movement and noise. Ivor decided to follow their example. He had seen and heard enough. On his way down the hill to where he'd parked his car he came to the Union Inn. He stopped outside and then, deciding he had a little time at his disposal, went inside and ordered himself a half pint. He thought he'd earned at least that.

THIRTY-ONE

Ivor ran into Father Edward quite by chance when they were both in the queue at the bank in West Street. Although the priest was wearing civilian black trousers and a raincoat Ivor had memorised his appearance at Mass and had no doubt about who he was. He caught him up when they were both outside again in the street. 'Excuse me,' he said, 'but I want to find out about Confession.'

'Oh,' said the priest, looking startled for a moment but then relaxing as he recognised Ivor as the customer who had stood next to him in the queue for the tellers. He went on lightly, 'You haven't just robbed the bank, have you?'

'No,' said Ivor. He didn't trouble to smile at the priest's question, or else was unable to. He knew you were supposed to call a Catholic priest father, but somehow he couldn't quite manage that either. 'No, it isn't that.'

Ivor sounded so serious that the priest became serious again himself. 'Are you a Catholic?' he asked.

'No,' Ivor said.

'Then what is it you want to know about Confession?'

'I want to confess. I want to have my confession heard – if I've got the right expression – by a Catholic priest.'

Father Edward frowned slightly. 'Ah. It's not quite as straightforward as that. But if you would like me to explain what I mean by that – and it is quite a serious subject as well as a complex one – I'm sure you realise that the pavement of a busy street is not the best place. If you care to, walk up the hill with me and we can have a chat in the parlour of the friary.'

'The friary?'

'It's where I live. A friary is a monastery for friars – a monastery is technically for monks, but we needn't bother ourselves with the precise differences now. Enough to say that both kinds of establishment have got smaller in recent years. I'm the only friar in Rye. You could think of my bachelor pad as a Catholic vicarage if that makes it any easier.'

They walked up the steep cobbled slope of West Street, past the view down Mermaid Street that Gemma had painted on her first visit to Rye, and past Lamb House, where Ivor's repair to a windowsill had had such epic consequences a few years after that. They rounded the corner by the Anglican parish church, then, in Watchbell Street, where the smaller St Anthony's stood, the priest opened with a Yale key a door alongside the church. Chiselled in the stone lintel were the words 'Franciscan Friary'. Ivor was surprised he hadn't noticed them on his previous visit.

Across the hallway the priest showed Ivor into a small, very bare room. He sat Ivor down in an armchair and switched on a tiny electric fire. Then he sat down opposite Ivor. 'The thing is,' he began, 'if someone is not a Catholic they can't just go to a priest on a whim and ask him to forgive their sins. Confession is just one part of a bigger package of sacraments and a whole system of belief.'

'My grandmother was a Catholic,' Ivor said, and heard himself sounding a bit desperate as he did so. 'She used to come here to this church. I think she even brought me once when I was small. She was a member of Opus Deus.'

'Opus Dei,' the priest corrected gently.

Ivor frowned. 'I thought Latin words always agreed with each other,' he said. He'd learned that somewhere, probably from Gemma.

'They do, but in this case it's a genitive: the possessive case. The work *of* God. Anyway, never mind. But I'm afraid membership of the Catholic Church – or of Opus Dei for that matter – is not hereditary.' He smiled. 'It's not transmitted with your DNA.'

'You mean I'd have to be a Catholic first, before you'd let me confess? How long would that take?'

The priest sighed, then quickly covered it with a smile. 'There is a course of instruction.' He saw Ivor's horrified reaction and went on immediately, 'It's not like a university course, it's more like a series of private chats with a priest – like the one we're having now. And for an adult there's usually a bit of reading to do too. It usually takes place over a period of weeks or months.'

'But people confess on their death beds, ' Ivor objected. 'That doesn't take weeks or months.'

'That's a special case. From the sprightly way you came bounding up the hill just now – I was hard put to keep up with you – I'd rather guessed you don't fit into that category quite yet.'

'But...'

The priest stopped him with an upraised hand. 'Before you go any further, and before you think any further about becoming a Catholic, especially if your only motivation is to go about obtaining the benefits of Confession, there are two things about the sacrament you need to know.' He saw that Ivor was bursting to interrupt, so ran on quickly, hardly giving himself time to breathe, to prevent him doing so. 'The first is this: the priest does not actually forgive sins; God does that. Confession is a meeting between the penitent and God. The priest, in reciting a standard rubric, a liturgical formula if you like, is merely acting as God's mouthpiece. When absolution is given, that forgiveness is God's, not the priest's. But God's forgiveness is conditional; it requires contrition – the penitent has to be sorry, to repent – and there must be a firm purpose of amendment, which means a determination not to commit the same sin again. In practice, in many cases, this also involves restitution. That means that if the penitent has stolen something they must give it back, or if they've slandered someone, told lies about them and damaged their reputation, then they have to try and put that right – which is much more difficult in practice than returning stolen goods. In the same way, if they've committed a sin that is also a crime against the state – the breaking of a law that is agreed to be just, then they must take the appropriate action to put that right too.'

Ivor couldn't stay silent any longer. 'You mean like turning themselves in to the police?'

'I'm afraid I do. Now, in the confessional box as it's called, the penitent is obliged to say that he or she will carry out all those conditions. He has to recite a short prayer called an act of contrition. He may mean those words as he speaks them or he may not. The priest has no way of knowing. If he hears the words pronounced solemnly and seriously he will respond with the words of forgiveness, the words of absolution. But if the penitent is simply reciting the formula of contrition in a pretence of sincerity, the way an actor says his lines, that forgiveness will not take place. Because, although the priest can't know whether the penitent means what he says or not, God certainly does.'

Ivor started to get to his feet. Father Edward stopped him with another little movement of a hand. 'There is one last thing you need to know. You've probably heard of the seal of the confessional. That priests may divulge to no person, nor to any state authority, what has passed between them and any penitent during the rite of confession. That is true. But this doesn't apply in the case where a stranger approaches a priest in the street and announces that he has stolen the Crown Jewels. That doesn't count as a confession in the sacramental sense. In that hypothetical situation the priest would have the same moral duty as any other citizen to report the matter to the appropriate authority, presumably the police.'

Now Ivor did get to his feet. He felt that he stumbled his way to the door and hoped it didn't show from the outside. The priest said mildly to his departing back, 'I hope I've answered your question: told you what you need to know. If you do decide you'd like instruction in the Catholic faith, just ring the doorbell here and I shall welcome you in.'

At the door Ivor turned, though he hadn't thought he was going to, and said, 'Thank you, Father,' the *father* slipping out by accident as he turned the door-handle and let himself out into the cold cobbled street.

As he walked down the hill Ivor considered what he had learned. There seemed no point in unburdening yourself of a load of guilt if that release was conditional on another captivity. If he served even twenty years in prison for murder he would be approaching fifty when he came out, the best years of his life behind him. Sonia had waited years for Roddy to finish his sentence, but Ivor didn't believe that Feri, or anybody in the twenty-first century, would do the same. As Gemma might have said, different times, different people. And as well as losing Feri Ivor would lose his business and his house. Feri might be able to hang on to them in the aftermath of a divorce but he could not. All he had worked for would go to waste; Jack's death would have been in vain.

He arrived at his car, parked, like everybody else's was these days, in the supermarket car-park at the bottom end of town. He had no choice, he decided, but to put the lid back on his secret just as Mark, the wonderful Mark, had promised to do. He could not rid himself of his guilt in the sight of God. (A bit of an impertinence to attempt to, since he didn't believe in God, but there you were.) But he could do something for Mark at least. He'd already promised to buy the oast. He would get that project under way. Make himself go inside when he got home and start to measure things up. He didn't believe in God and he didn't believe in ghosts either, he reminded himself. Heinz would not be speaking to him as he drove home. Jack would not appear to him, dropping as he did in dreams through the trap-hatch in the oast. He had simply to pull himself together, get the better of his subconscious and of his too vivid imagination and soldier on, the knowledge of what he'd done somehow walled deep inside him, buried like radioactive waste. Perhaps he could manage to bury it so deep that, like his childhood visit to Welstead House, it could never be retrieved by memory. Perhaps there were self-help books that taught you how to do that. He would look on Amazon later.

Two miles outside Rye Ivor drove past Welstead House, tall and grey on its bank beside the road. He passed it often without giving it a thought: it was just a part of the scenery on this very familiar drive. But today he found himself wondering for the first time who had bought it when it had been for sale a quarter of a century before, whether they still lived there, and what ghosts, if any, they had seen in all that time.

A lorry came towards him, passed him on a bend. Were the roads getting narrower, Ivor wondered, or the lorries getting endlessly bigger, or both? To take the tight curve the lorry had to steer well over the white line and into Ivor's path, so that he had to swerve to avoid it. He felt his wheels make contact with the wet grass verge as, inches from the lorry on the other side, he squeezed past. A fine drizzle was falling again now and the lorry's slipstream coated Ivor's windscreen in a film of filthy wet, so that he had to switch the wipers onto a faster setting to clear his line of sight. At least he hadn't had to listen to any misleading instructions from Heinz. That was something.

Back at Birdskitchen Ivor made his way a bit apprehensively into the oast house. He hadn't been inside the building for years, certainly not since it had become Trevor and Mark's property rather than his. He switched on lights, and everything was much the same as he remembered from the past. The ground floor was still a bit of a death-trap of outmoded tractor attachments, though at least the old crows' nests that had sat on the hop trailers had gone. There were memories, of course, but no ghosts. Ivor saw this as another good sign. Converting the oast house for Mark would be a new beginning for him, the beginning of a battle which he would win. He left the oast; he had other things to do today which could not wait; he would come back tomorrow with a tape-measure and begin to rough out some plans.

That night he made love to Feri with an intensity that had become rare, but with a tenderness that was entirely new to her and which reminded her oddly of Mark. Feri was pleased that Ivor had gone along with her wish to try for a baby, not just in principle but in practical terms as well.

In the morning Ivor returned to the oast as he had planned, tape-measure, note-pad and sketching block in hand. As he opened the door into the dark interior he had the sudden sensation of a light coming on, not on the ground floor but from the storage floor above the staircase and the trap. Then he saw it, hanging below the trap-door, with arms outstretched on its burnished, fiery cross: the Christ in Majesty as he'd seen it in St Anthony's in Rye, the ivory face impassive and gentle, yet unable not to judge. 'Go away,' he heard his voice say in a shaky whisper. 'Go away.' The sounds he was making were by now disjointed, inarticulate: the gobbling rattle of a turkey cock. He turned his eyes away for half a second then looked back. The image had disappeared. Light could not have been streaming through the hatch as it had appeared to do at first. The trap-doors were firmly shut. He ran from the oast, not knowing and not caring if he was making any sound or not.

Mark was stepping out of his Land Rover just a few yards away. He could see clearly that something was wrong and trotted quickly towards Ivor. For the second time in days he grasped his arms, the memory of that last occasion overlapping with the memory of Feri clutching him in the same way just after he'd discovered his father's corpse. 'What's up?' he asked.

'I need your help,' Ivor said in a flat quiet voice, the dull old voice that Mark remembered from their shared classroom days.

'Ivor,' Mark said gently, 'I'd help you if I could but I don't know how. It's a doctor's help you need for whatever's happening to you. Not mine.' He paused, then added, 'I would do anything to help you if I could, you know. I care about you very much.' But hearing his own last words he winced, and Ivor saw that he did, and Mark saw that. How could he claim to be Ivor's friend while carrying on an affair with his wife? It was true – and a small mercy – that Feri and he had not made love for two days now. Mark vowed at that moment that they never would again.

'Not a doctor, Mark,' Ivor said. 'A priest.' And while Mark watched him in astonishment Ivor, calm suddenly, walked to where his own car was parked, got in and drove off.

Father Edward showed no sign of surprise when he answered the friary doorbell to find Ivor waiting outside. He greeted him with a smile and let him in. As soon as he was seated in the parlour Ivor began. 'Can you do excommunications?'

The priest looked startled for a moment but then his smile returned. 'Only the Pope can excommunicate people. But I don't think you have anything to worry about there. Excommunication means kicking people out of the Church. And you can't very well be kicked out of an organisation to which you've never belonged.'

Ivor frowned and a dark look appeared on his face. 'Exorcism was what I meant.'

'Right,' said Father Edward, settling himself into his chair like someone preparing to answer a question they have been asked many times before. 'Well, the answer, which may turn out to be unsatisfactory from your point of view, is that I can and I can't. All priests have the power to cast the devil out, in theory at least, just as they have the power to marry couples, baptise their children and forgive their sins. But in practice there's an issue of administration. Exorcisms, which are very rare these days, have to be carried out according to certain protocols and with permission from someone pretty high up. They are also done, when they're done at all, by priests with fairly special backgrounds. Maybe, these days, by priests who are also trained in psychiatry or something else. To be honest with you, I'm not sure. I believe there's an official exorcist in the diocese but I've never met the man.'

Ivor looked surprised and disconcerted. Father Edward continued to explain. 'The other issue is this one. Situations which for hundreds of years appeared to require the reading of the rites of exorcism these days hardly exist. They are explained by psychology and medicine and a hundred other areas of knowledge that were unimaginable in the past. At one time even, infestations of tapeworm were believed to be the devil's work, hence the stories of several dozen devils inhabiting the same poor chap at once. It's very rare today to find a case of what used to be called possession that can't be explained in a less alarming way.'

'Are you saying that not even priests believe in the devil these days?' said Ivor, sounding disappointed somehow.

'We seldom meet the devil nowadays,' said the priest blandly. 'The great saints of the past may have confronted him face to face, but these days he hardly has to lift a finger in order to get his way. The world and the flesh provide stumbling blocks for most of us, and they do his work for him.'

'So you do still believe in him,' Ivor said. 'As something objectively real, I mean. Even if he seldom has to bother with us these days.'

'I suppose I'd have to say yes, or lose my job. But it hardly matters one way or the other – if you're not a religious sort of man. Objective or subjective? Makes little difference, I'd say. You're old enough to have noticed that evil gets done in the world. That it comes out of men's hearts. You must have noticed that.'

Ivor nodded slowly, and they both pretended not to notice that he had started to cry. 'Then for most people the question of how it gets there is an academic one. From the devil outside, or from the person within. As a non-religious person you can take whichever view you prefer. But you know as well as I do that evil's there.'

Ivor had managed to pull himself together. 'I'm not sure I want a devil casting out. It's just that...' Ivor was about to talk about hearing voices in the car, but decided that if he did the priest would simply think him mad. 'In an oast house I'm converting – I was there this morning – I saw the cross you have here in the church, the big gold fiery one that hangs in the roof... I saw it appear there.'

'Well,' said Father Edward. 'Even if I was able to perform an exorcism for you, you could hardly expect me to drive over and cast out our Lord.' He gave Ivor a mischievous look, then became serious again. 'It seems to me that you have things troubling you, things deep inside, that you need to sort out. Priests can't do these things for you. We can help sometimes to focus people's thoughts when they talk to us, and tell us, if they want to, what their real troubles are. Maybe whatever is troubling you has a physical, or a mental cause. There are doctors and psychiatrists to help with those. But if it's something else, then by all means come and talk to me again, if you find out that there's something you really want to say.' He stopped and looked at Ivor as if he found him a very interesting specimen indeed.

'Is that it?' Ivor said. 'Is that all?'

'I'm not really into spooks and hauntings, I'm afraid,' said the priest. 'They usually turn out to be something coming from within. But if you have a problem with this oast house of yours, something that makes it difficult to work in there – and I appreciate how inconvenient that is when you've money to earn – then I could come over and sprinkle some holy water about the place and say a blessing with you.'

'Holy water?' said Ivor, shocked. It didn't sound nearly powerful enough for the task he needed doing. 'What good would that do?'

'Oh, none at all,' said the priest lightly. 'Holy water is nothing but a symbol. Sprinkling it around simply tells us, tells you and me, that in taking the trouble to do so, we want to distance ourselves from the power of evil, to grow stronger than evil is. But it's only a statement of intent, of course. Like a promise to marry someone – or an IOU.'

'How long have you been here in Rye?' Ivor asked. He had good reason to want to know.

'Two years,' the priest answered. 'They move us around quite regularly – like military police in other countries – to stop us getting attached to places and to the people there. Another year and, sad to say, they'll move me on. Pity. Every friar that ever comes to this beautiful spot thinks he's died and gone to heaven. But, sad to say, the church needs us more urgently in places less lovely than Rye.'

The two years news was reassuring. Father Edward was unlikely to have heard gossip about what had happened in the oast at Birdskitchen nearly ten years ago. 'Can you come, with holy water, if I give you the address?' Ivor asked.

'Today, no,' said the priest. 'But tomorrow. I'll come at four in the afternoon, then perhaps you can make me a nice cup of tea.' Ivor wrote the address down, drew a rough sketch of Starvecrow Lane, and then the priest showed him to the door.

Ivor found that he couldn't sleep with Feri that night. He didn't know why. He went off to bed in the room in the attic that had been his when he first came to live at Birdskitchen. When, more than ten years before, he'd been taken in, saved from homelessness, by Jack. This night was a cold one. The rainy weather had given way to an icy spell, although in theory spring was on its way. Feri was almost in tears as she pleaded with him to share her bed. 'We get through things together,' she told him. 'Always have done. Together. Not apart.' She wondered if he somehow knew about Mark and herself. As Mark had done earlier in the day she made a promise to herself that she would end the affair. Full stop. It would be as if it had never happened. Null and void. Cancelled out.

Ivor resisted Feri's pleas. She had to watch him climb the narrow enclosed stairway that led coldly to the attic floor. Viewed from this unusual vantage point his figure seemed pathetically small and shrunken, the fragile figure of a child.

For some time Ivor lay awake. The narrow bed was too cold and damp to allow immediate sleep. He stared up at the crown-post in the wall beside him, following its rise to where it branched and disappeared through the plaster of the ceiling above. He tried to make sense of what was happening to him but could not. At last, with the bedside lamp still shining, he shivered himself to sleep.

He dreamed of his father – whoever his father was. His father, all white, stood among a silent unmoving group of figures, all of them also robed in white, on a floor that was laid with straw, a floor that led away to a distance so immense that no horizon brought it to an end. These people looked like chessmen. Like the Lewis chessmen, cold and hard and made of ivory or bone. Ivor tried to speak to his father, but could not. Nor could his father speak to him. His father's eyes were blank. Ivor felt a sense of hopelessness about the scene. Though perhaps a sense of waiting too. He had time to notice, though without surprise, that his father was wearing a white crown, but then the dream was fading and Ivor beginning to wake.

He got up early. He had to drive to Brookland on the Marsh for a meeting with a farmer who was a potential client: there was a barn on his land that he wanted to sell. But before setting off Ivor wanted to have one more crack at the Birdskitchen oast, to get those initial measurements done. The business with the holy water was a silly thing, he realised, but in a way he saw what the priest had meant. It was a symbol of your determination to be strong in the fight against – well, against whatever it was, the demon, for want of a better word, inside yourself. Somehow, he felt, even in advance of Father Edward's afternoon visit, he had been given new strength.

It was grey dawn, the sun not yet up, but already it was possible to see your way palely across to the oast without needing to turn on the yard lights. As he got near to the door of the oast Ivor heard a noise, a crashing, blundering sound, coming from just around the corner of the building. He thought he knew what was making the noise and changed his course to go and sort it out.

Rounding the corner he found himself face to face with a large wild pig. You always said wild boar, but half of them were sows of course, and Ivor was looking at the front end of this one, not the rear, so he couldn't be entirely sure. But the pig was heavily endowed with tusks and built on a massive scale, so a male it probably was. If it were to charge at him those tusks would rip into the tops of his thighs or worse. Ivor and the boar both froze, equally astonished. They looked each other in the eye. The boar's eyes were hard and dark. For a moment they reminded Ivor, absurdly, of Robbie's. Its bristly coat was darkly grizzled in the morning dimness, the bristles were raised in a dark ridge along its back and all around the animal they seemed to make a halo of almost porcupine-like quills. Then the boar spoke to him. 'It's all a load of hooey, if you ask me,' was what it said. 'Nothing but a load of old hooey.' The voice, just like the expression it had used, was unmistakeably Jack's.

'What did you say?' Ivor said to the animal, his voice little better than a terrified gasp. 'What did you just say?'

Of course the boar had said nothing at all. Its lips hadn't moved. Nor had Jack spoken. The voice was in Ivor's head: he did know that. Ivor tried to control his racing thoughts. But before he could the pig – Jack – spoke again. 'Oh Ivor,' it said – he said – in the most piteous and despairing tone Ivor had ever heard, 'Oh Ivor, there's no-one here.'

Ivor collapsed onto his knees, then lowered his head in front of him till it touched the ground. Let the boar skewer him with its tusks, let it trample him, let it do what it would, let him be dead. He heard his own voice call – in a sort of groan – 'Where are you?' Then, 'Dad? Daddy? Where are you? Who are you? Who am I?' Then he collapsed onto his side and rolled on the ground, howling in terror, like a child.

'Ivor. Ivor.' His arms were being shaken. Someone was pulling him to his feet. 'Ivor.' The voice, the hands, were Mark's. Ivor looked around him. The boar had gone, the daylight was getting stronger, and he stood now by the corner of the oast, being held by Mark and holding on to him. He wasn't sure how long he'd lain on the ground. A minute? Maybe two? He wasn't sure if he'd stopped bawling before or after Mark had come. 'It's OK,' Mark was saying. 'It's about the oast, I know. You don't have to go inside. Get Robbie to do it. It doesn't have to be you.'

'It's more than that,' Ivor managed to say. 'I heard Jack's voice. He spoke through a wild boar. He told me...'

'I saw the boar,' Mark said. 'It ran off down the track. But you didn't hear it speak. You know that. Those things are in your mind. See the doctor. See a shrink.' Mark pulled at Ivor's arms, gently shook him. 'Look, mate, I'll take you to the doc myself. I'll drive you there today. We'll do it together. You and me. You'll be OK.'

They were still holding each other, looking into each other's eyes. For a moment Ivor had the strange impression that he was looking into a mirror, for in Mark's face he seemed to see a version of his own: a little broader, bigger boned, ruddier of complexion, yet oddly resembling the face he saw each morning when he shaved. He said, 'I love you, mate.'

Mark said, though it was a bit of a mumble, 'I love you too.'

That was Mark, Ivor thought. Dependable and nice. Best friend. Then he suddenly realised something else about Mark. For a moment anger rose in him like fire, a volcano going up, but then, as suddenly and as surprisingly, it died. Ivor blurted his discovery straight out. 'You're fucking Feri.' There was infinite surprise in his voice but no rancour.

'Ivor,' Mark began, but stopped. He had no idea how he could go on. Ivor continued to look into his eyes and, to Mark's growing alarm, began to smile at him.

Ivor found himself thinking, taints and honours, his taints and honours waged equal in him. Where had he heard that phrase? From Gemma, no doubt.

'It's over,' Mark finally managed to say. 'It's in the past.'

Ivor felt that he was surfing on a volcano's molten lava flow. He didn't know what would happen next. Didn't know what he would do. He gripped Mark's forearms tightly, which made Mark flinch. 'We've done worse things,' he said. 'Every man fucking Jack.' The words coming out in the wrong order like that, a very Freudian slip, made him suddenly laugh. The laugh frightened Mark even more. Ivor relaxed his grip. 'I've got to go to Brookland now. See a man about another barn. Back midday. There's a priest coming at four o'clock to bless the oast. If anything... Look after her – Feri, I mean – till then.' He let go of Mark completely, then, seeming to change his mind about something, leaned in towards him and, perhaps through a minute miscalculation, perhaps because Mark tried to pull his own head away, kissed him on the nose. Then he turned away and walked towards his car, noticing as he went that Feri had come to the farmhouse front door and was standing there: presumably she had watched the previous scene. Ivor gave her a cheerful, almost childlike wave, and smiled, then got into his car, started the engine and drove off.

The floods had begun to go down in the last few days. Still, there was plenty of wet about and when the temperature dipped below freezing as it had done during the last couple of nights the mornings presented themselves all covered with skins of ice. Driving, you would skate on the fringe of a puddle and then crash through into its deep centre, as into a pot-hole, your front tyre working like an ice-breaking ship. So it was this morning as Ivor made his way towards the Marsh. Starvecrow Lane was particularly icy, but you had to go slowly there anyway and there was little traffic to come the other way. Passing Rye Foreign and Welstead House he found the main road almost dry. The same went for the road that skirted Rye and led out through East Guldeford to cross the levels towards Lydd. But then, as he crossed the Kent Ditch and the road changed course towards the Woolpack Inn, the old smugglers' haunt, Ivor found his way covered with ice again. This stretch of road was mainly straight but at intervals, because of the piecemeal way in which the Marsh had been drained in medieval times, it lobbed you a right-angled bend. Looking ahead Ivor noticed through gaps in the bare hedgerow a container lorry approaching, about a mile away across the flat. As the bends came and went it was periodically hidden from view by trees, and then would reappear again, a little nearer each time. Presumably it was coming, as most lorries on this road did, from the ferry port at Dover, twenty-five miles east. Eventually it appeared in full view, coming onto the straight stretch of road in front of him, safely rounding the bend.

A second later it was all across the road in front of him, the container sliding one way, the cab the other, and then back again. It was like watching a giant figure-skating routine going wrong. There was nothing you could do but gasp. One second Ivor thought he might be able to swerve to the right and pass the sliding monster on that side, throwing himself on the give-and-take mercy of the hedge, the next he knew he would have to try to scrape by on the left. Crazily – and he was self-aware enough to know how crazy this was – he expected to hear Heinz's voice instructing him to go left or right, and Jack's voice contradicting him, in a cacophony of conflicting advice. But he heard only silence beyond the din of engines and the howl of brake-locked wheels upon the icy road. He was conscious of feeling aggrieved at that absence of advice. He had time to think, though no time let alone any voice to utter the idea – *Tell me, Dad, what to do.*

He was partly conscious a little later on. Perhaps for whole minutes, or maybe it was seconds only. He struggled to know where he was and what had happened to him but failed. He knew only that it was dark and very, very cold. There seemed to be activity around him, but he didn't know what the activity was. It somehow registered with him that he felt no pain and he just about managed to understand that this mattered a lot and was something to be grateful for. This brief return of partial consciousness occurred while the Fire Brigade were struggling to cut him from the wreck – the wreck of his car, himself, his dreams and everything – but he didn't survive long enough ever to discover that.

Later that day Father Edward drove up to Birdskitchen and, finding nobody about, made his own way into the oast house, found the light switch on the stairs and sprinkled holy water about the place, blessing it upstairs and down.

THIRTY-TWO

You never 'got over' the death of someone you loved. Gemma knew that. Especially when they had died in disturbing circumstances. Even so, there came a morning, more than ten years after Dieter's death, when Gemma found herself thinking, as she cycled along the leafy avenues of Göttingen towards the Kunst Akademie, that she had reached a point of equilibrium where grief was balanced by enjoyment of ongoing life. It had something to do with this particular glorious morning of early summer of course. Sunshine really did do good things to the heart and brain. Gemma arrived at her place of occasional work, padlocked her mount to the railings and went inside. A note was in her pigeon-hole, politely asking her to call on the principal when she had time. She went at once.

He wasn't the principal who had employed her in the first place. Gerhardt Ritter had retired some years before and this was his successor, a very much younger man. He asked Gemma to sit down, then, assuming a suitably compassionate half-smile told her the bad news. It was the recession, of course. The disaster that had overtaken British farming at the turn of the millennium had proved no more than a dummy run for the global economic catastrophe that was unfolding now. The effects of the debacle seemed to reach out, tentacle-like, to touch everyone and everything. Even the Kunst Akademie. Funding difficulties, the principal told Gemma, meant a paring down of the college's many activities to its core courses only, and Gemma's teaching of the subject of book illustration on two days every week would come to a stop at the end of term.

For years Gemma had opened envelopes, in Britain as well as in Germany, that contained offers from the banks she dealt with to lend her money for everything she might want or need or merely hanker after. Lend without end had seemed to be the mission statement of the mission-statement decade. Gemma had thought to herself as she binned the mischievous enticements, where would this end? Today she knew. The mischief was costing her her part-time job. Even as she took in the news she thanked whatever gods there might still be that, as an artist whose work was still in demand, whose books still sold, who had some savings and a house that was all her own, she was one of the luckier ones. But there was no particular reason for her to remain in Germany now and so, a few months later, she took advantage of the departure of the latest tenants of Gatcombe to return there to live.

Within a week of her arrival she ran into her old friend Jane in Rye High Street and they walked up the hill together to drink coffee at Simon the Pieman's. Despite Jane's transformation by silver hair, it felt to Gemma as though the past eighteen years or whatever it was had never intervened.

Gemma – her hair still honey-blond thanks to those modern genies that live in bottles – sat with her back to the door and the serving counter, so she was hardly aware of the woman who came in to buy chocolate cake. Until she spoke. Then Gemma spun round on her wheel-back chair. 'Feri!'

Feri, like Gemma, had kept her figure well. Her cheekbones remained keen and fine, her dark brown eyes still wore the shining bloom that made them appear blue. Her black hair had not started to show grey. But she had matured into someone grand and statuesque, South American elegance blooming in the streets of Rye.

Feri said, 'Gee?' a bit uncertainly, because the beamed and lamp-lit interior of the tea-shop was hard to see into after the brilliance of the sun-swept street outside. Gemma stood up and walked towards Feri, who remained standing still. Silently each inspected the other's face for a moment but found no clue there as to what would happen next. Then Feri said quietly, 'Give me your hand, Gee.'

Gemma didn't extend her hand. Not in that way. Instead the two women embraced each other. They kissed, then laughed absurdly, till Gemma's make-up ran. There were things that should have made this impossible: letters that cried for help had gone unanswered, a boyfriend had been stolen half a life ago. But those things slid away in the joy of reunion in the way that water slides from sea-birds as they rise from it into the air.

'We must...' Feri began and Gemma, nodding her head to where Jane sat, said, 'I'm with one of the... I'm with a friend.'

'I have to get back,' Feri said. 'Come to Birdskitchen. There's someone you must meet. Can you make tomorrow afternoon?'

The assistant was wrapping Feri's purchase in a box and bag. Feri pulled a note from her purse. Gemma couldn't help remembering that when she'd last lived here it would have been coins.

It had never crossed Gemma's mind before – she was realising it for the first time now – that as you drove away from Gatcombe up Float Lane you found yourself looking straight across the Tillingham valley towards Birdskitchen Farm when you got to the main road at the top. You couldn't see the farmhouse itself, that was hidden by the folding hills, but Birdskitchen's outlying fields lay less than half a mile away, tumbling down towards the Eggs Hole brook. Because of the river Tillingham, though, you couldn't go there straight. You had to drive west, halfway to Brede, before diving down Hundredhouse Lane, grinding up Ludley Hill when you'd crossed the river bridge, then double back along Starvecrow Lane and up-down through Eggs Hole. It made a journey of about five miles. Of course it was the route that Ivor had cycled to work during that brief time between his starting work at Birdskitchen and Gemma's throwing him out of her house. But it was a beautiful drive, especially on a sunny September afternoon like this one. The valley was no longer filled with hop gardens. Gone were the spiders' webs of overhead wires and no longer was the scene busy with pickers and the slow-moving tractors with their trailers and crows' nests. The valley bottoms were mainly pasture now. Even the oast at Gatcombe had been sold off by Bob Jameson and converted into a family home. This had given Gemma a family of new neighbours to get to know and, with luck, perhaps like.

Gemma didn't think she had driven past Birdskitchen since the day she'd seen it from the window of Jane's car, decided it was the kind of house she wanted, and then bought Gatcombe, its lookalike, on the strength of that. But she hadn't forgotten the way there and as soon as she saw the house across the fields she was struck again by its resemblance to her own. The afternoon sun was lighting its white paintwork and pink brick, just as the morning sun lit Gatcombe. The twin white cowls of its oast – also now converted, by the look of it – gleamed brightly above the roof. At the gate a neatly lettered sign advertised Hop Bine Country Crafts and another, Bed and Breakfast. How farms had had to change, Gemma thought as she turned onto the track. The track was still grass-grown along its centre line, which was reassuringly like old times, and as it brushed the underside of her car the grass made a soft rushing sound.

Before Gemma had even reached the house she saw Feri emerge from a brick outbuilding on the other side of the yard. She waved Gemma towards a suitable place to park and a moment later the two women were walking together towards the front door.

Gemma couldn't stop herself from saying, 'How like Gatcombe it is.'

'You'll think it all the more so when you've seen inside,' Feri answered. That made it inevitable that before even sitting down they embarked on a tour. 'Even some of the furniture's in the same style as mine,' Gemma said, and Feri heard for the first time in eighteen years that little sleigh-bell laugh. 'Though I don't own a square piano.' Gemma had caught sight of the small instrument in the old parlour. 'Does this get played on?' she asked, fingering a chord and noticing it was in tune.

'It does and it doesn't,' Feri said. Then, 'Of course it was Ivor mainly who wanted the place to look as much like Gatcombe as it could. When he wasn't trying to make it look like Great Dixter, of course.' They both laughed.

Feri had told Gemma there was someone she wanted her to meet. Mark presumably, though there had been no sign of anyone else about the place. But it was mid-afternoon and he would probably be busy around the farm: it wasn't quite teatime yet. 'And Mark?' Now that Ivor had been mentioned it seemed to Gemma that it was time to show an interest in Feri's second husband. For Mrs Broackes had told her years ago about Feri's marriage to Mark in the wake of Ivor's death. She'd learnt of that death from Feri herself. The news had come in one of those letters she'd been unable to answer. Until now. 'How's Mark?'

Feri looked at Gemma. A strange flatness seemed to come over her face. It came over her voice too as she said, 'Oh, didn't you know? Mark's dead.'

The inappropriate things that went through your mind at times like this, Gemma thought. *To lose one husband might be regarded as a misfortune; to lose two looked like carelessness.* Impossible to let Feri even guess that that had floated into her consciousness. 'I'm so sorry,' she said instead. 'Darling Feri.' Standing in the kitchen now she took her younger friend in her arms.

They walked out into the garden. This had not been one of Ivor's preoccupations nor especially one of Mark's, but Feri had taken some trouble with it over the years, fencing it securely to stop sheep and chickens, as well as the wild boar, getting in. Now at summer's end the small lawn was framed with borders that blazed with the varied colours of golden rod, Michaelmas daisies, rudbeckia and early chrysanths. On the lawn were white wooden chairs and a table and here Feri and Gemma sat.

'Mark died three years ago,' Feri said. 'We'd been married just over five.'

'Died how?' Gemma said gently. 'I can't not ask.'

'Cancer of the stomach.' Involuntarily Feri touched herself near the diaphragm. 'Incredibly rare in someone as young as he was. Just thirty-five.'

'Like Mozart,' Gemma said. 'And Jesus Christ. Only the very best of us die so young.' She paused a second, wondering if her trite generalisation could be extended to Ivor too; decided not to pursue this. She said, 'I never met Mark, of course. Was he tall and blond, like a Viking? I might have seen him once, helping to collect Ivor's things.'

'That would have been Andy,' Feri said. 'He manages the two farms now, for Mark's old mother. He's no longer blond, alas. No, Mark wasn't tall. Same size as Ivor actually. And dark. I'll show you photos when we're back inside.' She smiled. 'But not too many, I promise.'

Gemma said, 'You can show me as many as you like.'

'But you,' Feri said, frowning slightly. 'I'm sorry. I haven't asked.'

'Yes, you have,' Gemma said. 'You wrote me two letters in the space of a month nine years ago and I didn't answer either. You needed my friendship and my help and – I'm dreadfully sorry – there was none that I could give. I need to explain...'

'Don't, please,' Feri said, and Gemma saw her two hands tremble on the table. 'Past is past...'

Gemma went on doggedly. 'I'd lost my husband, as you know. But I couldn't bring myself to tell you I'd lost him twice.'

Feri leaned towards Gemma. 'What...?'

'He died in a train crash. In a train that ran almost past my house. But he wasn't coming to see me. He was on his way to Hamburg, where his ex-fiancée lived. Throughout our marriage he'd been seeing her. Contentedly leading a double life. That's why, when your letter told me you'd started an affair with Mark... I mean, you didn't write that but that's what I understood...'

Feri's agitation made her stand up. 'Poor Gemma. Poor, poor you.'

'Not poor me. Not poor anyone. Life happens, we treat each other badly, and that's how it goes.'

As suddenly as she had stood up Feri dropped back into her chair. 'We started an affair just days before Ivor died. It was a terrible thing to do. We didn't think so at the time but, goodness, later on we did. When Ivor was so vulnerable, so fragile, in the middle of a breakdown. It's easy to see now how things were but it wasn't then. I only knew that I was fragile just then, too.'

'Did Ivor know?'

'I don't think so. Mark always said he didn't. But I don't know for sure. There were secrets the two of them shared, I think. Things I didn't know.'

'There are things it's better not to know,' Gemma said. 'If Ivor didn't know about you and Mark, and died not knowing, that was good. I wish I hadn't known about Dieter. I'd have less complicated memories of him – I'd be deluded, of course, but life would be easier and his death easier to bear.'

'Gemma...'

'You were all so young,' Gemma said, looking down at the table for a moment. 'The three of you.' She changed the subject slightly, wanting to talk of things that would hurt them less. She looked up and around her. 'The farm. Ivor's business. Didn't he convert barns?' She looked beyond the garden, scrutinised the converted oast.

'After Ivor died his partner Richard bought my share of the barn conversion business. He runs it with a man called Robbie, who you wouldn't know. I keep going with the country crafts and doing B and B. It's not so much that I need the money, but empty rooms... You know.' Gemma nodded. For a second they both remembered the days when Gatcombe's many bedrooms had been full of kids from the American School. Then Feri went on. 'The two farms remained Mark's mother's property and they still are. As I said, our blond Viking Andy manages them now.' Silence fell for a moment. Then Gemma said,

'You told me there was someone you wanted me to meet. I'd assumed it was going to be Mark.'

'There is someone.' Feri glanced at her watch. 'You'll meet him any second now.' And a second later, with precision timing, Gemma did. He came round the corner of the farmhouse, wheeling a bike, and pushed open the garden gate. He was a striking-looking little fellow, with very large blue eyes framed in starbursts of black lashes and with a shock of black curls that had got rather over-long but which – Gemma imagined sympathetically – his mother probably hated to see cut. He stopped still when he saw Gemma, his hand still on the open gate. Then he looked at his mother and said, 'Who's your friend?'

'Tell you later,' Feri said.

'She must have a name, though,' the boy objected reasonably.

'You can call her Aunt Hattie for now,' Feri said. 'Explanation in full to follow, I promise.' She turned back to Gemma. 'My son Vincent.'

'Oh, don't be stuffy, mum,' the boy said, dumping his school bag on the lawn. To Gemma, 'Just call me Vince.'

'And call me Gee,' said Gemma. To Feri, 'What's this Aunt Hattie nonsense?'

'It was his favourite book a year or two ago,' Feri explained.

'Oh, mum, not a year or two. More like three or four.'

'And then, of course...' Feri began apologetically.

'I know,' said Gemma, smiling. 'Then Harry Potter came along.'

Feri spoke to her son. 'There are some fresh yoghurts in the fridge. Go and get one. Bring it out here if you want to join us. Otherwise don't. But put the kettle on while you're in there.'

Vince disappeared indoors. From the look of him, Gemma thought, he was of an age – eight or nine – to have been conceived around the time of Ivor's death, around the time when Feri and Mark had begun their affair. 'He looks like Vince in the book,' she said.

'He looks like Ivor, you mean.'

'And is he...?' Gemma let the question hang there, for Feri to answer as she chose.

Feri waited a second before she did. Then, 'Actually, I
don't know. This may sound crazy but Mark and I didn't
want to know. OK, I know you're thinking that Mark
could have taken a paternity test and settled it one way
or the other. But there's another thing. You know how
Ivor didn't know who his father was.'

'And didn't seem to care much,' Gemma said. 'Which
I always found odd.'

'Well, that changed at the very end,' Feri said. 'I'm
coming to that. His mother – Ivor's mother – told me
very solemnly once that she thought his father might
have been Jack. A farmer who lived round this way who
called himself Jay. Norma put two and two together and
made Jay into Jack. And I blurted that out to Ivor, very
stupidly and at a very bad moment. I told Mark too, but
only that Ivor's mother thought Jack was his father. It
wasn't until a few months after Ivor died that I told him
– told Mark – the bit about Ivor's father being called Jay.
His face went nearly white, which was a rarity for him.'
Feri leaned a little closer to Gemma across the table. 'He
said that his own father had been called Jay when he was
a young man. His father and grandfather both had the
same first name. But Mark's dad was Trevor Joshua
Harris, so got called Jay to avoid confusion. Like George
Dubbya Bush.'

'Which would have made Ivor a brother of Mark's.'

'Half brother, yes. Ivor by five months the younger of
the pair. And if that really was the case a paternity test
wouldn't have told us anything at all. Half brothers with
the same Y chromosomes... Believe me, we looked all
this up.'

'But you might have been able to establish that they
weren't brothers...'

'Mark didn't want to go there. Didn't want to find out
either one way or the other. His mother was – is – still
alive. He couldn't have borne to have to tell her his

father was putting it about while she was pregnant with him. And he said he couldn't have borne the secret if he'd known and not told her. "Too many secrets," he said.'

'Meaning...?' Gemma wanted to know.

'Meaning I don't know what. He and Ivor seemed to know things about each other that no-one else did. There was a closeness between them. At one point I even thought they might have been lovers in their teens. Now I'm sure they weren't. Being brothers, almost half twins if you like, would explain it better.' Gemma thought it would explain things more comfortably from Feri's point of view but was not going to say so. 'After Ivor died Mark and I arranged to get married within a few months. We were in love and there was going to be a child. Though actually Mark wasn't able to make love again for nearly a year. The same thing had happened to Ivor when we married. Seems to have been my fate. Though in both cases the problem put itself right with time. But in both cases time was shorter than we'd thought.'

'Feri, darling... But what did Mark's mother think? About Vince, I mean. She'd want a grandchild. Whatever did you both tell her? Ivor's mother too.'

'We simply announced a baby was on its way and let them think what they liked. They were welcome to ask who the boy's father was but neither of them did. Vince has Mark's surname, Harris, and Norma was fine about that. I don't remember if you knew her. She was a very calm person, very accepting of what happens in life. She became a Quaker around the time I married Ivor.'

'Good heavens,' Gemma said.

'Actually, people were more shocked by my marrying Mark just six months after Ivor died than they were concerned about Vince's parentage.' Feri shook her head and almost smiled. 'A never-ending source of surprise, that's what people are. Well, Vince has ended up with three grandmothers, if you include my mother in New York – which is one more than most people get.'

'And he himself?' Gemma asked. 'Vince Harris, who – this makes my head swim rather – shares not only his looks but first and second names with the boy in my books: what does he think about it?'

'Some boys know who their father was,' said Feri matter-of-factly, 'some don't. Ivor didn't, Mark did.' But she went on in a way that was far from matter-of-fact, looking Gemma steadily in the eye. 'What does it matter, so long as the boy is loved, really loved, the way Mark and I loved Vince, the way I still do? The way Ivor would have loved him if he'd lived. Vince knows that. He doesn't worry about the rest.'

Gemma doubted that Ivor would have loved the boy quite as much as Feri imagined if he'd believed him to be Mark's son, but she kept the thought to herself. 'And which of them does he take after, do you think?' she said instead.

'He has Ivor's amazing looks,' Feri said, 'as you saw for yourself. But his temperament is gentle, more like Mark's. I'm sorry you never met Mark. He was kind and good and strong, and when he could no longer be strong, then he was brave. He struck me, when I first met him, as rather ordinary compared to Ivor. I got involved with Ivor because he was sexy, exciting and somehow dangerous... All of which you know. It was what I wanted back then. But later it was the very ordinariness of Mark that I fell in love with, if you can understand.' Gemma nodded. She had no difficulty with that idea. 'Even so, Ivor did begin to change towards the end. He found a gentle, giving something deep inside himself. Began to respond to other people more, more generously. Caught it off Mark, perhaps? Anyway, Vince shares Mark's sweet nature. Has none of Ivor's melancholy. None of his demons.' Feri paused and smiled at Gemma. She went on,

'I loved both those men. You know how it is with brothers. Alike but different. I remember once saying – you won't remember this – I wanted to marry a Sussex farmer. I never expected to marry two.' Some connection occurred in Feri's mind just then. She said, 'Do you remember, I wrote to you offering their help with that book we used to talk about? In case you still wanted to write it. Though I think you probably never did.'

Gemma gave a tiny snort. 'There's nothing I'd like to do less,' she said. 'The book of Ivor's ghosts. Time they were laid to rest, I think.'

Vince emerged from the kitchen door at that point, carrying a yoghurt pot, from which he was already eating with a spoon. 'I've put the kettle on,' he said. 'So Auntie Hattie can have her tea.' He moved out of the shadow of the house towards them, into the sun, which made mirrors in his curly hair.

THIRTY-THREE

It was not long before there were cats again at Gatcombe. Vince took it upon himself to name the four of them. He called them after various characters in The Lord of the Rings. He was in many ways the child that Gemma would have liked to have herself. Bright and intelligent, courteous without being over-respectful. He did call Gemma Aunt Hattie when he wanted to tease her, but he seemed to find her a pretty acceptable honorary aunt. 'Not quite as good as having J. K. Rowling as a family friend,' he said to people, 'but, you know, beggars don't get to choose.'

His precocity could be a little wearing sometimes, but then Gemma herself had been quite precocious at his age: she knew that he'd grow out of it in the natural course of things. She was glad that he liked books. Moving on from Harry Potter he'd downloaded the whole of The Lord of the Rings and was into Ruth Rendell now, and P. D. James. It would be Henry James before long, Gemma thought.

He had the run of Gatcombe, of course, and treated it very much as a second home, turning up out of the blue on his bike just as often as he arrived with his mother in the car. It was hardly surprising that he felt so much at home there. The house had an almost identical ground-plan to the one he lived in, after all, and he loved to examine the king-posts in both attics, searching for minute differences between them. One day it would be his, of course, though he hadn't yet been told that. Within a year of meeting him Gemma had decided to leave him the bulk of her estate in her will. Although he would in theory come in for Birdskitchen – both the house and the farm – and a certain bungalow along the coast at Winchelsea Beach, Gemma knew how easily things could go wrong. It might yet be proved conclusively that he was not Mark's son, in which case Mark's mother, dear old lady though she was, could conceivably change her intentions. Alternatively, if it were ever established beyond doubt that he was not Ivor's son, Norma might do the same. Gemma had wanted to make assurance double sure. Jonathan Lyle, who drew her will up and read the name Vince Harris in Gemma's rough draft, joked that she was leaving her estate to the character in her books, although he knew the boy's mother and had known both his might-have-been fathers perfectly well. It was just one of those things, Gemma told him. One of life's little strangenesses.

Gemma spent as much time at Birdskitchen as Vince did at Gatcombe. It had seemed the most obvious thing, in this era of recession and reduced demand for everything except bread and funerals, for her to become Feri's partner in Hop Bine Country Crafts, and now her pictures brightened the walls of the shop and showroom just as Ivor's had once done. 'We are the Fogresses now,' Feri said. Working alongside Feri, Gemma had soon learned the circumstances of Ivor's death. 'Officially it was an accident,' Feri told her. 'But Mark and I thought it might have been a sort of suicide. As if he had a subconscious wish to die. Trevor's death unhinged him in some way, just as Jack's had years before.'

Of course Gemma heard details of the deaths of Trevor and Jack, two men she'd never met. 'They were oddly different situations, somehow,' Feri said. 'I mean the feeling that surrounded them. While everyone accepted that Trevor had killed himself, in Jack's case... Well, although it was clearly an accident – old Mrs Fuggle saw it all – there was somehow a terrible feeling in the neighbourhood that it couldn't have been. Sometimes it even got to me.'

'But if it wasn't an accident...?'

Feri didn't give Gemma a chance to finish whatever question she had in mind. Shaking her head, she'd said, 'I couldn't live with myself if I thought that.' She had gestured around the workshop, the old apple store, where this conversation was taking place. 'Look at all this. The business, the house, the farm... Not that the farm's mine, strictly speaking, but it will belong to Vince one day. How could I justify having those things, having Vince himself, if I thought I owed it all to...?'

'You don't,' Gemma had said stoutly. 'You can't make someone walk through a trap-door.' Though in bed that night a few memories had surfaced uncomfortably. She wondered if Feri remembered their light-hearted tour of the oast at Gatcombe in search of a murder plot more than twenty years ago. She would not remind her of it now. Of course Feri knew nothing about a certain conversation in a Marrakesh hotel, when Ivor had answered that very objection by saying, 'You could if the doors were off.' And had he said, or had she dreamed it...? Or had he muttered it in his sleep that night? '...If you had a sort of gauze...' A hot and chilly feeling had come over her as she lay awake. She had to make herself forget this. For Feri's sake. For Vince's.

It was Saturday afternoon at Gatcombe. Gemma had been back in England for two years. Vince was in the room that still got called the parlour, busy on his lap-top, playing some adult-baffling game. Feri and Gemma had been in the garden but a sudden July shower had driven them temporarily indoors. They sat in the big dining-cum-living room, their conversation inaudible to Vince through the huge chimney-stack and one closed door. This was just as well, since they were talking about him.

'It just seems so weird,' Feri said.

'But you shouldn't worry about it,' Gemma reassured her. 'Lots of kids of ten go through a religious phase. They grow out of it.'

'He could at least have got interested in the Anglican branch,' Feri said. 'With Peasmarsh church just down the lane from where we live. And the architecture's much finer, plus we've known the rector for years.'

'You're forgetting your Latin American roots,' Gemma told her. 'That's probably subconsciously in his mind.'

'I don't think it's that. He has this little friend called Roddy...' A wisp of a thought flickered through her mind but she carried on. 'Roddy's family are Catholic and they took him to St Anthony's one day. Now I never hear the end of it. Wanting to have instruction in the faith... Of course, Roddy's an altar boy.'

'It'll be the vestments, the ceremony and all those things,' Gemma said, wanting to reassure. 'They can have quite an impact on impressionable minds. Let him go with it, I suggest, until it's run its course. And if it doesn't... If, improbable though it sounds, he grows into a religious young man, well, there are worse things he could be.'

That flickering thought, like a shadow, like a wraith, crossed Feri's mind again. This time she gave it voice. 'Did Ivor ever have a friend called Roddy? That you knew of, I mean.'

Gemma frowned. 'No, I don't think so. Not that I remember anyway. Why?'

'Before he died Ivor talked to Mark about a friend he had, called Roddy. Mark asked him, don't you mean Robbie?, but he said something like, No, Roddy's the man for me. It was so peculiar. Talking of Vince's little friend brought it back. That's all.'

'Well,' Gemma said, now that she'd had a moment to think, 'There is a character in Crime and Punishment called Roddy. Rodion Raskolnikov's his full name, but his family call him Roddy for short. I got Ivor to see two Shakespeare plays once, and to read one book. Crime and Punishment was the one.' Gemma peered at Feri. 'You haven't read it yourself?'

'I tried Anna Karenina once, but didn't get all the way through.'

'Different author,' Gemma said. 'You should give Crime and Punishment a go. I remember it made a huge impression on Ivor. He talked about it a lot afterwards. And yes, now I think about it, he did talk about Raskolnikov a lot. Referred to him as Roddy, just as if he was real.' She had got up now and was scanning the book-shelves in search of her Penguin paperback. She returned, smiling, the book in her hand, and she put it into Feri's.

'It's at least as big as Anna Karenina,' Feri said. She made a weighing movement with it in her hand, then starting to flick through the pages. And as Gemma watched Feri doing this, all sorts of things tumbled into place in her mind. 'Oh no,' she burst out suddenly, and snatched the book back. 'Don't read it. Don't. It would be... It would be an unnecessary thing to do.'

Feri looked at Gemma in astonishment. Gemma's face had turned white. Her behaviour was extraordinary. 'What on earth...?' Feri began, but before she could go on or Gemma could answer her, the door opened and Vince walked in.

'And what are you two up to?' he asked. 'Fighting over a book?'

'Gemma's behaving very oddly,' Feri told him, smiling and making a joke of it. 'Behaving quite like Aunt Hattie. Telling me to read a book and then telling me not to in the next breath.'

'What book is it' Vince said, picking it up from the arm of the chair on which it now lay between them. He answered his own question. 'Crime and Punishment.' He looked at Gemma. 'From the size of it it looks like a punishment in itself.' He turned to his mother. 'Perhaps we could read it together. Like A Book at Bedtime on the radio.' He opened a page at random and read aloud:

'Why don't you see a doctor?'

'I know without your telling me, of course, that I'm ill, though I honestly don't know what's wrong with me. I'm sure I'm five times as healthy as you are. But I didn't ask you whether you believed that ghosts appeared to people. What I asked you was – do you believe in ghosts?'

'No, I shall never believe that,' Raskolnikov cried, even with a sort of resentful note in his voice.

'People say, "You're ill, so that what you think you see is merely a delusion." But that's not strictly logical. I'm ready to admit that only sick people see ghosts, but that merely proves that ghosts only appear to sick people. It doesn't prove that there aren't any ghosts.'

'It doesn't prove anything of the sort!' Raskolnikov insisted irritably.

'Doesn't it? You don't think so?' Svid ... Svig...' Sorry, can't pronounce him. Mr Swigalov. Whatever. Anyway, Mr Swigalot *went on, looking hard at him. 'What if we should reason like this; ghosts are, so they say, bits and pieces of other worlds, the beginning of them. There is no reason, of course, why a healthy man...'*

Vince stopped reading and looked at his mother, then at Gemma and then back at his mother again, with a frown on his face. 'Bor-ing,' he said. 'I like Gee's second suggestion best. That we should skip that one.' Then he and his mother both laughed. Neither of them saw the tremor of relief that passed through Gemma's body and across her face. 'Is there anything to eat?' Vince asked his mother.

'We'd better ask Gee,' Feri said. 'And ask her nicely. This is still her house.'

'There's cake in the fridge,' Gemma said, getting out of her chair again. 'From Fletcher's or Simon the Pieman's. I forget which. Let's go and look for it.' Gemma moved off towards the kitchen. When she got there she heard the other two come in behind her. She turned to see them, mother and son, she with her arm around her boy's shoulder, laughing and talking together. Outside, the rain had stopped. The sun blazed suddenly, and the garden's dripping tears became like jewels.

****

Author's Note

Although Ivor's Ghosts is a work of fiction it contains several accounts of events which are either non-fictional or, at least, not fiction invented by me.

The account in chapter one of Ivor's visit to Welstead House is the same account that a four-year-old boy called Harvey gave of a visit to Broomhill Lodge, near Rye, in 1974. His story was relayed to me ten minutes afterwards. The coincidence of a second account emerging to support Harvey's tale (the end of chapter eight) reflects a conversation to which I was party at Bellhurst Farm, Beckley, in 1976.

The account of the visit to Lydd in chapter four makes use of details given in a published report of a visit to Kersey by three naval cadets on a training exercise in 1957. Their stories were published in *Adventures in Time*, by Andrew MacKenzie, in 1997. I have met none of the people concerned in this event.

An Adventure, which I have quoted in chapter twelve, is a real book. First published in 1911 it is currently in print under the title *Ghosts of the Trianon*, by Moberly and Jourdain.

Lastly, I have used the account that Daniel Day-Lewis gave of his reason for dropping out of the RSC's 1989 production of Hamlet, as reported in the press at the time. Day-Lewis is an actor I admire enormously, but have never met.

In using these sources I have not sought to trivialise them. If anything, the reverse is true. But I have used them purely as building blocks in the architecture of my narrative, and not to make a point, either pro or contra, about the objectivity / subjectivity of such 'hard to explain' experiences. As for my own view, I can only echo Ivor's thoughts on the matter. He didn't believe in ghosts, but knew that some people (himself included) experienced them. Whatever that meant...

Anthony McDonald

***

Anthony McDonald is the author of more than twenty novels. He studied modern history at Durham University, then worked briefly as a musical instrument maker and as a farmhand before moving into the theatre, where he has worked in every capacity except director and electrician. He has also spent several years teaching English in Paris and London. He now lives in rural East Sussex, England.

Also by Anthony McDonald

GETTING ORLANDO

SEVILLE TRILOGY

ADAM

BLUE SKY ADAM

SILVER CITY

TENERIFE

These and other titles are all available from Amazon as paperbacks and as Kindle e-books.

22902337R00255

Printed in Great Britain
by Amazon